There was treasure down below. Aisha was so sure of it she could taste it.

She wasn't thinking about gold and jewels. She meant to find something much more important. Something that would save the expedition, and keep them from having to leave the world she'd been born on.

A Rosetta Stone, Mother had said. A key to languages that no one alive read, not even the nomads who followed the herds of giant antelope across the plains. They had no written language, no books, and precious few old stories. It was as if their whole culture had been mindwiped.

That was why Mother had named this planet of endless, empty ruins—which was designated MEP 1403 on the star maps—Nevermore.

Forgotten Suns
Copyright © 2014 Judith Tarr
All rights reserved
Published by Book View Café
www.BookViewCafe.com

ISBN: 978-1-61138-491-8

Cover art:
Copyright © Rolffimages | Dreamstime.com - The Eternal Explorers

Cover and interior design copyright © 2014 Knotted Road Press
www.KnottedRoadPress.com

FORGOTTEN SUNS

JUDITH TARR

Book View Café

www.BookViewCafe.com

FORGOTTEN SUNS

JUDITH TARR

ACKNOWLEDGEMENTS

Sincerest thanks to the backers of the Kickstarter campaign, without whom this book could not have been written. You are all Awesome.

Marty, Dr. Alice Ma, Rick Kirka, William F. Bowen, Oz Drummond, Robert Glaub, Gwyndyn Alexander and Jonathan Farr, Marie A. Parsons, Mark Vandervest, Adam L. Crouse, Kari, Cora Anderson, Joni Teter, Geoff Cooper, Rhel ná DecVandé, Ingrid Emilsson, William Lewis, J. Quincy, Alan Hamilton, C. Joshua Villines, Lisa Clark, R.K. Bentley, K&K Case, Jeanne Kramer-Smyth, Yaron Davidson, Pete Newell, Amy Sheldon, Noe Medina, Miles Matton, Houman, Estara Swanberg, Burt Beckwith, CE Murphy, Zuhur Abdo, John A, Hannah Steenbock, Trygve Henriksen, Donna P., Clinton W Harpman, Phil Johnson, K Liu, Kathleen Hanrahan, Anne, Jan Hendriks de Geweldenaar, Adrianne Middleton, Joseph Hoopman, Mike Weis, Evaristo Ramos, Jr., Max Kaehn, Linda Antonsson, Bryant Durrell, Lynne Glazer, Rachel Neumeier, Meredith Tarr, Ray Rischpater, Melita Kennedy, Mary Spila, Jase, Cosma Shalizi, Mike Zipser, Soli Johnson, M.L.K. Ondercin, Megan Beauchemin, Blair MacGregor, Twila Oxley Price, Ruth Stuart, Anatoly Belilovsky, Paul Weimer, David K. Mason, Nick Bate, Gregory Norman Bossert, April Steenburgh, Karen Grennan, B. A. Lawhead, Ashley McConnell, Tainry, Tara S, Melissa Scott, Robin D. Owens, Johan van Selst, Tony Fiorentino, S. L. Gray, Emily Mah, Katharine Kerr

Help me to shatter this darkness,
To smash this night,
To break this shadow
Into a thousand lights of sun,
Into a thousand whirling dreams

Langston Hughes

PART ONE

NEVERMORE

A isha had blown the top off the cliff.

It was an accident.

The parents had been excavating a circular mound on the eastern side of the old riverbed. While they argued over whether it was a palace or a temple, Shenliu wangled permission to explore across the long-dead river, where the cliff rose up sheer. He had climbed most of the way to the top, and found the opening of a cave there.

Shenliu was an artist with nuplastique. In the old days he would have fought in wars and blown up trains. Now he was a xenoarchaeologist, and he planned to blow a little hole, a tiny one, then drill down and open up whatever was below. Instruments didn't work so well on the cliff; all they could tell was that there was a larger cave inside, without any apparent way in or out.

Shenliu was set to open up the cliff before the end of the season, but then Mother and Pater found the room full of broken pottery. Shenliu had to forget about his cave and get to work cataloguing boxes of shards. He left the explosives in their locked box, away up in the cave where nobody was likely to go.

The night after he had to give up his project, Aisha had been awake long after bedtime, finishing just one more book. After she put the reader away and told the lights to go out, she heard the parents talking in their room down the hall.

Lately she'd been able to hear people through walls and even if they whispered. She had to close her eyes and listen very, very closely, but the words as often as not came through.

She might not have done it tonight, because it was late and she was sleepy, except Mother had that tone she'd had too much this year. Tight. Just a little too soft.

"I can't find any way to keep the expedition going past next season. We've put everything we have into it. Outside funding is getting leaner every Earthyear, and what sources we can scrape up are getting more and more insistent on actual, measurable, marketable results. Now Centrum's trying to gut the Department of Antiquities. We're done, Rashid. It's time we faced it."

Pater was harder to hear, but Aisha pushed herself almost to the point of headache, and his answer came clear. "We've been here twenty years. That's a good run by any standard. If we have to back off, regroup, we'll do it. The planet is a Perpetual Preserve. It will be here when we come back."

"Will we ever come back?" Mother had raised her voice. That was so rare it startled Aisha. "Once we've packed up and gone, you know what will happen. Centrum will find an excuse. The designation I fought so hard to get will evaporate. All those untouched resources, those empty continents, those seas that no one's sailed on or fished from in five thousand Earthyears—the feeding frenzy won't end till the world's stripped bare."

"We'll fight," Pater said. "The family has some power still. We'll hold off the Goths and the Vandals and even bloody Psycorps, at least for long enough to get new funding."

"If there is any," Mother said.

"Marina—"

"Rashid," she said, flat and hard and so unlike herself that Aisha's stomach clenched into a knot. "You were raised like a prince. I wasn't. I know when doors are slamming shut. We're being pushed off this planet. There's nothing more we can do."

"There is one thing," he said. "We can find something that even the idiots in Centrum will notice."

"What? More potsherds? More scrolls and tablets in languages no one can read? Even a burial wouldn't do it by this point—if there had been one single bone left anywhere that we've ever been able to find. It would take a Rosetta Stone to even make a dent, and then we'd have to explain it to the idiots in ways they might begin to understand."

"I won't give up hope," Pater said. "I will not."

Mother didn't answer that. She'd shut herself off, turned away from him and gone inside herself where no one could reach, even Aisha.

Aisha never did sleep that night. By morning she'd made her plan. She crept out while it was still dark, sneaked into the stable and saddled her horse and led him out, to find her brother Jamal blocking the way. He had his own horse, whose empty stall she hadn't noticed in the dark, and he was looking even more like Pater than usual: scowling and trying to loom.

Since he was still half a head shorter than she was and built like a runner bean, that didn't play well. "You can't stop me," she said.

"I wouldn't waste the energy," he answered. "Whatever you're up to, promise it doesn't involve explosives."

She set her lips together.

He sighed. "Of course it does. Look, Aisha—"

"I have to do this," she said. "If there's any chance at all of saving the expedition, I've got to try."

"You know we'll be all right if we can't. Beijing Nine has been after Mother for years to take that endowed chair. We like Beijing Nine."

"To visit," Aisha snapped. "Not to live on. It's not home. This is home."

He didn't point out that when she was older, if she wanted those doctorates she planned to get, she'd have to live off Nevermore for years. That wasn't important, and he knew it.

He pulled himself up on Ghazal's back without another word. She mounted Jinni much more gracefully. The spotted gelding was off and cantering by the time she landed in the saddle.

Which was bad of him, but this morning she was as impatient as he was.

She'd watched Shenliu often enough that she thought she knew how to set a charge. There was treasure down below. She was so sure of it she could taste it.

She wasn't thinking about gold and jewels. She meant to find something much more important. Something that would save the expedition, and keep them from having to leave the world she'd been born on.

A Rosetta Stone, Mother had said. A key to languages that no one alive read, not even the nomads who followed the herds of giant antelope across the plains. They had no written language, no books, and precious few old stories. It was as if their whole culture had been mindwiped.

That was why Mother had named this planet of endless, empty ruins—which was designated MEP 1403 on the star maps—Nevermore. Pater held out for Lethe, but nobody else liked that. Nevermore it was.

Aisha knew that there was a key to the mystery somewhere, and she was going to find it. The cave was as good a place to start as any.

First she had to get in. It was hardly Aisha's fault that she mistook the amounts, and thought a unit of nuplastique was a whole stick. Afterwards, when the top of the cliff had fallen in and she and Jamal had barely got out before the earth swallowed them, she found out that a unit was a hundredth of a stick. Her little hole, just big enough to let a narrow-bodied girlchild through, had turned into a terribly big hole.

She was too crushed even to cry. There was a cave, but there was nothing in it. There had been a little gold and a jewel or two—mostly vaporized—but no real treasure at all. Not even a bone, or a word carved in a fragment of stone. Certainly no key to the mystery that they were all trying to solve. That they had to solve this year, or never do it at all.

Now the cliff looked like a broken tooth, starker than ever above the long-dead river, and Aisha and Jamal were on lockdown. No intersession off planet for them. Everyone else got to go back to civilization for a handful of tendays, but Aisha and Jamal stayed on Nevermore with Vikram, who had been in Spaceforce when he was younger, and Aunt Khalida, who was not talking about why she had shown up in midseason and gone to work cataloguing artifacts.

It was supposed to be a dire punishment. Pater hadn't said a word to Aisha since the cliff blew. Mother had. Aisha could still feel the blisters on her conscience a tenday later, after the shuttle had carried them off to the tradeship.

Usually Aisha looked forward to intersession. Mother and Pater went off wherever they had to, to pull together staff and funding, and Aisha and Jamal spent the time on Earth with the grandparents and a pack of aunts and uncles and the tribe of cousins.

This year she had a mission, and she had the whole world almost to herself. Jamal would do whatever she told him. Vikram was barely there, and Aunt Khalida spent most of her time in her room. Except for making sure Aisha was not about to blow up any more portions of the landscape, and checking the schoolbot's records every evening for evidence that the prisoners had done their day's assignment, she left Aisha and Jamal completely and gloriously alone.

Aisha wished Blackroot tribe was still in their camp outside the ruined city, but they had left for the summer pastures. That was too bad: some of them, especially Aisha's friend Malia, would have been interested in a treasure hunt. Aisha and Jamal had only themselves for company, and the horses, who were happy to spend most days roaming and grazing.

Within the first tenday they had covered every quarter of the city, and spotted a new edge of it, too, buried under grass out on the plain. That left the territory on the other side of the riverbed, and the broken cliff.

"I want to go back up there," Aisha said halfway through the second tenday.

"Oh no," said Jamal. "That's strictly off limits. You can't even think about—"

"I can't stop thinking about it," Aisha said. "I saw something before it all came down. I want to see if it's still there."

"Of course it's not," Jamal said. "It's all blown up with everything else."

"Most of what blew was the roof of the cave. There's still plenty left underneath. What I saw was down below. I'm betting it's still there."

He narrowed his eyes at her. "What was it? All I saw was rocks flying."

"I'm not sure," she said. "I just know there was something down there."

"Well, if there was," he said, "it's buried twenty meters deep."

"Maybe not," she said.

He was stubborn, but she was worse. They were both bored. At the very least, he finally allowed, they could ride over there and look—from a safe distance. It was better than dangling around the house.

Neither of them mentioned the other thing, the thing that made Aisha so determined to go back and look. She might not get another chance.

Not just because of the problem with the expedition. This was much nearer and more terrifying. She'd been carefully not thinking about it all year.

Aisha would turn thirteen after the new season started. Psycorps would test her then. If she passed, the Corps would take her.

Aisha did not want to pass. She wanted to be a xenoarchaeologist like Mother and Pater, and discover Nevermore's secrets, and keep it safe from Goths and Vandals and the bloody Corps.

Aisha didn't just hear things she wasn't supposed to be able to hear. She saw things, too. Once in a while, in the empty squares and the broken and deserted buildings, she could see people coming and going, and hear their voices. They walked in her dreams.

She had a good imagination, that was all. She had no psi. She was nothing that Psycorps would be interested in.

This close to noon, thunder was brewing over the plain. That set Jamal off again. "We can't go out in that," he said. "What if there's lightning?"

"It's a long ways off," Aisha said. "We'll be there and back again hours before it hits."

Jamal glowered and muttered and kicked a bit, but when Aisha finished saddling leopard-spotted Jinni, he was right behind her with bay Ghazal. The horses were fresh and full of sparks, like the air. They were glad to get out and run.

Nobody saw them go. Vikram was doing something in the house, and Aunt Khalida was locked up in her room as usual. Aisha made sure her lunch was safe in her saddlebag and her water bottle was full, and set off toward the dead river.

Horses did not like the area around the cliff. They had that in common with the native tribes. Horses, like tribesmen, thought there was something bad there—or not so much bad as powerful, and not in a comfortable way.

It made Aisha's skin shiver and her head itch deep inside, but it had never frightened her. Whatever was there had nothing against her.

The cliff felt different now its top was broken off. The strange feeling was still there, but it was much weaker. The horses barely shied from the cliff's shadow, and that was mostly habit. Whatever had been inside was—not dead. But the pent-up power had blown away, or else sunk so deep in the earth she could hardly feel it any more.

The storm rolled toward them over the plain, but it was still klicks away. Aisha and Jamal left the horses in the pen at the cliff's foot, slung on their backpacks and started to climb.

The horses had grass, and water that bubbled from a spring into a stone basin. Aisha carefully shut her saddle and bridle in the shed outside the pen, well out of reach of inquisitive noses. Jamal was lazy, and therefore not so careful, but that was his lesson to learn. If his saddle was still on the fence when he got back, Aisha would be surprised.

It was a long, steep way up. She took a deep breath and went at it.

2

The top of the cliff was empty. The sun had scoured it. The rain that had fallen since Aisha's mistake had sent the last of the summit sliding down into the cave. There was nothing left to get into, and nothing to see, except rocks and rubble and tumbled earth.

Aisha's whole body sagged. She had been so sure there was something here. But it was all gone.

It really was dead. The power she'd been feeling was her imagination again, and hope playing tricks with it.

Jamal very kindly said nothing. He hardly even grumbled when she turned around without stopping and trudged back down the long, twisting trail.

Someone was in with the horses. Aisha thought it was Vikram at first; the horses were all over him, mugging him for cookies. But Vikram was taller and nowhere near as wild-looking as the person who stood with one arm over Jinni's back and the other hand scratching Ghazal's withers.

He really was wild. He was all hair and nails and bare blue-black skin—darker than Vikram, even. He wore very little except for a surprising lot of gold around his neck and arms and waist, hanging from his ears and braided into the wild mane of his hair. A few tatters of cloth hung from his belt, but they disintegrated while she stared, blowing away to dust in the wind off the storm.

He looked like a naked sage from Govinda. Aisha had seen them under their trees, sitting each in his bubble of silence, communing with the infinite. But they never wore anything at all, let alone enough gold to fill a small museum.

They never spoke, either. This one did. He was sweet-talking the horses. Aisha recognized the tone—any horse person would. The language was odd, as odd as he was.

She had a gift for languages. She could put words together and have them make sense, even when they were in a language she barely knew. He was speaking the old language of the tribes, but his accent was completely different from any she had heard. "What are you, then?" he was saying to the horses. "Where do you come from? You like that, do you? *Ah!* No teeth, madam!" That to Jinni, who liked to nip.

"He's not a girl," Aisha said. Her accent was fairly horrible, but not any worse than his.

He whipped around. She stepped back before she thought. He had a sword and a knife. They were less gaudy than everything else that was hung on or around him. Aisha did not doubt for a nanosecond that he knew how to use them.

Jamal was babbling; had been for a while. He pulled at her, too, but she ignored him.

"Those are our horses," she said. She had to use the Earth word, because the closest one in Old Language meant *giant antelope*. Which helped prove the point Mother liked to make about their use as riding animals, but that was not exactly important now. "They like you. Do you mind telling us where *you* came from?"

He frowned. He did look like Vikram, or like someone else from Govinda. There was no one in the tribes like him, at all. They were all gold or brown, and their faces were much blunter. He had a nose like one of the eagles that hunted along the river.

"Horses," he said. He mimicked her pronunciation exactly. "A horse is this?"

"A horse is this," she said.

"Tell me where I am," he said. "How did I come here? Who are you? What are you? What are these animals, these *horses*?"

Aisha could not answer half of what he asked. The part that she could, she did her best with. "You're on Nevermore. We're from Earth. We're digging here—my parents are. They're with the Cairo Museum. In Egypt, you know. In Greater Eurafrica."

His eyes on her were perfectly blank. Not one of those names meant a thing to him. He turned his head from side to side without taking his glare off her. It was hot enough to crisp her skin. "No," he said. "No, that's not—where is this? Who brought me here? *Where is my city?*"

At almost the same instant, Jamal howled at her, too. *"Aisha!"*

Him, she could slap some sense into. The wild man, not so much. His hands were on his weapons, gripping them so hard his knuckles had gone grey, but he had not drawn them. She noticed that. He was not trying to hurt her.

"I don't know," she said to him. "I'm sorry. I think your memory must be—"

"My memory," he said. Maybe his face twisted. It was hard to see in all the hair. "I remember—I was—I can't—"

"I'm sorry," Aisha said again. It was pathetic and useless, but it was all she could think of. "You can come home with us. We can see if—"

Jamal's yowl nearly ruptured her eardrums. The wild man's face went blank; his eyes rolled up. He dropped like a rock.

She laid Jamal flat, then hauled him up and shook him until he stopped shrieking. Which he did eventually. Jamal was an idiot, but if she hit him hard enough, he usually came around.

"*Now* look what you did," she said through the ringing in her ears. "You've killed him."

"*Good!*" Jamal half-yelled, but only half. Her hand was waiting to smack him again if he tried any more than that.

The wild man was alive. He was breathing fast and shallow. His heart when she dared to touch his chest was hammering. He shook in spasms, as if he'd taken a fit.

Lightning walked down the dry riverbed. Wind plucked at Aisha's hair. She smelled the electricity in it, and the faint sharpness of rain.

They would be lucky to make it back to the house before it hit. Aisha threw Jamal toward his saddle—on the ground and half trampled as she'd expected—and ran for her own.

Sometimes the horses liked to play at being hard to catch. Today they knew better. Aisha and a loudly reluctant Jamal pulled and hauled and heaved and shoved the wild man up onto Ghazal, who was quieter. He was too far gone to sit upright; they had to tie him face down and plan to apologize if he woke up on the way.

Jamal had to ride double with Aisha, which he didn't like, either, but she was long past paying attention to him. As soon as he was solid behind her, with his arms around her waist, she got a grip on the bay's rein and urged Jinni into a canter.

The storm chased them all the way to the gate of the compound. It broke just as they clattered into the barn.

"That's luck," Jamal panted.

Aisha had her own theory, but she kept it to herself. Jamal had stopped yowling and made his peace with the world, or close enough. A hard ride in rough weather could do that. He hardly complained at all about having to cool the horses out by walking them around the barn while Aisha fetched the hay cart and eased the wild man onto it.

He was no lighter now than he had been across the river. Even with Jamal helping, he was a sturdy weight to move. She had been thinking to get him up into the loft, but that was not happening. She hauled him down along the covered porch to the staff quarters instead.

Shenliu wasn't there to mind that Aisha stole his apartment for the wild man. It was the closest one to the stable, and she knew the key for the lock. She also knew where things were, which made it easier to get the bed made up and the stranger into it.

Then she just stood and breathed. He needed things, but she could hardly think what.

"We have to tell Aunt Khalida," Jamal said.

He was wobbling in the doorway, darting glances at the wild man, like a horse shying and then coming back to the scary thing and then shying again. "The horses are all cooled off?" Aisha said.

"Pretty much," he said. "I put them in their stalls and gave them hay."

"Water, too?"

"Of course water, too," he said. "We have to tell Aunt. She'll know what to do about him."

Aisha had been thinking the same thing, but because Jamal had said it first, she had to say, "No! We'll figure it out ourselves."

"What's to figure out? This is a crazy man. We found him in the middle of nowhere. He could be an escaped criminal. He was mindwiped, wasn't he? He can't even remember his own language."

"He knows Old Language," Aisha said.

"That's what I mean," said Jamal. "He's not from the tribes. He's got to be from offworld. Either he went native or he went crazy, or somebody wiped his mind for him."

Jamal was an idiot, but he was anything but stupid. All the while he had been yowling and kicking, his mind had been working. He'd put it all together even better than Aisha had.

She had to give him credit. Even when he said, "Aunt is MI—Military Intelligence. If anybody knows what to do about a criminal or a hostage or whatever he is, it's Aunt."

The fact he was right didn't make Aisha any happier about it. "So what do we say? That we were where we were told flat out not to go? We'll be grounded for the rest of our lives."

"We don't have to tell her exactly where we found him. Just that he was out there, he passed out, the storm came—it's all the truth. She can take it from there. Then if he wakes up and tries to kill us all, we won't be the ones he goes for."

"He won't try to kill anybody," Aisha said. She was absolutely sure of that. She had taken the sword and knife off him and hidden them in Shenliu's closet, but that was mostly to keep him safe from himself.

"Look," she said. "Let's just let him sleep until morning. Then we'll decide what to do."

"What if he wakes up and runs off again?"

"I'll make sure he's locked in," she said. "Just until morning, all right?"

It was not all right, but the fight had gone out of Jamal. He gave in.

Aisha should have felt better about it than she did. She always won; that was the way things were. But this was too odd for anyone's comfort.

3

The Brats were up to something.

They usually were, but this one had an exceptionally odd feel to it. They were quiet at dinner, kept their eyes down, ate everything they were fed, and most damning of all, offered no objection when ordered to bed early.

Khalida would have welcomed the quiet, but the quality of it raised hackles that should not have been there. The nightmares were back, and so were the other things, the things that had got her sent away on psych leave.

She had been rationing her computer time, because that was another symptom: compulsive escape into the mysteries of a planet that had gone from extensively populated to nearly deserted in the space of days. Rashid thought months or even years, but Khalida did not think so. What must have taken years was stripping out every image of humanoid or domestic animal, everywhere, in every inhabited place. That meant they had had warning of whatever it was, and time to prepare. But they had left quickly.

Even thinking about it was an evasion. While she sat at the window, staring into the dark, she avoided sleep and the dreams that waited in it.

Her head ached. Phantom-psi syndrome. Psycorps had taken what little psi she had out of her when she was Aisha's age, declared her fully and acceptably neutered and free of abilities too defective to develop further.

She could still feel them. Still, when she was tired or disconnected or close to sleep, reach down into herself and for a few brief instants know she was whole.

This was whole, she told herself. This, now, with all the damage it had taken in the disaster on Araceli. Normal, human, ordinary traumatic stress, duly and officially treated. Not some complication of a quarter-century-old procedure for a moderately common birth defect.

"You," she said to the blur of her reflection in the window, "are a right mess." She pushed herself up, meaning to stagger off to bed, but as she paused, swaying in the darkened room, she saw shadows against shadow flitting outside.

The Brats were headed toward the stable. That was enough to send Khalida in pursuit.

They did not, after all, steal horses and slip away into the night. They went on past to the staff quarters, the row of cabins down along the south wall. Those were deserted: Vikram had an apartment above the stable, and everyone else was offworld.

Aisha and Jamal had something hidden in Shenliu's quarters. Whatever it was, it kept them busy and bickering for close to an hour. Khalida considered walking in on them, but decided to wait instead and see how long it took them to finish whatever they were doing.

It was dark and cool in the shadow of the covered porch. There were no stars tonight; the storms had moved off, but the sky was heavy with clouds. Khalida breathed the smell of rain.

Every world was different. Here on Nevermore the rain had a sharpness as in the deserts of Earth, but with an undertone that was alien. She had yet to put words to it. Spice, a little. Greenness. A faint, cold note, like wind in empty places.

The Brats came out of the cabin, still bickering. She could not make sense of the words, nor did she try overly hard. She sat for a while after they had gone back toward the house and their beds, not sure what she would or even should do until she found herself in front of Shenliu's door.

Someone was inside. She could feel the life and warmth in the darkness behind her eyelids, and hear the rush of breath into and out of lungs. Human—an animal felt and sounded different.

She opened the door.

The children had left a light on, heavily shaded but bright enough after the dark outside. Khalida stood over what they had brought home.

It was certainly not what she had expected. If she had had to guess what he was, she would have guessed Govindan, with a few rather extreme modifications. But the treasure trove he was loaded down with was distinctively of this world, and rich enough to widen her eyes. The xenoarchaeologist in her catalogued and provisionally dated it at some centuries before the Disappearance—Nevermore's late Bronze Age, more or less. The craftsmanship of the belt, the sheer weight and mass of the torque around his neck...

He must have got into a tomb. Or someone had shut him up in one and left him for years, feeding him just enough to keep meat on his bones.

He burned with fever. When she laid her hand on his forehead, she recoiled from the heat of his skin.

His head tossed. She reached by instinct to steady it. His eyes opened.

There was nothing sane about them. They fixed on her face as if it had been the most fascinating thing in any world. He spoke a running stream of words in a language she knew just enough of to recognize. It was a very old ritual language of the tribes.

"I'm sorry," she said. "I haven't studied enough to understand—"

He went still. His eyes were still completely crazy, but his voice was soft and steady, and he spoke perfectly comprehensible PanTerran. "A bath," he said, "would be a welcome thing. And a razor, if you have one."

"Not if you're going to slit your throat with it," she said.

It was next to impossible to tell, but maybe the corner of his mouth curved upward. "I will not do that," he said gravely.

If she had been a suitably modest daughter of the family, she would have called Vikram to do the honors. But she had not been either modest or proper in a long time, and Vikram would add complications that she was not, at the moment, in a mood to face. She ran the bath herself and found a razor in one of the other cabinets, and a set of shears, too. While she was at it, she raided the common storeroom for clothes that she hoped would fit, and a few other useful things.

He was still in Shenliu's bed when she came back, and still awake. The pure madness had retreated from his stare, but was still there underneath.

She knew that madness. She had a fair share of it herself. She contemplated carrying him into the bath, but although he was weak, he could walk. He was a little taller than she was: not a big man at all, but well-built and compact, and surprisingly fit. When he was back to himself, he would be quite strong.

He had no modesty that she could detect, and nothing like shame. He acted as if it was perfectly natural for a man to be bathed and shaved and turned into a civilized being by a woman.

He was much younger than she had thought. Under the thicket of beard he had a young man's face, though not exactly a pretty one. Distinctive, that was the word. Whatever modifications had given him that skin like black glass, she suspected the features were the ones he was born with.

He had scars, which meant the modifications were years old. Most were on his arms and chest; there was a deep one in his thigh. His right hand was a fist; it would not open for any pressure she could put on it. His fingers and palm must have fused together with some old injury.

He would not let her cut his heavy curling mane, though it hung clear to his waist. She combed it out as much as she could and twisted it into a braid as thick as her arm. That contented him, and got it out of the way.

He was still feverish, and weaker than she liked to see. He hardly argued when she helped him back to bed, though when she ordered him to sleep, he said, "I've slept enough."

"You're sick," she said. "You need to rest."

"Not any more," he said.

She shook her head. If she had to sit on him to keep him down, she would.

She bullied water into him, and tipped a pana-tab in with the last of it. He choked and tried to spit it up, but it had already dissolved. "Stop glaring," she said. "It will help with your fever."

"It will not." He was breathing hard. Panic attack, she thought. She knew about that, too. Oh, did she. The shakes, the sweats—all of it.

By the time she realized that he was not panicking, he was actively sick, it was too late to head off the reaction. She cursed herself ferociously. Any three-year-old knew not to give medication before asking if the patient was allergic. Even a pana-tab. Especially a pana-tab, when the patient had an unknown quantity and variety of modifications.

"Never," she said. "Never without a scan. *Damn*. If I've killed him, I'll kill myself."

With luck he would kill her first. The first assault of fever laid him flat and kept him deathly quiet. She did what she could: ice baths, cold cloths, prayer to a God she had stopped believing in when she was Aisha's age.

Then came the delirium.

It was daylight by then. She noticed it because the door was open and the children were standing in it, all eyes and shock.

She gave them something to do: mine the house computer and the schoolbot and find something, anything, to counteract a severe allergic reaction. Miraculously, they did as she told them. They were gone before all hell broke loose.

The convulsions and the raving were easy. Soft restraints, then hard ones. More cold baths. The bed was soaking wet. If she survived this, she would have to get Shenliu a new one.

What came after that was harder.

If Psycorps had neutered this one, the neutering had not taken. He was not only completely unregulated, he had aberrations she had never even seen.

Most of it had to be illusory—trapping her inside his hallucinations. He had not really destroyed the whole city and everything in it, then put it back together again exactly as it was, ruins and excavations and all.

He had not remade the city, either, as it must have been several thousand years ago, bright and sharp and new, full of people and animals, life, light, voices and laughter and song. Giant antelope in saddle and bridle or drawing wagons or chariots. People of what must have been a dozen nations, some of whom looked like the tribes she knew, and some were fairer but most were darker, and all of them were taller. The darkest were the tallest. They looked like him when she had first seen him, with black eagle-faces and exuberant beards and a clashing array of ornaments.

That had to be a fantasy. He was certainly no giant.

It was a wonderful dream, vivid and strikingly real. She could feel the pavement underfoot, and smell the complex smells of a thriving city, and hear the song a woman sang: a woman with skin like honey and hair like fire. It was a love song she was singing, and she smiled as she sang, with warmth that reached across all the hundreds of years.

Such sadness struck Khalida then, such grief and such rage that it broke her mind apart. She felt it breaking. She felt it healing, too, as the dream melted around her: wounds knitting, scars fading, places that had been stripped bare filled up again with light.

4

Aisha and Jamal brought Vikram in when Khalida collapsed. As she clawed her way out of whatever had happened to her, she was more than glad to see that well-worn face with its web of old radiation scars.

During a lull in the delirium, Vikram helped her get the stranger into the main house. The walls were more solid there, and there was in-house security—not much by MI standards, but better than nothing.

"We need a name for him," she said as they finished rigging the restraints in one of the guest rooms. He, whatever his name was, was unconscious for the time being. The house medbot had already confirmed that he was breathing, his heart was beating, and he had a dangerously high fever.

Vikram rubbed his jaw where a flying fist had caught it. "Rama," he said. "Call him Rama."

His expression was odd. So was hers, she supposed. "Rama, then. We'll let him tell us what it really is when he comes to."

If he did. She did not say it. Neither did Vikram.

On a civilized planet there would have been resources. Medics; hospitals. The medbot here was programmed for the ills an archaeological expedition was prone to. It had only the most basic accommodations outside of that. For what ailed Rama, it was next to useless.

There were no ships within two tendays' reach of the system. Vikram had determined that before Khalida even thought of it. Khalida was almost desperate enough to load the Brats into a rover and order them to fetch a shaman from a tribe when the storm of delirium stopped.

It was abrupt, and it happened in the deep night. An hour before, he had been throwing off sparks. When Vikram tried to hold him down, he was nearly electrocuted.

That, the medbot could treat. Vikram was in his own bed recovering. Khalida sat at a prudent distance, wide and painfully awake.

The silence grew on her. It was more than a lull. Rama lay on his back, perfectly still.

She leaped. At the last instant she remembered lightning, but that was gone. His forehead was cool. He was breathing, deep and slow.

He was asleep. It *was* sleep; the bot confirmed it. He was not in a coma.

The tension ran out of her so quickly her knees buckled. She did not need the medbot to tell her the fever had broken. There might be brain damage; he was probably insane. But as far as the bot could tell, he would live.

He slept for a day and a night. The bot fed him a glucose drip, but not— cautiously—anything pharmaceutical.

Khalida woke at dawn. She was restless and irritable and ready to claw the walls, but she could not bring herself to leave the patient alone. She curled up in the corner with a reader and a box of databeads, running through expedition files.

She had most of the finds from the southwestern quadrant of last season's dig organized and catalogued when something made her look up.

He was watching her. He seemed perfectly calm. As far as she could tell, he was sane.

"Good morning," she said.

"Good morning," he replied.

"You've been sick," she said, "but you're getting better."

"How long?"

He said it quietly, but it seemed to matter a great deal to him. "Four days," she said. "I made a mistake. I gave you something I shouldn't have. I wasn't trying to kill you."

"Four days," he said. It was a sigh. "No wonder I'm hungry."

Probably she should not have laughed, but he actually smiled, which was a relief. She preferred that to being blasted where she sat.

"Breakfast," she said. "Let me see what I can find in the kitchen. Promise you won't go anywhere."

"I promise," he said without irony.

She was ravenous, but she made sure to feed him first. Not much, and nothing solid—not yet. He obviously was not impressed with the mug of liquid ration, though he drank every drop.

"Good," she said. "A meal or two more and we'll try you on something you'll like better."

"I do hope so," he said, but he sounded more wry than annoyed.

She kept a close eye on him, and kept the medbot running. He showed no sign of a relapse. Toward noon she fed him again. By evening she was as ready to feed him solid food as he was—and she was beginning to believe that he had come through intact.

Next morning when she woke from an entirely unplanned and nearly nightlong sleep, he was gone. The bed was neatly made. The clothes she had found for him were gone.

Part of her was purely and whitely panicked. Part knew exactly where he was. She could feel it the way she felt her own hand, twitching at the end of her arm.

It was part of what he had done to her. She was not ready to think about that yet. She scraped the sleep out of her eyes and the hair out of her face and stumbled into the early-morning light.

He was cleaning the spotted gelding's stall, slowly, with frequent stops to rest. Aisha had done the whole of the opposite row and started on the end of that one. Khalida swooped down on her like the wrath of Spaceforce. "What are you doing? How could you let him? He almost died!"

"I made her show me," he said behind Khalida. "If anybody's earned a whipping, I have."

"He already knew how," Aisha said. "I showed him where things were. The horses like him."

That was obvious. Jinni was wrapped around him, nibbling his hair.

"Back to bed," Khalida said. "Now."

"No." There was nothing defiant about it. He simply refused. "I've had enough of beds and sleep. Let me finish here. Then let me lie in the sun. That will heal me better than any pill or potion."

He was amazingly hard to argue with, and not because Khalida had seen what he could do when he was out of his head. He was so very reasonable, and so very sure of himself.

She threw up her hands. "Do what you like. Die if you want to. I don't care."

He bowed, which nearly tipped him over. The gelding propped him up.

Khalida turned her back on him and left him there.

He lay in the sun of the courtyard all morning and part of the afternoon, basking like a lizard on a rock. Any unmodified human would have burned to a crisp. He bathed in light.

"He's charging," Khalida said from the upper floor of the house, where she had been trying to put together fragments into something resembling a statue.

"Like a solar panel," Vikram agreed.

"Have you ever seen anything like it?"

He shot her a glance. "You're MI, and you're asking me?"

"You were Spaceforce," she said. "If there's anything to hear, Spaceforce hears it. MI gets the leavings."

He grunted. "Somebody somewhere has to have come up with the mod, or he wouldn't have it. Unless..."

"What?" Khalida demanded when he did not go on.

"Unless he was born that way."

"What, gengineered?"

"Do you have any other ideas?"

"Not offhand," she said. "I've sent inquiries on the subspace feed. There's no telling how long it will take to get anything back."

"I sent a few myself," said Vikram. "So far all I've got is nothing. If he's one of ours, he's so classified even he probably doesn't know what he is. If he's one of yours..."

"I suppose we'll find out eventually," she said. "Are you going to report him to Psycorps?"

"Are you?"

She shrugged. It was more of a shiver. "I'm thinking about it. If he's theirs, I'm not sure I want to be anywhere near him when they find him."

"I'd worry more about them," Vikram said.

That, Khalida had to agree with. There were rumors about what happened when a psi went rogue. A psi of the level of this one would have the whole Corps out after him.

Which would explain why he had turned up here, at the back end of nowhere, on a planet with effectively no inhabitants. Either he was hiding, or someone had been hiding him.

Her inquiries would trigger searchbots, if there were any. So would Vikram's. It was small comfort that he had failed as badly as she had at thinking things through.

Too late now. It would take a while in any case. In the meantime Rama or whatever his name was was as safe as she or Vikram could make him.

He certainly seemed happy. When the sun vanished behind clouds and the thunder began its daily walk, he came in to be fed. He was walking steadily, and he looked orders of magnitude better.

The implications of that for MI were enough to tie her stomach in knots. She was here on psych leave. She could not be thinking what she was thinking. Because if she did, she would start remembering. And memory was deadly.

She put on a smile and showed him how to make his own lunch. "We don't do room service here," she said, "unless you're on your deathbed. Breakfast and lunch, you're on your own. Dinner, we take turns. Be warned: when it's the Brats' turn, the menu can get creative."

He smiled at that. "Do I get to be creative, too?"

"Not too much," she said. "I'll show you how to work the cooker. It's not that hard."

"Everything is easy here," he said.

"Like magic," said Khalida.

All the lightness drained out of him. "Oh, no," he said. "There is nothing easy about magic."

Vikram called the wild man Rama. That was not his real name, but he liked it. He wanted to keep it.

He was not so wild now, with his face open to the world. Aunt Khalida had dug clothes and shoes and even a pair of boots out of the storage room for him, raiding the boxes of castoffs and extras and I-forgots. He could never look ordinary, but at least now he looked civilized.

Aisha had looked up his new name on the house computer. She had guessed right about what Vikram had really wanted to call him. He looked just like Lord Krishna.

Maybe he was an avatar. She had looked that up, too.

"That's just mods," Jamal said. "He must be a Ramayanist. They all want to be Krishna. Or Kali or Lakshmi Bai or Vishnu."

"You've been hacking the schoolbot again," Aisha said. "Why didn't you tell me?"

"I was going to," he said. "You were busy cleaning stalls with Lord Krishna."

"Don't call him that," Aisha said. "It's bad luck."

"There's no such thing as luck," said Jamal. But he stopped tempting it with a god's name.

Not that there were any gods but God. Aisha just liked to cover all the possibilities.

With Rama in the house, it was much less tempting to wander off. He got over his fever in no time at all; then he settled in to make himself useful around the house and the stable. Mostly the stable. He liked horses, and horses loved him.

He sat in on lessons, too. First because he came wandering in in the middle and the bot thought he was another student and asked him a question, and then because he got curious about the answer.

Aunt Khalida said he had amnesia. If he did, he picked up new memories fast. Aisha gave him one of the spare readers that they kept for interns, and the box of databeads that went with it. After that, if he wasn't mucking out stalls or grooming horses, he was parked somewhere, usually in the sun, with the reader perched on his nose.

A whole tenday went by without any of them going outside the walls. Rama didn't seem to remember there was anything out there, and Aisha and Jamal found enough to do around the compound.

Aisha was anything but bored, but Jinni had been stuck in the paddock for all that time. He let her know that if she kept him in much longer, he was going to do something about it.

The day she caught him eyeing the back fence, she knew she had to get him out of there. Jamal was up for a ride, for a change. She said to Rama, "You can come, too."

Nobody told Rama what to do. Even Aunt Khalida had learned to ask, and not to argue if he said no. But Aisha could hand him a halter and point him toward the fat pinto they kept for beginners, and be reasonably sure he would go.

Of course, being Rama, he didn't bring in the pinto. He brought in the red mare.

Nobody rode Lilith but Mother or Aunt Khalida. Nobody else could stay on her.

Rama could. He got on without even bothering with the stirrups, and when she started to buck, he rode her out almost as easily as if she'd been cantering around the paddock instead of turning herself inside out trying to get him off.

Lilith was evil but she wasn't stupid. She stopped all once, ears flicking back and forth, and tried one last, half-hearted twist-and-kick. When he didn't budge, she let out an explosive, two-ended snort, shook herself all over, and made up her mind to behave herself.

He laughed. He was not being unkind, at all. She made him happy.

Aunt Khalida would be jealous. Aisha looked forward to seeing that. Meanwhile the horses were saddled and the water bottles were full. Aisha was ready to go.

They went in the opposite direction from the dead river and the broken cliff, down along the edge of the city. Aisha thought she might find the river where it was now, and see if she could catch some fish for dinner. She had hooks and coils of line in her saddlebag.

This part of the city was still under the grass. Here and there a wall stuck up, but mostly you had to know the hills and hollows hadn't grown there on their own. The track they rode on had been a road a long time ago; it was more or less smooth and mostly straight.

Lilith liked to lead, but she was out of shape. Soon enough, Jinni caught up with her. Aisha grinned at Rama and got his white smile in return.

Some days it was hard to remember he was really old—as old as Shenliu at least. Maybe even as old as Aunt Khalida. He looked at Aisha and Jamal as people, not children, and treated them accordingly. It made all the difference.

His smile widened to a grin. "Race you up the hill," he said.

Lilith had a few sparks left in her after all. She left Jinni in the dust.

It was a long hill and not very steep, but from the top it dropped off more sharply, plunging down to the river. Rama never even hesitated. He gave Lilith half a dozen strides to get her back legs under her, then let her go.

Aisha's heart tried to jump out of her chest. Jamal wasn't even trying to keep up. He was smart. Aisha was completely crazy: she sent Jinni after Lilith.

Nobody died. Nobody fell, either. They slowed down when they were neck and neck, cantering along the bank. Aisha was breathing harder than Jinni, but her grin stretched from ear to ear.

Without saying a word, they curved around together and settled to a walk. Jamal had picked his way down the hill before he speeded up daringly to a trot. His expression was thunderous.

Aisha laughed at it, which only made it worse. She tossed him a coil of hook and line. "Let's go fishing," she said.

Jamal was much better at fishing than he was at riding. Rama was about the same at both. Aisha wasn't patient enough, but she had been using it as an exercise, and she actually caught two fish to the others' half-dozen apiece.

With fish on strings and horses and riders lazy and smiling, they made their leisurely way back to the house. Aisha deliberately went a different way, farther along the river where the bank went up in terraces. The top had the best view of the city that Aisha knew: it was high enough to see most of the excavations and a good part of the rest, clear across to the old riverbed and the cliff.

She was ready to explain to Rama how her parents liked to come out here and plot the work for a new season, but when she opened her mouth to begin, something stopped her.

He sat perfectly still on Lilith's back. Aisha had seen effigies on tombs that looked more alive than he did then.

She looked where he was looking. There was nothing new or different there. Just trenches and markers, the market square with the colonnade that they had spent two seasons digging out, the round temple on its low hill, and a great deal of grass and ruins. They could dig for decades, Mother said, and barely begin to uncover it all.

He could see it. Not everybody could. He saw what was there, and what must have been there before time and weather broke it down.

"It's gone," he said. He was speaking Old Language, which he hadn't done since he came out of his fever. "All of it, gone. Even—"

His eyes lifted. They fixed on the cliff and its broken top. "Even that? But how—?"

"That's my fault," Aisha said. It was a bad idea, maybe, but she had to say it. "The rest of it, nobody knows."

"How can no one know? Where is everyone? What happened to the people?"

"That's the mystery," she said. "The planet's empty. It's all ruins."

"All of it?"

"The whole planet," she said. "We've scanned it all."

"How long?"

"Five thousand planet years. A bit more than that in Earth years."

"Five thousand years." It seemed to be more than his mind could take in. "They all went away? Where? Why?"

"We don't know," said Aisha. "This planet is at the top of all the Most Mysterious lists."

"They must have left something. Some word."

"We can't read their writing," she said. "Even if we could, I don't think we'd find anything. They took out all the statues and the paintings. Every likeness of a human, and most of their animals. Smashed them or wiped them out. Completely destroyed them. We can guess what they looked like, but nobody can be sure. It's as if they wanted to keep someone, or something, from ever recognizing them."

He sucked in a breath. "No. No, they can't have been that afraid of—"

"Whatever it was, they can't have liked it much."

His fists were clenched on the pommel of Lilith's saddle. Aisha watched him get his breathing under control. "To keep something from recognizing them. That would be something that had never seen them. Not—"

"That's what I think," she said. "There are all kinds of theories. But if it already knew them, why hide? Even if it was so awful the whole population had to run away, what would be the point in covering up what they were?"

"Yes," he said. Then: "There are books still?"

"Books and inscriptions. We've never found anything to help us translate them."

"I'd like to see them," he said.

"Even if you can't read them?"

He shrugged. "I'm curious. That's all."

Aisha eyed him sideways. She could tell when a person wasn't telling the whole truth. She could also tell when he wasn't going to answer any more questions. "They're in the vault with the rest of the really valuable finds. I don't have access to that."

"Someday you will."

"Yes," she said. Refusing to think about what might happen if the expedition ended next season. "Years from now. After I've grown up and gone to university and got all my degrees. Then I'll get a key."

"When you're terribly old," he said.

He was teasing her. He must have got over whatever shocked the breath out of him. "Yes," she said with a hint of a snap. "When I'm almost as old as you."

That shut him up. A little too completely, maybe, but she refused to feel guilty. It served him right for treating her like a child.

6

Khalida knew about the Brats' excursion. She also knew who had gone with them. If she wanted to think like MI, she could wind herself into a glorious fit of paranoia.

The person they all called Rama was not about to kidnap the offspring of the Doctors Nasir and Kanakarides. Whatever he was here for, she was sure it had nothing to do with the Brats.

He liked them. It was as simple as that. They kept him out of mischief. As for what he did for them—she had seen the way he moved. Somewhere, whether he remembered it or not, he had been trained to fight. The Brats could do worse than attach themselves to a bodyguard.

They came back windblown and loaded down with fish, which by house rules they had to clean and cook. Rama, too. He was better at it than they were.

Khalida happened to notice how quiet he was in all the bubble and babble. She also noticed when she went through the kitchen that he had the boning knife in his right hand, and it worked as well as the left. Whatever had been wrong with it when he first came, he seemed to have got over it.

It was one more odd thing about him, of more than she had the patience to count. She recorded it, tagged it, and passed on by.

There was still no response to her inquiries. Searches had turned up nothing. As far as she or Vikram could determine, the man did not exist.

The latest results were waiting when she came up from dinner, with Vikram's tag on them: *Spaceforce Intel. Can't get any deeper without setting off alarms.*

She had already tried and failed to convince him that they could hack into Psycorps. That was insane, he said. Which it was, but Khalida was reaching the point of not caring.

Here was the best Spaceforce could come up with: a deep gene scan that made no sense at all. He was, according to the scan, distantly but definitely related to Khalida. He had also, the scan declared, originated on Nevermore.

She had committed the most basic of all errors: she had contaminated the samples. She moved to delete the message, but paused. As humiliations went, it was minor, and it was a useful reminder. There was no excuse for sloppiness, no matter how distracted she was.

There was a second message attached to the first. That was even more ridiculous. *Physiological age, thirty to forty-five years. Chronological age—*

"Six thousand years?" Khalida dropped onto her bed and let out a small, cathartic howl. "Now that's not my mistake. They should know better than to test the artifacts instead of the man."

She kept that, too. The rest was less egregiously wrong but equally useless. He was not, Spaceforce Medical opined, modified. This was his original form, as indicated by the genetics.

Vikram had been right, then. Gengineered. The scan was not set up to speculate as to where or how.

Khalida shut off the feed and pressed her hands to her eyes. "A mystery on top of an enigma," she said. "He couldn't have found himself on a more appropriate planet."

She should get up, undress, get ready for bed. She was much too comfortable to move. Sleep had been harder and harder to come by lately. Tonight she thought she might manage it. She might even keep the nightmares down to a statutory minimum.

She lowered her hands. Her arms stung. She did not remember cutting them.

She sat up and stripped off her shirt. There were scars on top of scars, up and down her forearms. The new ones crept close to the veins again, to the deepest and oldest scars, the ones she had almost died of. Would have, if Max had not been there to—

Max was dead. So were Sonja and Kinuko and John Begay.

Because she made a mistake much worse than contaminating a genetic sample. Much, much worse. So much worse that she could not let herself die for it. She had to live. To remember. Because there was no more fitting punishment.

Her nails were cut to the quick, to keep her from doing what they tried to do now: claw the skin off, let the blood out.

It was all perfectly reasonable. She had been repaired. Psych had smoothed over the rough edges, cut away the worst of the mental proud flesh, lasered off the scars. Just a little therapy, they had told her when they discharged her, and she would be as fit as she ever was.

All of this—side effects. Normal. Nothing to trigger alarms. The blood was a nuisance, but when it was all gone, so would she be. Then there would be no alarms at all.

Fingers closed around her wrists. Their grip was light, but it was too strong to break.

There was no mistaking whose they were. She raised her eyes to Rama's face. "Don't you know what it means when a door is locked?"

"Yes," he said.

The lock on this door was nothing to what else he could hack into. He was wearing the torque she had found on him that first night. "That was in the vault," she said.

"It's mine."

"Technically," she said, "it's the property of the Department of Antiquities for Ceti quadrant."

"It belongs to me," he said.

"So that's what you are," said Khalida. "An interstellar thief. I'd had you down as a mass murderer."

"I took what was mine."

He was stubborn. She already knew that. "You're the thief," she said. "I'm the murderer. Do you know how many people died because of me? Two hundred thousand six hundred and fifty-four. The last four were my direct responsibility. I looked them in the eyes when I hit the trigger. They knew exactly what I did to them."

He said nothing. His face was blank.

"You're lucky," she said. "You got the mindwipe. I didn't qualify. I acted to the best of my capacity to forestall a greater disaster. That's how they put it. Word for word. I appealed. They said, *You performed a service. You also committed a substantial error. The decision is just. It stands.*

"Just," she said, "but merciful? Not even slightly."

"Sometimes there are no right decisions," he said.

"What, are you the wise sage now? How many people have you killed?"

"With my own hand? Hundreds. By my order? Thousands. More than you, maybe. I stopped counting."

She gaped. Then she laughed, sharp and bitter. "Don't make fun of me."

"I never do that."

"They seeded you with false memories," she said. "In extreme cases, that's what they do. Wipe the mind clean, give it a new set of programming, drop the result somewhere out of the way. If he survives, he'll never know what's real and what isn't. If he doesn't, how convenient."

"Memories find their way out," he said. "Even through this thing you people do."

"'You people'? Who do you imagine you are? Some alien warlord pulled out of a tomb?"

"Something like that," he said.

"I can't deal with you tonight," she said. "Go away. Go to sleep. Forget I ever said anything."

"No," he said.

She would have knocked him down, if he had not still been holding on to her wrists. Damn, he was strong.

"Sleep," he said. "Dream peace. For this night, forget."

That bastard. He was turning her orders back on her. Making them stick.

"You're Psycorps," she said before she slid down into the dark. "That's the only thing you can be."

"Not the only thing," he said.

She was floating: drifting through infinite space. His eyes were dark, but they were full of the sun.

A solar-powered man. MI would be all over him when it found out.

Not from her. MI should have mindwiped her when it had the chance. She owed it nothing now. Not one thing.

Rama never mentioned that night. Khalida made sure he never had occasion to try. She had the rest of the cataloguing to do before everyone came back. He had stalls to clean and Brats to chase and locks to hack. But if he stole anything else, Khalida did not know about it.

Most of the antique gold he had come with was safe in the vault. The torque never did turn up there, nor did one of the armlets and a ring. Khalida quietly adjusted the inventory to fit. Just as quietly, Rama appeared wearing none of the articles he had liberated.

He had settled in so seamlessly that unless she stopped to think, she could not remember this place without him. That was disconcerting in its way, but so far it managed not to be dangerous. She had him under surveillance. That was the best she could do.

7

Intersession was ending, and not just because the chrono told Aisha so. The summer storms were shorter and weaker, and the heat was gradually getting less. Some of the nights were almost cool.

Birds had started flying south. The herds of antelope had come back to the plain. Very soon, the tribes would come back, too, and so would Mother and Pater and the rest of the expedition.

She hadn't forgotten her mission. She'd changed tactics. She had questions to ask the tribes. She might find ways to get hold of a rover, too. She was still pondering that.

Aisha and Jamal took Rama out one morning to see the antelope. It was the schoolbot's day to be down for maintenance. They could do what they wanted, as long as they had adult supervision.

That, these days, was Rama. Vikram had the bots out in force, cleaning cabins and getting them ready for the new crop of staff. Aunt Khalida was where she usually was, holed up with the computer.

Aisha was worried about Aunt Khalida. She was working too hard and not sleeping enough, and she bit one's head off if one said anything. Pater would talk some sense into her. For sure nobody else could.

But today was a free day, one of the last before everybody came back. Aisha planned to enjoy it.

The antelope were just beginning to fill up the winter grazing grounds. There were hundreds now, compared to the thousands that would pour in later, with the tribes following. Antelope were the best hunting of all, and they brought smaller animals with them, and birds, enough game to feed half a world.

Aisha was not out to hunt anything. She just wanted to see.

Jamal had his reader with him. Watching animals was not his favorite thing, though he was always glad to get out of the house. She thought Rama might bring his, too, but all he had was his water bottle and a bag full of lunch.

Aisha's favorite herd was back already. The old male with the crooked horn was still alive. He had a dozen babies, most of them striped dark brown and gold like him, and a band of new wives that he had won from another male.

Aisha was glad to see him. "He's old," she told Rama, "but he just keeps going on, collecting wives and scars."

Rama lay beside her in the tall grass. He had a hungry look—not kill and butcher and roast a fat doe hungry, but as if there was something here that he wanted so badly it hurt. When some of the babies came bounding and leaping and mock-sparring over near where they were, he almost forgot to breathe.

"They're beautiful," she said.

"Yes."

"I think people rode them once. Don't you think so? They're not really shaped like Earth antelope, not in the back. They're more like horses. Though the males with their horns might be a problem. They could put your eye out."

"Not if you knew what you were doing," he said.

She had to agree with that.

The old male's herd moved on after a while, grazing its way down to the river. A new herd wandered by. This was much smaller. Its male was young, with horns barely longer than her arm. He had three wives, and just one baby, which was red with a white foot. He was black, which told Aisha it was probably some other male's baby. Blacks didn't sire reds out of red females.

"Look," she said. "He just won those ladies. He's all proud of himself."

She looked to see what Rama thought, but he was no longer beside her. He was up and walking through the grass, not even trying to hide. She opened her mouth to yell at him, but that would only spook the animals sooner.

The females were still grazing. The baby was bouncing around its mother. The male had seen Rama: his head was up, his horns as straight and sharp as spears.

His eyes were ruby red. Aisha had only seen that once or twice before, and never in a black. The others were normal brown or amber, and the baby's were blue.

Rama walked right up to him. By the time Aisha realized what he was doing, it was too late to move.

He was talking to the antelope. She was too far away to hear what he said. The rhythms weren't PanTerran. They weren't Old Language, either. He sounded very polite.

He reached out his hand and laid it on the male's forehead between the horns. The male's head lowered. Aisha sucked in her breath.

The male didn't spit Rama on his horns and trample him to death. He lowered his nose into Rama's palm as if he had been a horse, and blew. Rama's other hand rubbed him around the base of the horns and behind the ears, working his fingers into the thick mane that grew like a horse's on the long neck.

Tears ran down Rama's face. He pressed his forehead to the antelope's forehead and cried.

And the antelope let him. He stood the way Jinni stood when Aisha needed a hug more than anything.

Then Rama did something completely, totally insane. He caught hold of the hank of mane at the antelope's withers and swung onto his back.

That was it. Aisha was done with him. She couldn't watch him die.

She couldn't stop watching, either. The explosion wasn't any worse than Lilith had given him. It was the same kind of thing: testing, feeling him out, getting the balance.

Just the same. Rama rode it the same, too. If anything he was more comfortable with that big, long neck in front of him and those horns spearing the sky. They couldn't put his eye out unless the antelope aimed his chin straight up, which he wasn't built to easily do—any more than a horse was.

This was a wild animal. Feral, Mother would say. Mother was precise with her terminology. Domesticated once, but gone wild for thousands of years.

Aisha would never have known it to see this one. Rama didn't ride long. Just long enough to get the bucks out, get a sensible walk and a bit of trot, then he slid off and smoothed the black mane and said in Old Language, "Come."

The antelope came. So did his wives and his stepdaughter. They followed the horses—and Jamal wide-eyed and as speechless as Aisha was—away from the plain and into the city and straight to the corner paddock with the shedrow shelter, that happened not to have horses in it at the moment.

Nothing ever surprised Vikram, but Aisha thought he might be as close to it as he ever got. He took in the new additions, checked that they had water and hay, then found Rama in the tack room, taking apart one of the old saddles.

"Horse backs aren't quite the same," Rama said when Vikram came in, as if they'd been in the middle of a conversation and not right at the beginning. "We'll need to rig the bridle differently, too."

"You're planning to ride those things?" Vikram said.

Aisha bit her tongue. It wasn't her place to say Rama already had.

Rama smiled at Vikram. "Wouldn't you like to see me try?"

"Why?" Vikram demanded.

"Why not?"

"Your funeral," Vikram said, the way everybody did sooner or later with Rama.

Except Aisha. She had observed that when Rama set out to do something, he knew he could do it. He never tried anything totally impossible.

"Before you lay me in my tomb," Rama said to Vikram, "will you help me with the saddle? I can see what it needs, but I'm not familiar with this kind of tree. Show me what to do."

Vikram shook his head, but he sat down on the workbench and pulled the half-dismembered saddle over toward him and held out his hand. Rama put the seam ripper in it. A moment longer and their heads were together, wavy black and steel grey, turning a horse saddle into an antelope saddle.

Jamal was a menace with a computer. Mother said it, and she would know. She was fairly dangerous herself.

Aisha caught him the day after Rama brought the antelope in, pretending to take a nap but actually deep inside the house web. She'd been looking for Mother's articles on antelope, but a tweak in a search string led her to Aunt Khalida's files and a fragment of code that Jamal hadn't quite got around to hiding.

She slipped out of the web as stealthily as she could, ducked down the hall to his room and sat on him. She was still heavier than he was, though just barely.

He came out of the web with a lurch and a squawk. "*Hey!* What do you think you're—"

"What do *you* think you're doing?" she shot back. "You know what happens when Aunt Khalida catches people hacking her files. Do you really want to be locked out of the web for a tenday?"

"The way you were?" He scowled at her. He'd been practicing Pater's patented expression again; it didn't work as well on his thin boy-face, and he'd have to grow much more imposing eyebrows. "Do you think she knows what Rama is up to?"

"Why?"

He pushed at her. She stopped sitting on him and perched on the end of the bed instead. He sat up and hugged his skinny knees. "You don't think it's weird that he's training wild antelope to ride?"

"I think everything about him is weird," she said. "What were you doing in Aunt Khalida's files?"

"Nothing."

He barely looked guilty, which told her all she needed to know. "You couldn't get in."

That stung him. "I would have, if you hadn't ripped me out."

"You're lucky I caught you before she did."

"I was almost there," he said, and now his scowl was almost of Pater proportions. "She has to be running searches to find out who Rama is. Or what. I want to see what she's found."

"She hasn't found anything," Aisha said. "You should have asked. I could have told you."

"I hate you," he said mildly.

"I hate you, too." Aisha fixed him with her firmest stare. "Look. Whatever happened to Aunt before she showed up here, she's a right mess. I don't think we should cross her any more than absolutely necessary. And that includes getting caught hacking her personal files."

"I won't get caught."

"No, you won't. Because you're not going anywhere near them."

"Says who?"

"Says you, if you just wake up to yourself. It's not worth getting grounded to come up with nothing, and you know it. If anything does show up, we'll find out. One way or another."

One thing about Jamal: if she pushed hard enough, he actually stopped to think. He was still scowling, but he'd stopped arguing.

"What Aunt doesn't know won't hurt us," he said. "Fair enough about the files. But, Aisha, there are *antelope* in the barn. Sooner or later, she's going to—"

"Make it later," Aisha said.

Aunt Khalida might not have found out at all until everybody came back, except that one day she wandered down past the barn, looking for something in the staff cabins and not paying attention to anything else, and walked right through the antelope pen.

She found herself face to horns with the male. It wasn't a threat exactly. His stepdaughter was playing with her shadow in the corner, and Khalida had come between her and the rest of the herd.

Khalida stopped. The baby, encouraged by her mother's calling, skittered past. The male backed away, bowed to Khalida, and left her standing there with her mouth open.

Aisha found that out later. The first she knew of it was a bellow like a drill sergeant's, loud enough to lift the schoolbot off its moorings and set it bouncing against the ceiling.

Aisha had never heard Aunt Khalida in full cry before. It brought Aisha and Jamal out of the classroom and Vikram out of the cabins, but she wasn't calling them.

Rama took his time answering. He had a polishing cloth over his shoulder and a bridle in his hand.

Once she had him in front of her, Khalida went back to her normal volume. "I'm sure you can explain this," she said, jabbing her chin toward the herd.

"They're lovely, aren't they?" he said. "The mares are all in foal. By spring we'll have a proper herd."

"What do we want a herd of antelope for?"

Aisha could feel the thunder rumbling in that. She could see Rama wasn't going to do anything to calm it down, too. She butted in with as much wide-eyed innocence as she could. "It's an experiment, Aunt. Remember that paper you and Mother wanted to write about alien riding animals? We're going to prove your thesis."

"The children are," Rama said smoothly. "I'll be the illustration. I've adapted a saddle for the stallion, and rigged a bridle. Would you like to see?"

"You can't call them mares and stallions," Khalida said through clenched teeth. "They're not horses."

"No," he said, "but they were bred for riding. I've been teaching the stallion his basics. See."

He held out his hand. The male snorted at Khalida and danced on tiptoe around her, and slid familiarly and comfortably in under Rama's arm.

He was smaller than the average male of his kind, about as tall as Jinni, but he was sturdy and well made like Rama, and he was laughing at Aunt Khalida. Aisha could feel it. It tugged at her lips and made her want to laugh, too.

Khalida's eyebrows had gone up. "Basics are turning a wild animal into a lapdog?"

"Basics are obedience and discipline and"—Rama raised his arm and sent the stallion out in a circle around them all, tossing his head and flagging his tasseled tail—"the skills essential to a ridden animal. Correct gaits and paces. Balance. Ability to carry a rider with ease and grace."

"First a thief," Khalida said. "Now a riding master. What will you turn into next? A starpilot?"

"That's your skill," he said. "When I'm done with this gentleman, he'll consent to let you ride him. Then you can write your paper from experience as well as knowledge."

"Experience is no authority," Khalida nastily. She stalked away. Her back was stiff; it got stiffer the more Rama laughed at her.

Still, Aisha thought, most of that was temper. She actually was fascinated. Give her a day or two to get over it and she'd be out there with Rama, trying her hand with one of the mares.

Rama had bet on it. He had a second saddle started, and the bridle in his hand wasn't a horse bridle. It was made for the wider-set ears and smaller muzzle of an antelope, without the extra buckle on the side that he needed to get the headstall over the stallion's horns. Mares had none, which made bridling them much simpler.

"You're evil," Aisha said approvingly. He grinned at her. He was as pleased with himself as a male ever was when things were going his way.

Khalida was losing her grip. Walking through a paddock she had assumed was empty, not even seeing the herd of horse-sized animals until she was in the middle of them, was worse than idiotic. It was dangerous.

She was damned lucky the animals were, somehow, domesticated. That needed examination, but not today. Today she had to examine herself.

She could keep falling apart without any effort to stop it. She could kill herself. Or she could scrape together what was left and make the best of it.

Everything should be so simple. MI had run her through therapy, declared her repaired, and sent her on leave to finish the process. She had another six tendays to reinstatement. It was fully expected that she would return to active duty.

What had not been expected was that she isolate herself so completely. On an actual inhabited planet she would have had ongoing therapy, constant supervision, and an expectation of complete recovery.

That was why she had come here. She had not wanted to get through it. She wanted to feel the whole of it. Every corrosive drop of guilt. Every nightmare.

Now she was seeing things even when she was not asleep. Hearing voices. Plucking feelings from the air. When she walked through rooms in the house, she could taste the people who had been in them since they were built, layer on layer of memories.

That was her mind dissociating. Disintegrating. It was supposed to be putting itself back together.

She had no appetite for dinner. Jamal pounded on the door and went away. When Khalida gave way to the jabbing in her stomach, she found a tray, and dinner still hot inside the tiny stasis field.

She ate a few bites and pushed the tray aside. The computer pinged at her. *Subspace message incoming,* said the crawl across her vision.

It was from MI. Again. She let it file itself as unread, yet again. The computer informed her that she had forty-seven unread messages. Forty-three were from MI in its various incarnations. Most of them were flagged as urgent.

The computer did not count all the other messages she deleted as they came in. She considered deleting the ones from MI, but she was not that far gone. Yet.

The walls of her room closed in on her. Ah, claustrophobia. It had been a while since she had a bout of that. She should have seen it coming today when she went on an errand she never had finished, even if she could have remembered what it was.

The house had quieted down. Everyone was in bed. Khalida went up the ladder to the roof.

Whether the people of this world had used their roofs as rooms for sleeping or eating or cooking in hot weather and for growing gardens all year round, the archaeologists were still arguing. In this house, because Rashid and Marina had restored it, the roof was an extension of the rooms below.

The Brats were supposed to tend their mother's garden up there with its boxes of vegetables and its row of fruit trees in pots. One corner, which had a view of the city, had a long table and a crowd of chairs and benches. The staff had meetings up there in season; they could sit for hours arguing about this find or that theory.

If Khalida half-closed her eyes, she could see them: Rashid in his usual spot wearing his usual scowl, Marina up and pacing as she argued, Shenliu stretched out long and lazy on a bench, and last year's interns in a huddle, wide-eyed and too shy to speak.

One of the figures in the vision stayed when she opened her eyes to the night. The moon was rising, huge and red, with its cratered face and its white cap: it was winter in the north of the moon, and the icecap had spread as far as it would go.

Rama leaned on the parapet that rimmed the roof. His head was tilted back. The moon's light bathed his face in blood.

Khalida's first impulse was to turn on her heel and stalk back into the house. But why should she have to leave? Let him go if he wanted to be alone.

He did not move, but he knew she was there. She felt him feeling it, a uniquely strange sensation, like being two people at once.

His voice came soft in the bloody light. "I don't suppose you know what happened to the other moon."

"What other moon?" Khalida said. "There's only the one."

"There were two," he said.

"No, there weren't," she said. "This is all there is. If there had been a second one, there would be evidence. Rubble in space. A ring. A crater in the planet, or in the other moon. Evidence of major tidal disturbances. There's nothing."

"Nothing at all?"

"Not a thing."

"I suppose they could have taken it with them," he said.

"That's crazy."

He shrugged, no more than the lift of a shoulder.

He had the torque on again. It looked odd with a work shirt and a well-worn pair of Spaceforce uniform trousers. They were both leftovers from the storeroom, and they both fit, which was all that mattered to him.

"We've got to get you some clothes of your own," Khalida said. "I'll have Vikram put in the order tomorrow. With luck there's still enough time for it to come in with the supply ship."

He said nothing about how long it taken her to think of it. Not because he was being kind; he honestly did not care. There was too much else to care about. Giant antelope. Ruined cities. Missing moons.

"Don't mock," he said.

Her body went hot, then cold. She measured each word precisely. "Get out of my mind."

"Stop shouting at me, then."

"I am not—"

"One thing Psycorps has right," he said. "An unschooled talent is a menace to itself and everything around it."

"You *are* Psycorps," she said. Her stomach had done a duck and roll, and then gone to ground.

"I am not," he said.

"That you remember."

"I am not Psycorps," he said.

She scoffed. "Oh, stop! Of course you are. Maybe they mindwiped you and tossed you, but nobody with that much talent can escape the Corps. I wonder what you did to earn the mindwipe? It must have been impressive."

"What I did..." He closed his eyes and shook his head. "It was more what I would have done, and was starting to do. But it wasn't Psycorps."

"They gave you false memories," she said. "But they didn't neuter you. I wonder why? Is it possible they couldn't?"

"I am not—" He gave it up. Not because he yielded. He was still determined to believe that he had nothing to do with the Corps.

"That's part of the programming," she said. "When they're ready to reactivate you, it will all come back."

"I should be so sure of myself and my world," he said.

He meant the words to sting. She gave him a brick wall. It was authentically antique: glazed brick, with a dragon stalking across the top.

He laughed. "Oh, wonderful! Where is that?"

"Earth," she said. "Babylon." Then: "Get *out* of my mind!"

"I am. It's mine you're in."

"I am not."

He counted breaths. She counted with him. At a hundred and three, he said, "I do apologize. I was not in my right mind when I did what I did. I opened doors that were bricked and plastered shut. I filled wells that had been drained by the most ham-handed, the most ineptly brutal—" He stopped; he brought himself under control. "I did this. I will not undo it. But I can make amends."

"You *won't* undo it? That means you can."

"I will not mutilate you all over again," he said.

"I was defective," she said. "Psycorps repaired the defect."

"Psycorps gutted you and left you a mass of scars."

His disgust was so deep, his anger so fierce, that Khalida could hardly see. "I was still defective. I still had to—"

"You were *not!*"

The force of that flung her back into a chair and knocked most of the wind out of her.

He dropped to his knees in front of her. His hands gripped the arms of the chair. "I see what Psycorps does. It chooses and trains the middling and the weak, and binds them to its rules and regulations. The strong it destroys. You are strong. That is the defect. That is what had to be cut out."

"I'm not—"

She stopped. If her psi was not weak—if he told the truth—it all finally made sense. Why the Corps had taken her. What it had done.

Those memories were buried deep, below even nightmares. Mindwiped. But what they must mean...

"Strong is dangerous," she said. "Strong can't be controlled. Strong can destroy."

He dropped back onto his heels. "So it can," he said, soft again, sounding unspeakably tired. But the anger was as hot as ever. "So can bodily strength or high intelligence. Are there agencies to destroy those, too?"

"Of course not. Brawn and brains are normal human attributes. Psi is different."

"How? Isn't it born in you? Is it not as much a part of you as your eyes or your hands?"

She looked at him. At his eyes; at his hands. He had something in his right hand. In that light it looked like a bleeding scar. As if something had cut out the palm and filled it with—what?

His fingers closed over it, clenched as they had been when she first saw him. He rubbed it along his thigh. It hurt, she thought. Badly, from the way it trembled.

She was evading. Again. "My eyes can't kill. My hands can't break a person's mind."

"Of course they can." He looked her in the face. "Psycorps is afraid. It knows so little and understands even less. It breaks what it should cherish, and destroys what it should keep."

"You're saying it's a pack of amateurs."

"Isn't it?"

"Then what are you?"

He did not answer. His face had closed in on itself.

"You're its worst nightmare," she said.

"It doesn't know I exist." He stood. Even exhausted, even shaking all the way down to the bone, he had grace. He always knew exactly where the parts of him were.

His hand brushed her hair. Before she could remember to flinch, it was gone. So was the sensation of wearing her skin inside out.

The world was its normal self again. She deliberately refused to find it dull or her senses muted.

He was gone. She refused to regret that, too. No matter how hard it was.

A tenday before everyone was due back, Aunt Khalida called a family council. That included Vikram. It did not include Rama. He was out with the antelope, teaching the stallion to canter under saddle.

Aisha would rather have been watching him or riding Jinni. But Aunt Khalida was not in a good mood. She hadn't been for days. In fact, though Aisha would get her mouth washed out if she said so, Aunt Khalida had been a raving bitch.

Even with that, she looked healthier. The hollows weren't so deep under her eyes. The places on her arms where she cut herself, which Aisha was not supposed to know about, were healing. Her nightmares had stopped shaking the house quite so hard. She was even sleeping, though maybe she didn't realize it.

Now she sat in the kitchen over the last of breakfast and glowered at Aisha and Jamal and Vikram. "All right," she finally said, catching Jamal just as he reached for the last of the cloudberry juice. He snapped his hand back as if she'd slapped it.

She paid no attention. "I heard from Rashid this morning. They're getting in early—half a tenday from now."

Aisha wanted to cheer, but didn't dare.

Vikram was braver. "We're all ready. Just need to make sure the cabin assignments are sorted out, and finish tuning up the rovers."

"Good," said Khalida, who'd barely been listening. "That's good. There's just one thing."

"Rama," Jamal said.

Everybody stared at him. He was never the one to blurt things out—that was Aisha. He went red, but he stood up to them all, even Aunt Khalida. "Well? He does need explaining."

"Rama," said Vikram, "is my cousin from Govinda, who got himself into a bit of trouble with a certain young lady's family. Our family judged it best to send him out of the way for a while."

"That doesn't sound like Rama at all," said Aisha, now everybody had got to talking.

"Do you have a better idea?" Khalida asked her.

Aisha was been thinking, too, and noodling around in the computer, and she knew what to say. "He's Vikram's old shipmate's son, and he's from Dreamtime. He's on walkabout. A tradeship dropped him off here."

Vikram rubbed his chin under the curly grey beard. "Now that," he said, "is downright plausible."

"It is, isn't it?" Khalida only sounded halfway bitchy. "So do we change his name? I don't think there's anybody named Rama in the Dreamtime."

"Let's not get any more complicated than we have to," Vikram said. "I called him that and he liked it. It stuck."

"That's the truth," Aisha said.

"Yes," said Khalida. "You understand why we're doing this, don't you? As long as we don't know who he really is, it's safer to give him a cover story."

"Like MI," Jamal said. "I get it. The less everybody knows, the less there is to find out."

And, Aisha thought, the less trouble Aunt Khalida would get into for letting a total stranger babysit her brother's offspring when she was supposed to be doing it. The fact Rama was completely trustworthy in that respect would make no difference whatsoever. Pater was hard line about responsibility, and Aunt had been slacking it.

Everybody had reasons for wanting to keep people in the dark about Rama. "I'll go tell him who he is now," Aisha said, and got out of there before anybody could stop her.

They did try. Jamal was loudest. "*Hey!* It's your turn to put the dishes in the cleaner!"

"That's a good story," Rama said.

He'd had Jinni saddled, and Lilith too, when Aisha got to the barn. She thanked him for that.

The antelope stallion was not happy. Not in the least. *He* wanted to go out. *He* wanted to do the running and the carrying. But he wasn't ready for that yet. Not because he'd been wild only three tendays before; Rama didn't worry about such things. The stallion needed more practice carrying weight.

So he stayed with his wives, roaring and ramping and screaming, and Rama and Aisha rode toward the middle of the city. They stopped beside last year's excavation, the building with the round paved floor that was probably a temple.

While the horses grazed around the broken pillars, Rama and Aisha sat on one that had fallen down, and shared a fruit pastry. Aisha had told him who he was supposed to be once everybody got back, and he smiled. "Walkabout," he said. "That's like a journey, yes? Such as a priest would take, to discover the world and himself."

"People on Dreamtime don't do priesthood," said Aisha. "They're not that formal. They go 'way back, did you know? Thirty thousand Earthyears, more or less."

He widened his eyes. "That's old," he said.

"About as old as anything human gets. When everybody went into space, some of them went walkabout. One way and another, most of those ended up on Dreamtime. Now when the young ones go out, they go all over, but they always head back home. Just like in the old times, when home was an island continent on Earth."

He nodded. His eyes were dark and as soft as they ever got. "I went walkabout when I was young. Maybe it's time I did it again."

The bottom dropped out of her stomach. "You can't leave! You just got here."

"Did I say I was leaving?"

"You said—" She sucked in air. "Never mind. It was the way you said it. Are you really from Dreamtime, then?"

"No."

She went still. "You remember, don't you?"

"Yes."

She didn't ask. She wasn't sure she wanted to know the answer.

His eyes understood. Without stopping to think, she said inside her head, "Thank you."

"You're welcome," he said.

He hadn't said it aloud.

She stilled even more. "I've got it, haven't I? The thing. What Aunt Khalida had. Has."

He bent his head. Neither of them needed to hear him say it.

"You do, too. Lots of it. Lots and lots. But Psycorps didn't take you. Did it?"

"It never found me," he said.

"I wish it would never find me."

There. She'd said it. She hadn't been thinking about it. Much. About how the tendays were spinning on, and she was getting closer and closer to the day when Psycorps would come. Because it always came. Even to the remotest places, where a person turned thirteen Earthyears, and the law said she had to be tested.

On populated planets, parents took their offspring to Psycorps stations. In places like this, Psycorps came to them. She had her appointment. It had come in yesterday. She would get a present for her birthday: a Psycorps agent with his testing protocol.

"That's what they call it," she said. "Testing protocol. Like who gets to speak first at the summit meeting. Or who gets taken off to a processing center."

"Is that what they do? Take you away and turn you into sausage?"

She didn't want to laugh, but she couldn't help it. "Just about. You get more testing. The more you pass, the more they teach you. Eventually you turn into an agent. Or they decide you won't work out, and neuter you."

"Yes," he said in his throat. "That I have seen. Your aunt was there for a while, wasn't she?"

"Half an Earthyear," Aisha said. "She never talks about it."

"She doesn't remember."

"I'm sure she doesn't want to," Aisha said. She had to say it, because if she didn't, it would tear her up inside. "I'm just like her. Everybody says that. I don't think I'm that bitchy, but I haven't been through all she has, either."

"Nor will you," he said.

"How do you know? Can you see the future?"

"That's not my gift," he said. "I'm making you a promise. Psycorps won't do a thing to you."

"Look," she said. "Don't go killing the agent to save me. That will just make everything worse."

He bit his lip. It was kind of him not to laugh. "I will not kill the agent. Here," he said. "Look."

He held out his hand. He had the sun in it. The real, literal sun. She could see the swirls of superheated gas, and the streams of plasma licking out from the edges, and a spot drifting across the center.

It was an incredible thing. Really incredible—unbelievable. She stretched out a finger, terrified to touch it, but positive that if she didn't, she would never stop wishing she had.

It didn't sear the skin off her bones. It was warm, and there was a weirdness to it, a snap and tingle. But mostly it felt like the palm of a hand—as if his skin was transparent, and the sun was underneath.

"Remember this," he said. "When the agent comes to test you, keep it in your mind, directly behind your eyes. Let it be all you think of."

"What—" said Aisha. It was hard *not* to think of it, with it burning and flaming in front of her. "What in the worlds is it?"

"Magic," he said.

"There's no such thing," Aisha said.

"Of course there is. You just call it something different. This, Psycorps would say, is a highly evolved manifestation of psi talent."

"'Any sufficiently advanced technology is indistinguishable from magic,'" said Aisha. "That's one of the Clarkean Laws. There's another one, from someone else I don't remember, that says the opposite is true, too."

"Is there a law that says psi and magic are essentially the same thing?"

"I don't know," she said. "Probably. Can that thing in your hand really help me with the test?"

"One of the things it is is a key," he said. "It can open any door. It can also lock that door, and keep safe what's inside."

"Like me? And the thing inside me?"

"Just like that," he said.

"I think you might be dangerous," she said.

"I am," said Rama.

She wasn't afraid. She never had been, even when she first saw him, when he looked and was so wild. She took his hand and held it in hers, to cool it a little. "I won't tell anyone," she said.

The expedition came in on the usual tradeship from Marduk: one of Mother's family connections. Rashid had done a little trading of his own; the ship would stay in orbit for a tenday, and a flock of tourists would flutter and flap its way around the planet, escorted by genuine xenoarchaeologists.

That was not the first time Rashid had paid his passage in that particular way. It explained the range and apparent excess of Vikram's preparations. Khalida should have known, but she had had too many other things on her mind.

One of those things proved not to be nearly as fragile as she had expected. When the shuttle came down on the plain outside the city, Rama was there with the rest of them. He watched the ship descend with open fascination and no perceptible fear. He lent a hand with the unloading and the sorting out of people, and helped set up the tents for the guests.

She did not know why she should have expected him to hide in a corner with his arms over his head, babbling about metal birds and fire from the sky. Maybe because she was tempted to do just that. A world occupied by four other humans and an assortment of animals, she could handle. This onslaught taxed her narrow limits.

She had to expand them, and fast. The shuttle offered an opportunity she could not afford to waste.

It came with a pilot and a handful of crew, all of whom were taking a few days' leave planetside. That first day, in the confusion of unloading, she calculated would be her best chance.

She wandered onto the bridge on the pretext of looking for lost luggage. The pilot was young, bored, and desperate for someone intelligent to talk to—by which she meant, able to talk about ships and flying and the yacht races around Earth system.

The old skills came back fast. So did the sense of familiarity when Khalida sat at the console, leaning back in the chair, arguing the relative merits of solar sails and cosmic-dust propulsion. Well inside of an hour, she had Meichan convinced to take a well-earned break under an actual sky. Meichan set the security locks before she went, but she made the mistake of letting Khalida see what she was doing.

It was blissfully quiet after she left. There were still voices and banging and rumbling of machinery elsewhere on the ship, but those were muted here.

Khalida took a deep breath. There was nothing quite like the taste of ship's air, with its faintly canned, faintly stale undertone. It made her surprisingly homesick.

The security locks were standard models, childishly easy to hack if one was MI and trained to memorize keycodes on sight.

It all came back in a rush. She would pay later, but not until she had what she came for. The shuttle's system lay wide open. Through that, she got into the main ship's system—and that was connected to the worldsweb.

The sheer, overwhelming *rightness* of being open to the universe again was as much as she could stand. She let it roar on past her while she found her balance. That took a while, but she had allowed for it.

Her MI codes still worked. That had not been a sure thing. She still had her clearances. She set up a flock of proxies and sent them off in carefully random directions while she aimed for the target.

Psycorps was hell to hack. She had had tendays to plot a strategy. The codes she fed in, with search strings embedded in them, were designed to mimic Psycorps' own internal systems.

Subspace relay was fast, but it was not instantaneous. She filled the time by calling up the flight simulator and running the latest pilots' testing module.

Both sets of results came up at the same time. She had renewed and upgraded her license, and there was no reference anywhere in Psycorps' accessible system to a humanoid entity of Rama's genetic description.

Something else had come up, too. Something that pinged a dummy string, or so she had thought when she coded it—just before the hacker alarms went off.

That ping nearly laid her open to Psycorps' internal security. A voice pulled her out just before it swallowed her whole. "Have you seen a pink tesser-bag? Sera Lopakhina will die, simply die, if she can't find it."

Khalida blinked stupidly at Rama. The weblink had cut off. He was smiling at her, completely oblivious. She pointed at the object he was looking for, which glowed pinkly under the auxiliary console.

It was amazingly pink. He fished it out and held it gingerly, regarding it with a kind of horrified amusement. "I don't think I've ever seen that color before. Does she really keep all her baggage in here?"

"Wait till you see what comes out of it," Khalida said. Her focus was coming back, along with some minimally useful fraction of her intelligence. "We caught a thief once who had stowed a whole shuttle in one of these, complete with cargo."

"Was it pink?"

"God, no," she said. "That would have taken hiding in plain sight to a whole new level."

So, she realized, had he. His accent, his expression, his whole tone and presence, had changed in ways she would never have expected. While she digested that, he tucked the bag under his arm, saluted her with a fair imitation of a Spaceforce snap, and sauntered off the bridge.

She stayed until the pilot finally remembered to come back. Her mind chewed over and over what she had stumbled across while she searched for something else. It was a file label, to which a file should have been attached, but the alarms had triggered before it could download. All she had was the file name, *Araceli*, and the designation, *Operation Incomplete*.

She was not quite crazy enough to reactivate the search. She had covered her trail just well enough this time, thanks to pure chance. If she tried it again this soon, she might not be so lucky.

Dinner that night was a mob. They ate on the roof, where there was table space enough for them all; the Brats, who had done most of the cooking, played host until Marina chased them off to bed. Their protests had the air of a formality: they were worn out.

"I see they didn't blow up the planet," Rashid said long after dark. The tourists had been herded to their tents, and the staff and students were either asleep in their cabins or snoring under the table. Rashid and Khalida and Marina sat together under the moon, finishing off the last of the coffee.

Khalida blatantly and selfishly emptied the pot. "You've been gorging on it for tendays. I haven't even seen real coffee since before you left."

"This time we brought enough to last us," said Marina.

"We'd have had enough last time if it hadn't been for greedyguts here," Rashid said, grinning at Khalida.

She bared her teeth in return, and paused for a long, bitter-blissful sip. When she came up for air, her brother went back to what he had been talking about before. "So you kept Aisha away from the explosives and Jamal from hacking into Spaceforce Central. I salute you."

"They found other things to get into," Khalida said.

"Less destructive, at least," said Marina. She stretched and yawned, looking no older than her daughter, and not much larger, either; but the glance she darted at Khalida was wickedly sharp. "How long did you say the antelope have been in the paddock?"

"Three tendays now," Khalida said. "Almost four."

"And they've never even tried to take the wall down?" Marina shook her head in wonder. "Who would have thought it?"

"Vikram says we're not to blame the Brats for that," said Rashid. "That's his new assistant's project."

"It is," Khalida said.

"Vikram never mentioned that he felt overworked," Rashid said.

"He doesn't," said Khalida. "But when your old shipmate's offspring shows up looking for a berth, what do you do?"

"Yes," said Rashid. "What do you do?"

Khalida knew what he was waiting for. She gave it to him. "He's clean. No civil or criminal complaints anywhere in the system."

Nothing at all in the system, but neither of them needed to know that.

Rashid sat back, cradling his mug in his hands. "So I've got a new hire to do the paperwork on, and he'll probably up and take off before I get it all filed."

"Why bother?" Khalida said. "He's on walkabout. He'll earn his keep while he's here, and the rules won't let you pay him, just feed him and give him a place to sleep. Vikram can look after him."

"That's what Vikram said," said Rashid. Khalida held her breath, but he did not seem to find it suspicious that they had their story so carefully rehearsed. Marina, who was more likely to smell a lie, had curled up with her head on Rashid's shoulder and fallen abruptly and deeply asleep.

Khalida observed her with envy. Most people lost that talent when they grew out of childhood.

Rashid was still wide awake. His eyes rested on Khalida, clear-sighted in the crimson moonlight. "You're looking better," he said.

She shrugged. "It had to happen sooner or later."

"I'm glad it happened sooner."

That was as close to sentimentality as anyone in their family was likely to come. Khalida shot it down before it reduced them both to mawkish sobs. "Can't wait for me to go wandering off again, can you?"

"Just make sure you get everything catalogued before you go."

"Oh no," she said. "I'm not staying here for the rest of my life."

"That's too bad," said Rashid. Half of it was mockery, and half of it was not.

Khalida pushed herself out of her chair and kissed the top of his head where the hair was starting to thin. "Don't worry. I'll stay till the hordes have blown off down the spaceways. I'll even help clean up after them."

11

The first few days after everybody got back were always crazed. The schoolbot stayed on shutdown, and Aisha and Jamal had to help get all the new people settled and deal with the tourists and make sure nobody got into anything they shouldn't. Mother and Pater were itching to get back to excavating, but the best they could do in the uproar was make sure last season's work was still there.

To add to the confusion, the tribes had finally followed the antelope to their winter camps. Of course the tourists wanted to take their shuttle and harass the "*dear* primitives"—that was what they were saying, loudly, as often as they could find someone from the expedition to screech at.

It was never any use to try to explain the difference between a real primitive, if there had ever been any such thing, and a postapocalyptic remnant. The most one got for that was a blank stare and, if one was Aisha or Jamal, a cloying, "Oh, *isn't* that darling?"

The parents had the usual plan in place, but that always waited for the tourists' next-to-last day. Meanwhile everybody suffered, and staff got to take turns leading tours of ruins as far as possible from any tribal camps. The city by the eastern ocean, which was built all in circles, was especially popular—and it took so long to get there by rover that people had to stay overnight.

While that went on, the rest of the expedition could finally start setting up the next round of digging. Some of the Blackroot men came straggling in to help, hung with amulets and smelling of the smoke they'd bathed in to keep the curses off. There would be more later; Aurochs and Far Passes weren't hopelessly afraid of the ruined city, either, and they had a great liking for the bolts of cloth and the copper ingots they got in return for digging in the dirt.

There was no way Aisha could get away to visit Blackroot camp until everything was set up for the season. She was supposed to be studying patience.

It helped that she was terribly busy. That morning she was running back from the staff cabins with a load of laundry for washing in the main house when she heard a squawk from inside the barn. It sounded as if someone was getting strangled.

She dropped her basket with no regret at all and went to investigate. What she found was about what she had expected.

Rama had been cleaning stalls: the cart and the fork were in the aisle. He had the invader by the throat. There wasn't much to see of that one but black robes and veils and a pair of amber-yellow eyes glaring out of them.

Aisha was careful not to laugh. "Rama," she said. "It's all right. This is Malia. She's a friend."

Rama's glare was as baleful as Malia's. He moved so fast that Aisha could barely follow, and stripped out every knife, sword, throwing star, mace, knout, rope, cord, and chain that Malia carried. He even found the coil of copper wire that could be either a garrote or a set of shackles, depending.

"*Now* she is a friend," he said.

Malia spoke perfectly decent PanTerran, but she was so mad at him, she spat words in her own language.

He spat back without missing a beat. He had all the tones exactly right, and an intonation that said he was so far superior to her, she didn't even deserve to slit her own throat in front of him. It was too fast for Aisha to catch more than a handful of words, but it reduced Malia to wide-eyed silence.

Then, sweetly and in Panterran, he said, "That's better. Next time you try an ambush, make sure the quarry hasn't heard you coming since you came over the wall."

"I was practicing," Malia said.

"Clearly," he said. "You're by no means perfect."

Aisha moved in before they went to war all over again. "Malia, this is Rama. He's usually much more polite. Rama, please give her back her weapons. I promise she won't use them against anyone here."

"Won't she?" Rama said, but he stood back and let Malia put everything back where it belonged. She never took her eyes off him, even when she had to bend down and slip the smaller armaments into their various pockets.

He never took his eyes off her, either. When she was all put back together he said, "The truly great warrior walks in through the front gate, and no one thinks to question him."

"I'm a long way from greatness," she said. "I have to learn how to get there."

He burst out laughing. Not at her—even Malia could tell that, by the way she stood. He saluted her with a flourish. "Oh, well played! And well met. Someday you'll be a credit to your upbringing."

"I don't think I can say the same about you," Malia said darkly.

"That's what everyone always said." He picked up his fork and went back to his cart.

They were dismissed. He was good at it. Malia kept shooting glances back at him, but when Aisha had her out of there and in the house, helping with the laundry, she wouldn't talk about him at all.

Aisha didn't try to push her. When she was ready, she would talk. Meanwhile there was a whole season's worth of news to catch up on, how Vayel was married and Jana had had her baby and Malia had earned her second sword. Which Aisha had seen. Rama had taken it off her with everything else.

Most of Aisha's news had Rama in it, which was a problem, but Malia had more than enough to keep them going through the day. Then they had the new crew to talk about, and the tourists, who were about as awful as they usually were. Aisha did not mention the fact that this might be the last season. It wasn't time for that, yet.

She got permission to eat her dinner with Malia instead of with everybody else. They took it up to the roof, which was empty tonight. There were clouds coming in, promising rain by morning, but the sky to the west was clear.

Malia took off her veils and let the wind blow through her hair. It was cropped into curls, and it was the same color as her eyes. Her face was a much lighter shade of gold.

Before she put on the veils, the sun used to dye her all one color, except for the spray of freckles across her nose. Now she was her natural ivory, with a thin white line of a scar running straight down her cheek: her first rank-mark. The higher she went, the more she would get. She was determined to win all nine.

She looked completely human except for the eyes. There were no whites to them unless she opened them wide. The xenobiologist who came through a few seasons ago had said the natives checked out human to some vanishingly tiny degree—which disappointed him terribly. He had so wanted them to be an example of parallel evolution and not just another interstellar remnant.

Not that anybody had traced the original stock to its source yet, or figured out how it got scattered across several hundred similar worlds. That was an even bigger mystery than the emptying of Nevermore, and much, much older.

Now here was Malia, sitting on the parapet with her legs hanging over, watching the sun go down. "You'll get more people for your digging this winter," she said. "That thing you did, blowing the top off the Sleeper's Rock? The shamans are saying you let the evil out. Some think the whole world is cursed now, but the rest want to make you a goddess for breaking the curse."

"I don't want to be a goddess," Aisha said, "or Pandora, either."

Malia knew what she meant by that. Malia had as much Earth-style education as Aisha did, what with spending so much time around the house and being there when Jamal hacked the schoolbot so they could jump ahead with assignments. "Grandmother says whatever was in there is out now, and it's up to the gods which way it will go."

"Do you believe that?" Aisha asked. "That there was a demon in there?"

"I know what the stories say. That something very old and very dangerous slept inside the Rock. The old ones tried to destroy it before they left, but all they managed to do was knock the spires off the top."

"They didn't have nuplastique," Aisha said. She shivered, and not because the air was cold. "I thought I saw something inside, but whatever it was, it's buried now. There's nothing left alive down there."

"I hope you're right," said Malia. "I don't like the thought of some *thing* stalking the earth."

"Do you have an idea what it's supposed to be?" Aisha asked. "Like a dragon or a demon? Or some kind of prehistoric monster?"

Malia spread her hands. "Nobody ever really says. Just that it's terribly powerful and terribly dangerous, and it's supposed to wake and either destroy the world or save it."

"Maybe it already did," said Aisha. "Maybe that's what caused the Disappearance."

"Grandmother says no," Malia said. "That's why we stayed behind. Waiting for it."

"What will you do if it comes?"

Malia swung her legs over and stood up on the roof. "That's a Mystery. I'm not even supposed to know as much as I do, while I'm still barely a fledgling, and only one rank-mark to fly with. If anybody finds out I told you…"

Aisha nodded and set her lips together. That was their signal. Silence till death, it meant. "Stay here tonight," she said. "We'll help mark out the new dig in the morning. Mother wants to see if she can find where the ordinary people used to live. That's more interesting than temples and palaces, she says."

"Your mother is odd," Malia said, but she smiled. Malia was very fond of Aisha's mother.

She stayed the night, curling up in Aisha's bed and sleeping soundly all night long. Aisha kept waking up. She had dreams of monsters stalking the city, and a dragon flaming from the top of the broken cliff.

They were just dreams. Even in the middle of them she knew there were no dragons on Nevermore—though there might be demons. Demons were everywhere.

The last time she woke up, she remembered what Rama had told her. She filled her mind with the sun. Then finally she could sleep until morning.

The day before the tourists finally left to torment some other helpless planet, they went to visit Blackroot camp. It was a village really, with stone houses that people lived in from year to year, and fields and orchards where they planted winter crops and harvested fruit. They hunted for the meat they ate, but they had a kind of oxen to pull their wagons, and something like sheep that gave them wool and milk.

It always disappointed offworlders to discover that the simple primitives lived very well, and weren't totally ignorant, either. Still, they were exotic, especially the blackrobes who moved around the edges and kept watch over everybody else. They were entertaining enough to keep the tourists satisfied.

Vikram led the tour this year. They rode on horses as always, which got rid of the worst idiots right there. Some of the staff went along with the pack string, taking gifts and trade goods to the tribe and riding herd on tourists.

One of them was Rama. He rode Lilith, and for the most part he kept to the rear. Aisha had seen how totally he could charm anybody he had a mind to, but today his mood was strange. He hardly talked to anyone, and he didn't smile. That wasn't like him at all.

Aisha went because she wanted to visit her friends in the village, and because Vikram needed all the help he could get. Blackroot people were used to tourists;

they weren't likely to take offense at anything any of them said or tried to do. But it made sense to have plenty of backup, just in case.

Rama might be backup, or he might be trouble. Aisha wasn't sure which. He and Malia hadn't met again, and that felt deliberate on both sides. If anyone had asked Aisha, she would have said he shouldn't be here.

But he was, and so far he hadn't said or done anything difficult. He kept the stragglers from getting lost, made sure girths and bridles were adjusted properly, and glared down the idiots who wanted to race off after a herd of antelope. They were on the slowest and pluggiest horses, but that wouldn't have stopped them. Rama's look of ice-cold murder did.

The straight route to the camp only took about an hour. They took the long way, which used up most of the morning. By then the tourists who weren't saddle-sore were tired enough to be mostly quiet. In that condition, they were as ready as possible to be guests of Blackroot tribe.

The plain only looked flat from a distance. Up close, it was a landscape of long rolling hills and sudden hollows, crisscrossed with streams. Some of the hills had been towns and cities; the grass covered them now, and their walls had tumbled down.

Blackroot camp filled one of the hollows. A stream ran through it. The hill that rose up over it had a tower at the top, which was not nearly as broken as the rest of the things that people had built in this country. The tribe used it for a sentry post, and for keeping track of sun and stars.

When the caravan came into view, all the children came out, singing a welcome. Aisha sang back, and called to people she knew. That was almost everybody; they clapped and danced and swirled around her.

For a while she lost sight of Rama. When she found him again, they were all in the square in the middle of the camp, and he was helping herd horses into the pens at the far end. Aisha had her own herding to do, getting humans to sit down and be quiet.

There was a feast for them, and singing and dancing and mock warfare. The sword dance would come at the end, when all the blackrobes came out of the shadows and showed off their art.

Rama might have preferred to stay with the horses, but Vikram needed him to keep the troublemakers from wandering off. He had to lift one of them bodily and drop him in between Vikram and Sera Lopakhina. Then, one way and another in the crush of people, he ended up beside Aisha.

Food came out in its usual profusion; that concentrated the mind of even the flightiest offworlder. Aisha snared a bowl of bread filled with stewed antelope, but before she could eat more than a bite, Malia slid in beside her.

She opened her mouth for a greeting. Malia said, "Grandmother says come. Bring him." She tipped her head toward Rama.

Now that was interesting. It was also an honor. Most people, including people who came to study the tribes, thought the chief of the blackrobes was the chief of the tribe. They never paid much attention to the Wisewoman, but she was the real power behind the people.

Blackroot's Wisewoman was Malia's twice-great grandmother, though nobody counted the greats; they just called her Grandmother. She was very old, and she had been blind for most of her life. But that meant she saw the important things more clearly.

Usually when Aisha visited her, she was in her house by the stream. Today Malia led Aisha and Rama clear up to the top of the hill.

The grandmother sat at the foot of the tower on the side away from the camp, warming her bones in the sun. She wore no veils, nor had Aisha ever seen her in them, but even through the many wrinkles on her face, one could see the nine thin rank-scars.

She tilted her head at the sound of feet scrambling on the steep slope. Her blank blind eyes turned toward them. Aisha felt the warmth of her smile as it passed over her.

It only lasted an instant, before her whole self fixed on Rama.

She could see him. When Aisha looked in the same way the grandmother looked, he wasn't a shortish dark man in boots and breeches and a worn red shirt. He was a shape of fire, towering up to heaven.

Aisha blinked hard to make the vision go away. Rama had his alarming moments, but this was terrifying. She made herself see the person she knew, with his long black braid and his white smile.

"So," the grandmother said to him in Old Language. "It is you."

He answered in the same language. "You know me?"

"We stayed for you."

He dropped to one knee in front of her. Half of it was respect. Half, Aisha thought, was that his legs had given way. "You know? You remember? Where did they go? What happened to them?"

She held up her hands to stop his rush of words. He caught hold of them. "Please," he said.

Rama never pleaded. Hearing him do it now made Aisha's throat hurt, as if she were holding back tears.

The grandmother's head shook. Her face was sad. "I can't tell you. I only know what came down from the first who waited, who stood at the gates of the dark. 'If you are what we hoped for, you will know how to find us.'"

"If I am…" His breath caught. It sounded like a sob. "And if I am not?"

"Then they are safe from you."

"It wasn't fear of me that drove them away."

"No," she said. "You were all the hope they had left in this world."

"Then I've failed them," he said. "I'm several thousand years too late."

"Maybe," she said. "Maybe there was a reason it took so long."

"They're all gone now. All dead. How could they not be?"

"We still live," she said.

He had no answer for that. She slipped her hands free of his and ran them over his face.

He held still. There were tears on his cheeks. She paused at that. "Demons don't weep," she said.

"I'm a very human monster," he said.

"We all have that in us," the grandmother said.

He bowed his head. Her hands came to rest on his hair. "I don't know where to begin," he said.

"You will," said the grandmother.

She seemed sure of that. Rama was not, at all, but for once he had found someone who could face him down.

Aisha didn't often remember that this wasn't really her world. Just then, the feeling was so strong it made her dizzy.

The others were all born here. Rama, too.

Aunt Khalida and Vikram had spent so much time looking for him around the worlds, and trying to track him as if he came from Earth or a world settled by Earth. They hadn't found anything because there was nothing to find.

Where he came from on Nevermore, or how, Aisha wasn't ready to think about yet. Because the right word, the one that nobody had thought of because it was impossible, might be *when*.

She'd gone looking for treasure, and after all she'd found it. But whether it could help her or the expedition, or whether it would, she didn't know. All she could do was wait and hope.

Aisha didn't remember much about the rest of the day. When everybody came back to the city, so late the last of the light was dying from the sky, she went straight to her room.

She was almost too tired to keep her eyes open, but before she went to sleep, she linked in to the house computer. She and Jamal had made a back door for the two of them, with a password that let them in.

There were the files Aunt Khalida had saved because they were so outstandingly useless: the genetic analysis of the person called Rama, and various data related to it. Aisha stared at them for a long time, till she stopped trying to make them make sense. Then she knew what they meant.

Her world had tipped over. Malia had grown up with stories that her grandmother thought were finally coming true. Aisha hadn't even known they existed.

And it was her fault.

In the end she made the only decision she could make: to carry on the way she had been doing. Rama was still Rama, or whatever his name really was. He hadn't changed just because she knew more about him.

She was going to learn the rest of it. She promised herself that as she slipped out of the link. It might not solve Nevermore's greatest mystery, but there was a whole world's worth of stories apart from that. Those were the ones she would find. Then the expedition would have to stay, because it finally had something to show Centrum.

At long last the invaders left, lifting off in a bright and windy morning. The expedition could finally get back to its real work, and life could settle to a sensible routine.

Khalida had had enough of cataloguing and archiving to last for a while. She was also, if she admitted it, avoiding the overload of messages from offworld. She attached herself to the team that was carrying on with last year's excavation.

They had cleared the circular floor with its white stone paving and its remnants of mosaic tiles. Now they were working their way underneath it, opening up a complex of rooms that the sensors said were there.

No one expected much. Underground crypts and secret chambers on this world always proved to have been cleaned out thoroughly or else buried so deep there was no getting into them. But archaeologists were perpetual optimists, and insatiably curious. At the very least they might find an interesting floor, or a wall painting with all the people and animals scoured away.

The entrance was blocked with rubble that took three days to clear—most of it spent scanning every millimeter to make sure the blockage had nothing of value in it. Khalida dug in with a pick and shovel, helping to clear away the last of the bits of broken stone from a flight of stone-carved steps. Rashid sifted the most interesting remnants beside her, and Marina inched ahead of them with the scanner.

The scanner showed one large room below, and a smaller one leading off it. Nothing of any size lived there—a snake or two, the usual crowd of insects, but no cave bear or plains lion. Not that there would have been. Animals avoided the city as carefully as most of the tribes did.

There was no gold, either. Nothing metal; no tomb or treasury. Something did show up in a smaller chamber off the large one, but it was blurred and ambiguous.

The last few centimeters of rubble took forever to clear and carry off in baskets. Rashid's eyes gleamed with excitement, but he had never rushed an excavation yet, no matter what the temptation.

The sun was straight overhead when one of the interns carried the last basket off to the rubble heap. The entry stood open. Like most of the others that they had found in this part of Nevermore, it was wider and higher than Earth standard, as if designed for people who were over two meters tall and proportionately broad—though if there ever had been such people, they were long gone. The tribes tended toward the shorter end of human norm.

This particular doorway was made of stone, and there was a carving over the lintel, a common motif: the disk of the sun with a halo of rays. Often it was gilded. Here it was carved simply out of the pale gold stone.

The steps went down into the dark. The air that wafted up was cool, almost cold, and smelled of old stone. It was clean: the scanner had found nothing toxic in it.

Rashid had a biolume ready, the white light with its faintest hint of green barely visible in the sunlight. Khalida fished hers out of her pocket and shook it to life.

Marina was already on the stair, going down slowly, testing each step. Rashid followed. So did Khalida. The others had to wait. If there were paintings or manuscripts or artifacts made of something other than metal or stone, they were much too fragile to withstand a sudden invasion of trampling, breathing, sweating humanity.

Caution first and always. That was Rashid's mantra.

The room was huge and surprisingly high. It seemed to mirror the structure above: a circle of pillars in the same pale-gold stone as the rest, each pair framing an arch and an empty niche. Statues might have stood in the niches, but those were gone.

The walls were plain. If they had been painted, they were no longer. They might have been hung with tapestries once. The floor was a mosaic of pale gold and white and an occasional fleck of crimson, intricate in its way and pleasant to look at.

At the far end was a wider arch than the others. Rashid and Marina were determined to walk completely around the chamber, in case there was something hidden in a niche or carved on a pillar. Khalida let curiosity lead her straight to the next room.

It was much smaller, and square. When she amped up her biolume, she almost bolted back out again.

She caught herself up short. Of course there was no one sitting there. It was a statue, which must be life size, or near enough.

It sat against the wall in a stone chair. The chair was starkly simple, carved of pale grey stone, almost silver, with a translucent sheen. The back was as striking as the rest was plain: yet another gilded sun, with rays that stretched to the far walls and the ceiling.

The figure in the chair was male, and looked as if it was carved in obsidian. It was bare above the waist, dressed in a kilt below; the kilt was painted a vivid and beautiful shade of scarlet. There were gilded sandals on the feet, laced to the knee, and a massive gilded belt around the statue's middle, and a golden torque around its throat. On its head was a golden lion's head. It could have been a helmet, or it might have been a crown.

The statue's arms were weighted with golden ornaments. Its left hand rested on its knee. The right was lifted, palm outward. Painted on it was yet another image of the sun in splendor.

Her eyes insisted on taking in the whole, because she was trained to do that. Finally they let her focus on the thing that was most truly improbable.

The statue had Rama's face. It was a perfect likeness, right down to the fierce curve of the nose and the slight upward tilt to the corner of the mouth.

Khalida let her breath out slowly. Rashid and Marina were talking behind her, as excited a babble as she had heard from them. The niches, it seemed, had inscriptions. Not that anyone could read them, but they were rare, and they were there.

When it came to rarity, this thing in front of her trumped them all. She found she wanted to keep it to herself for a few moments more.

It really was remarkably lifelike. Maybe he had been a priest, if the building was a temple. More likely he was a king. It was possible he was both.

There were inscriptions everywhere that the statue and the sun were not: up and down all the walls, over and around the door, even marching across the floor. Rashid would be beside himself. Khalida would rather have something she could read.

She backed out of the room—shrine, archive, hiding place, whatever it was. It felt right to do that. Kings in Earth's history had not been fond of subjects who turned their backs. Kings here might have been different; she tended to think not.

The statue and its storeroom made Rashid ecstatic. If he recognized the statue's face, he said nothing about it. His mind was so full, it was possible he never made the connection between Vikram's assistant and the alien king.

Marina had to be dragged off at sundown and forced to eat and, Khalida hoped, sleep. Rashid might have camped in the room himself if he had not had Marina and the Brats to think about.

Khalida lent him a hand, and made sure he ate and slept, too. The house quieted down slowly. A buzz vibrated through them all, a thrum of excitement.

As everyone else fell asleep or tried to, she lay in her room, staring at the ceiling. On an ordinary night she would have fled to the computer. Tonight she pulled on boots and jacket and stuffed an extra biolume into her pocket, and went for a walk.

The temple's site was dark and completely silent. With the excavation gone underground, there was nothing to see except the sealed door.

She had the code for that. She keyed it, waited for the door to phase off and let her through, then carefully rekeyed it behind her.

Nothing had changed down here. It had been night underground for several thousand years.

Rashid or Marina must have left a biolume in the smaller chamber. It was amped down to a dim glow, gold rather than green.

There were two statues in there. The new one stood upright, turned toward the left-hand wall.

Then he moved. His hand ran down the written lines. He murmured words, as if he were reading. They were not in a language she knew.

A shiver ran under her skin. What she had spent most of the day trying to convince herself was not so, what had brought her here tonight because she had to make sure she was wrong, was alive and breathing and standing in front of her.

It was not just the face. Those ornaments, or ones remarkably like them, were locked in a box in the vault, all but the armlet with the herd of antelope running in a skein around and around it, the gold ring with the rayed sun carved on it that looked like a signet, and the torque that was gleaming now, as if generating its own light.

The person they called Rama never had worn the other two things while she could see him, but he seemed sincerely attached to the torque. It must mean something. Rank, prowess—whatever large, heavy, ridiculously expensive ornaments could mean in a culture.

"Priesthood," he said, turning toward her.

His voice was soft in the dim golden light. Usually he spoke without identifiable accent. Now there was a distinct lilt to his speech, which reminded her of the words he had been reading off the wall.

In the day she might have scoffed, mocked, denied. Tonight she let it simply be. "Sun cult?"

He nodded.

She tilted her head toward the statue. "That's your high priest?"

"No."

"King?"

His head bent slightly.

"Ancestor?"

That he did not answer.

Physiological age: thirty to forty-five years. Chronological age...

Stasis, she thought.

There had been no such technology on this world. Before they all vanished, its people had reached the age of steel and simple mechanical devices. They never discovered gunpowder or steam or internal combustion. They never got that far.

Had they needed to?

"What were you?" she asked. "The captain who went down with his ship?"

"The threat that had to be contained."

His voice was bleak but his face was calm. "All this is your fault?" she asked him.

"Do you know," he said, and that seemed to bemuse him, "I don't think it was. No one was abandoning the world on my account."

"What did you do?"

"Too much, and not enough. Your king who wept because he had no more worlds to conquer? For me, it was rage."

Psychically powered rage. Magic, they probably called it. "They couldn't neuter you. They wouldn't kill you. So they shut you off."

"I think you would say they reset my programming."

Khalida bit down on laughter. There was nothing humorous about it, but thinking of what she was doing here, and what she was talking to, and how preposterous it was—what other reaction could she have? "I gather you're not mad any more."

"Oh," he said, "I am as thoroughly devoid of sanity as I ever was. But angry? No. That faded away in the long dream."

"So you know what happened. Where they all went."

"No," he said.

Khalida blinked. "But you said—"

"Whatever happened, it happened long after I paid for my sins."

"You can read the writing," she said. "There must be something there."

"Not here," he said. "Not in your archive, either."

"So what is this?" She swept her hand around the room with its treasury of alien words. "What does it say?"

"It's a king list," he said. "A chronicle. It stops before the end."

"Just stops."

"History generally does, on the day you write it."

"How far does it go?"

"A thousand years, more or less."

"Then it stops."

"Then it was written. And someone carved a statue."

"A portrait."

He stood in front of it. His head tilted as he studied it. "You think it's a clue."

"Isn't it?"

"Maybe they blamed me after all."

"Or else they expected you to come out of stasis, look for answers, and end up here. It's the only statue left intact on this planet."

"And it leads me straight to myself."

"I agree," said Khalida, "a map would have made more sense. I don't suppose you've found one anywhere around here?"

"Nothing but lists of kings and priests, and chronicles of reigns."

"Well," she said, "now we know you can read all this, you can teach the rest of us. We can help you look."

His face shut down. "There is no *we*."

"Why? We're all commoners, so we're not good enough for you?"

"You are all archaeologists."

Khalida's fit of temper evaporated. She was not an archaeologist. Her mind had a different slant.

She had had questions. This, however improbable, was an answer.

That was not what an archaeologist would see. Rashid and the rest had been praying for a stone, a dictionary, a translator, something, anything to open this world to them. That would allow them to continue their work in a universe of fading funding and bureaucratic idiocy.

A living relic, a being who had lived in that world, spoken some of its languages, read the writing that recorded them, known its history and culture not just as an observer but as a participant, was their fondest and most impossible dream. They would want to wring every scrap of knowledge out of him, and study him down to the subatomic particles that he was made of.

Right up until the moment when Centrum came to take him.

A discovery of this magnitude would never be allowed to remain in the hands of an already struggling expedition. Once United Planets discovered his particular talents, that would be the end of any hope of freedom that he might have had. They would never let him go.

"You see," he said.

"Yes."

He did not plead with her. He left her to think about what she should do, and whether, when she had discovered what that was, she could bring herself to do it.

It was amazing what people saw and didn't see. The ancient statue and Vikram's assistant didn't connect in their minds at all.

Rama kept his head down and his mouth shut, which didn't hurt. As far as anyone took the trouble to notice, he was just the Dreamtimer who lived in the stable and looked after the animals.

Aisha had the hardest time keeping quiet. This was the treasure she'd been looking for, and she couldn't talk about it to anyone without causing all kinds of complications. Even Jamal would want more explanations than Aisha could come up with.

What could she say? That she'd blown open some kind of stasis chamber and let out Nevermore's version of Alexander the Great? She wouldn't believe it, either, if she hadn't been in the middle of it.

It didn't matter, anyway. Mother and Pater had the statue. That was all they needed to keep the expedition going.

Life wanted to go on in its normal way. The schoolbot was back up and running, and Pater had upped the difficulty level. There were horses to ride; Rama was still training antelope in the increasingly cooler mornings.

She went down once to look at the statue. It was a beautiful thing, and whoever made it had caught the expression perfectly. The ancient king had been proud and happy and full of himself, and absolutely sure that he was meant to rule the world. She could see people bowing in front of him and being glad to do it.

The Rama she knew was all damped down. The old king was still in there; she could feel it, and sometimes he showed flashes of it: when he rode a horse or an antelope, or when he had an audience he wanted to play to. But the long stasis and whatever had happened right before it had broken him inside. It was taking him a while to heal.

She tried to help. Most of that involved grooming antelope and learning how to saddle and bridle the stallion properly, and cleaning stalls and paddocks and feeding horses and patching them up when they got hurt, and when there was no one around, showing him how to navigate the computer system.

He didn't have any implants or uplinks. He didn't need them. He could go right in and do what he wanted.

"It's easier than reading minds," he said. "It's simpler. Trails are easier to follow."

"This is just the house computer," Aisha warned. "The worldsweb is 'way bigger and 'way more complicated."

"Can you show me how to get to it?"

"I don't have that implant yet," she said. "I'm supposed to get it after my birthday. If I don't—if Psycorps doesn't—"

She couldn't get any further than that, and he didn't ask her to. He pulled up the expedition archive instead, and got her to teach him how to run search strings through the database. New scans came in every day now: they were recording the inscriptions under the temple.

He wasn't interested in those. He could go down and read them for himself. He wanted the older ones, and the scans from other sites. Anything with words on it that they had in the database, he wanted to see.

He was looking at other things, too, mostly from Jamal's files that Aisha wasn't supposed to know about. Star maps. Ship's schematics. He ran through Jamal's collection of space-pirate stories in two days, swallowing them in one huge, mind-boggling gulp.

That might not have been a good idea, but by the time Aisha realized he was doing it, it was too late. Then he went off and had Vikram teach him to drive a rover, and repair one, too.

He had a plan. Aisha was fairly sure she knew what it was. She knew what she would do if she were Rama.

She couldn't do anything about it, even if she'd had any idea how to begin. She had to get through her birthday, and the thing that was coming with it.

Maybe Psycorps would lose the record that said she existed. Maybe everybody else would forget she was turning thirteen Earthyears in six days, then three, and then it was tomorrow. They were all caught up in the new find. Aisha barely pinged their radar.

That night Pater cooked dinner, and he had all her favorites: tagine made with woolbeast meat, which was better than Earth lamb, and a huge platter of roasted vegetables from Mother's garden, and most special of all, a pie made with real apples from Earth, and real cinnamon. He had that particular look when he brought it out, half mischievous, half excited.

She had to be thrilled with it all, and eat a big piece of pie. Everybody was there on the roof on maybe the last really warm evening of the season; the stars were out, and people sang, and some of the interns had got up a band that wasn't bad at all.

It was one of the best night-before-birthday dinners she could remember. She wished she could have enjoyed it, and not been all knotted up thinking of what was supposed to happen tomorrow.

The transport was on its way. It would hit orbit around midnight. In the morning the shuttle would come down.

Mother went with Aisha when it was time for bed, and tucked her in. It hurt to take the kiss and the hug the way she used to when she was little, and not be able to tell Mother all the things that were spinning around in her head.

"It's going to be all right," Mother said. "Just relax and let it happen. It will be over in no time, and then you'll never have to worry about it again."

"I hope so," Aisha said.

Mother smoothed Aisha's hair back from her forehead and smiled. If her smile was a little shaky, Aisha couldn't blame her. "Go to sleep," she said. "Don't worry about school tomorrow. I'll come get you when it's time to get ready."

All Aisha could do was nod. Mother kissed her again and went away. She lay with dinner sitting like a rock in her stomach, and thought about throwing up.

She'd been practicing the sun-shield that Rama had taught her. She was getting good at it, she thought, but other things had started happening, maybe because of it. Those, she wasn't as sure of.

A few days ago, she'd woken up to find herself floating half a meter above the bed. It wasn't a dream. She didn't crash down when she realized where she was. She stayed there, drifty and peaceful, until it dawned on her that this was really impossible. Then the air dropped out from under her.

It had been wonderful when it happened. Terror came after, when she remembered the Corps. But there was the sun, wrapped around her, roaring and flaming. Keeping her safe.

Tonight she opened the door in her mind where the floating was, and let the bed sink slowly away. She couldn't sleep like that—if anybody found her, Psycorps wouldn't even bother to test her, it would just take her away—but as long as she was awake, it was hard to resist.

It felt like floating in the ocean. Things like fish swam around her, a flicker of shadow and gleam: people sleeping or thinking or wandering through a dream. If she wasn't careful she could slide right inside them, but Rama's sun worked to keep her in as well as Psycorps out.

Thinking about him brought him up beside her. Unlike everybody else, he knew she was there. Warmth washed over her. If he'd been there in person, she would have seen him smile.

Then she could sleep. Nothing could touch her. Anything that tried would have to get past him first.

The Psycorps agent came in on a Spaceforce shuttle: leaner, quieter, and much faster than transport and tourist shuttles. It landed on the plain with not so much as a bump, right in front of Aisha and the parents and Vikram with the rover.

The agent's name was Lieutenant Zhao. He was young, pretty, and shockingly cheerful. He looked nothing like the grim psi master Aisha had been expecting. He wasn't wearing black, either. His uniform was dark green, like conifers, and he even smelled a little like one.

She had slept better than she ever thought she would, thanks to Rama, but she still felt scratchy and out of sorts. Mother had let her sleep through morning barn cleaning, then brought her breakfast in bed, and helped her get dressed and braid her hair.

She had a headscarf over the braids now, like a grownup, and a new dress in her favorite color, which was the soft deep purple of Nevermore's sky after sunset but before the dark had completely come down. Aunt Khalida had given her thirteen silver bracelets, one for each year of her life. They felt strange on her thin brown arm, but she liked the way they slid up and down, chinking softly together when she moved.

Lieutenant Zhao smiled at her and kissed her hand, which made her blush all over. She *knew* he was doing it because he was trained to, so if there was anything to find, she'd be too relaxed and trusting to hide it. But she also knew he meant it. He did think she was pretty, and he was glad to meet her.

She was so far off balance she almost forgot to hide behind the sun. She remembered just in time. She even managed to smile, though she couldn't look him in the eye.

He was probably used to that. He had three gold buttons on his collar. Level three—that was high. They only went to five, though there was a rumor of more that nobody talked about. All the way up to nine.

All the more reason to keep her barrier up. He bowed to the parents. "Dr. Nasir. Dr. Kanakarides."

They bowed back, not as low. Pater's thick black eyebrows were even closer together than usual. He didn't like Psycorps. At all. Most people didn't. Mother had to smile for both of them and invite Lieutenant Zhao back to the house—as if he wouldn't go there anyway, whether she wanted him to or not.

It was Mother who sat next to Lieutenant Zhao in the rover. Vikram was up front, driving, and Aisha was in the back, trying not to cling to Pater. She was determined to keep her chin up and her best face on.

This was going to take forever. There would have to be greetings and coffee and a tour of the house and the site. It would be hours before the test could even start.

But when they got to the house, Lieutenant Zhao smiled as brightly as ever and said, "I know you're eager to get this over with. Doctors, is there a room we can use, with full computer access?"

The schoolroom was ready, with the bot shut away in its cabinet, and Jamal off doing whatever he wanted. Mother and Pater had trouble leaving Aisha there. She had trouble letting them go. Lieutenant Zhao's smile drove them out, and he shut the door and sealed it behind them.

Lieutenant Zhao was still smiling when he turned back to Aisha, but there was a strong tinge of sympathy in it now. "This won't take too terribly long," he said, "and I promise it won't hurt."

She was so stiff inside she could hardly move. She sat where he told her to sit, in the chair that Jamal usually sat in, and he sat facing her. His expression was more serious now as he linked in to the house computer and overrode the passwords.

She held her breath, but he didn't go exploring in the system. He just wanted to patch through to the shuttle and from there to the worldsweb.

His eyes changed when he closed the connection. Someone else was there, too: someone older, sterner, and closer to what Aisha had thought he would be.

This other person didn't introduce itself. It said, "Sera Nasir. Relax, please, and focus here." Lieutenant Zhao held up his hand. There was something in it. It looked like a databead, but databeads were inert. This had light in it, and colors swirling around and around.

The sun shone inside her. It was made all of light, with coils and swirls of plasma, and a herd of spots that had come around from the far side just this morning. She watched them follow one another across the face of the sun.

On the other side of that, she could feel small pricks and stabs and the occasional jolt, like a spark of electricity. It was like being examined by a slightly out-of-sync medbot. It poked here, prodded there. It tried to get a reaction in one place that she knew should have yowled back, but the sun was so bright, nothing could touch it.

After what might have been a nanosecond or an hour, the sequence of irritations stopped. Aisha looked through the sun at Lieutenant Zhao's face. The stranger was still there, just for a moment, staring hard at Aisha as if it suspected something. But it went away, and he blinked and took a deep breath and smiled with a touch of wistfulness. "There, Sera Nasir. That's it. You're done."

She needed to take a breath, too. "What happened? Did you find anything?"

"Nothing significant," he said. "I'm afraid you're not a candidate for Psycorps."

She couldn't collapse right there. She had to stay upright, stay awake, and say something that didn't sound too terribly elated.

She had to keep her barrier up, too. Nobody had to tell her not to let her guard down for one instant as long as Psycorps was in this system. She'd failed the obvious part of the test, but Psycorps hadn't got where it was by being easy to fool. Lieutenant Zhao would be keeping an eye on her until he left.

Still. The worst part was over. All she had to do now was keep her head down and not do anything stupid.

Khalida fully intended to stay out of Psycorps' way. She spent the day in the vault, labeling and inventorying artifacts.

Through the computer she knew when Aisha's test results came through. Minimal psi, barely enough to measure. Aisha would not be leaving Nevermore with the agent.

Khalida was happy for her—surprised, but happy; she would have sworn Aisha would test positive. She was happy for Rashid and Marina, too. The last thing they needed to do was lose their daughter to the Corps.

There would be a real celebration tonight, now the elder of the Brats was safe. Khalida saluted her with a cup that, according to its label, dated from a century or so before the Disappearance.

As she lowered it, she looked up into a stranger's face.

Level Three Psycorps, with lieutenant's bars and the name *Zhao* above the pocket of his uniform. He was one of the meet-and-greet unit: attractive well past the point of prettiness, open-faced and honest and ferociously well-intentioned.

That did not mean he was any kind of idiot. It took more than strong psi powers to make level three. It took brains, and a certain talent for working the system.

She set the cup down on the sorting table. His glance asked permission; she shrugged. He picked it up.

Testing for impressions. She hoped he got a mind-full. She had been handling it with gloves; the last human touch the cup had had was some five thousand years ago.

It must have worn off: Lieutenant Zhao put the cup down with a faint sigh, as if disappointed. "It's finely made," he said. "Very beautiful."

She nodded. The silence stretched to the awkward stage.

That was an old game, and MI played it as well as Psycorps. Khalida reached for the next artifact in the series, a bronze dagger with an inlaid ivory hilt, and recorded its image and the label attached, with keyword strings and cross-references.

Lieutenant Zhao broke first. He retrieved something from his pocket and slid it across the table.

Her mind took a while to put it in context. It was a set of captain's bars. "Don't tell me they promoted me."

"They did," he said, "Captain Nasir. You have orders also, which I'm to see you download and acknowledge."

"MI is using Psycorps to do its dirty work? When did that start?"

Lieutenant Zhao's smile was wry. "Shocking, isn't it? They've tried every possible permutation of computerized message. Rather than send a hardcopy letter to be further ignored, they happened to discover that I would be passing through at this convenient time. I'm to observe and record your receipt of the orders, and then accompany you to the transport. MI will direct you from there."

"What if I refuse? I'm on leave."

"Your leave ended six Earthdays ago," Lieutenant Zhao said, "and you failed to apply for an extension. Technically you're AWOL, but your superior officer in this system chooses to be lenient. She has to dock your pay, that's regulations, but she won't put you on report."

That was better than Khalida deserved. She studied her hands, which had closed tightly around the dagger. Its blade was sharp: she felt the sting of the cuts.

She really did feel it. Amazing. She was barely tempted to experiment, to cut deeper and see what happened.

It seemed she was starting to heal after all.

Lieutenant Zhao was waiting. This time he won: there was no point in fighting it any more. Khalida opened the file that was strobing and screaming at her through the house link.

It was official. She was Captain Nasir.

She had not asked to be promoted. She certainly had not wanted it. But there it was.

The orders were short, blunt, and to the point. Report soonest to Spaceforce vessel Leda. Await further orders.

When orders came in stages, that was never good news. Without explanation or apology, Khalida ran back through the file of unread messages. The first third were all about the commendation, the second third informed her that she had been promoted, and the last third all said the same thing: Report somewhere and wait.

That meant it was really bad. But not, she noted, absolutely or desperately urgent, if it had taken this long for them to send someone to fetch her.

She clicked on another file, one that she had been thinking about sending, but had never quite brought herself to do it. There it was, her resignation, signed and sealed but not, yet, dated.

She called up today's date, tipped it in, but when the Send key blinked at her, she sent it back into storage instead.

"Give me time to think about it," she said to Lieutenant Zhao.

"I can give you forty-eight Earth hours," he said. "After that, I'm afraid I'll have to arrest you."

"Not if I resign," she said.

"They won't accept your resignation."

"They have to."

"Not since you've gone AWOL," said Lieutenant Zhao. He honestly seemed to sympathize. "Do take the time. I've always wanted to visit the mysterious Nevermore. But in forty-eight hours, I have to bring you in. Willingly or otherwise."

He saluted her crisply, softened it with a smile, and left her there with her captain's bars and her orders and her hopeless state of confusion.

It was her own damned fault for avoiding what she knew would have to happen. MI was spread thin. Any operative who was even close to functional was expected and required to function.

Which left open the question: Was she functional? Regulations forbade her to make that determination. Command would decide—and Command well might decree that she was.

She finished what she was doing. She cleared the table, got everything inventoried, and backed up and saved the files. Her chrono said it was still daylight. She was expected at dinner, to help Aisha celebrate her reprieve and her new, untrammeled future.

Khalida could do that. Someone ought to be happy. Why not Aisha?

She was maudlin already, and there was not a drop of wine or liquor on this side of the planet. Rashid was traditional that way.

Now there was a reason to head back into space. Khalida opened a file for it, labeled and saved and stored it. There was already a file for reasons to stay, which had swelled past a hundred a long time ago.

Everything wanted to happen at once. Instead of leaving on the same day like a polite and sensible Psycorps agent, Lieutenant Zhao stayed. He stayed in the shuttle and not in the house, but the shuttle was still on Nevermore. Aisha was getting very tired of keeping her barriers up.

He stayed because of Aunt Khalida. MI had called her back, and he was supposed to make sure she got there.

That meant she was leaving. And so was Rama.

"Did you know he's rich?" Jamal asked that afternoon.

Aisha was supposed to be resting. She had a bit of a headache, but she'd started to think about going out to ride Jinni. A long ride, as far away from everything as possible.

Jamal showed up in her room before she could get her riding clothes on, and perched on the hoverchair that she mostly kept tethered in the corner. She didn't know why she let him stay. It was obvious he'd come to annoy her.

A buzzing began in her back teeth and worked its way around to the top of her head. That was the firewall going up, and the parental controls turning off. No one outside could listen in.

"All that gold Rama had on him," Jamal said. "It's worth more than you would believe. He could buy most of a small planet, if he had any use for one."

She frowned at him. "How did you find that out?"

Janal shrugged the way he did when he was determined not to feel guilty. "I caught him while you were having your test, forging travel papers. He's good. Not as good as I am, but good."

"You didn't."

"I had to," Jamal said. "If he'd messed up, it would have traced back to us."

"So you helped him." Aisha sighed. "You know those artifacts belong to the Department of Antiquities."

"Not if he can claim them under the aboriginal property laws."

He actually said that as if he knew what it meant. Aisha only did because she ran a search on the term. "You know about him?"

"It's kind of hard not to," he said. "He's nowhere in any database. Considering where we found him and what he was wearing, I had to conclude, logically—"

"Stop talking like a schoolbot," Aisha said irritably.

Jamal stuck out his tongue at her. "I set up an account for him, and showed him how to build an identity. He'd already figured out most of it. He learns fast."

"You know what you're unleashing on the spaceways," Aisha said. "The Dread Pirate Gallifrey was nothing to what he'll be."

"I know," Jamal said. "It will be beautiful."

"I think you lack a moral compass," Aisha said.

"Now *you're* talking like a bot."

Aisha was past ready to get out of there, but she knew her brother. "All right. What are we really doing here?"

He bounced in the hoverchair, up and down and up and down, the way he used to when he was five years old. She kicked him to make him stop.

Finally he came out with it. "It's over. The message came on the shuttle. The expedition has to shut down. We get to finish the season, but then we're done."

Aisha wheezed. His words had punched all the air out of her. "What—they can't—"

"The statue did it," Jamal said. "That was their excuse. *Significant archaeological discovery,* they said. *For the protection and preservation of the artifact and the site.* They're taking it away from Mother and Pater. Someone else will come in. I looked her up. She's a Department drone. They send her when they think they can make money off whatever's been found."

Finally Aisha had her voice back. "How can they do that? All these years and all that work and now we finally found something spectacular, they just take it away?"

"I don't know," Jamal said. "I just know it's happening."

"Mother will fix it," Aisha said. She wasn't as confident as she wanted to sound. "Mother can talk sense into them. They have to see how important it is that we stay. They have to understand—"

But they wouldn't. She knew it even while she said it. All her life she'd heard the parents snarling about idiots and bureaucrats. Once the idiots got their claws in something, they never let it go. Especially when there was money in it.

She didn't ride Jinni after all. Jamal had to go: he was supposed to help cook her actually-on-her-birthday dinner. Aisha stayed in her room. Thinking. Making up her mind.

By the time dinner was over, with everybody pretending to be happy and nobody talking about the cliff they were all going to fall over, she knew what she had to do. It was the hardest decision she had ever made, but she couldn't see any other way.

The next morning she woke up long before sunrise, and couldn't get back to sleep. She pulled on riding clothes and crept out toward the barn.

A dark shape perched on the fence by the antelope pen, watching the baby play. Even in the very early dawn, the black robes and veils were hard to mistake.

It was Malia. Aisha would have known that set of the shoulders anywhere.

"He's still here," Aisha said, swinging up beside her. The baby shorted and shied and pretended to be horrified, but a few bucks and caracoles later, she had her nose pressed against Aisha's leg, demanding to have her ears rubbed.

Malia slid her shorter sword out of its scabbard and set to work sharpening it.

Aisha got the message. She was unperturbed—oddly, maybe. "I don't think he's that easy to kill."

"Legend says he can't be killed at all." Malia ran the stone down the blade and up again, working by sound and feel more than sight, being precise about strokes and edges. Blackrobes took pride in being able to take care of their weapons in pitch dark if they had to. "I think a stake in the heart or the sweep of a sword through his spine will do what it needs to."

"Why?" Aisha asked. Still not afraid, though she knew she should be. "Is he really that bad?"

"Grandmother says," said Malia, "that he has a destiny, and I am not to get in the way of it. Especially since he's following it away from this world. To which I say he might follow it back, and then where will we be?"

"Don't you want to wait and find out?"

"I want," said Malia, sheathing her sword with a sharp *snick*, "to keep my world and my people safe." She slid to the ground outside the pen. "Grandmother says come."

For a long few seconds, Aisha forgot how to breathe. How could the grandmother—what could she—

Of course she didn't know what Aisha was up to. She wanted to see Aisha, that was all. Maybe to find out if Rama had said anything about the tribe or the world or where he intended to go. Or else she'd found out, somehow, about the Department of Antiquities. Aisha had learned never to be surprised by what the grandmother could know.

Aisha thought about refusing, but that would be suspicious. Unless she lied and said she had to stay home today—but Malia would know, if the grandmother didn't. Malia always knew when people were lying. It was a gift. A magic, Rama would say.

While she wibbled, Malia brought Jinni out and tied him for Aisha to brush off, and fetched Ghazal for herself. Aisha could still say no, but by the time Jinni was clean and saddled, there was no point in fighting it.

They slipped out the back way, through the gate in the wall that was barely wide enough for a horse, and mounted outside. The sun was bright but the air was chilly; Jinni felt fresh enough to buck, but settled before Aisha could have words with him.

Jinni was glad for the run. Ghazal not so much, but Malia wasn't Jamal. She didn't put up with his nonsense.

"Lazybutt," she said. "For me you'll move."

For her he would actually consent to a grudging gallop, before he broke to a pissy-eared, tail-swishing canter. She laughed and kept him going.

They rode into Blackroot camp just as the sun was coming up. The grandmother sat in front of her house with her face turned to the light that she could feel but not see. She almost looked like Rama, the way she drank the sun.

One of the children had brought her morning tea; the rest of the pot bubbled over the fire. The little boy, who was one of Malia's cousins, filled each of the two cups that waited beside him, and gave them to Malia and Aisha.

Aisha had grown up drinking tea in Blackroot camp. This was waking tea, strong and bitter but pleasant. She thought it was nicer than coffee.

She drank the first cup to be polite, and the second to honor the host. Then she could turn the cup upside down and set it in front of her and say, "I've come, Grandmother. What do you need of me?"

It was borderline rude to be that direct, but Aisha was careful with her intonations. She tried to indicate respect and attentiveness, and just enough curiosity to put an edge on it.

The grandmother held her cup to be filled a third time. She took her time drinking, while Aisha and Malia had to wait. Malia could afford to be patient. Aisha didn't have a choice.

Finally, the grandmother drained the cup and set it in front of her, right side up. She had things to say, that meant, and Aisha might not like them.

Aisha bit her tongue before she started defending herself. *Never explain yourself to authority,* Mother always said, *and never volunteer information.*

That was hard, if you were Aisha. Still, she managed it. She waited for the grandmother to speak.

Which also took forever, but she held herself still, not fidgeting the way she desperately wanted to. Having to look calm actually helped her stop twitching. She was breathing deep and steady by the time the grandmother said, "If you do what you intend to do, your soul will never be the same."

Aisha let her breath out more quickly than she meant to. "What? What would I be—"

The grandmother said nothing. At all.

Aisha flushed. Lying to the grandmother was not possible. She knew that. She'd known it since she was small.

"You're not sending anyone with him," she said. "You're letting him go out alone."

"I have no authority to 'let' that one do anything," the grandmother said.

"You hate him that much?"

"He's somewhat beyond either hate or fear," the grandmother said. "Love I can't speak for. Or loyalty. We were left here to guard him, not to serve him. Our service was given to those who came after him."

"All of which is to say that you don't want to give him one fraction more than you absolutely have to."

"Out of all the oldest stories," said the grandmother, "one repeats in every tribe. That the Sleeper hunts alone, and the people hold the world behind him. When he comes back, if he comes back, the world and the people will be waiting."

"To do what? Kill him?"

"That remains to be seen."

"I believe," said Aisha, "that he'll do everything he can to find out where all the people went. If any of them can still be saved, he'll save them."

"I believe that may be true," the grandmother said.

Aisha studied her, narrow-eyed. She looked calm, the way she always did. "What if he comes back, and the world isn't here? Or it's so changed, there's nothing to come back to? What if he's not what you should be afraid of?"

The grandmother didn't flinch. "I think," she said, "that if this world suffers at anyone's hands but his, that person should be very much afraid."

"I think so, too," Aisha said.

She resisted the urge to duck down under the grandmother's stare, those blank silver eyes that shouldn't have seen her at all. The grandmother leaned toward Aisha. Then it was obvious she was blind: she traced Aisha's head and shoulders with her hands, touching very lightly. Aisha's hair crackled and tried to stand up.

The grandmother sat back. "Be careful, child. Think hard about what you will do, and how, and with whom. He is difficult to resist. He's not even aware he does it. He makes people do as he wills, because neither he nor they can imagine any other order in the world."

"I see what you're saying," Aisha said as respectfully as she could. "What I don't see is any other way through this mess we're in. People out there—my people—want to tear apart this world and sell it for scrap. He just wants to find out what happened to his people. And rule them, maybe, though I'm not entirely sure about that."

"I don't think he can help it," the grandmother said. She spread her hands. "His is a long road, and a dark road, and no one who travels on it will come back unchanged. If you follow him, it may be your death."

Aisha knew that, down deep inside. It didn't make any difference. "If I don't, this planet might die."

"So it might," said the grandmother. "But it's not as clear a choice as you may imagine. You think you know him; you see what he is and what he does, and how he makes his way through this world he's awakened to. What you see is a dreamer still more than half in his dream, barely beginning to wake."

"I see that," said Aisha. "He's in shock. Everything he knew is gone. He's having to learn to live all over again. I studied—I looked it up. People who are in stasis for a long time can take years to get over it."

"So they can," the grandmother said, "but has any of them ever been what this one is? Your people have no kings or emperors. You outgrew them, you say, long ages ago. You have never had or allowed the kind of powers that were born in this man, that he mastered in his first life and has in no way lost. He's quiet now, and seems gentle, because as you say, he's in shock—and even in this state, he studies, he observes, he learns the ways of this new world."

"He's not a monster," Aisha said. "That was the trouble all along, wasn't it? Everybody thought he was this terrible, outlandish *thing*. So they shut him off and left him for somebody else to deal with."

"No," the grandmother said. "He was no more a monster than any other great lord of his world. There were others as powerful, if not more—some of those shut him in the rock. He did what he had to; he acted as he believed he should. He tried to be a good man and a good ruler, and for the most part he was. Even those who were afraid of him or of what he tried to do never called him evil. There was never any malice in him."

"So why?" Aisha demanded. "What was so wrong that he had to be punished all the way to the end of time?"

"He changed the world," the grandmother answered, "but he wasn't able to change with it. When the time came to accept that not everything could go exactly as he wanted it, he refused. He could conquer, you see, and he could rule—well, by all accounts. But he never knew how to let go."

"I think he knows now," said Aisha.

The grandmother's head shook. "This is not a tame animal. He may like you, even love you, for yourself, and appreciate the qualities of your people and your world, and do his best to do no harm. But as with the lion cub who grows into a lion, the day will come when you or your people do something or say something that wakes the native instincts. Then nothing else will matter. He won't mean to destroy you, but he will. He won't be able to help it."

"Maybe not," Aisha said. "And maybe I'm not the one he'll destroy. I'm taking that gamble, Grandmother. I have to."

"Child," said the grandmother, and the word was meant to dig in and twist, "his own family could not teach him to be other than he was. They were the ones who laid the sentence on him. His wife, his child, the man who raised him—they had to turn on him to save all that he had made. What makes you think that you, who are not even of this world, can so much as sway him?"

Those were hard words, with terrifying thoughts in back of them. But Aisha was born stubborn. "Everything is different now, including the people he's dealing with. He was supposed to learn a lesson. Someone has to believe that he could. *They* believed that. Or they'd have killed him and got it over with."

Aisha had done the impossible. She had argued the grandmother to a standstill. The grandmother hadn't given in, not hardly, but she stopped trying to talk Aisha out of what she'd made up her mind to do.

"Go with such gods as you believe in," the grandmother said, "and may those gods protect you."

Because no one else would. That meaning was perfectly clear.

Aisha was not going to get any help from here. These people weren't any more hers than Rama was. They had an obligation to him, and they had met it. But they didn't have to like it, or really understand it, any more than they liked or understood him.

It didn't matter. What mattered was that Nevermore was in trouble, and no one else had the power to save it. Rama might not, either, but Aisha had to help him try.

It was fair enough. After all, it was her fault he was awake.

One thing Aisha could be sure of when she left Blackroot camp: the grandmother wouldn't report her to her parents. In the tribes, if you were set on doing something insane, they tried their best to talk you out of it; then they let you go. Really determined insanity, in their religion, came from the gods. It wasn't any mortal's place to get in its way.

That made it obvious, at least to Aisha, that the people who put Rama in stasis weren't tribesmen. His own family—that must have hurt badly enough to break him.

Malia followed her back toward the horses. Aisha would have liked to avoid her, but there was no sensible way to go about it.

After Aisha had Jinni saddled and ready to mount, Malia held Ghazal's reins out of reach when Aisha moved to take them. "Tell me one thing," she said. "You were so determined not to leave here with the green man. Now you want to leave anyway. How does that make sense?"

"The green man would have taken me away to turn me into someone just like him," Aisha said.

"You'd rather turn into someone just like the Sleeper?"

"*He* won't open my head and scramble my brains."

"Oh, won't he?" said Malia.

"Malia," said Aisha, "if he finds his people, and brings them back, Centrum won't be able to keep this planet. Its own laws won't let it. If it breaks those—Rama will do what Rama will do. He's a weapon, you're always saying so. I want to be sure he's *our* weapon."

"He'll turn in your hand."

"But Nevermore will be safe."

"You hope."

Aisha let that sit for a handful of seconds. Then she said, "Will you look after Jinni for me while I'm gone?"

Malia ran Ghazal's reins through her fingers. Her eyes above the black veil were impossible to read.

Aisha couldn't read her inside, either. Not that she was anything like perfect at that, yet. But tribespeople had barriers that she hadn't found in anyone else.

Malia blinked. The blankness was gone; in its place was white-hot rage. "You're going away. You're going to die—and that's if you're lucky. And you want me to be your stablehand? Isn't there anyone of your own people who can do it?"

Aisha twitched, stung. "No! No, there isn't! Nobody else knows what he likes. Nobody rides him right or feeds him right or—"

"All *right*! I'll do it!"

"Good!"

They both stopped, breathing hard. Aisha's eyes wanted to run over. She couldn't let them. Not because anyone here would laugh at her, but because once she started, there was no way she'd ever stop.

She swallowed hard. "Behave yourself," she said. "Don't forget about Jinni."

"Not in this life," said Malia. And that, in the tribes, was a solemn oath. "You come back. Alive or dead. Don't you dare go away forever."

"I promise," Aisha said. "We'll do what we set out to do. We'll find what we're looking for. Then I'll come home."

PART TWO

LEDA

At forty-seven hours and thirty-six minutes, Khalida presented herself in front of the shuttle. Her uniform felt stiff and unfamiliar, the captain's bars oddly weighty on the collar. The hair that had grown down to her shoulders during her leave was cut military short.

The wind blew cold on her bare neck. Seasons changed quickly on Nevermore; literally overnight, summer had turned into autumn. It would rain before dark, Vikram had said. Vikram was wise to the weather on this world.

Rashid and Marina had come out to see her off. Jamal surprised her by wandering in behind them. Aisha was not there, nor did Khalida expect to see her. She had pitched such a roaring fit when she discovered both Khalida and Rama were leaving that her father had confined her to quarters.

That was Aisha: drama to the last. Between Aisha and the antelope stallion, which had been screaming since the sun came up and seemed likely never to stop, Khalida's ears were ringing.

Khalida would miss Aisha, though maybe not the animal that Rama had taken and tamed and then abandoned, damn him. She would miss everyone in the expedition. She would even miss the planet. The quiet, when it was not broken by stallion rage; the cleanness of air and water and sky. The emptiness, with not even a ghost to remember the people who were gone.

Nevermore's one and only ghost waited with her on the windblown grass. For once in his life, he looked almost aggressively ordinary: like a moderately well-to-do planetsider in a plain grey suit and a long coat, with a hat drawn down over his eyes.

Khalida knew with absolute certainty that he should not be allowed off Nevermore. It was her duty and obligation to preserve the safety of the United Planets. If she let this man loose on the spaceroads, God and Allah and Great Cthulhu knew what would come of it.

She kept her mouth shut and her eyes forward. Crew were loading cargo in the corner of her eye: boxes of samples from the excavation for the museum at home, and trade goods from the tribes.

As the last of them slid into the hold, the passenger access finally opened. "All clear to board," the pilot's voice sang out over the comm.

Marina caught Khalida in a fierce embrace. Her husband was directly behind her. Between the two of them they squeezed the breath out of her. "You be careful," Marina said. She sounded angry, which meant she was trying not to cry. "Don't get into any more trouble than you can help. Come back soon."

"As soon as I can," Khalida said.

They let her go. Rashid kissed her forehead and her cheeks and murmured a blessing in Arabic. Unregenerate atheist though she was, she was glad to have it.

"Five minutes," the comm said. "Five minutes to liftoff."

Khalida had to go now or she never would. That alternative tempted her sorely, but Lieutenant Zhao was waiting at the top of the ramp, flanked by burly marines. She could go under her own power or under arrest. That was all the choice she had.

She opted for dignity, such as it was. Rama had already disappeared into the shuttle.

She had to give him credit for courage. When the doors shut and sealed and the shuttle powered up, he sat perfectly still across from her. The only sign of tension was the greying of his knuckles on the arms of his seat.

As they lifted above the plain and set course for outer orbit, he relaxed visibly, and probably with intent. Lieutenant Zhao and his marines had taken over the rear seats, and they were watching.

Khalida wondered what they thought of Rama. His clearances were beautifully forged. She would not have suspected that they were false if she had not known who he really was.

According to the records on file with the shuttle and the transport, he was one Madhusudana Rama, citizen of Dreamtime, certified traveler-on-walkabout, moving on from Nevermore, destination indeterminate—as it should be: that was the meaning of walkabout. The list of previous stopping places went back a handful of years, fading into a somewhat dull and thoroughly blameless existence on his supposedly native world.

It was rather impressive, as covers went. MI would have done better, but not by much. The fact that an eleven-Earthyear-old boy had done it with a house computer, even with a psi master to help, would terrify Khalida when she had the energy to spare. Psycorps would never get their claws on Jamal, but MI would be all too interested in him when he was older.

Once the shuttle was in the air, Rama let out the breath he must have been holding since the flight began, and leaned toward the viewport. There was no telling what was in his mind as he watched his world drop away beneath him.

The blue of the sky gave way to the blackness of space, with the planet's curve diminishing below. Rama sat back. There was still a deep tension in him, but on the surface he was a traveler of worlds, marveling at their various wonders. He took off his hat and unfastened his coat.

He was not so ordinary to look at now. He wore the torque that Khalida distinctly remembered not seeing while he waited for the shuttle. Now there it was under the high collar of his suit—right in front of Lieutenant Zhao. Was he trying to flip the bird in the agent's face?

Khalida closed her eyes and sighed.

She caught what scraps of sleep she could. There had been too little of that last night. Her head ached dully, as if her skull were too small for her brain.

The slight jolt of docking startled her awake. The crewmember who had been looking after the passengers, a slender young woman nearly as dark as Rama, glided through the cabin. The shuttle had gone to half-gravity to match the setting in the landing bay: easier for unloading.

Khalida should have thought to warn Rama. He was holding himself together, probably by sheer will.

Lieutenant Zhao and the marines were waiting for Khalida. There was nothing she could do for Rama but hope he lost control after Psycorps was out of there.

She could make that happen, at least. She stood up, taking a moment to remember how to balance. It came back fast. Her first step had a fraction too much bounce: she caught herself before she hit the ceiling, recalibrated, and settled into the low, gliding motion that the crewmember had demonstrated before her.

She felt Rama's eyes on her, recording and studying. She felt when his attention turned away, too. It was rather too much like living with her skin off.

The shuttle bay opened in front of Khalida. Half a dozen other shuttles were docked along it. *Leda* was a heavy cruiser, big enough for troop transport; this was a patrol run through Ceti Quadrant, which happened to be convenient for both Psycorps and MI.

She forced herself to put Rama out of her mind. He was the universe's problem now. She had problems of her own, beginning with the detachment of marines that fell in around her as she reached the end of the bay.

"Am I under arrest?" she asked the one at her right shoulder.

He did not even flick a glance at her. Bad sign, that. Her headache went from distinctly annoying to blinding.

Khalida would hardly have been surprised to find herself in the brig. The captain's office was only marginally more reassuring, even with the person at the desk slipping smoothly out of at least four uplinks and a comm ping, rising and stepping around the desk and pulling Khalida into a long, fierce hug.

The marines and Lieutenant Zhao had discreetly evaporated. They would not have gone far, but for now it was enough.

Captain Hashimoto held Khalida at arm's length and shook her so hard her teeth rattled. "*Damn* you, woman! Don't you ever answer your messages?"

"I was hiding," Khalida said.

"On a planet with a total human population of five." Captain Hashimoto dropped Khalida a good few centimeters, which was a feat: she was barely taller than Khalida's chin. "Don't do that again."

She tipped Khalida backward into a hoverchair and dropped into one that drifted around to face it. Khalida sat for a moment and concentrated on breathing.

Hashimoto Tomiko had that effect on people. Khalida found herself smiling—and that was not what she had intended at all. "I suppose several dozen of those messages were to crow at me about how you got yourself a ship."

"And that I was coming to get you, whether you wanted it or not," said Tomiko. She tucked up her feet, frowning. She looked like a child, but anyone who made the mistake of treating her like one lived to regret it. "You did pick an interesting place to disappear to. Whoever slapped the Perpetual Preserve designation on it was either damned lucky or had damned good connections in high places. If U.P. Admin had any way to touch that much pristine Earth-class real estate, they'd have it colonized before you could blink."

"The planet is not empty." Khalida surprised herself with a rush of anger. "It has inhabitants."

"A few thousand primitive tribesmen," Tomiko said. "U.P. would fence off an island somewhere and turn them loose." She waved the subject aside before Khalida could erupt. "Never mind. They're there and you're here, and the universe is back the way it should be."

"You think so?" Khalida said.

Tomiko kicked her chair over toward the wall, which opened at her approach. She pulled out a bottle and a pair of glasses, filled them deftly as she floated back toward Khalida, and handed her the fuller of the two.

Khalida drank a long swallow of smoky fire. It burned its way to her stomach. She held the second swallow in her throat until her head spun with the fumes, then let it slip down to join the first.

"Tell me there aren't any orders," she said. "You pulled rank and abused your privileges shamelessly to get me off Nevermore."

"I did that," said Tomiko, "but there are orders. MI's calling you back."

"Voluntarily? Not because you exploited a few connections?"

"I didn't have to: they'd already cut the orders. I'm taking you to Centrum."

"The long way or the short?"

"Mostly the short," Tomiko said with regret.

"That's still a solid tenday," Khalida said.

"Most of it in jump," said Tomiko, "and cut off from the subspace feed." She saluted Khalida with her glass. "To mystery and suspense."

Khalida returned the salute. "To hiding your head in the sand."

They grinned at each other. Soldiers' humor: coal black and sharp enough to draw blood.

It was good to be back. That feeling was strictly temporary and had a great deal to do with Tomiko's bottle of brandy, but Khalida enjoyed it while she had it.

A isha's plan had succeeded beautifully so far. She and Jamal had worked it out when he was in his pirate phase, in case they ever needed to stow away on a spaceship.

Not that she'd said a word to him or to anyone but the grandmother and Malia. What her brother didn't know, he couldn't tell.

All it took was a shipping container, a portable life-support system with backup chargers, and a supply of food and water. They'd commandeered the equipment last year and stowed it in one of the outbuildings. The supplies weren't too hard to siphon off from stores.

With everybody busy excavating or cataloguing or researching or hacking systems for Rama, nobody had noticed Aisha coming and going around the shuttle. Adding one more container to the manifest was a little harder, but Jamal wasn't the only hacker in the family. He always got the blame, but as often as not it was Aisha who'd done the hacking.

She'd figured three earthdays to get off Nevermore and onto the ship, then wait for the first jump. Once they were in jumpspace, turning back was much harder. And *Leda* had orders that didn't allow much room for unloading a stowaway.

They might space her. She had considered that. The ship had lifepods and she knew where they were; she'd have to hope she could get to one before the marines got to her.

But that was in the future and might not happen at all. Her chrono said she was two days in. She'd run through most of the databeads she'd brought with her reader. She still had enough space rations for another shipday. She wasn't quite ready to run screaming through the spaceways. Yet.

She was horrendously bored and missing Mother and Pater and Jinni and even Jamal so badly her insides hurt. The rumble of sheer terror underneath, not just for Nevermore but for herself now she'd done this enormous and irreversible thing, made it almost impossible to think.

She could hang on for one more day. One more endless round of hours until jump.

An alarm went off, so loud and close she jumped like a rabbitzoid.

Jump alarm. One hour to jump.

But it was only—it wasn't supposed to—

She peeled herself off the ceiling, literally in the half-gravity of the cargo bay. She had no intention of riding through jump in a shipping container. Strapped into a cradle at full ship's gravity, with the ship ready to feed in meds against the nausea and the disorientation and the potential brain damage, was bad enough. Inside a metal container at half-gravity, even with what she'd done to make the container fit to live in, was really not on. She needed a better place to hide, and she needed it fast, while ship and crew were busy prepping for jump.

She pulled on the clothes she'd brought. She was careful about it, though the alarms made her gut tie up in knots. When she was dressed and had everything with her that she was likely to need, she slipped out the back door of the container and crept away through the maze of boxes in the cargo bay.

She had the *Leda*'s schematics memorized. She knew where the main corridors were, and where crew went when they needed to get around fast. She wasn't sure exactly where Rama was, but there weren't many guest cabins on a military ship, and they were all on the same level. He was the only passenger on this leg of the voyage, which meant the other rooms would be empty.

Once she thought about Rama, she knew where he was. She could feel him. He was part of the sun she was still using to keep Psycorps from finding her.

She did her best to keep him from feeling her. She crept through the maintenance ducts that ran through the whole ship. For someone thin and not very tall, like Aisha, they were big enough to walk upright in, and the lights there were emergency lights, just bright enough to see by.

She counted levels as she went up the ladder, then went off sideways. Nobody came at her from any direction. The crew must be all battened down for jump, or else busy making it happen.

She wouldn't let herself think about what it would be like if she didn't get to a cabin before jump. She moved as fast as she could, as quietly as she possibly could.

The ship relied on the crew's implants to keep track of them. Anybody who didn't belong there would trigger alarms. But she hadn't triggered any.

Maybe not having real implants yet, just the house-computer model, meant she was basically invisible to the ship. Or maybe the ship knew, and wasn't doing anything about it.

She didn't dare link to its web to find out. All she could do was keep on going, and hope she didn't run into a troop of marines.

She made it to the hatch. The passage on the other side was wide and high enough for the larger end of human norm. It felt huge after the one she'd been in.

Now she had to hope the cabins weren't locked. That was the down side of not being linked in to the ship. If the *Leda* couldn't see her, neither could the doors.

Maybe she hadn't been as smart as she thought she was.

She had to keep going. The hallway was empty, but it might not stay that way. She went on past the door where she felt Rama, down two to be safe, and pressed her hand to the touchpad on the third one.

"Ident code, please," the door said.

Then the ship said, "Jump warning. Ten minutes."

Aisha lost fifteen seconds to a panic attack. Her eyes darted up and down the corridor. It was all closed doors with numbers on them.

The door to cabin 7 slid halfway open. A shadow leaned out. "Get in," Rama said.

Aisha didn't try to pretend she wasn't there. She dived into the kind of cabin she'd traveled in since she was small: six jump cradles built into the walls, two of which were open and waiting, and everything else tightly stowed until the ship made it into subspace.

Aisha's panic wasn't screaming as loudly now. She dived for the nearest cradle, but she took an instant to say to Rama, "Get strapped in. It's almost time."

He was already moving as if he knew what to do. She fastened the straps the way she'd been taught, and thought about hitting the panel that brought the wall up over the cradle, but decided not to, the way she always did.

Rama left his cradle open, too. She hoped it wasn't a terrible idea, but just about the time she started to say something, the thirty-second alarm went off.

That was the longest and the shortest time in the world. Aisha made herself breathe deep, in and out. Breathing helped.

Then the world fell apart.

Supposedly it was different for everyone. For Aisha it was like being blown up in slow motion, with each piece of her spinning away into infinite dark. The dark was full of stars, but they were all stretched and twisted and their light had collapsed into itself. They flowed around her like water.

Chronos said jump lasted a minute at most. Inside Aisha's head, that minute was forever. She had heard of people going into that place and never coming out. Even people who did come out could keep a part of it in them, a piece of infinity that floated up at odd moments and sometimes drove them insane.

Aisha could see Rama, because she'd turned her head right before the jump took her. He was lying on his back like an effigy on a tomb, and his eyes were open.

They were full of stars. Galaxies wheeled under his skin. He reached up his hand, though the straps should have kept him from doing any such thing, and gathered a handful of suns.

He was smiling. It was a sweet smile, nothing evil about it at all, but it made Aisha's skin shiver. Nobody ought to be *happy* about being in the middle of jump.

As quick as that, they were out. The walls were solid again. The *All Clear* rang through the ship.

There was not supposed to be any difference from inside between truespace and subspace, but Aisha had always been able to tell. Subspace felt deep and cold and quiet, like being under the ocean. It was supposed to be empty of life, too. It was just her imagination that filled it with vast shapes. They swam all around the ship, paying no attention to it, except to slide past when it got in their way.

She unfastened the straps and got up slowly. Rama hadn't said a word since he pulled Aisha into the cabin. He stowed the cradles he and Aisha had been in, and ordered the cabin to rearrange itself into a proper stateroom. Then he sat cross-legged on the bunk farthest from the door.

He was in the ship's computer. Aisha felt it like a tickle in the back of her skull.

He could walk inside a system without triggering any of its security alarms, because he wasn't accessing it in any way they'd been programmed to recognize.

He was even more invisible than Aisha was—and he could get into systems she couldn't get near.

He was terribly dangerous. He didn't scare Aisha, though she supposed he should have.

"Your parents are beside themselves," he said. He was still in the computer, but he was in the room, too, looking straight at her. "They think you're somewhere on-planet; that was clever of you, setting a rover to fly out to sea the day after you left. Were you planning to let them know where you really are?"

"Eventually," Aisha said. "Are you going to tell them?"

"I might," said Rama. "Tell me why I shouldn't."

"I need you to help me find a way to keep Nevermore from turning into a U.P. colony. And you need me to help you make your way through this universe you've found yourself in," she said, though she wasn't as sure of that as she'd been when she worked it all out. "You can get into the computer, but you don't know how people are when they're face to face: what kinds of things they do and say, and how they keep from strangling each other. I know those things. I can take care of them while you follow the trail. There is one, isn't there? You're not just running around at random?"

"All I know is that the answer is out here," he said. "I'm following my gut, you would say. I can't explain it any more clearly than that."

"I know about gut," said Aisha. "You do that, and I'll keep people from figuring out that you're *really* not from around here."

He raised an eyebrow at her. "You have a plan?"

"I always have a plan," said Aisha.

People laughed when she said that. So did he, but he wasn't laughing at her, exactly. He appreciated her.

It was good that somebody did. She narrowed her eyes at him. "You're not sending me back?"

"That's not possible from this place," he said.

"What about Centrum? What will you do there?"

"I don't know yet," he said.

"Look," said Aisha. "Just keep quiet and I'll take care of the rest. I promise I'll send a message to Mother and Pater and Jamal when I can."

He didn't like being told to do anything. She knew that already. She braced against his glare, and didn't more than half wilt under it.

When he relaxed, so did she. She shouldn't have. "So you're going to swear yourself as my servant," he said.

She looked down at her clothes. She'd decided on black robes and veils— not like Malia's, exactly; the tribes weren't the only people in the worlds who followed that tradition. She didn't have any weapons, and she wasn't likely to get them. "I'm not swearing anything," she said. "This makes it easier to be invisible, that's all."

"You know what these robes mean where I come from," he said.

"Yes, but who else in the universe does?"

"I do," said Rama.

Aisha resisted a sudden urge to shrink down small. "My religion has these, too. They're called the burqa. It's *very* old-fashioned and some people think it's horrible, but we can use it. I don't need to turn into a fighting machine."

"No?"

"No," said Aisha.

"Then what will you be? My concubine?"

Aisha knew what the word meant. She didn't mean to blush. "You're 'way too old for me," she said.

He stared; then he laughed. "Oh! My wounded heart. A warrior you'll be, then. I'll teach you enough to keep you safe."

Aisha could argue with that, but she decided not to. "I know some of it already," she said.

"Good," said Rama. "You'll be learning much more before we're done."

"I'm ready for that," said Aisha. Maybe she even believed it. Some of it.

19

Ship's night found Khalida unable to sleep. The consensus that dimmed the lights in the public areas and put the majority of the crew off duty was out of sync with the time zone she had left. Her body still, after three shipdays, insisted on waking up halfway through ship's day and staying awake well into the night.

Tomiko was sound asleep, curled in a ball in the middle of the doublewide captain's bunk. Khalida kissed her ear, which made her stir, but barely; then slipped softly out of bed.

She was hungry, maybe. The buzz of last night's brandy had worn off. The headache was no better than it had been when she started, if no worse.

The captain's quarters had a direct link to the ship's main computer. Khalida's clearances got her in; she found the files where she knew they would be.

Hands slid across her bare shoulders and down over her breasts. Tomiko's arms clasped tight around her.

She clasped them in return, but most of her mind was on the link that Tomiko had refrained from mentioning. Her orders were here, not on Centrum. She could go that far to get them from someone higher up, or she could access them now.

If she did that, there was no getting away from them. No last few T-days of strictly relative freedom. No blissful ignorance.

She keyed the codes. The locks let go one by one. Her orders from MI streamed through the implants into her brain.

"Khalida?"

She was lying on her back. Tomiko bent over her. Her headache was gone.

"God damn," said Tomiko. "What the hell was that?"

"I don't know," Khalida said. She caught herself groping around inside her mind, hunting for the pain that had been part of her for so long that she had forgotten what it was like to be without it.

What she found instead made no sense at all. It was like the strongest, clearest, highest-security uplink she had ever been part of, but the ship's feed was off. She should have been alone inside her head.

She looked at Tomiko and saw layer on layer on layer. Worry on top, love and fear below that, calculation down deeper, a quick run-through of possibilities, including the one that Khalida might be a security risk or worse. Psych repair was supposed to be foolproof, and Khalida had been duly repaired—but she had refused followup therapy. She might have been more broken than anyone knew, or have broken all over again for reasons Tomiko could not know. She had been isolated on a nearly deserted world, after all, with only the most basic medical services.

That barely stung, even the parts that were true. Tomiko was Spaceforce. She ought to be thinking that way.

Khalida should not be inside Tomiko's head. She was not psi-five—because that was what it took to be doing what she was doing.

What was Rama? Was there even a number for what he was?

That thought appeared completely at random. It shut off the stream of thoughts that poured from Tomiko. It put her face to psychic face with the man—psi master—mage—whatever he was—from Nevermore.

Nothing ever seemed to surprise Rama. He did something that she would replay over and over in her memory, to try to understand it. It felt as if he had tucked in all her flapping edges, smoothed and secured them, so that nothing could get in and she could not, inadvertently, get out.

All of it passed in the fraction of a second. She reached up and pulled Tomiko down and kissed her until they were both dizzy.

With luck Khalida might have kept Tomiko distracted until the alarm called her to her day's duties on the ship, but Khalida had never had much of that. When their breathing had quieted and the sweat had dried on their bodies, Tomiko propped herself on her elbow and said, "I'm putting you in for a psych evaluation."

"Good," said Khalida, and she meant that.

Not just because she needed it, either. A new evaluation would delay the orders, if not invalidate them. Whatever had knocked her flat on her back had not even touched that memory.

Report to authorities in Centrum. Secure transport to Araceli. Mission specifics attached.

Those were secure in her head, too. She had been breaking apart by then, but the download had completed before the blackout.

The situation she had supposedly resolved, was not. All those lives were gone for nothing. Castellanos was still at war with Ostia. Ostia, broken, battered, be-nuked Ostia, would not stop fighting. Would not stop demanding that she come back, not because it wanted to indict her for high crimes and misdemeanors, but because it would not negotiate with Castellanos unless she served as mediator.

It was insane. It was impossible—which was why Ostia was insisting on it; she needed no terabytes of analyses to be sure of that.

She could not go back there. She was broken already. That would crush her to powder.

A psych evaluation would show MI exactly how damaged she was. It would end her career, too, but by now she was ready to let it happen. No one had any business using Khalida for anything more challenging than cataloguing artifacts on an archaeological site at the back end of nowhere.

It was all so simple after all. Clean, almost. Clinical. Insane, no question, but insanity was good. Insanity would keep her away from Araceli—and Araceli far, far away from her.

"I owe you," she said to Rama in her head. She had no sure way of knowing if he heard, but she suspected he did. He sent no answer that she was aware of. He had his own insanity to wallow in, and his own obsession to chase after.

Khalida smiled at Tomiko. It was a great relief to have everything settled.

Tomiko did not look relieved at all. But there at last was the bell for the day shift, and she had a ship to run. She left Khalida with stern orders not to get into any more trouble than she could possibly help.

Those were orders Khalida could easily obey. She found she could sleep then, and when she woke she treated herself to a long, blissful session in the cleanser.

When she was clean inside and out, she dressed in a fresh uniform and ate a solid meal of shipboard rations. Even those tasted good in the mood she was in.

A ping waited for her in the ship's system. Captain's dinner tonight. She was expected to attend.

Captain's dinner was a formality she could hardly avoid. Whatever Tomiko was to Khalida, Captain Hashimoto of the *Leda* and Captain Nasir of MI were expected to observe certain proprieties. Which meant at least one official gathering during the voyage, and suitable courtesies paid to the ship's officers.

It also meant that she would have to face the boy from Psycorps. She braced for that, fortifying herself with the assurance—even if it might be false—that he could not get into her head. There were protocols for that, and MI had backups of its own. She was safe.

So, she hoped, was the other guest at the captain's table. Civilian passengers were always invited, and if they were wise, they accepted. Rama was wise.

He seemed to be on his best behavior. He wore the plain grey suit that Vikram had given him, and no torque. No jewelry at all that she could see. He still refused to cut his hair, but tonight it was clubbed at his nape: enough of a Govindan style to avoid attracting notice.

For the most part he kept quiet. He ate enough to be polite, and sipped the wine that came with each course. The conversation flowed over and past him.

It dawned on her gradually that he was controlling it. He was very subtle. A glance, a word, a brief question: he steered them all in the direction he wanted.

She could not tell exactly what that was. War stories, old jokes and older gossip, the virtues of this wine over that—there seemed to be no particular order in it.

Lieutenant Zhao had got married not long ago. He linked them all to an image of a handsome young woman in Psycorps green, with five pips on the collar.

He was transparently proud. No one said what most of them must be thinking: that the Corps was breeding for more than looks. This was an island of civility; the response that was expected was to share one's own joy, one's spouse or family or child, or if one had none, one smiled and asked after those who did.

What it must be like for someone whose whole world was so long gone that no one else alive remembered it, Khalida could not imagine. Rama was perfectly opaque, and perfectly polite.

Then Lieutenant Zhao said, "You're from Dreamtime, yes? Bai was stationed there before we married, in Woomera. Have you been there?"

His gaze was limpid, his expression perfectly innocent. As traps went, it was not too badly laid.

Rama smiled. "There is no Psycorps station in Woomera."

"She was liaison to the ambassador from Araceli," Lieutenant Zhao said.

Khalida's spine went stiff. This was a trap, yes, but maybe it was not laid for Rama.

He raised a brow. "Ah," he said. "So you are both from Araceli."

"Bai was born there," said Lieutenant Zhao. "I was born on Earth, in Chengdu."

"In the old city?"

Lieutenant Zhao nodded, with some regret. "We left before I was old enough to remember. I grew up on Araceli, near the Ara itself."

Rama did not move and his expression did not change, but Khalida felt his alertness like a prickle on the skin. "Is it true what they say of that? That it's a remnant of a race that went before?"

Khalida opened her mouth to decry the myth. The flick of his glance stilled her.

Lieutenant Zhao shook his head and smiled. "That's very pretty, but it's just a story. It's a natural formation, a stone arch. Someone a long time ago carved glyphs in the rock, but those are forgeries. Araceli had no human inhabitants before Earth colonized it."

"That you know of," Rama said.

"We're sure," said Lieutenant Zhao. "There's no evidence of such people at all. Just that one arch and the carvings on it. Stargates are an old story, a fiction from Earth. There's never been any such transport in this universe."

"Too bad, too," said *Leda*'s XO. She was a wry and wickedly humorous woman, and she had been greatly enjoying the wine. "We'd be out of a job, but imagine opening up a gate and walking from one world to the next. The whole universe would be as close as the bodega down the street."

"We'd still need security forces," Tomiko said. "First-contact units. Armies."

"Right," said the XO. "You never know what you'd find on the other side, if you opened up a new one. Still—the possibilities!"

"All sadly mythical, I'm afraid," said Lieutenant Zhao. "There are only two ways to get from world to world: sublight slog or subspace jump. You can't tame a wormhole and turn it into a gate."

They all nodded and sighed. All but Rama. He sat back, and Khalida could swear he was biting back laughter, or possibly tears.

Maybe she imagined it. His face was expressionless. He reached for his cup and drank slowly, as if hiding behind it. Or else he simply admired the captain's taste in Shiraz.

Tell me about this Dreamtimer with the Govindan name," Tomiko said. Khalida had not expected Tomiko to miss a word or a glance, but she had rather hoped not to have to explain Rama. They were still in the captain's mess, finishing off the last bottle of wine. Everyone else had long since rolled off to bed.

Khalida turned the goblet in her fingers. In that light, the wine looked like blood. "He does have Govindan relatives," she said. "You know Vikram, on Nevermore? That's his cousin."

"I've read the dossier," Tomiko said. Her tone was as dry as the pinot blanc she was finishing off. "It's as interesting for what it doesn't say as for what it does. Is he one of yours?"

"MI's?" Khalida was stalling. They both knew it. "If he were, would I be able to say so?"

"No," Tomiko said. "He looks modified, but the scans say he's not. Whoever gengineered him, they were good. They weren't trying to hide it, either."

"Truth in labeling?"

Tomiko bared her teeth in a grin. "If I swung in that direction, I'd be jumping his bones. Have you noticed the way he moves?"

Khalida had noticed. No one with eyes could avoid it.

"He was doing katas this morning," Tomiko said, "down in the cargo bay with his ninja. He's better at them than she is. In half-gravity, he was literally flying."

"His—" Khalida bit her tongue.

Tomiko's grin stretched even wider. "Oh yes, he omitted to declare that part of his cargo. I've docked his account accordingly. So far he hasn't said a word about it."

Khalida was on her feet. Her head only swam a little. When she roared out of the captain's mess, she was aware that Tomiko followed.

Good. She was going to need the backup—and the authority.

Aisha was asleep in the bunk closest to the cabin's door. Her black robe must have been appropriated from Blackroot tribe, though she seemed not to have borrowed the weapons to go with it. The veils lay crumpled beside her.

Rama was awake. He had the walls set to show a star field approximating the one they were jumping through. It looked as if he was floating in space.

Khalida's grand fire of outrage died, but the ember was hot enough to keep her going. "That," she said, perfectly reasonably, she thought, "is my niece you've kidnapped."

"She kidnapped herself," said Rama. "She stowed away. I believe she found the inspiration in a novel about pirates."

Khalida opened her mouth, then shut it with a click. "And you *let* her?"

"Didn't you?"

"I had no idea she'd even try it!"

"You should have," he said. "That is a very determined child."

"Determined to do *what*?"

"Solve mysteries. Find answers. Save the world."

That was Aisha to the life. Khalida was near to hating this alien, this creature out of time, for understanding Aisha so much better than her own family did.

"You let her do it," Khalida said. "You abetted it."

"I never knew she was here until just before the jump," Rama said. "Should I have let her go through it in the hallway? Or in the cargo bay?"

"How could you not know?"

He let the echoes die before he answered. "I do not know everything."

Was that a flicker of regret? Khalida was too angry to care. "The minute we come out of jump, she's going straight back to her parents."

No one argued with that. Even Aisha, who was awake: dark eyes, stricken face, staring at her. Khalida held out her hand. "Get up. You're coming with me."

Aisha sat up but made no move to take Khalida's hand. "Where?"

Khalida had not thought that far. Yet. "Out of here. Where you'll be safe."

"She's as safe here as she is anywhere," Tomiko said.

Khalida spun toward her. That was betrayal, that salt-in-the-wound sting. "You *knew*!"

Tomiko shrugged, a lift of the shoulder, a graceful spreading of the hands. "Like Meser Rama, I didn't know she was here until right before the jump. I didn't know who she was until today. There were other priorities, and I had her under surveillance; she wasn't a threat to the ship."

"You should have told me." Khalida was not sure which of them she spoke to. Both, she supposed. All of them.

None of them reproached her, or gloated at her, either. She settled on Aisha as the cause of it all, but it was Rama she spoke to. "If she gets so much as a sniffle between now and the time I ship her home, I'll hold you personally responsible."

"I do take that responsibility," he said.

"Does it mean the same thing to you as it does to me?"

Rama met her glare. His eyes could be hard to meet: there was so much in them, so many years, so many things she could never understand. At the moment she was too angry to care. He said, "It's quite possible it means more."

That was a rebuke. She shook it off. "You had better be telling the truth," she said.

She slept alone that shipnight, in the cabin that had been nominally hers to begin with. Tomiko did not try to force sense or reason on her.

In the morning, directly after shift change, she went down to the cargo bay. There were other people going down there, too, and not many of them had official reason to be there. They were circulating in that direction, that was all.

The cargo bay was useful for troop maneuvers and martial training. The gravity made a soldier work for her balance, and the open spaces away from the cargo could host a whole mock battle.

This morning a small crowd had gathered halfway down the bay. Most of them were watching. A few, dressed for exercise, were doing katas.

That at least was what they looked like. Khalida had seen something like them before, in one of the sword dances in the tribal village on Nevermore; but this was the root from which they must have sprung. They had a great deal of elegance and a great deal of speed. They were completely merciless.

Rama led them, wearing the bottom half of a *gi* and nothing else. It was not surprising Tomiko had called his shadow a ninja: she did look like a secret warrior of old Japan in her black robes and veils. He had a real sword, slim and slightly curved like a katana. Hers was a practice sword, made of plasteel, with a blunt blade. The others had hands or staves or practice blades or whatever they happened to have brought with them.

Aisha must have spent time training with the Blackroot warriors. She was good, though not perfect: sometimes she had to stop and redo a step.

So did everyone but Rama. He was teaching children. He was not patronizing and he certainly did not insult their clear and visible talents, but Khalida knew the difference.

He reached the end of the sequence, turned and bowed. The line of students bowed back. There were a good dozen besides Aisha. They were breathless and sweat-streaked, and some were grinning.

He grinned back with a sudden, wild edge, and whirled into motion.

Then they saw what this art was supposed to be. He was a blur of darkness struck through with the flash of steel. With each leap he sprang higher, until he was spinning in the air, striking with fist, feet, blade.

Tomiko had told the truth. In the half-gravity, he flew.

After the first startled instant, Khalida got the measure of the dance and the speed. Some of it was still too fast to follow, but most she could. She could use her full-G strength in the half-G, let it balance and speed up the spins, keeping her eye on the imaginary target, striking to wound, disable, kill.

Especially kill.

It had been much too long since she did anything more physical than shift an artifact from a shelf to a table. She pushed through the pain. She ignored the exhaustion. She could not match him—quite. But she did not embarrass herself, either.

He wound down gradually. She followed a fraction of a step behind.

She was going to pay for this. She was wringing wet, shaking, sobbing for breath. But she stayed on her feet. She bowed when he bowed, and was gratified to see him sweating, too. Then he really did look like obsidian, black glass born of volcanic fire.

For an instant in his eyes she saw what he was. It shook her in ways that she was not ready to define, and steadied her in others that she was even less ready for.

Then he had drawn the veil across them again. They were only eyes, dark in a dark face, and rather more human than not.

She walked away on her own feet. People were applauding—giving him his due.

"Yours, too," he said.

He was beside her, not touching her, but his presence was holding her up.

"Stop that," she said. She had just enough breath to say it.

He ignored her. When they were in the lift, and full gravity weighed them both down, he caught her before she fell over.

His breath was still coming faster than usual, but most of his strength was back already. She glowered at him. "What are you feeding on? Blood?"

He shook his head. His smile was wide and sweet and a little crazy. "This ship has a core like a sun."

She sagged in his arms; then she struggled until he set her on her feet. "The fusion reactor. Of course."

"Yes," he said. "I was afraid, I admit it. Away from the sun, what might happen to me? But the ship is here, and it sustains me. I'm free of all the stars."

"God help us," she said.

The lift stopped. The door opened. The handful of crewmembers who stood there got an eyeful of Khalida wringing wet and clinging to a half-naked man.

Too bad Tomiko would never believe it. Khalida was not feeling charitable toward her at all.

Rama went with her down the corridor, though the way to his own cabin was three levels farther up. At her door she turned on him. "That's far enough," she said.

He bent his head in the way he had. It must be a habit from when he was a king. Without a word he turned and walked away.

She surprised herself with disappointment. A fight would have felt good then—since Tomiko was not there to get what she deserved.

No one could give Khalida what she deserved. Not Tomiko, not Rama, not anyone. She punched the lock and let herself fall through the door as it opened, not caring where she landed or what happened when she did.

Aisha was worried about Aunt Khalida. Not because Aisha was in unbelievable amounts of trouble, though she was, but because Aunt Khalida looked awful. When she came to the cargo bay and matched Rama in his katas, that was impressive, but it was crazy. It felt all wrong.

Rama made sure she got safely to her room, but that was as far as he went. When Aisha yelled at him for it, he said, "She didn't want me there."

"Should that even matter?"

"With her it does," he said.

Aisha had to think about that. When she was done thinking, she went to someone who could actually do something, though she might be as stubborn about it as Rama.

Aisha could have worn normal clothes for that, since she wasn't really invisible any more, but if she did that, she might have to explain to Rama what she was doing. Then he would try to stop her. She stayed the way she was, then, and hoped it would keep people from getting in her way.

She went the back way, through the access ducts. It was faster, and she was less likely to meet anybody. The ship had surveillance in there after all—she couldn't believe how wrong she'd been before—but it didn't seem to care what she did as long as it could keep an eye on her.

The captain had an office she worked in when she wasn't on the bridge. Aisha would stake out the office and wait, and eventually the captain would come in.

It was a foolproof plan, especially the part where she convinced the door to let her in. She didn't hack it so much as persuade it. Jamal wasn't the only one in the family who could make a computer do things people insisted it couldn't do.

She made herself comfortable in a hoverchair, after she discovered and used the lavatory. There was a bowl of nuts to nibble on—real nuts from a tree on a planet—and water from a dispenser. She could stay for hours if she had to.

It was not even an hour before she heard people in the outer room. One was the captain: Aisha could feel as well as hear her. The other one made her shrink down in the chair.

Lieutenant Zhao was talking fast. Aisha had to strain to understand the words. "Please, you must understand. This is urgent. No one else can do it."

"Why not?" the captain shot back. "Rinaldi is barking mad. As soon as he gets his hands on her, he'll rip her to pieces."

"No!" The word came out as a yelp. "He's not like that. He's insane, yes, most of the nines are, but he sincerely believes that there is no other choice. What she did won his respect. He hates her, fears her, but he trusts her judgment. He knows she'll judge fairly."

"Will she?" said the captain. "He manipulated her into nuking Ostia. Do you have any idea how much that damaged her?"

"She's been repaired," Lieutenant Zhao said. "Whatever residual damage there may be, we can take care of on the way there. She will be fit for duty when she gets to Araceli."

"What if she isn't? What if I'm right and you're wrong, and she's still broken and Rinaldi wants to gnaw her liver? Will you take responsibility for what happens then?"

Lieutenant Zhao sputtered. "I'm not—I don't have—"

"I didn't think so," the captain said. She sounded tired and disgusted. "Go away. Leave me alone. Above all, leave her alone. I'll get her evaluated. If Psych says she's not fit, she's not fit. Do you understand me?"

"I understand," Lieutenant Zhao said, "that the need is strong enough to bypass a Psych hold. She won't get out of this, and you won't get her out."

"We'll see," the captain said grimly.

Aisha would have run away if she could, but the only way out was past Lieutenant Zhao. She stayed in the captain's office. When the captain came in, she was still there, sitting stiffly upright in the hoverchair.

The captain stopped. She wasn't even as tall as Aisha; she looked like a flower carved in ivory. But Aisha knew how strong she was.

She loved Aunt Khalida, and Aunt Khalida loved her. That was one of the things the parents didn't talk about: that Aunt Khalida was never going to marry a man. If she married a woman, the family back on Earth would pitch a fit, but Mother and Pater would still speak to her. Probably more than they would to Aisha by the time she finished doing what she had to do.

Knowing all that made it easier to keep her chin up and say, "You can't let him do that to her."

The captain's brows went up. "You heard that?" Then she answered herself. "Of course you did. Did you understand even half of it?"

"Don't talk down to me," Aisha said. "Maybe I don't know all the whos and whys, but I can tell when my aunt is in trouble. Whatever Psych did to her didn't fix her. It made her worse."

"Did it? And you know this how?"

"I lived with her on Nevermore for almost a T-year. She's not repaired, Captain. At all."

The captain dropped down into the chair behind the desk and rubbed her forehead as if it wouldn't stop hurting. "That's not supposed to happen."

"You know it has," Aisha said. "You can see."

Captain Hashimoto kept talking as if Aisha hadn't said a word. "Traumatic-stress repair is as effective as any therapy we have. Results are guaranteed. They *can't* fail."

"Who says that?" Aisha asked. She really wanted to know.

Captain Hashimoto frowned at her. "Everyone. All the literature. Psych. Those protocols always work. No matter who or what they work on."

"Nothing *always* works," Aisha said. "You know what I think? I think people need it to work, so they make a lie and tell it so often they believe it's the truth."

The frown turned into a narrow-eyed stare. "How old did you say you were again?" Before Aisha could answer, the captain said, "I'll fight this. I will. But if they're determined to send her back into the unholy mess that broke her in the first place, they will do it. Nothing I can do will stop them."

"I don't believe that," Aisha said.

"*Now* you're acting your age," the captain said. "I hear you. I believe you. I'll do my best. That's all I can promise."

"I would rather be my age than yours," Aisha said. She shaped each word carefully. "Thank you for listening to me. I won't bother you again."

She stood up. Before she turned to go, the captain said, "Think before you do anything. Think long and hard. Promise."

"I won't do anything without thinking about it first," Aisha said. The captain wasn't happy, but neither was Aisha. They both had all they were going to get.

Every shipday, Rama spent hours on the observation deck. There was nothing to see—really nothing; subspace was completely blank. Most people found it disturbing. He seemed to like it.

When Aisha sat near him, he lifted his head. His eyes moved as if he watched something above him.

Something big, swimming huge and slow, trailing fins as long as the ship, and thrusting itself through subspace with a tail so wide even Rama couldn't see its edges. It was singing, a song too deep and at the same time too high for human ears.

It was easier if she closed her eyes. Then she could feel and see and hear.

He was singing back to it. He couldn't use his voice; it didn't have the range. The power in him, the psi that was 'way, 'way above a nine, could make the fabric of subspace thrum and ring.

The huge creature swam on past. There were others around the ship, but none so big and none so close. Aisha opened her eyes.

Rama lay back on the padded bench with one knee drawn up. He looked as if he was asleep.

"What were you singing?" Aisha asked him.

He answered without moving. "It asked me who I was and what I was and where I was going. I answered it."

"What did you say?"

"That I swim through the other world, the one so barren of song; that I was born to both worlds; that I was going to find what I had lost."

"Your world? Your time?"

"Nothing can reclaim time," he said.

"But—"

"There are things that can travel as freely in time as in space. I am not one of them."

"Really?"

He didn't answer that.

"I think you don't want to. There would be no place for you there. You'd tear yourself to pieces."

"And everyone and everything around me."

Rama sounded most cool and distant when he was hurting the worst. It had taken Aisha a while to figure that out. "You're not a bad person," she said.

"I don't need to be bad to be too dangerous to live."

"Do you have to be dangerous? Why is it so awful to have as much psi as you've got?"

"You know what they say about absolute power."

"You had it," Aisha said. "I don't think it corrupted you. I think you got set on a particular way of doing things, and it turned out not to be the right one. People do that all the time. Now you have a chance to make up for it."

"People aren't all like me," he said.

"You might be surprised."

He turned his head to look at her. His eyes got very wide and very sharp. He came up in one motion, so smooth it didn't look human, and knelt in front of her.

He took her chin in his hand. She didn't pull away. She wasn't afraid, either, though he had gone completely strange. He turned her face from side to side, and then looked into her eyes, so deep she felt him walking on the bottom of her skull.

"No," he said, all the way down there. "Oh, no, you aren't. That is just too—no."

He wasn't speaking PanTerran, or Old Language, either. She didn't know what language it was. It didn't matter; where he was, all languages were the same.

"You turned against me," he said. "Even you. Most of all you. How many eons do you think it will take me to forgive?"

Aisha didn't want to understand that. That he saw something so deep inside her that she hadn't even known it was there. That he recognized it. And that she could—if she wanted; if she tried—let it speak through her.

She wasn't ready. She might not ever be.

She twisted free. But she didn't run away. "Whatever you think I did, or was, I don't remember. All I know is what I am now."

"Do you?"

"Don't push," she said.

He shied at that, a little bit shocked, a little bit offended. She wasn't about to apologize, except sideways. "Whatever you think you have to do, just make up your mind to it. Then do it. You can do anything you set your heart on."

"Not anything. I am not all-powerful. I'm not a god. No matter what people said or will say."

"Oh, no, you're not a god. But you're not the normal run of human, either."

"Neither are you."

"I'm starting to think," said Aisha, "that there is no such thing as normal. People who try to make just one kind of human the right kind and get rid of everybody else, or cut them down to the same size, are making a terrible mistake."

"You could argue that I'm not human," Rama pointed out.

"Genetically you are," she said. "We've got all but the tiniest tiny fraction of bits in the same places. We're just not from the same planet. Lots of us aren't. There's a hundred inhabited worlds. It's not just Earth any more."

"Or Nevermore."

"Or anywhere."

She sat and he knelt, thinking about that. His hands were on his knees.

She took his right hand and turned it so she could see what was in it. It was still his own sun, with spots and a flare.

"You know," he said, "before I went to sleep, or into stasis if you prefer, it wasn't like this at all. It was gold, like an inlay in the skin. Doubters said that was what it was. Somehow in the long years, it changed. Now it looks on the outside the way it feels on the inside."

"See?" said Aisha. "Things can change. Even you."

He laughed. It wasn't much: just a gust of breath. But it was real. "You keep waking me up, do you know that?"

"I'm sorry," said Aisha. "The first time was an accident. Really."

"And this one?"

"Well..." she said.

He smiled. She did love his smile, when he wasn't being wild.

It made her remember why she was here in the first place. She went straight to it. "Can you fix Aunt Khalida before we get out of jump?"

That killed the smile. "How do you mean?"

"You know what I mean. Mend her broken bits. Make her whole again."

"I've done as much as I can."

"As much as you can? Or as much as you will?"

"I've given her everything she needs," he said. "The rest is hers to do."

"You're just like the captain," she said, and it was hard, because her throat was suddenly tight, "and I'm just a baby, because I think nobody is doing enough."

"Oh, no," said Rama. "Some of us are doing altogether too much."

"Including me?"

"You love her. That's exactly right, and exactly the right amount. We're doing what we can for her. Do believe that."

"But it's not enough!"

He let those echoes settle down into silence. In it, another of the huge beasts swam below the ship and sang. Its song was the saddest thing in any world.

That was why Aisha burst out crying. Rama didn't say anything, didn't laugh at her; didn't push her away when she held on to him and bawled.

She'd be horribly embarrassed when she got done with this. At the moment she didn't care at all.

Tomiko had never been one to waste time. She was not above stacking the deck in a game, either. She sent her own morale officer to evaluate Khalida.

Dr. Sulawayo had the manner polished to a fine art: soft, quiet, scrupulously non-threatening. Khalida knew from his dossier that he was barely a decade older than she was, but he had modified his appearance to the most comforting percentile: wise lined face, dark liquid eyes, pure white hair. She found it ironic that he looked so much older than the oldest living thing on the ship.

She tried to imagine Rama wearing the face of age, but her imagination failed. That species of antique conqueror never grew old.

One day she was going to remember to ask him what his name really was. Names were important. She was Egyptian; she was born knowing that.

She needed to focus. Dr. Sulawayo was standing in her closet of a cabin, watching her. She ordered the wall to present him with a place to sit.

The cabin was scrupulously, clinically clean. So was Khalida. Her uniform was new, crisp, and impeccable. Her mind might be ricocheting all over creation, but her physical surroundings would, by Allah, be perfectly organized.

"Doctor," she said. "This is a pleasure."

He smiled. It was genuine; so was he, with all his modifications. He honestly believed in what he did. "It's been a little while, hasn't it, Captain? I still remember our visit to the tomb of Menes—such a find; such pride for all of you, that your father was the one to find it."

Khalida remembered, too, but it was bright and distant, like someone else's memory. Everything was like that, that had happened before the suppurating wound that was Araceli. "Our family does have a certain gift for archaeology," she said. "A tropism, I suppose. We've been robbing tombs for millennia. Now it's not only legal, it's respectable."

"Your father argues that your ancestors were not the robbers but the occupants of the tombs," Dr. Sulawayo said. "There have been tests, have there not? Proof of kinship."

"Just about everyone in Egypt is related to a pharaoh," Khalida said, "one way or another. It's the same in Asia: if you're not Genghis Khan's descendant, you're a rarity."

"Genetics," said Dr. Sulawayo, "are a wonderful thing." He smiled at her. "Tell me about Nevermore. Is it as mysterious as it's reputed to be?"

Sudden shifts of subject where the psych officer's favorite tool. Khalida had enough training herself to have expected this one. "It's a planet-sized nature preserve with minimal human inhabitants and an impossibly large number of ruins. It's beautiful. It's driving my brother to happy distraction. He wants so badly to decipher all the inscriptions—thousands, millions of them. And no key to them anywhere."

"Not in the inhabitants?"

"They don't read. It's a religious restriction. We don't even know which of the different scripts would have belonged to their ancestors, if any of them did." But someone did. Someone on this ship. Someone whom Khalida had no desire to explain to anyone.

"A great mystery," Dr. Sulawayo said. "Quite wonderful, wouldn't you agree? The universe needs unanswered questions."

"It's my job," Khalida pointed out, "technically, to make sure all questions are answered. That's what intel is."

"Do you believe that?"

"I'm here, aren't I?"

"Voluntarily?"

Khalida met his calm gaze. "Actually, no. If I tender my resignation, will you accept it?"

There: she had got him to squirm. It was subtle; he was very well trained. But she felt it.

She pushed. She did not care if it hurt either of them. "They're not going to let you, are they? I'm going back to Araceli if I go in a box, screaming."

"Will you do that?"

"Will it make any difference?"

"To me," said Dr. Sulawayo, "yes. Not only because you were repaired, and it seems the repair may not have been as successful as Psych believed. Because we are friends, and I have a personal investment in your welfare."

"We were friends," Khalida said. "I don't feel it any more. I don't feel much at all. Everything before, it's globed in glass. And here I am. I'll shrink to a point in space and disappear. I realize people will notice, and some will even care, but I? I can't make it matter."

He reached toward her. She watched him realize that might not be the best course of action, debating it inside himself, in the endless stretch of a time-out-of-time between one second and the next.

He completed the gesture. He took her hands. "Oh, my dear. This is a gross failure of treatment. Whether it is the fault of the mechanism or the technicians—no matter. They left you in this state; they let you go. That is unconscionable."

She stared at his hands. He had no psi. His touch did nothing but grant her a small gift of warmth. Trickles of thought came in with it, worry and fret and gratifying anger and a dangling bit of reminder that he had another appointment within the hour. Which he could change.

"No, don't," she said before she could stop herself.

He let her go. She caught the stab of his guilt. He had no way to know what she was telling him not to do; of course he would think it was his touch.

She could correct him. She could tell him why. Then he would be sure she was insane. She was neutered. She had no more psi than he did. She certainly had not had it restored by a legend out of an ancient and completely forgotten tomb.

Stasis chamber. Enchanted tower.

"My dear," said Sulawayo, "we don't have the facilities here for the care you need. I will arrange for it in Centrum. I promise you."

"Before or after I'm shipped off to Araceli?"

"Before, I hope," he said.

"You know," she said, speaking the thought as it came to her, "I believe I understand why Rinaldi wants me back. He knows I'm as crazy as he is. Finally, there's someone who can understand him."

"Do you believe he caused this?"

She laughed—honestly; that was mirth. "I'm not that far gone! Whatever went wrong with the repair, it has nothing to do with him. This is my very own damage."

"I prefer to blame Psych," he said. He actually sounded fierce.

She patted him as if he had been one of the expedition's horses. "You do that," she said.

"We will undo this," he said. "I promise you. Whatever it takes, we will do it."

She sat for a long while after he had gone. On the other side of the glass, she was astonished and touched and even humbled. She always had been rich in friends.

Max and Sonja and Kinuko and John Begay.

"Hand-pick your unit for this one," said the Under-Undersecretary for Damage Control and Intraplanetary Affairs. Civilian clothes, as drab as bureaucracy in Centrum could tolerate, but a dossier that read like a pirate's tour of flashpoints in the United Planets. The fact that she was dispensing the orders, from well above the stratosphere of MI's channels, told Khalida just how anomalous, and critical, the situation was.

She sat in her featureless cube in an anonymous office tower out of Centrum proper, linked in to more feeds than Khalida could count. Khalida wondered if each of the rest of them had the same sense of being the Under-Undersecretary's first and only focus.

"It's that bad?" Khalida asked.

"They're all bad," the Under-Undersecretary said. "This one is slightly more delicate than usual. Pick a team you can trust implicitly."

She was stating the glaringly obvious. Khalida suppressed the first, reflexive retort, as training and field sense woke up and started to function. Of course this one would be difficult. Psycorps was not only involved, it was one of the warring parties.

The Under-Undersecretary nodded, following her train of thought through their mutual web link. "Exactly. Godspeed, Major."

Easy for her to say from her safe bunker in the heart of U.P. The link was already cut, and Khalida's mind had gone straight to the answer—no question as to who should ship out with her to Araceli.

Max and Sonja, joined at the hip since training camp. Kinuko, eleventh generation of MI noncoms, dragged kicking and screaming through officer candidate school and still fighting it, but not quite hard enough to up and quit. Big, quiet John Begay, exempt from Psycorps testing by a treaty so old it predated the first starship. Sometimes Khalida wondered…

MI had thrown them together for a routine mission to the outer worlds, shutting down that earthmonth's drugs-and-sedition cartel and slamming the lid on it hard enough to keep it from cropping up again for at least the next earthyear. They clicked well together: Max and Sonja young enough to find it all a grand adventure but intelligent enough not to make idiot decisions, Kinuko absolutely ruthless when it came to facing down the inevitable opposition, and John Begay a genius at tracking both people and cargo through the tangle of the outer planets' web systems.

Araceli on the face of it was a much more standard intraplanetary political mess, but the Under-Undersecretary's subliminal message and the crawling sensation between Khalida's shoulders promised enough adventure to satisfy even Max and Sonja.

"Not hardly," Sonja said the day it all went sideways. "You think Captain Batshit is telling the truth? Ostia wants to blow up Castellanos?"

The shuttle was prepped, the coordinates set, the weapons armed. Captain Batshit—Meser Rinaldi to his nonexistent friends and his many enemies—had requested that Major Nasir command the mission remotely. In his company. "For protection," he had said, smiling his too-sincere smile.

Khalida was stretching the limits of her orders by meeting her team in the crew lounge of one of the shuttle bays in Castellanos' spaceport. It was deserted except for the five of them; its shields were on high. MI of course was recording. For internal purposes. As Rinaldi might say.

"I don't believe a word Rinaldi says," Khalida said, "but every other form of intel we can gather indicates that a revolutionary cell in Ostia is aiming a dirty bomb at Castellanos. We're ordered to take out the cell by any means possible."

"They're desperate," Kinuko translated.

"Which 'they' do you mean?" asked John Begay. "I don't like the smell of this place. There's enough rot here to reach all the way to the top."

"Still," Khalida said. "A hundred million human lives. A whole planet, with all its biosphere. Rotten or not, it doesn't deserve to be poisoned."

"That might be up for debate," John Begay said.

"You can refuse the mission," said Khalida. "Any of you. I'll take the heat, and whatever penalties MI slaps on us."

"No," said John Begay, and the rest nodded. Good soldiers, all of them, no matter what their dossiers might say. "It's highly probable we've been lied to. That doesn't put the planet in any less jeopardy. We'll fly the mission."

Khalida had known he would say that. The ache in the back of her skull, the sense of deep and subtle wrongness, had grown stronger, the closer they came to departure. "You fly," she said, "but I make the call: execute, or abort. If it gets bad, it's on me. My head on the spike."

Every one of them wanted to argue: faces growing tight, eyes narrowing. They all knew better. The alarm buzzed. Fifteen minutes to departure.

Khalida followed them out into the bay. The shuttle waited, all systems optimal, all clearances granted. Specs for the mission were loaded into the shuttle's computer, set to download when it came in sight of the target.

Khalida knew the substance of them. *Locate target, take over target's system, disarm target.* With protocols for various possible modes of resistance, from small-arms fire to electromagnetic pulse.

Standard procedures. Standard disposition of forces: Max in the pilot's cradle, John Begay linked in to the web, Kinuko and Sonja manning weapons.

Nothing about it felt standard. The universe around her seemed thin, brittle, as if it could crack at a touch. "Listen to me," she said as the team filed into the shuttle. "If anything—*anything*—strikes you as off, get out of there. Don't stop, don't question. Just go."

Max arched an eyebrow. "Premonition?"

"Political instinct." Khalida eyed the interior of the shuttle. Orders be damned, and Rinaldi be triple-damned. She was going.

"Don't," Max said. She knew Khalida too well; could always read her, no matter how she schooled her face to blankness. "Whatever Captain Batshit is up to, we're all better off if you're near enough to stop it."

"Stop talking sense," Khalida said. "You'll ruin your reputation."

Max grinned and pulled her in, kissing her until her ears rang. "Keep the bed warm for me."

The shuttle powered up. Khalida stepped back away from it. Hating herself; hating her orders, and the bastard who had laid them on her.

Max was the best kickass shuttle pilot in the quadrant. If anybody could get out ahead of a dirty bomb, she could.

Unless the intel was off by fourteen minutes, and the bird started to go up directly below the shuttle, just as it entered Ostia's airspace.

The bomb could blow right in the heart of Ostia, or on the way to Castellanos and take out that whole sector of the planet, or hit target and turn Psycorps' heart and center to radioactive slag.

Khalida had Max on the comm and the bomb in her sights. One single, simple command. That was all it took.

She looked into Max's eyes, and Max understood. She nodded. Khalida blew her into the next universe.

Over and over and over again.

"Enough."

Oh, of course *he* would be there. "What are you?" she asked. "My personal *deus ex machina?*"

"You are giving me a mother of headaches," said Rama. He was speaking Arabic. He was also physically there, in her cabin, locks be damned as usual.

He was unusually ruffled; his eyes were narrowed as if the light were too bright. Since he could stare directly into the sun with no ill effects, that was noteworthy.

"Don't tell me you have a weakness," she said.

"I have a host of them," said Rama. "Of which you happen to be one."

"Not interested," she said.

He blinked. He really did look as if the thought had never occurred to him. Which was insulting in its way.

"I have a habit," he said with some care, "of trying to mend what is past mending. I brought a man back from the dead once. He was never especially grateful, though he did allow as how he had by no means done all he needed to do in this life. I gave him the room to do it. The second time he died, he made sure I let him go."

"That's very sad," said Khalida.

"Sad? No. He was the best of friends; of all the allies I had, he was the closest. He was happy, once he got over raging at me for violating Nature. He was part of me."

"I definitely am not part of you," she said.

"Unfortunately you are. When I mended you, I wove part of myself into the working. You were so horrendously badly cobbled together, there was no other way."

Khalida stared at him. "So I'm not just crazy for myself any more? I've got your crazy, too?"

"That," he said with a distinct wry twist, "is one way of putting it."

She did not need his humor, black or otherwise. "If I kill myself, will it kill you?"

"No."

"You're sure?"

"I am sure," he said.

"That's a relief," she said. She studied her hands. They were thinner than they used to be. She had gone down a uniform size. Which was not a good thing, but there it was. "I am a mess, aren't I?"

"Yes, and you are wallowing in it."

That, she had not expected. No kindness; no sympathy. Not even a leavening of understanding.

"I'm not your morale officer," he said, "or your brother, or your lover. I am certainly not the machine-happy fools who ran you through their standard program and never bothered to verify the results. I am only a bloody-handed Bronze Age warlord, but it seems even I know more of the science of the mind than your so-wise Psych Division."

He had backed her against the wall with nothing more physically forceful than words.

"Your machines are clever and ingenious and occasionally brilliant," he said, "and your worldsweb would make the sages of my people weep for envy, but you know next to nothing of this thing you call psi, and as for the workings of the mind and the heart, it seems you have forgotten what little of it you ever knew. Machines have failed you, because you are what you are, and your Psycorps so maimed you that the rest could not help but happen. I've done what I can, but I have neither the talent nor the training to make you whole. That, you have to do for yourself."

"How?"

"Piece by piece," he said. "First believe. Then do."

"You sound like a bad martial-arts vid."

"Not all mindless entertainment is false. Some of it is rooted in the truth."

"*You* are a bad fantasy vid." She slid down the wall, squatting on her haunches, and hugged her knees. She could not tell whether she wanted to laugh or cry.

He could be a figment of her imagination, a nightmare like the one he had banished with a word.

He squatted in front of her. He was solid, for a figment. She could hear him breathing. He had a faint scent to him. It reminded her of Nevermore: the smell of earth and grass and rain.

That was alien. He had never had any rankness about him at all, even fresh out of stasis, with a beard to the waist and nails longer than his hands.

"What you suffered is part of you," he said. "What you did was terrible. But it's done. You can't undo it. You can blunt the edges. You can learn to live with it. You can even, if you work at it, be happy."

"You're talking to yourself, too, aren't you?" She blinked away tears that were there for no reason, that she had not even been aware of until they blurred her vision. "What if you have to do it all over again? What if you're called back to the place where you did all those terrible things, and all the same choices are waiting? What do you do then?"

"Whatever I must," he said.

"You're stronger than I am," Khalida said. "Or colder. I wasn't brought up to be a warrior king."

"You are a warrior," said Rama. "Captain or king, it's much the same. You do what you have to. You pay for it. You atone if you can. You hold it together, because tomorrow you may have to do it all over again. That's as much mercy as you get in war."

"What did you drive your troops with? Scorpion whips?"

"I never drove an army in my life," he said, flowing to his feet. "I led."

She glared at the door long after he had stalked out of it. "'Just get over it,'" she snarled at the memory of him. "If it's that easy, what are *you* doing in this age of the universe? Why aren't you happily dead?"

He could have answered if he chose. The silence had a distinctly mulish quality.

One thing he had done. He had broken the feedback loop. It would come back—Khalida was hardly foolish enough to think it was gone. But she could function again, at least for today. That was worth something, whether she was happy about it or not.

W hat *is* your name?" Aisha finally got around to asking Rama. They were nearly done with jump. She'd been lying low, expecting Aunt Khalida to corner her any moment and try to ship her back to Nevermore, but everything had been suspiciously quiet.

Everybody was waiting to get back into real space again, so real life could start up again, along with the worldsweb and all the news and orders and messages that brought with it. The night before that happened, there was captain's table again, and this time Aisha was included.

She was helping Rama get ready. He never needed help with his clothes, but his hair was so thick and long, and he flat refused to get rid of it. It was like the torque he was wearing tonight: it had come with him from his own world. He wouldn't let it go.

He said she was good at sorting out all the twists and tangles. He didn't have the patience himself, if someone else was around to do it. She didn't terribly mind. It was like curling blue-black silk, and once she got it to cooperate, with help from a brush and a comb and a tube of gel she'd begged off the purser, it looked perfectly presentable.

Meanwhile she had time to ask questions, and he was her captive. "I know your name isn't Rama, or Krishna, either. What is it really?"

He knew better by now than to twist around and make her have to redo half an hour's worth of work. "Does it matter?" he asked. "I like my new name. I want to keep it. My old one is best forgotten."

"Why? Is it ugly? Silly? Would I think it was stupid?"

"No!"

She grinned as she finished weaving plaits and started working them together into a club at his nape. "So what was it?"

"Mirain." He bit off the word.

"Mirain," she said, feeling all around it with her tongue. "I like that. It's nice. What does it mean?"

"It means Firstborn, and it was an old family name, and my mother gave it to me. Are you happy now? Mirain is six thousand years dead. My name is Rama, and I live in this world, where no one has ever heard of the horror that I used to be."

"You were not a horror," Aisha said. "I have another name, too, you know. My grandfather wanted to call me Meritamon, which is a very old name in Egypt, but Pater said that was no kind of name for a Muslim. So I'm Aisha. But when I visit Grandfather, I like to be Meritamon."

"Meritamon," he said. He put a lilt in it, that was his own original accent. "That is beautiful."

"It means 'Beloved of Amon,'" she said. "Amon was one of their sun gods: the great one, the one who ruled the rest. So you see, I can be two people, and have two completely different names. You can, too."

"Was Meritamon a destroyer of worlds?"

"Of course not. Neither were you."

"Only because my family stopped me."

"You would have stopped yourself," Aisha said.

"No," he said. "Not by then. The one I loved most in any world was gone. She kept me from losing my grip on humanity. Without her, there was nothing left of me but fire."

Aisha bound up the last of his braids, but played with them for a while, to keep him talking. "I can see the fire inside," she said, "but you're human. I'm absolutely sure of that."

"That's because I haven't been tested yet. No one has tried to provoke me. I can afford to play at being human."

"You're not playing at it," Aisha said with a snap of annoyance. "This is what you are. Not all of it, maybe. But enough."

"So you hope," Rama said.

Aisha shook her head, but she'd run out of time to argue. Captain's table was in ten minutes, and she still had to put on her own clothes.

Dinner was formal and polite and perfect. They drank from crystal and ate with silver, and the food tasted wonderful.

Even Aunt Khalida behaved herself. She looked a little better, but she was avoiding Rama so carefully that it was obvious. She talked around him, and when she had to look toward his end of the table, her eyes slid past him.

Aisha could understand that. She was doing the same thing to Lieutenant Zhao. But Rama wasn't anything like Lieutenant Zhao.

Except, Aisha thought, for one thing. Which happened to be the one thing Rama couldn't let Psycorps know he had. They'd do worse than neuter him. They'd study him till there was nothing left of him.

That was true of too many people in this universe. Rama didn't seem to care. He had people telling stories, so he could sit back and listen. That was one of the ways he studied the universe he'd woken up in.

People loved to hear themselves talk; Rama could get them going for hours. Aisha had seen him do it on Nevermore, when everybody got together for dinner and stayed on afterwards, drinking coffee and nibbling dessert and falling in and out of friendly arguments.

Thinking about it made her miss it so fiercely that her eyes stung. When she got herself back under control, Lieutenant Zhao was looking right at Rama and smiling, and saying, "What of you, Meser Rama? You must have wonderful stories to tell, from your wanderings through the worlds."

It was an ordinary enough question, and anybody might ask it. But something about it made Aisha's head hurt. Lieutenant Zhao was pushing—testing.

Rama didn't seem bothered by it. "It does fascinate me," he said, "how many stories are the same from world to world. There is always a hero who endures great suffering in order to come to glory, or a villain who causes suffering and in the end pays a high price. Humans of any world, it seems, do insist on justice in their stories, though not always in their rulers."

"You don't believe in stories, then, Meser Rama?" Lieutenant Zhao asked.

"I believe in what is real," Rama said.

"Not everyone has the same definition of reality," Aunt Khalida muttered.

Aunt Khalida had been going for the wine while other people talked. There were reasons why Pater didn't let people drink wine or spirits on the expedition, besides being a good Muslim, and this was one of them.

Aisha tried to think of some way to change the subject, but Lieutenant Zhao had already got his teeth in what Aunt Khalida said. "Really? How do you define it, Captain?"

Aunt Khalida looked him in the face. "How do you think?"

That confused him. He blinked. He even seemed a little sorry, though not enough. "There are certain standards that we all agree on."

"Are there?" She shook her head as if she felt sorry for him. Very, very sorry indeed. "Rama's wrong. Justice isn't only for stories. It's mercy we're all short of."

"Stories are meant to be true," said Captain Hashimoto. "They're life without the dull parts. All the best and worst: those things go into stories."

"Usually the worst," said Aunt Khalida.

"Light and dark are balanced," Rama said. "One should never outweigh the other."

The way he said it made Aisha's skin shiver. The words were full of memory and sorrow and pain.

Aunt Khalida didn't care. "You would know, wouldn't you?" she said.

"Too well," he said.

"The rest of us tell stories," she said. "You are the story."

He didn't answer that. He hadn't tried to stop her, either. She was getting them both in trouble. Really bad trouble, if Lieutenant Zhao understood even a tenth of what she was saying.

Captain Hashimoto saved them, maybe. "Everyone is a story," she said. "Sometimes we know what it is when it happens. Sometimes it takes a while."

She stood up. That was a signal for the final toast. If it came a little earlier than it should, nobody argued with her. There were so many currents swirling around the room, most of the people there must have been baffled. They seemed glad to escape.

Rama was so good at hiding what he felt that Aisha didn't think anyone else knew how dark his mood was. Aunt Khalida must; she'd caused it. But she was busy getting reamed by the captain. Aisha could feel that even through the door.

Lieutenant Zhao wasn't going to let Rama get away. There wasn't much Rama could do to avoid him, but Aisha didn't think he wanted to try. When Lieutenant Zhao followed him toward the lift, he paid no attention.

"Meser Rama," Lieutenant Zhao said. "The hour is early, and I have a bottle of Dreamtime Cabernet in my cabin. It's already open; jump will turn it to vinegar. Would you care to finish it with me?"

Aisha would have bet Rama would ignore him. She was horribly shocked when he said, "That's kind of you," and instead of getting on the lift, went down the corridor toward Lieutenant Zhao's quarters.

The last thing Aisha wanted to do was get trapped in a ship's cabin with a Corps agent. She ought to bolt; Rama wouldn't blame her. But she couldn't do it.

This was exactly what Rama needed her for. He might not know it and he certainly wouldn't like it, but that didn't matter. It had to happen.

She didn't get offered any wine, but there was a case of synthorange. "I have a weakness for it," Lieutenant Zhao confessed.

Aisha wasn't thirsty. She didn't much care for synthorange, either. But she took a bottle because it was the polite thing to do.

Rama was doing the same thing with the wine. He must have a plan after all. Aisha shouldn't have doubted him. She probably shouldn't have followed him, either. But she had, and so far it was all perfectly harmless.

If she'd ever stopped to think about what a Corps agent's cabin was like, she'd have said black leather walls and spy screens everywhere, and a jab like a spike into her mind the minute she came inside the door. What she found instead was an ordinary cabin with jump cradles stowed and a bunk and a desk and a hatch into the lavatory. There weren't any personal things. No pictures or databeads or scattered underwear. No evil machines for scooping out parts of brains.

Not that Lieutenant Zhao needed one of those. He was psi-three. He had one in his brain.

He was trying to use it on Rama. What had got his suspicions up, Aisha didn't know. She wasn't Corps. Please God she never would be.

Something had him sniffing around Rama's edges, and Aisha's too because she was stupid enough to be here. On the surface it was one of those deadly dull adult conversations that went on and on about nothing. Winemaking, weather, the difference between one glass of strong-smelling red stuff and another. Underneath, Lieutenant Zhao was trying to get inside Rama's head.

Adults would never just *ask* what they wanted to know. Lieutenant Zhao must be getting very frustrated. As far as he could possibly see, there was nothing much to Rama but a stream of random thoughts and a taste of wine. He liked his wine sweeter, and not as strong.

Almost too late, Aisha remembered to hide behind the sun. Lieutenant Zhao had come so close she could feel him breathing. Maybe he couldn't touch Rama, but he could definitely get at her—and the Corps would get her after all.

She lay as low as she could. He was focused on Rama, who was giving him smooth glassy surfaces to slide off.

Lieutenant Zhao said, "Do you know, I've found no record of your having been tested for psi. Do you happen to recall the name of the agent who tested you?"

"Should I?" Rama asked.

Lieutenant Zhao shrugged. "People usually do. Mostly they're terrified of it. A few are actually eager."

"I don't believe I would have been either of those things," Rama said.

"It's no matter," said Lieutenant Zhao. "Just curiosity."

"Why?"

Rama was pushing. It was fair enough considering how Lieutenant Zhao had been doing the same thing, but Aisha wanted to scream at him to stop.

Lieutenant Zhao seemed a bit startled. People didn't talk back to Psycorps. "It's just a feeling," he said. "A hunch, if you like. Sometimes I think we miss the best ones by testing so young. Not all talents mature at the same rate."

"Whatever I am," Rama said, "I've been since I was a child."

"Still," said Lieutenant Zhao. He lowered his eyes; he was sitting down, but he seemed to be shuffling his feet. "I wonder if I might ask permission to test you again. You're under no legal obligation, of course. Testing is only compulsory for citizens in their thirteenth year."

"What happens if you find something?" asked Rama.

"I'll invite you to accompany me for further testing."

"May I ask where that would be?"

"In the sector we're about to jump into," said Lieutenant Zhao, "we would go to Araceli."

Aisha felt Rama come alert. "That could be interesting," he said.

She wanted to kick him. One psi agent wasn't much compared to Rama, but Psycorps had thousands of them. No matter how strong he was, if enough of them got together, they could swarm over him and drown him.

And they would. The minute they found out what he was, they'd eat him alive. They wouldn't even leave a molecule for the archaeologists to fight over.

Lieutenant Zhao almost seemed as if he might save the day after all. "I could be wrong," he said. "Sometimes, especially in jump, we pick up false readings; we think we see things that aren't there. I hope you won't be disappointed if you turn out to be perfectly normal."

Rama shrugged and smiled. He was straight out of his mind.

"We can begin now," Lieutenant Zhao said. "It won't take long."

That was all Aisha could take. She jumped up. "Rama, you've got to go. It's getting too close to jump."

"You go," said Rama, "I'll be back before the last alarm."

"But what if you aren't?" Aisha demanded, not even caring if she sounded desperate. "You can do this later."

"I'm going to do it now," Rama said.

That was his iron voice. Nothing Aisha could say would budge him, even if she could have said it in front of Lieutenant Zhao.

She dropped back down into her seat. "It's on your head," she said.

"But not yours," said Rama. "Go."

She stayed where she was. Her heart was hammering and her eyes kept blurring, but she wasn't moving unless he was. He could take them both down if he was going to do this.

"Not you," he said.

She hadn't seen his lips move. She folded her arms and set her chin and showed him who else could be stubborn.

Aisha was ready to fight if Lieutenant Zhao tried to send her out, but he hardly seemed aware of her at all. He sat in front of Rama, looking hard at him. Rama looked back calmly.

He was used to people staring at him. He wasn't either embarrassed or uncomfortable.

After a while Lieutenant Zhao flushed and looked away. "I promise I'll do you no harm," he said. He sounded oddly distracted.

"Nor I you," said Rama. He had that faint smile, the one carved on his statue back on Nevermore.

Aisha gave up then. Whatever happened after this, it wouldn't have anything to do with her. She just had to hope she didn't get caught in the backlash.

It was not the same as Aisha's testing. There was no uplink to the worldsweb in jump. Lieutenant Zhao was alone, with only his own powers to draw on.

He had a good share of those, and no way of knowing what he was getting into. He leaned forward in his chair.

The air started to hum. The hairs on Aisha's arms stood up. She shivered all the way down inside.

Rama sat perfectly still. Whatever Lieutenant Zhao was beaming at him, he was like deep water. Nothing rippled the surface.

Lieutenant Zhao frowned. He was almost touching Rama now, eye to eye and nose to nose. His breathing was quick and shallow. Rama's was deep and slow.

Lieutenant Zhao sucked in a single enormous breath. He almost choked on it. When he started again, he was matching Rama.

So was Aisha. It was impossible not to. The air in the room pulsed in the same rhythm.

Her nose wrinkled. She caught a faint smell of hot metal.

She squeezed her eyes shut. There were wide rolling plains behind the lids, and a sky stretching from horizon to horizon, dark with storm clouds. Shapes of metal moved under it, pouring over the dry brown grass.

They were people and animals. Men, mostly, in armor, and giant antelope under saddle or pulling carts or chariots. The hubs of the chariots' wheels were set with bronze blades, sharp and whirling and deadly.

Banners flew over them. Aisha would never in her own life have recognized them, but in this waking dream, she could put names to the lords and domains that they belonged to.

She stood in a chariot. Its floor was woven leather, firm but yielding. She was dressed in armor, and her team of golden duns were mares and therefore hornless, but their headstalls were set with horns of sharpened bronze. When she looked down at her hands, they were rounder than her own, and not as brown. They were the color of the honey that Blackroot tribe harvested from hives in their orchard.

She looked from side to side down the line of chariots, people and animals that she knew. They were all waiting on the command to charge. She could feel the eagerness in them, and taste the sharp tang of fear. But none of them was so afraid that he couldn't bring himself to fight.

They were angry. The army that stood against them had sworn treaties and promised loyalty, then gone home and bred treason.

A flash of gold and flame sped down the line: a man in golden armor on a red-eyed black stallion, with a blood-red cloak streaming out behind him. Aisha knew him in her bones, long before she recognized the lion helmet or the face under it.

The Rama she knew when she was awake was a dim and faded shadow of this warrior king. He drew every eye and focused every mind on both sides of the battle. When he called out to his own army, he hardly needed to raise his voice. Every one of them heard him.

He halted not far from Aisha. His stallion snorted and tossed his horns and pawed the grass.

He was looking down at something in it. Far down—much farther than a man on a horse-sized animal might ordinarily look.

Lieutenant Zhao stood in an empty circle, surrounded by men in chariots. Most of the men looked like Rama, but they were much, much taller. The smallest of them must be over two meters.

Those were the people the doors in the ruined city were made for. In armor and in chariots, they were gigantic.

Rama was not. Nor was his mount. But he managed to tower over everyone.

He smiled at Lieutenant Zhao. Lieutenant Zhao stared blankly back. "This isn't real," he said.

"It was," said Rama.

Lieutenant Zhao shook his head. "You won't control my reality. I won't let you."

Rama swung his leg over the pommel of his saddle, which had no stirrups, and slid down. He paused to stroke the antelope's neck, lingering over it, but only for a moment. When he stepped away from the stallion, his hand flicked.

The army vanished, all but Aisha. The plain was still there, an endless stretch of windswept grass.

The storm looked ready to break. So did Lieutenant Zhao. But he was tougher than he looked. "I was right about you," he said.

"To a point," said Rama. "You'll be taking me to Araceli. But not to dance to Psycorps' drum. I have other uses for you."

Lieutenant Zhao had gone pale, but he kept his head up. "I'm not usable, I'm afraid. Go any deeper and you'll find the blocks. I'll break before I'll bend. It's built into the system."

"I see," said Rama. He meant exactly what he said. He tilted his head. "Does none of you have the faintest sense of how your powers work? You're like a pack of apes in a goldsmith's shop."

Lieutenant Zhao did not like that at all. He reared up; he actually snapped the words. "Who are you? What right do you have to say such things?"

"Who am I?" Rama said softly. "In this age, I am no one. I pass from dark into dark. I hunt a track gone cold as stone."

"Poetic," said Lieutenant Zhao. "You have a passion for heroic-fantasy vids and a flair for drama. We might be able to use that."

"I'm sure you could," said Rama, "if I would let you."

"Show me more," Lieutenant Zhao said. He was getting cocky. "What else can you conjure up?"

"What would you like to see?"

It was hardly Aisha's place to warn Lieutenant Zhao when he was getting into trouble. He wouldn't have listened anyway. "Take us back to the ship," said Lieutenant Zhao, "but bring something from this reality. Make it as real as you can."

He didn't believe anyone could do that. Aisha could hear it in his voice. He thought he was asking the impossible.

She tried to will Rama not to do it. It was useless, of course. With no fanfare at all, they stood in Lieutenant Zhao's cabin on the *Leda*, and Lieutenant Zhao was wearing much the same thing that Rama had been wearing when Aisha first saw him.

The kilt stayed whole—it was made of leather dyed deep green—and the necklaces and armlets and rings and earrings and the massive belt were mostly copper instead of gold. There were so many necklaces that they weighted down Lieutenant Zhao's narrow shoulders; he had to strain to lift his arms and stare at all the bracelets and rings.

"What in the—"

"I did as you asked," Rama said. His voice was terribly gentle.

He was back in his grey suit again. No more golden armor. Aisha was a little sorry. But there was life in his eyes: not as much as there had been when he rode down the line of the army, but more than she had ever seen in him.

Lieutenant Zhao started pulling off ornaments. His hands were shaking so hard he could barely keep a grip on anything, but when Rama moved to help, he backed away so fast he crashed into the wall. "No," he said. "No, don't. Don't touch me."

Rama stepped back and lowered his hands. Lieutenant Zhao got everything off, even the kilt, throwing it as far away from himself as he could. But then he dropped to his knees and scrambled the scattered bits together, hunting down the last ring and bead, till he had a pile in the middle of the floor.

He sat back on his heels. "This is real," he said much too calmly. "As real as I am. Which must mean—"

"This is the universe you were born in," Rama said.

Lieutenant Zhao picked up one of the copper bracelets. It was made of twisted wire, set with green glass beads. Pater would kill to get his hands on it. "No one can do this," he said.

"No one in your Corps," Rama said.

"What are you?"

"I am nothing the Corps would understand," said Rama.

"Obviously. What *are* you?"

"You wouldn't understand me, either." Rama pulled a handful of something out of the air. When he dropped it in front of Lieutenant Zhao, it had the shape and color of a Psycorps uniform.

There was nothing left of the things that Lieutenant Zhao had brought back from the memory or dream or whatever it was. But there was Lieutenant Zhao with nothing on and a look of deep shock on his face, and a sick feeling in Aisha's stomach that was not going to go away.

"That was the craziest thing I ever saw you do," Aisha said. She waited till they got to their cabin to say it.

"I was perfectly safe," Rama said.

"You're perfectly arrogant. You may be stronger than any one of them, but there's a whole universe out there, and we're about to jump back into it. You try too many stunts like that one, you won't last long enough to start hunting. Then you'll be gone and I'll be stuck here and Nevermore will be turned into a tourist trap. And it will be all your fault."

Rama let her wind down, but nothing she'd said had sunk in at all. "He won't betray me. Even now he's telling himself he drank too much of his sour wine and watched one too many of his epic-fantasy vids. I should have told him what I really am. Then he would never believe anything strange of me at all."

"So you're not letting him take you to Araceli?"

"I didn't say that."

She picked up the nearest thing, which was a water bulb, and threw it at him. He caught it out of the air. She spat at him. "You—are—*crazy!*"

"Always," he said.

Khalida swam through jump in a sea of wine. She woke to the blare of the alarm and a command override, downloading urgent orders into her numbed brain.

MI was done with coddling her. She was ordered forthwith via the *Leda* to Araceli. They were not to stop at Centrum. A transport waited to take the cargo that had been meant for that part of the quadrant; nanoseconds after the ship emerged from jump, the transport had docked and begun offloading.

There were no orders for disposal of her wayward niece. There should have been. Khalida could well guess who was to blame for that, but she would have to rip him apart later. MI was doing the ripping now, force-feeding her the entire dossier on Araceli.

Most of the download overwrote files she already had, but one file refused to drop down out of sight. *Eyes Only,* it said.

That was never a good sign. If Khalida had been in her right mind she would have deleted it on contact. But she triggered the *Open* function and dropped back in her bunk as the blue-green sky of Araceli arched over her in all its virtual glory.

A man stood under it, posed on a long strand of white sand. Waves crashed just short of his booted feet. He smiled, baring white teeth in a face that had been modified with exquisite subtlety. "Captain," he said. His voice was rich and melodious. "May I congratulate you on your promotion. It is well deserved."

Khalida suppressed her first impulse, which was to destroy the message before it delivered one more oily, lying word. Rinaldi was as crazy as he was dangerous. When she first came to Araceli, he had decided, somewhere in the convolutions of his psi-nine brain, that she was the only intelligent member of MI's deputation.

That intelligence had played directly into his hands. A quarter of a million people were dead because of it. And he was smiling as if he had never done anything in his life to cause him a moment's guilt.

She hit the override on the message. It was petty, but it killed the special effects. He addressed her from a much more mundane cubicle somewhere on Araceli, dressed in a plain suit and ordinary shoes instead of pirate bravura. But his face and voice were still their expensively modified selves. "I sincerely beg your pardon for calling you back from your extended leave—and on so fascinating a planet, too. But it seems our solution to the problem of Ostia Magna was neither as compelling nor as final as we had hoped. The Ostians are being obstreperous again—insisting that their status as psi-normal entitles them to equal protection under our law. Which of course it does, but their definition of equality, as you know, is somewhat skewed.

"The nuclear missile that you were able to detonate was no more than a feint—a mockery, if you will. Now they threaten us with a weapon that should not exist, which our intel assures us not only exists, it can do what they claim it can. They are threatening, my dear Captain, to destroy the planet from the core outward unless we surrender to their demands. One of which is that you and only you be permitted to negotiate with their emissaries." He lowered his voice; his expression altered to one of somewhat overplayed concern. "We do fear that their intention is not negotiation but revenge—but they are intractable. They will speak with you or they will speak with no one. And Araceli will be a band of dust among the stars."

"Dramatic," Khalida said to the ceiling as the message cut off. The ceiling persisted in showing her the link embedded in the message: a reference to a weapon called, among other things, a worldwrecker.

The last time Khalida had heard that word, she had been slumming in one of Jamal's pirate vids. The dread pirate Gallifrey had won a worldwrecker from the evil overlords of Maldonado and kept it in the cargo hold of his legendary cruiser—never to use, of course, but it was a terrible and thoroughly convincing threat.

Ostia Magna's version had none of the baroquely gleaming architecture of the pirate's weapon. It was much less concrete and much more deadly.

It was, at its simplest, a flaw in a system. Perfect power: tapping the planet's core, feeding power to the grids on the surface and in orbit, and drawing up rare and enormously valuable elements that just happened to be essential for starship drives, worldsweb systems, and terraforming planets. It was perfectly safe and ecologically sound.

Except for that one, tiny, potentially catastrophic flaw.

Khalida had a tendency to blank on scientific jargon, but this she managed to remember, because she appreciated irony. Pele Syndrome.

The core tap, under certain highly specific conditions, could create a runaway chain reaction that blew the tap out of the crust, with apocalyptic results. Earthquakes, eruptions, storms of radioactivity that sterilized the planet.

Rinaldi had been exaggerating about the band of dust, but the consequences would be much the same. No carbon-based life form would live on Araceli for the next few million years. As for those that already inhabited it…

She had seen the first victim of the syndrome from the safety of space: Pele, actively volcanic to begin with, now an object lesson in greed and corporate overreach.

"That was a confederacy of idiots activating the system before all the tests were done and the firewalls in place," Khalida said to Tomiko. *Leda*'s captain stood in the doorway, looking as harried as Khalida felt. "There are failsafes now: layer on layer on layer of redundancies and preventive measures. There's no feasible way to trigger the Syndrome. You'd need a database the size of U.P.'s. No single world has that much bandwidth."

"It does if that world has turned its entire network of machines, along with a truly remarkable range and variety of devices and implants offworld, into one massive computer. Stealing a few cycles here, a few bits of code there, steering the tap just to the edge of Pele Syndrome. Monitors? Alarms? Corrupted just as thoroughly as all the rest. It only needs one command, one single trigger, and the reaction is irreversible. Once that trigger is hit, Araceli has a handful of tendays at most, of escalating ecological and planetological disaster. Then it's gone."

Khalida shook her head slowly. It was beautiful. Diabolical.

Machines were everywhere, performing their functions, exchanging their codes, linking and connecting and serving the manifold needs of the United Planets. They all had firewalls, of course. Shields and barriers. Controls on access. But who paid attention to their constant and ubiquitous web-chatter? Or took the trouble to examine every byte of code?

"How long have they been at this?" she asked. "Decades? Centuries?"

"Ten years, give or take," Tomiko answered, "plus another twenty or so of building the framework. Ostia Magna holds the contract for all the electronics used in the core tap, along with household systems, rovers and shuttles, web implants…. Remember the slogan? 'Who needs psi when you have P.S.I.'?"

"Perrier-Souza Implants, Unlimited," Khalida said as the pieces clicked together, "of Centrum, Terra, and Ostia Magna." She drew a long breath. "It's brilliant."

"Isn't it? You hit Ostia before they could get the thing up and running, but they don't appear to have lost any critical systems."

"I don't think they intended to," Khalida said. "That was a feint. Concealing what they were really up to. Gambling—and losing—on our inability to make the hardest choice."

"Or sacrificing a city to push us over the edge; to drown us in guilt, so that when the greater threat was ready to go live, we'd give in to their demands."

"That's why they insisted on bringing me back," Khalida said. She felt very little; it was so inevitable, and so perfectly, cruelly logical. "Ostia bets that I won't commit mass murder again. The Corps postulates that I will. It's an impasse." She fixed Tomiko with her most unrelenting stare. "What would you do?"

Tomiko lifted her hands and let them fall. "There's no good choice here. I can guess what MI wants. Find the trigger and disarm it. Crush the insurrection. Protect this world—and oh so coincidentally, Psycorps' people and installations here."

"But of course," Khalida said with a bitter twist. "You've got half the planet breeding psis and the other half feeding them—and the feeders woke up, saw what they'd been lied into, and said, 'No more.' We can't have that, now, can we? We need our psis to keep the universe safe from only they know what."

"Itself," Tomiko said.

"Is that what you believe?"

Tomiko shrugged. "It doesn't matter what I think. I have orders. If I don't follow them, someone else will. You're going to Araceli if MI has to slam you in stasis and shoot you there in a life pod. Both sides want you. Both sides get you. That's going to happen regardless of anything you or I may want or try."

That, Khalida thought, was why she and Tomiko would never be more to each other than they were now. It was an old thought, worn smooth, with most of the sadness and even some of the anger gone from it. Tomiko was a good soldier. Khalida, even before she vaporized a city, was not.

"Don't," said Tomiko. "Don't try that. Don't even think it."

Khalida stared at her. Somehow, while Khalida's thoughts ran on, Tomiko had caught hold of her wrists. They stung. There was blood under her nails, so fresh it glistened.

Tomiko's eyes glistened, too. Tears? Khalida would have wiped them away if she had had a hand free.

"Maybe you need that stasis pod," Tomiko said. Her voice was hard.

"Maybe I do," said Khalida. "I won't have to suffer through all the briefings. I can go in cold. Will that be better or worse, do you think?"

Tomiko dropped Khalida's wrists with a sound of disgust, turned and left her there. Where the captain had been, Khalida looked into the faces of a pair of marines, as flat and hard as if made of metal. One held up a pair of manacles.

That was clear enough. Khalida spread her hands. "I'll behave," she said. "Am I confined to quarters?"

"For the moment," said the one with the manacles.

She had brought it on herself. She could hardly complain. And all the while she had faced Tomiko and then the marines, the download continued, filling her head with the minutiae of a world.

There was a way to let it break her. A way to die.

Either she was impossibly brave or she was a perfect coward. She shied away from it, from the thought and the memory.

She could die of this. She wanted to. But not by her own hand.

Cowardice, she thought. Courage would fling itself headlong into the dark.

There was only one thing left to ask. "Why me?"

No one was there to answer. Khalida had to do it for herself. "Because I'm the one they could use. I'm the one they broke. If I refuse, either the planet dies or Ostia does. I'll be a mass murderer all over again."

Once was enough. She compacted her orders into a tight, small blip of data and marked them *Received. Acknowledged.* And after a pause that she could not help: *Accepted.*

PART THREE

ARACELI

J ump from Centrum to Araceli was indecently short: half an Earthday to
the outer edges of the system, and the rest of the Earthday cruising at
sublight toward the inner planets. Khalida badly wanted to spend the time
locked in her cabin, but she was damned if she could keep on hiding. She saw
the end of jump in a cradle on the bridge, facing the screen that showed the
shift from nothingness to crowding stars.

The hum of the bridge went on around her. Everything was ordinary, quiet,
unexceptional. No ambush. No armada waiting to blast the *Leda* out of space.
All their clearances were in order. The system was open, waiting for them.

And yet...

Something felt off.

Of course it did. Everything about Araceli was off. The tightness between
her shoulder blades was as much memory as warning.

She pushed herself out of the cradle and stowed it. Tomiko was leaning over
the comm, exchanging rapid spits of code with planetary command. Khalida
had an almost irresistible urge to run a hand down her back.

That would not have been wise. At all. Even if they had been on speaking
terms.

A shadow caught her eye. She held back from spinning to face it. She let the corner of her vision take it in instead.

How long he had been there, she could not have said. He should not have been there at all. Passengers were barred from the bridge during and immediately after jump.

Rama was the last person in the universe to care about Spaceforce regulations. He was also the last person she would have expected to be invisible in the middle of a brightly lighted bridge.

She saw him because he was letting her see. His eyes were on the viewscreen. His expression was distinctly familiar: he was linked in to the ship's web. Khalida refrained from asking how he managed that.

His voice spoke inside her skull. "This is a trap."

She answered him in the same way. "I know."

"Yet you say nothing?"

"What's to say? It will spring when it springs. All we can do is go in and hope we're ready for it."

"And if you're not?"

She shrugged. "We die."

She felt his eyes burning on her. "I don't believe you."

"I don't care."

"Now that I believe."

He got out of her head then. It was an odd feeling, half relief and half emptiness, and odder for that he was still all too physically there.

Intentionally or otherwise, he had mutated from shadow into substance. Tomiko turned from the comm to find him standing behind her.

Her eyes widened slightly. Her voice lashed out. "What are you doing on my bridge?"

Khalida braced for royal wrath, but Rama smiled and said amiably, "Good day, Captain. That world yonder wants to eat your ship whole. Are you doing to let it?"

Tomiko looked him up and down. He was wearing both halves of a *gi*, as if he had been doing katas in jump. And, Khalida thought, during emergence: as if the distortion of spacetime meant nothing to him at all.

Tomiko jabbed her chin toward her office. "In there. Now."

Clearly he was in a mood to be cooperative. Khalida was not, but no one was asking. She followed them without a word, and got none from either of them.

In the much smaller, dimmer room, Tomiko and Rama between them seemed almost too much for one space to hold. The privacy shields when they locked down made it even worse. Khalida managed to find air to breathe, but it was an effort.

"All right," said Tomiko, and her glare fixed not on Rama but on Khalida. "No more games. If you know something about what's happening on Araceli, I need you to tell me now. Clearances be damned. I'm not losing my ship because of something you could have told me."

"I don't know any more than you do," Khalida said.

Tomiko's glare did not lighten even slightly. Khalida opened her mouth, but Rama spoke first. "She's telling the truth. The world and its rulers are playing a game of masks and shadows. They like to think they're playing the universe for fools. Mostly," he said, "they are."

"And you," said Tomiko. "What exactly are you? Intel? Corps? Both? Neither?"

"Most certainly neither," he said.

She moved in close. As small as she was, she almost made him seem tall, but no one in that room made the mistake of thinking it mattered. She tilted her head back and searched his face, taking in every line of it, noting it, cataloguing it with a taxonomist's precision.

"You're not human," she said.

His smile was wide, white, and dizzily joyous. It erupted into full-bodied laughter.

She let him finish. Eventually he did, still grinning, as if he had never heard a more hilarious or more delightful thing.

"Genetically you're close," she said. "So close, there's no distinguishing you from one of us. What differences there are, anyone would think that's modification. But it's not. Is it? You're just as accidental an organism as the most determinedly backwoods Earther."

"Just so," he said.

"You don't even try to hide it," she said. "That's genius."

"Only if it works," he said. "How did you guess?"

"I don't guess," said Tomiko, "and I don't pay attention to the hand tricks or the curtains. When I look, I see. Where are you really from? Nevermore?"

He bent his head.

She nodded. She never took her eyes from his face. "This is my ship," she said. "Those people you're seducing with your katas: they're my crew. You don't get to keep them. Do you understand?"

"Perfectly," he said.

"Then you also understand that whatever you're up to, whatever you're passing through in order to do, if you're any kind of threat to my ship or my command, or to the force I serve, I'll do whatever it takes to stop you."

"I'm no threat to you unless you threaten me," he said.

His voice was soft. There was nothing dangerous in it. It was a fact, that was all. But Khalida shivered.

Tomiko was perfectly still and perfectly focused. It seemed she was satisfied with what he had said. "Now tell me what you know about Araceli," she said.

"Nothing," he said. "But there is a smell to it that makes my hackles rise."

"What kind of smell?"

"Carrion," he said.

She snorted. "Serves me right for asking that, doesn't it? Yes, it stinks, but I need something solid. Something I can get Spaceforce's teeth into. Otherwise we've got orders to submit ourselves to planetary authorities, offer such aid and comfort as we can, and resolve the situation to the best of our ability."

"You should still do that," he said. "Running would help you, but not the ship sent in after you. This isn't going to end until someone takes the bait."

"Granted," said Tomiko, "but if I'm looking at a ripe worm, I want to know who's dangling the hook. You're psi. How high?"

The shift seemed not to rattle him at all. It did rattle Khalida, who should have expected it, considering what else Tomiko had seen. She blurted out the answer before he could. "High. Which, if he isn't picking up whatever's behind this, means—"

"It's shielded." He dropped back and down into the hoverchair that happened to be nearest. "I know it's there. What it is, what it's meant for, who's behind it—those things I can't touch. They're too well concealed."

"You can't break it down?" Tomiko demanded.

His head shook, sharp and short. "Not until I know what it is. I don't even know what part of it concerns us, and what part is simply the Corps being the Corps."

"Weapon?"

He frowned. Khalida could feel him seeking: a dull ache at the back of her skull. She felt the wall, too; crashed into it with force enough to split her head in two.

He held his together with his hands. His lips were the color of ash. How he managed to shape words, let alone have them make sense, she barely knew. "Not weapon. Not exactly. Not... harmless, either."

"Neither are we," Tomiko said.

"Bravura." His grin was back, wide and crazy. "If you go in now, and whatever it is attacks, your backup won't get here in time."

"Maybe not," said Tomiko, "but if this really is a trap and we really are the quarry, we'll be all the proof Spaceforce needs. Araceli may have Psycorps behind it, but United Planets is bigger."

"Yes, but is it nastier?"

"Much."

"Well then," said Rama. "Would you like to dangle bait of your own?"

Tomiko sat opposite him, leaning forward. "You?"

He smiled.

"Why? What's in it for you?"

"I owe a debt," he said.

Khalida blinked. Her head was suddenly, brutally clear.

"Bronze-Age honor." She had not meant to say that aloud.

It would hardly have mattered if she had not. He would have heard.

"What," he said, "have you grown out of it? I hope I never will."

"My family hasn't. Nor," she said with a glance at Tomiko, "has hers. But do you really want the Corps to see what they've been missing?"

"It might be good for them," he said.

She quelled an urge to spit. "God, you're arrogant."

"Is it arrogance if it's true? Those are weanling children who dream they hold the power of kings. They keep a hundred worlds in terror with their little tricks and sleights of mind. What they did to you and all who are like you I will never forgive. I'll bring them down, and gladly."

"All by yourself?"

Her mockery was so bitter she gagged on it. He actually flinched. But he came back as hard as his ancient steel. "I've done it before."

Tomiko spoke outside the circle of their combat, wry and bracingly practical. "Don't tell me Nevermore is empty because of you."

"Apparently not," he said. He sounded as tired as Khalida had ever known him to be. "I don't know why it's empty. This world may hold a clue. Or not. I don't know. I can't find it if the world is shattered, or if it's so torn with war that nothing can get near it. If I have to spring this trap in order to get where I need to go, I'll reckon it a fair exchange."

Tomiko took her time in responding. She rocked gently in her hoverchair, frowning. Her brows were knit, her eyes dark, focused inward.

Neither Rama nor Khalida broke the silence. He tilted his head back and closed his eyes. Khalida sat on her heels on the floor, since both the chairs were taken.

She felt strangely light. When Tomiko asked the question she had known was coming, she was ready for it.

"Do you trust him?"

"No," Khalida answered.

"But you think he can do this."

"I think he's too proud not to."

"And if he gives us all up to the Corps?"

Khalida's eyes were on Rama, who had not moved at all. "He won't do that. He may try to take them over, but he won't sell our souls for that. We're not worth enough."

"Not to them," he said without opening his eyes.

He sounded more than half asleep. He was in a trance, she realized: wandering away from his body, trying to penetrate the walls that the Corps had raised around Araceli.

"Don't do that," she said. "Hack the web instead. Easier. Faster. Lots less dangerous."

His eyes opened. For an instant so brief she almost missed it, there was nothing of flesh or blood in them at all. It was like looking into the sun.

He blinked, and they were human again, or close enough: dark eyes in a dark face. "I'm not as good at that as Jamal," he said.

"Not much of anybody hereabouts is," she said. "Except me. Who do you think taught him?" Her glance flicked to Tomiko. "Permission to access ship's web?"

"Granted," Tomiko said. Her face was completely blank.

Khalida remembered to breathe. She would have hacked the system regardless, but it was much less complicated with the captain's permission. "You rest," she said to Rama. "Be ready. I may need you."

His assent shivered through her synapses. He was in the web, woven into it as securely as if he were a part of it.

Not as good as Jamal? Khalida had a feeling he might be better.

Khalida crawled out of the web with a pounding headache and a head full of data, some of it useful, none of it close to what she had been looking for. Tomiko was back on the bridge, but with Khalida, too, like a hand holding hers through the ship's web.

Rama sat cross-legged in the corner of Tomiko's office, watching her with calm intentness. He was on guard. When she scowled at him, he took a breath and visibly relaxed. "An army of mages would have been easier," he said.

"Not for me." She winced at the sound of her own voice.

He handed her a cup. It was full of scalding-hot coffee. There was no way to brew it here, and he had been in front of her, fixed on her, for the better part of an hour.

Some things were best not looked at too closely. The coffee was real, it was hot, and it tasted fresh. She drank it in grateful sips, savoring the rich and bitter taste.

With that in her stomach, she could stand up and walk back out to the bridge. Rama followed, soft-footed, padding like a big cat.

They were an hour out from Araceli. The traffic of the system hummed around them, an intricate stream of data flowing through the web. It was all perfectly normal, considering that there was a war below.

Whatever the trap was, all they could do now was walk into it. "If there's anything you want to take with you," Khalida said to Rama, "get it while you can. The minute we get clearance, we're going down."

He dipped his head and vanished, moving almost too quickly to see. She shivered, caught Tomiko's eyes on her, forced herself to slow down, breathe, be calm. There was nothing she could do now but wait. She was as ready for this as she was ever going to be.

Planetary Control took hold of the *Leda* as it locked into its assigned orbit. Araceli's own shuttle waited to take passengers planetside. It was not exactly standard procedure, but it was common enough. Planetary governments and Spaceforce shared, at best, an uneasy alliance.

Rama had brought his baggage to the shuttle bay: a slight figure wrapped in black.

Khalida should have known. "No," she said. "Aisha, back to the cabin."

Aisha neither moved nor spoke. Her eyes within the veils were openly rebellious.

"She's safer with us," Rama said, drawing Khalida's fire.

"You," she said, "are insane. I'm not much better, but neither am I crazy enough to take that child into the middle of a war."

"The war is all around us," Rama said. "It's not being fought with the kind of weapons a starship can stand against. I promise you, while I live I shall protect her."

"And when you get killed?"

"I don't intend to die here," he said.

Khalida was not sure if she could say the same. "She's staying here," she said.

"No," said Rama.

Khalida's teeth set. "You are neither her parent nor her guardian. You have no right or authority—"

"Captain," said a voice in her ear. She spun on its owner.

Lieutenant Zhao flinched, but only slightly. "Captain," he said, "Control has instructed that all passengers be removed from the ship. If Meser Rama's assurance isn't enough, will you take mine? I'll take responsibility for your niece's safety."

Khalida had the satisfaction of seeing the horror in Aisha's eyes—but it was a small spurt of pleasure, and vanishingly brief. If Rama was bad, Psycorps was worse.

As always with Araceli, there were no good choices. Only a cascade of bad ones. Khalida hissed at the lot of them.

Tomiko stood between Khalida and the shuttle. Khalida had not seen her come into the bay; there had been too much else to fixate on.

Khalida saluted stiffly. "Captain," she said.

"Captain," Tomiko replied. Her face was set, her voice clipped.

There was little else to say, even if they had not been quarreling. Khalida said it regardless. "Don't do anything stupid."

"Likewise," Tomiko said.

She stepped aside. Khalida had a brief urge to knock her flat, and an equally brief one to hug her till she gasped.

She did neither. She marched past Tomiko into the shuttle.

Aisha was in the worst trouble she had ever been in in her life. Squeezed in between Rama and Khalida, dropping away from *Leda* to the blue-and-white ball in space that was Araceli, she had a sudden, powerful, and completely impossible urge to get up and walk away and not stop until she found herself on Nevermore again.

Of course that wasn't happening. Khalida was perfectly still and perfectly silent. Rama stared out the port, watching the world grow till it blocked out the blackness of space.

They were coming down on the day side, right along the line between night and morning. A continent stretched below, with sparks and flashes of light that were lakes and inland seas. A deep blue ocean curved away toward the bottom of the planet's arc, flaring white at the utmost bottom, where the polar caps where.

Cities spread like neurons across the night side, linked by chains of smaller lights. The day side was almost all green and dun and brown, with only a few grids or circles that marked the places where humans lived.

It looked empty, like wilderness—almost as empty as Nevermore. But that was deceiving. The cities were full of non-psis: feeder cities. The psis lived where people were few and far apart, with shields to protect themselves from each other.

Aisha looked for the crater that her aunt had made, but it wasn't on this side of the planet. Everything here was peaceful and whole.

She was supposed to be deceived. She was just a child, after all. But Aunt and Rama weren't supposed to know as much as they did, either. None of them was playing the game the way Psycorps and Araceli expected.

That could be either good or bad. Aisha's stomach was in knots. She took deep breaths the way Vikram had taught her. "Breathing is important," his voice said in her head. "Breathing is everything."

In her head, he sounded like Rama. Warm deep voice with a lilt underneath. Rama's sun surrounded her, shielding her.

They were dropping fast. Somewhere outside the sun, Aisha was screaming with panic.

Breathe in.

Breathe out.

The darkness of space around them felt like Rama's hand. The shuttle, cradled in it, fell down and down into the deep well that was Araceli.

MI waited in the shuttle bay, backed by a detachment of armored marines. They surrounded Khalida as soon as she stepped out of the shuttle. Even though she had expected it, the snap of the restraints around her caught her off guard.

She could not even look back to see what had happened to Rama and her niece. The web was still alive behind her eyes, but external links were blocked. All she could access was the direct feed from MI, and that contained a copy of her orders, a precis of the situation as it had evolved since she left the *Leda*, and a dataspurt from local command.

There was nothing she could do about the rest of it.

Not yet, she thought, deep inside, where no one could come.

Except one. And he was keeping to himself.

Biding his time.

The dark part of her was glad. The rest had work to do, whether she wanted it or not. Nor would MI care overmuch if it killed her.

There was comfort in that, of sorts.

None of the marines or the escort from MI was familiar. They were all new since Khalida left Araceli: fresh faces, new victims for the old war. She caught some of them sliding glances at her, then looking quickly away. It seemed her reputation preceded her.

Even MI headquarters had changed. The old building in a somewhat seedy section of the port was gone: a casualty of war, taken down by a suicide bomber after the fall of Ostia Magna. The new one had moved well inward toward the wealthier quarter, a squat block of fortified stone with levels of security that raised her brows higher as they penetrated each one.

"Just a little bit spooked, are you?" she inquired when, at considerable length, she found herself in the commander's office.

He was a new face on this world, too, though hardly unfamiliar. Shimon Aviram had his own reputation, and that was as the court of last resort. When he took charge of a situation, it had already begun to spin out of control.

"Captain Nasir," he said. He had a smooth cool voice and a face modified to match, but his eyes were perfectly level, unwavering, still and cold. For an instant as Khalida met them, she imagined she saw a second consciousness staring out, one she almost recognized.

She knew better than to dismiss the thought, but she buried it below a babble of undisciplined mind-noise. "Colonel Aviram," she said. "I'd salute, but as you see…"

The restraints sprang free. The marine on her left caught them and stepped back conspicuously out of fist-snap range.

If Khalida hit anyone, it would not be one of her escort. She flexed her numbed fingers but otherwise made no move.

"Give me your word," said Aviram, "that you are not a flight risk."

"I might be," she said. "If it seems advisable. In the meantime, I have orders. Do I have your permission to execute them? Colonel? Sir?"

"I can neither permit nor deny," he said. "You are, for the duration of this operation, my superior officer."

That set Khalida back on her heels. She had managed, in the flood of data, to overlook that particular and crucial fact.

"I did insist," said the man who deigned at last to show himself. He might have been there from the beginning: for a psi of his level, that was hardly impossible. He only had to encourage the unwitting eye to pass on by.

Rinaldi in the flesh was both more and less prepossessing than he chose to seem in vid. He was tall and well built but somewhat soft: a man who had no need for action other than the virtual sort, and no inclination to alter his body to look as if he did.

That was a mask, like everything else about him. "Isn't this a conflict of interest?" she asked. "If I'm mediating for both sides, where is your worthy opponent?"

"Waiting," Rinaldi said. "She requested we meet on neutral ground."

"Which this port allegedly is," Khalida said.

He smiled. "Allegedly, Captain?"

She had no reason in this world to trust him, but no choice but to let herself be taken where her orders commanded her to go. It was small consolation that Aviram had the same orders—and even less autonomy. If and when this fell apart, he would go down with her.

"I will go," she said, "after I have eaten, rested, and reviewed the situation. An hour, Meser Rinaldi. Colonel: I suppose you have a kitchen here?"

Aviram nodded stiffly. Rinaldi was amused. She was dancing in chains, and they all knew it.

It made a point. She was hungry, to her surprise, and she did want as well as need to examine her orders more closely. Aviram's revelation might not be all that was hidden in the knotwork of official phrasing.

As far as she could tell while she worked her way methodically through a small vat of pasta alla vongole and a bottle of rather pleasant red wine, her orders were no more or less complicated than they had seemed at first scan. Meet, separately and together, with representatives of the warring parties. Talk Ostia down off the ledge. Get the keys to the worldwrecker and relay them to Tech. Use the resources of MI on-world and the *Leda* off it.

And there it was. In collaboration with the Interplanetary Institute for Psychic Research.

Psycorps.

Officially, Psycorps and the city-state of Castellanos were separate entities. The fact that Castellanos was founded, inhabited, and governed by Psycorps, and only by Psycorps, was never, officially, acknowledged.

Khalida spoke aloud to the apparently empty office. "You're not even pretending that there's any hope of objectivity here."

"We all do what we must," Rinaldi said. His voice came from everywhere and nowhere, but her uplink found him in the hallway just outside the door, leaning against the wall. Loitering; or eavesdropping.

"And if I decide that we have to lock you up and find for Ostia by default?"

"I don't think so," he said. His amusement made her skin shiver.

"I begin to understand," she said, "why Ostia would rather see this world dead than in your hands."

"Understanding is the beginning of wisdom," he said.

If she hated him, he won the skirmish. She made herself cold and quiet and still. He was nothing to her. An obstacle, that was all. She would find a way over or around him. Or not.

Nothing mattered. This war was nothing. This man, this psi-nine—nothing. Nothing at all.

Was that a gasp from the hallway?

She must be imagining it. "I'm ready," she said.

If the envoy from Ostia had not insisted on meeting Khalida alone in a shielded room, Khalida would have done it for her. These negotiations could not be the normal and ordinary meeting of opponents across a table or a webspace. Khalida would speak with each party in that room, where psi was blocked and blanked. Then, if and when she was ready, she would bring them together. She might not even do that at all.

For now there was the representative of the people whose relatives and children she had murdered. Mem Aurelia was a woman of size and presence, composed and still. She sat on a cushion with her feet tucked beneath her skirts. Her hands were folded in her lap; her eyelids were lowered.

She might have seemed asleep, but even within the shields, Khalida could feel the force of her regard. "There's no escaping our enemies," she said. "No matter where we go. No matter what we do."

"You seem to have found ways," Khalida said.

"Desperation," said Mem Aurelia.

"You asked for me. Why?"

"Because you understand," Mem Aurelia said.

"You don't think I can talk you out of this."

"No one can."

"Tell me why," Khalida said.

"Not in words," said Mem Aurelia. "Watch."

Khalida had an instant's warning: the flash of the download alert; the ripple in the web that warned of data incoming before it crashed over her.

It was meant to overwhelm her. She sorted it almost by instinct, with reflexes that had not, after all, lost their edge. Every city, every town, every farm and ranch and station, had its own file. Collated, searched, and sorted, they transcribed a pattern.

She had seen parts of it on the first tour, before she destroyed Ostia. She had not known how large it was, or how pervasive. It had seemed to be a matter for an individual and rebellious city-state—not for the whole half of a planet.

More than half. One thread in the pattern was distinct. Children of talent and intelligence taken from their families—for schooling, those who took them said; to better their prospects and those of their towns and villages. But they never came back. Nor were they heard from, apart from a handful of bland messages: *Dear Father and Mother, I am well, I am learning, I am a credit to my teachers.*

That set of files linked to another from which the *Classified* seals had been visibly removed. There were not nearly as many of those, and they were incomplete in ways that spoke of files truncated or corrupted. But the pattern persisted.

On the surface it was not so different from what Psycorps did to every child on every world: tested, analyzed, took away those with the talent to be brought into the Corps. But these were younger, not yet come to puberty. They had been genemapped at or before birth, again as children were, and those maps had been flagged.

Not every flag led to a child's being taken. Only particular cases. Intelligence of a particular type, at a particular level.

And again, Psycorps bred for psi. That was common and accepted knowledge. But only, as far as anyone knew, within the Corps.

"Not just for psi," Mem Aurelia's voice said through the cascade of data. "For its opposite. For minds not only blind but locked. Unreadable; inaccessible. Not just non-psi. Psi-null."

"That doesn't make sense," Khalida said.

"This is Psycorps. When has sense ever had anything to do with them?"

Khalida felt the drawing of kinship, the bond of common understanding. That was dangerous. She must be objective. That was why she was here.

"Blind minds," she said. "Impenetrable walls. Perfect spies. Perfectly loyal, one would presume."

"One would," said Mem Aurelia.

Khalida went perfectly still. Mem Aurelia's eyes widened slightly.

Khalida was not going to say it.

There was more than one war. Not only psi against non, but psi against psi—using the nulls as weapons. But for whom, and against whom?

It was too complicated for Khalida's damaged mind. She focused on what was here and obvious and in front of her. Clear violations of the Compact of Worlds. Use and abuse of human populations without their consent.

Those populations had chosen to counter that abuse with a much more blatant violation of Compact. In return for the loss of their children, they threatened to destroy a world.

"Tell me what else there is," she said. "What justifies your ultimatum."

"Our children—"

"No," said Khalida. "As terrible as it is, it's not enough. United Planets has laws against such things. You have the right to invoke those laws. Why haven't you? Why do you see no other choice than planetary suicide?"

"You are an innocent," said Mem Aurelia. "Don't you know who owns United Planets?"

"Psycorps isn't that powerful," Khalida said. "Not yet."

"You don't think so?"

"I think it would like to be," Khalida said.

Mem Aurelia's composure was visibly strained. "We are what they would make of us all—every human on every world. Serfs and slaves, to feed and breed. They will rule. We will serve. That is what the Corps is for. Has always been."

There was a perilous logic in it. Khalida had had such thoughts herself. Still…

"What good will it do to destroy one world? There are hundreds of others, and the Corps has its claws in all of them. You won't be martyrs. You'll be criminals, deplored and despised."

"People will know," Mem Aurelia said. "Some will think. The Corps can't stop every mind from drawing conclusions. If even a few realize what has been done, and undertake to stop it, maybe—"

"I can assure you," said Khalida, "that mass suicide—or massacre—solves nothing."

"Not if we take the cream of the Corps with us," Mem Aurelia said.

"Now who's the innocent? You've given them ample warning. They've gone elsewhere, or made plans to go before the world breaks. You'll be dead, and they'll be safe. All of it will come to nothing."

"I don't think so," said Mem Aurelia.

Her voice was so soft that Khalida barely heard it. It echoed much louder on the connection between them, a pinprick of data that unlocked into a pattern of terrible beauty.

As nulls and normals were linked through their implants, so were psis—not only by their powers of mind but by certain enhancements. Connections that everyone took for granted. Technology so common, so simple and so ordinary, that not even a psi stopped to ask who made it, or what that person or persons might have built into it.

"They will find it," Khalida said, "if they haven't already. Even as we sit here—they know. If they didn't before, they do now."

"I don't think so," Mem Aurelia said again. "What they've done to our children: as soon as we knew, we developed our own countermeasures. Try to speak of this, or even think it outside of this link. I do mean that, Captain. Do try."

Khalida did not need to. She had her own defenses, and they had analyzed the nature of the link and reached the appropriate conclusions.

"What good does it do to tell me of it, then?" she asked. "If I can't report in full to my superiors, all I have is a grossly unequal provocation and response, and a finding against you."

"You'll find a way," said Mem Aurelia. "That's your gift, as you should know. To think around corners. To see a path where none seems to exist."

"And you reach that conclusion how? From the ashes of Ostia Magna?"

If that was a blow to Mem Aurelia's serenity, she did not show it. "Not all perception is measurable as psi. Nor is every non-psi strictly normal in the Corps' definition. That too you should know, Captain Nasir."

Khalida was past knowing what she knew. She hoped she excused herself with appropriate politeness. In her mind she was already far away, curled in a corner, trying hard to think of nothing at all.

29

The marines took Aunt Khalida away, surrounding her with a wall of black uniforms and broad upright backs. She wasn't a small woman, but they dwarfed her.

Aisha and Rama were not taken prisoner, exactly, but while Aisha was distracted with her aunt, they acquired their own large and imposing escort. Instead of marines they had Psycorps—and that made Aisha's skin crawl and the sun inside her shoot out a flare that she hoped blinded any of them who tried to spy on her mind.

They were herded onto a transport, quite a comfortable one if she had been in any mood to notice. Rama was perfectly calm, inside as well as out. He still refused to see any danger in these psionic amateurs, no matter how hard Aisha tried to convince him to be careful. He watched the city go by outside the transport's screens, taking it all in with wide clear eyes.

She knew where Psycorps headquarters was. It was the first thing she'd looked for on the worldweb after she left the *Leda*. They were not going toward it.

That didn't reassure her as much as it might have. They were humming down a clean and open street, for a port city, with barriers up to keep the squatters out, and not too many people loitering on the corners and trying to look as if they belonged there.

The houses that lined the street had privacy shields as well as physical walls. When there were shops or places to eat or drink, they were perfectly tidy. Nobody sprawled out in front or sleeping it off within sight of the street.

The transport stopped in front of one of the houses, most of the way down the street. There was nothing exceptional about it at all. It was just a house, a good bit smaller than the one Aisha lived in on Nevermore, with a plain brown door and nothing pretty painted or holoed on the wall either outside or in.

The privacy shields were planetary-prison strength. The two Psycorps agents who had gone inside with Aisha and Rama lurched when they crossed the threshold, and one of them looked if he'd have liked to faint. But he caught himself in time.

Aisha already had psi shields even stronger than that, and she didn't have her worldsweb chip yet. The only difference for her between inside and outside was that the web portal stopped reading *Araceli* and showed the Greek letter psi in flat black—Psycorps' logo, which made her shiver just to look at it. It was still the same heavily restricted web.

The house was as painfully ordinary inside as out. They built them from the same plan on every world that needed a quick and easy way to store people. Big open room past the entryway, smaller rooms along a corridor in back, each with its own bath. The kitchen was a wall unit off to the side of the big room. Another wall was a screen that could be made bigger or smaller depending on what one wanted it to do, from watching vids to monitoring the street outside.

The stronger of the two Psycorps agents tried to herd Aisha away from Rama. "You'll want to rest," she said, "and refresh yourself. We've prepared a room for you, if you'll come with—"

"No," Aisha said.

Even Rama seemed startled at that. Aisha had surprised herself, a bit. She was tired of being herded here and there. And she seriously did not like being captured by the Corps.

The agent visibly swallowed a sigh. "You'll be perfectly safe, and you won't be confined. This house is open to you entirely. It's only—"

"No," Aisha said again.

The agent spoke slowly, enunciating each word. "You are safe. We promise you that."

"No," said Aisha for a third time.

The agent's lips had drawn into a thin line.

Aisha was glad. "I'll pick my own room. Thank you very much."

"Let her be," the other agent said. He sounded as if he might like to laugh, if he hadn't been so tired. "They're both safe enough, however they decide to arrange themselves. And we're late for the meeting."

That got rid of them both. Aisha was almost sorry—she would have liked to see what she could get out of the weaker agent. If only to find out what meeting they were both called to.

The house seemed much bigger without them. There were spycams everywhere, of course. Probably psi monitors, too, though they wouldn't get much.

Rama had wandered toward the kitchen unit and started poking at it. The vat of pilaf that came out of it was almost as good as Pater's—which made Aisha's throat lock shut.

There really was no going back. Not from here. This was real. Not a game she was playing. Not a fight she had run away from for a day or a handful of days, till she crept home and everybody pretended nothing had happened.

She still knew all the way down that she had to do this for the expedition, and the family, and for Nevermore. It was the only glimmer of hope any of them had. That didn't keep her from wanting, suddenly, to burst out bawling.

She got no sympathy from Rama, and she didn't want any. She put her half-empty plate in the cleaner and left him still eating, and shut herself in the first sleeping room she came to.

Aisha lay for a long time in the unfamiliar dimness. The air's smell, the way the room felt around her, were subtly alien. This wasn't her world or her place. She didn't belong here. She should never have come.

On the *Leda*, mostly she'd been in jumpspace, which was its own reality. She'd made herself not think about what she'd left behind. Told herself she wouldn't miss Jinni, or Jamal, or Mother or Pater or Vikram or Malia or—

She could let go here. Nobody who mattered would see.

She cried for a while, till her throat ached and her eyes burned and her head felt heavy and thick. Sleep ambushed her, with dreams in it.

She was riding Jinni on the plain outside of the city. Jamal trudged along beside her, with grass stains on his breeches and a long lead in his hand, but it wasn't Ghazal on the other end, it was the antelope stallion.

"Don't tell me *you're* trying to ride him," Aisha said.

"You think I'm crazy?"

Aisha let that hang in the air.

"I've been trying to link through to you," he said. "You weren't on Centrum. It took forever to find you. I think I know where you are in space, but now you're firewalled so wide and high it's like a ring of volcanoes all around you. You aren't about to blow up, are you?"

"Are you sure you don't have any psi?" Aisha asked. She didn't expect an answer, nor did she get one. "I'm all right. I'm not blowing up. I don't plan to, either."

Her plans might not have much to do with what actually happened, but he didn't need to know that. "Tell Mother and Pater," she said. "There's nothing to worry about."

"You know that won't stop them." He looked up at her in the hazy light of the dream, scowling just like Pater. "You should have told me you were leaving."

"What you don't know, you can't suffer for." That was a line from just about every pirate vid they'd ever watched together.

She wanted him to laugh, or at least shrug and let it go, but she should have known better. He hit her, so hard that even in the dream it stung. "I hope you do blow up. Serve you right. You went away and didn't tell me. After we swore to each other. Pirate's Oath, Aisha. You forgot."

"I *didn't* forget. I was trying to save you!"

"Well, you didn't." He stood on the windblown grass, with a rope in his hand that wound away now into the sky. There were stars in it, and skeins of suns. "I'll never trust you again."

Aisha woke not knowing where she was. Her head ached, but not nearly so much as her heart.

Everything around her was strange. The only familiar thing was the sun roaring and shooting off plasma behind her eyes, and Rama's voice saying, "Come and eat your breakfast."

"I just ate," Aisha said before her eyes were half open. Then her stomach crunched, and the web told her she'd slept over half an Earthday. Her mind might still be remembering dinner, but the rest of her was ravenous.

By the time she stumbled into the common room, she was almost capable of making sense. Rama prowled like a big cat. If he'd had a tail, it would have been twitching.

"What's wrong?" Aisha asked him.

"Eat," was all he said.

She opened her mouth to argue, but shut it again. Psycorps was watching. She tried asking inside, where the sun was. "What is it?"

He didn't snap her head off, which surprised her somewhat. He didn't answer, either. Not exactly. He made her feel instead, and remember.

Lying on the observation deck on the *Leda* during jump. Drifting through absolute nothingness. Feeling huge bodies moving in the void. Swimming. Singing.

One song out of them all was different. It made her ears hurt. It tried to tear her heart out of her chest. It was beautiful, and it was screaming. It was making glory out of agony.

She sucked in a breath and almost choked. It was a wonder she didn't fall down. That terrible, beautiful, awful song filled her till her skin felt ready to crack and split and burst wide open.

Quiet. It was a word in Rama's voice. It was a thing: a cool and soothing wave of blessed silence.

"That—" she tried to say. "That—"

"Hush," he said. "Eat."

Food was the last thing she ever wanted to see, but the bread and hummus and pickled vegetables had to go somewhere. She ate what was in the bowl, twitching because she couldn't say any of the things that her tongue itched to say. She didn't dare think them at Rama, either. They tangled up inside her and lost themselves in the memory of the song.

Something shifted. She felt freer somehow. She could take a deep breath and not feel as if it stopped halfway down.

Rama stood up straighter. Aisha hadn't realized how quenched he'd been until he turned, quick as a cat, and said, "I can keep this going for a while, but the quicker we move, the better."

"What—" Aisha said.

"We're going out," he said. "Bring whatever you can carry—but not so much it weighs you down."

"We might need to fight," Aisha translated. She wasn't sure how she felt about that. She might be excited. Or she might be terrified.

"We will not seek violence," Rama said, sounding as prim as Vikram throwing cold wisdom on a hot adventure. Unlike Vikram, he threw a flash of a grin at it. It looked like light catching the edge of a blade.

The part of Aisha that mostly wanted to be a good daughter and grow up to be a good archaeologist was wibbling frantically. The rest built a long, slow burn over that tortured singer—whoever, whatever it was.

"We're going to rescue it," she said, though Rama wasn't in the room any more. "Aren't we?"

He didn't answer. She didn't need him to.

Nobody just walked out of a Pyscorps facility. Rama did it—not working too hard at it, either, as far as Aisha could tell. He had his old barn clothes on, the hand-me-down Spaceforce trousers and the faded red shirt and the riding boots that had seen better days. With the torque he'd worn when he came out of the ruined cliff and a pair of gold earrings that Aisha distinctly didn't remember seeing in any of his kit, but she had seen them go into the vault on Nevermore, he fit right in in the part of the port that she'd been warned never to go near on any world.

She looked dangerous, she reminded herself. She was all in black and her face was veiled and she had a pair of swords that she more or less knew how to use. They were plasteel practice swords, but they had an edge that could cut.

She could walk like a panther, too; she'd learned it at the same time she learned to use the swords. The rest was keeping her head up and her eyes hard and not letting anybody see how badly she wanted to shrink down and disappear.

People didn't stare here. They darted glances, or they carefully didn't look at all. Minding their own business, their body language said. Not meaning any harm. Just getting through what they had to get through in order to stay alive for one more day.

Vids showed the scenery often enough. Dirt and vomit and bodies in gutters. Most of the bodies were even alive. The dead ones hadn't gone too far off yet—the cleaners would come through sooner or later.

Vids didn't show the smell. Or what was under it, a taste almost, bitter and harsh and suddenly, overwhelmingly sweet. Aisha wanted to gag, but her throat had locked. Her whole body was stiff.

Rama walked through crowds and clots of traffic as if they hadn't been there. He seemed to know where he was going, which was more than Aisha could manage. This part of the city she hadn't mapped on the web, and she was not likely to try it now. Psycorps would leap as soon as she tried.

As far as Psycorps was concerned, she was linked in to the schoolbot in the house, studying Old High Marsian. Rama was in his room, meditating. Or sleeping. Being still. Biding his time.

She could have been happy with that, just now, as they passed a clot of very dirty people around a very clean one. He looked as lost as Aisha felt, but he didn't have Rama to keep him safe.

"They're going to eat him," she heard herself say. "Don't you think we should—"

Rama ignored her. Aisha slowed down, loosening her left-hand sword in its scabbard. She knew how deeply stupid it was, but she couldn't seem to stop herself.

Rama slapped Aisha's hand away from the sword and hauled her forward, half off her feet. Then he let her go.

He wasn't waiting for her to find her balance. A few more meters and he'd be gone, and she'd be alone in the back armpit of the port.

That might not be such a bad thing. Even while she thought it, she staggered after him.

By the time she looked back, she'd gone too far to see what had happened to the other lost outworlder. Aisha had to hope he'd got away somehow. Or that it hadn't hurt too much when he went down.

The city got filthier the deeper they went. Aisha slipped in blood more than once, and in worse things more than that. She kept her feet because if she didn't, and landed in some of the things she tried to step over, she would want to rip her skin off along with her clothes.

She knew inside that skin that the only safe place here was directly behind Rama. He didn't care enough about anything to be afraid. He didn't even care if he died. He'd just come back and keep on hunting for the world he'd lost.

People here could smell fear. They could smell its opposite, too. They left him alone and stepped wide of his shadow.

When he stopped, she almost ran into him. The street they were on was narrow and twisty, but it was different from the past dozen twisty streets they'd been winding down. The pavement was almost clean, and the piles of garbage seemed to be restricted to the areas around the disposer units.

Somebody cared, here. Or was paid to care. Aisha's eye ran down a line of shops with names that didn't mean anything to her, and signs in writing that she couldn't read. The one nearest seemed to sell spices, Old Earth curios, and, from the smell, high-quality ganja. Which Pater would not be pleased to know she recognized.

Rama wasn't paying attention to the shop. The place just past it looked like either a tavern or a brothel—Pater would not have liked her to know that, either. It smelled like beer and wine and lower-quality ganja, and voices babbled out of it.

Another sound wound above the voices. It wasn't the song Rama was still following and Aisha was trying not to remember too clearly. It was much more obviously human, and as clear and pure and strong as it was, it didn't feel mechanical at all. It was coming out of a living throat, with a living mind inside.

"That's Old Earth opera," Aisha said. "What is she doing singing it in—"

"She's weaving dreams," Rama said. He turned toward the tavern.

Taverns in vids were dark and full of people with strange mods and stranger addictions. There were mods enough here, and most of them made Rama look distinctly normal, but the lights were up. Except for the ganja, most of what went around seemed to be safe enough for a children's party back in Cairo.

Rama made his way to a table by the wall, not too far from the door, but close enough to see the singer, who floated in a hoverchair at the far end of the room. He sat with his back to the wall, leaving Aisha to settle beside him.

The singer looked as if she rode in a globe full of stars, wearing a gown of stars, with stars woven into her abundant black hair. Her voice was so pure it hurt.

Queen of the Night. Rama's voice swam beneath earthly sound, the same way the great shapes swam through jumpspace. The words woke knowledge in somewhat the same way a web-ping did: the name of the opera and the character and the song she sang—aria, it was called.

It was born on Aisha's home world and not his, but it spoke to him. Music: sacred song. Songs for the gods, and of them.

His long sleep had taken them away from him. This song, and this singer, brought them back. All of them. A whole soaring tide of them.

They were part of the other song somehow, the terrible one, the song of agony. They were a guide. A point of focus. Leading him to the singer.

"Drinks, meser? Food? Dreams?"

The person speaking to Rama had no discernible gender. Heshe was blue— blue eyes, blue spikes of hair, skin shading from sea-blue to just this side of midnight. Hiser features were smooth and round and vaguely piscine, and hiser movements were smooth and flowing, as if heshe swam through air like water.

Rama's eyes were slightly wider than usual, taking in the sight, but then he relaxed. The person inside was human, and quite ordinary. There still wasn't a gender, exactly; more a sense of a body that was one thing and a mind that was another.

That hurt him, for some reason Aisha couldn't understand. She wasn't sure she wanted to: it was an old hurt, as old as he was, but as fresh as if it had happened that morning.

He covered it quickly, and said, "Food and drink we've had elsewhere. Dreams, we make for ourselves."

The blue person giggled behind hiser hand. The fingers were webbed. "Yes! Yes, we do, don't we? Drink, then, if you would stay. Directly, meser!"

The blue person didn't wait for an answer, but air-swam away. The singer still sang. Her voice never wavered and never seemed to tire.

Aisha was almost sad when the aria ended. She hadn't understood a word, but it didn't matter. Everything she needed to know was in the music.

The singer floated away into the darkness of holographic night. Something else took the stage, but Aisha didn't pay attention. It wasn't music; it was a babble of nothing much.

The babble in the room rose to drown it. Aisha only had vids to go by, to judge the people that crowded around her, but she didn't think many of them ran on the high side of the law.

It wasn't the ones with the extreme mods who made her skin creep. It was the quiet ones, the ones with their backs to the walls and their eyes watching, watching.

They were watching Rama. He looked bored now the singer was gone, leaning back, ignoring all the eyes on him. The more he ignored them, the more they stared.

"I wouldn't do that," someone said gently.

She wasn't tall, but she held herself so straight that she seemed to tower over Rama. Without her robe of stars she wasn't much to stare at: not young but not old, either, neither fat nor thin, with warm brown skin that Aisha would bet she had been born with, and a cloud of black hair.

She sat down across from Rama, not caring at all that her back was to the room. "I know you mean to provoke them," she said, "and I'm sure you could take them, singly and together, but this is my house, and I prefer it clean and quiet. No blood on my walls, meser."

"What, none at all? Not even a little?"

"Don't test me," she said.

She was as gentle as ever, but Rama blinked. "Your song," he said. "That was a holy thing."

"All the more reason not to commit blasphemy in my temple."

He bent his head to her. She knew how to talk to him—Aisha was impressed. Nobody even had to tell her what he was. She just knew.

"We'll give you a glass of whatever you like," she said, "but then you'll leave."

"Even if I promise to behave myself?"

"Are you capable of it?"

"Maybe not," he said, "but I can try." He paused. "I need a place to rest in for a day, two—maybe three. You have rooms, yes? If I convince you that I won't destroy them, or you, may I stay?"

"Rest? Or hide?" she inquired. "There are hotels by the dozen around the spaceport."

"I could hide there if I were minded," he said. "This is where I need to be."

"Need?"

"Need," he said.

"I should refuse," she said. "If I discover you've put a witching on me, I'll call the Corps. Do you understand that?"

"Perfectly," he said.

"Then come," she said.

Aisha should have known better than to expect anything in this place, but she'd seen too many vids; they'd marked her for life. She stood in a suite of rooms as big and bright and clean as any she'd ever stayed in, with a view of the spaceport and the shuttles taking off, that she only realized after a long few minutes was on a screen and not a wide, very clean window.

There were no windows, but screens everywhere. The place was like a fortress. It was shielded in as many ways as she could imagine, and probably a few she couldn't.

The terrible singing was still there, but muted almost to silence. Rama stood a little straighter; his shoulders were a fraction less tight. "This will do," he said.

"You haven't asked the price," the woman said.

"They tell me I'm wealthy," he said. "You can have it all, if you insist. I'll find more."

"Oh, no," she said. "I'll ask for something that matters to you."

"Not my companion," he said.

Aisha was somewhat pleased at how quickly he said that.

"I don't think that is yours to give," the woman said. "You may rest. When the time comes for payment, you'll know."

"We could simply walk away," he said.

"I think not," she said. She turned to go, but paused. "My name is Marta. Speak it, and the system will provide whatever you ask for. Within reason, of course."

"Of course," said Rama. Aisha couldn't tell if he was being ironic.

After Marta left, Rama said, "Katas in an hour. Meanwhile, rest if you will. Eat."

"You sound like my grandmother," Aisha said. "Always telling us to eat."

"Food is life," he said. And that *was* ironic.

Aisha didn't trust him. The way he'd tried to provoke people down below, the quiet he was cultivating now—he was up to something.

She could play the game, too. "Marta," she said, "I want a bath. With real water. And soap. And then I want dinner. Something good, with chicken. Can you do real chicken?"

"*Gallus gallus redivivus* thrives on Araceli," the air replied in a sweetened version of the living Marta's voice. "Have you a preference as to cuisine?"

"You choose," Aisha said.

"Heard and recorded," said the air.

"Thank you," Aisha said, though it was only software.

"The port is full of pirates," Rinaldi said.

Khalida had been expecting a delegation. It consisted, apparently, of Rinaldi, a pair of aides so bland as to be invisible, and a prickling in the nape of her neck that made her feel as if she was being watched by a multitude.

Rinaldi seemed unperturbed by room's shields, though his aides held themselves tight and still. He sat where Mem Aurelia had sat, with no sign of sensing the presence that had been there before him. To Khalida's eye he seemed small beside that memory of calm and composure, like a little yapping dog that wants to be a king of wolves.

That was interesting in itself. She sat on a cushion of her own, deliberately relaxed, and raised a brow. "You have new enemies, then? I'm to negotiate with pirates, too? Does MI know?"

"Military Intelligence is well apprised of the situation, I would hope," Rinaldi said. "As for what they might choose to share with you…"

Khalida knew better than to let him provoke her. "Tell me what pirates have to do with the reason we are, ostensibly, here."

"Oh," said Rinaldi. "Such steel in that spine. Pirates, my dear Captain, have taken advantage of a peculiarity in planetary law, which allows them free access to the port city and limited access to the rest of Araceli—excepting our territories."

Khalida was not going to give him either aid or ammunition. If he wanted anything said, he would have to say it himself.

"The port is now full of them," he said, obligingly, "and there are reports of 'touring parties' throughout Ostia Magna and its neighbors. There's a fair conclave of ships in orbit. All with letters of marque, or safe-conducts from one or more of the carefully neutral worlds. Geneva Nova, most notably."

"Isn't that a little obvious?" Khalida asked.

"One would think," he said. "But considering the ultimatum under which we all labor, and the cargo capacity of the various ships, I do wonder…"

"Pirates," Khalida pointed out, "or free traders, as they prefer to call themselves, don't believe in charity. If your opponents are as poor as all evidence indicates, can they be planning anything close to what you imply?"

"Poor they may be," he said, "but if all of them have gathered what resources they have and—even more to the point, perhaps—their talents—"

"Talents?"

"Technical skills," he said. "Such as are rare and highly valued in the outer worlds."

"Speculation," she said.

"Informed speculation," he said.

"Which is well and good," said Khalida, "but I'm here, at your insistence, to resolve this conflict. I am not your speaker to pirates."

"Even if your mission requires you to do so?"

Khalida took care to breathe slowly; to cling to calm. She had never taken kindly to being manipulated—and he was not even trying to hide it. "I take orders from Military Intelligence," she said. "You are here to present your terms."

"Well then," said Rinaldi, "those are my terms. Clear the port of pirates. Prosecute those who can be prosecuted, and remove the rest. Then we'll come to the table."

He was smiling, damn him. Like the king in the old story, demanding impossible tasks for the hand of his daughter.

This would not be the only one, Khalida thought. Oh, no. He was just beginning.

Logically Khalida would go to Colonel Aviram, and then through channels to MI, and try to make sense of this game Rinaldi was playing. She was not here to run security sweeps through a spaceport.

Unless of course she was. Her orders dropped as soon as she left Rinaldi sitting in the shielded room, sitting and smiling.

The last time she had to cope with this nightmare of a world, she had had Max and Sonja, Kinuko and John Begay. They were all inside her, capsules of memory, but none of them was speaking, or had spoken since she dropped the bomb on Ostia.

All she had now was herself.

Delegate, her orders said. Port Security was at her disposal. Aviram had the roster of MI personnel for both remote surveillance and boots on the ground. There was little enough for her to do but sign off on authorizations already prepared.

Khalida had never been good at signing off on orders. MI knew that.

She caught Aviram on his way out of HQ, in riot gear with his helmet under his arm. "No," she said. "Mine."

"Surely we can share," he said.

"Unless it's a ploy to get both of us out of HQ."

He barely blinked. "There's nothing here to attract a spy. Everything's encrypted on the Worldsweb."

Which she should know, his tone implied—gently, but nonetheless. "Everything but us," she said, equally gently. Then she shrugged, shaking off the shudder under her skin. "Do what you will. We'll sweep both ends against the middle, shall we?"

Even while she spoke she was scanning duty rosters on the web, calling up teams, some with names that swam up out of memory, others whom she did not know at all. Aviram saluted and went on his way. Khalida strode where the web directed her, in search of her own gear and the dozen MI operatives who would sweep the port under her command.

They were waiting in the ready room: twelve and one. The thirteenth met her stare with the faintest of half-smiles. Khalida counted the pips on the woman's collar with a kind of acid pleasure. "A psi-five? We're honored."

"Major Li," the agent named herself, "detailed to Military Intelligence."

Very much by the book, that one. Without the stiff carriage and the stern expression, she would have been a remarkably pretty child. Though surely she was not as young as she looked.

"I am not," she said. Crisply, but with a flicker of bone-dry humor. Not so stiff, then, either. And making a clear point of what she was and could do.

Khalida stiffened her own spine. Best she not see any of these agents as human. Allah knew, the Corps itself was not.

"You are here," she asked of this agent, "for what purpose?"

Major Li replied with a ping on the web, a packet that unfolded itself into a set of short and remarkably concise orders.

Khalida has received the bulk of them already. Door-to-door sweeps. Executing warrants against the freer of the free traders—some of long standing, others suspiciously new. Clearing out the bars and brothels. Encouraging holders of letters of marque to hold them elsewhere. And, most directly to the point, searching for signs of psi-nulls—triangulating those signs with psis attached to other units, and agents at Corps HQ.

"Since," Major Li said, "nulls are, as the term indicates, blank. Non-presences. Not there to the sight that I can bring to bear."

"Rogue nulls?" Khalida wondered aloud, as pieces fell into place and patterns took shape. "Is any of you at all surprised?"

Major Li chose not to answer that. Instead she said, "Nulls are a sort of cloaking device. Whatever is being done around them, neither psi nor MI can detect. Therefore—"

"That must be terribly frustrating for you," Khalida said.

"I enjoy a challenge," said Major Li.

Khalida, at this stage in her life, did not. But here she was, playing policeman for Psycorps. It might be better than playing executioner for them—just.

Major Li refused to lead. She would follow. Khalida shrugged and took second, with the unit's sergeant at point: a solid, foursquare, no-nonsense woman who managed without moving a muscle to convey her utter contempt for the Corps agent in the rear.

The rest of the unit did not even offer her that much. She could come or go, they said with turn of shoulder and angle of eye. It made no difference to them.

Khalida was a different matter. They knew who she was, and what. From some she had a sense of admiration. From others, almost fear. But none of them offered contempt.

That was something, she reflected as they advanced into the port. Word had gone out, of course. This being a spaceport, that meant more people in the streets rather than less, a succession of clogs and blockages that could have been completely accidental, but were ongoing and persistent.

Major Li looked for zones of nothingness. Khalida and her unit aimed toward the opposite: firmer obstruction, heavier crowds. Those were protecting something, as often as not.

Interesting how often Li and Khalida agreed as to where to go. It was slow going, and fruitless. Every knot they unraveled had nothing in its center. Every crowd evaporated once they had penetrated its outer circles.

Khalida held tight to patience. Door to door, her orders said. Door to door it was, no matter how many bodies tried to set themselves in the way.

She mapped their progress through the web. From HQ east toward the port proper, and then north, into the old city. Parts of that were as old as the human occupation of Araceli, built of native wood and stone and what looked like cannibalized shuttle parts.

They caught their first rat there: a small one, with a warrant out in three systems, and enough cheap liquor on board to float him through a fourth. Major Li had no interest in him; she barely deigned to wait for him to be wrapped and sealed and shipped off to Deportation.

"Trouble?" Khalida asked, leaving the unit to deal with the rat and taking station with Major Li in the street outside the tavern. It was suspiciously empty, and silent: not even the sound of a snore from the gutter.

Major Li frowned. Her lips were tight, her face pale, as if she nursed the mother of headaches. "No more than I expected," she answered.

Her expression belied the words, but Khalida kept her mouth shut. The prickle in her nape told her there were eyes behind every door and window.

Between her unit and the rest, they had pirates running to the spaceport from every corner of the city. It had a slightly rancid smell about it: a script they all ran through, with everyone knowing her part, and no one minded to improvise.

The unit emerged from the tavern, minus the rat's escort, which would deliver him to the nearest Port Security post and then rejoin the rest. Major Li had that look again, the hunter's glare, aimed still deeper into the old city.

32

Major Li had stopped pretending to do anything but hunt a single quarry. Khalida kept her mouth shut and her troops in line, and let her lead them toward the real target.

Not a pirate. Those were running like a herd of antelope, bounding toward whatever shelter they could find. Major Li pursued a different prey.

Triangulating emptiness. Khalida felt it ahead of her. The world around it was ordinary, the sun sliding down the sky but still casting a painfully bright light on the nether parts of the port. The place toward which they were going was blank. Simply, starkly blank.

Trap.

"Too obvious," Khalida said, though she knew what she was doing to herself by saying it. She found she no longer cared. "It's not the empty you're looking for. It's the imperceptible."

They were fanned out across a wider street than most, with Major Li on point and Khalida behind her. Doors were shut and windows blanked. Any vehicle that had not got out of there long since was pulled over and shut down.

Major Li turned in the empty street. "What—"

"Down!"

She dropped before the word was fully out. A bolt pierced the air where her head had been and blasted the facing from the building across the street.

Khalida's troops were moving before she could get the words out, tracking the source of the shot and converging on the wall.

There was no one there. No heat signature. Nothing but the track of a bolt, and a sense of...direction. That was the best word Khalida could lay on it.

"That way," she said.

Major Li said nothing. Her eyes had narrowed, maybe with anger, maybe with concentration. She set her lips together and followed where Khalida led.

The marines spread out as much as the street would let them, covering land and air and the walls between. The back of Khalida's neck prickled, but she kept her head up and her riot shield over it.

She was moving fast, not quite running. The thing she aimed toward had started to move, too, sidling away from the direct line of the street. Side alleys, connected tunnels—in this part of the port, it could be anything.

Khalida stopped abruptly. "I'm going in alone. The rest of you, keep on with the sweep. Make it look good. Catch a rat or two if you can."

She got no argument from the unit, though the sergeant's lips had gone tight. Major Li's dissent was equally physical: when Khalida handed off her shield and slipped through the massed and armored bodies toward the shadow of the wall, the Corps agent did the same.

Khalida had expected that. She set her own pace and let Li work to follow. Which, to be fair, she did well enough.

The trail of nothing led down an alley so narrow Khalida could touch both walls with outstretched hands. The sense of being funneled into ambush was strong enough to make her breath come short, but deeper instincts told her the walls and roof were clear. If anyone was lying looking to take another shot, the aim was outward, toward the unit.

This alley was no more than middling foul, which for this part of the city was worth noticing. It ended in a blank wall.

"May I?"

Khalida moved aside. Major Li slipped past her and laid both hands on the wall.

Her face twisted briefly; her fingers flexed. The wall shifted, divided, opened.

There was nothing supernatural about it. It was a door concealed behind the façade. It led to a corridor, dimly but adequately lit, and perfectly anonymous.

Major Li took the lead. Khalida loosened her sidearm in its holster and slipped the safety.

The passage had no exits: no doors on either side, and another blank wall at the end. To Khalida it felt like one of her less memorable nightmares, a cascade of blankness culminating in nothing.

Between one step and the next, the walls opened. A room formed itself around her. It was the same room in which she had met with Mem Aurelia, or a close facsimile.

That place was nowhere near the part of the city in which she had thought she was. Psi tricks, she thought. She was too tired of it all to be angry.

It was some small consolation that Major Li looked ever so slightly disconcerted. The room was empty. The shields must be up: Khalida's ears ached faintly.

"This is illusion," Li said.

"You think so?" Khalida turned completely around. "Suppose she's right," she said to the walls. "The game's up. You've trapped us. Now show yourselves."

The walls said nothing. There was no door; no sign of entry on any side. They stood in a bubble, and there would stay, until their captors were inclined to let them out.

"I don't think so," Khalida said. She raised her pistol and took aim straight ahead: one direction being as good as any other.

A coiling in her backbrain brought her half around away from Li, flicked the pistol from kill to stun, and fired into blankness.

The walls melted. She caught a flash, a flicker of shadow, but the living presence she had been sensing was gone.

This must be a warehouse, abandoned for some time, by the thickness of dust on it. Major Li crouched in the middle of it. Her arms were over her head; she rocked back and forth as if in agony.

Khalida knew better than to touch a psi in crisis, but her voice, even at its sharpest, won no response. She dialed down the power in her pistol, aimed and fired.

Li dropped as the shadowy presence had, but stayed solid once she hit the floor. Khalida hauled her up and heaved her over a shoulder.

The unit was halfway to the other side of the sector, and time had gone strange. Khalida would have admitted to half an hour at the most, but the worldweb marked three hours since she entered the building.

She set her teeth. Maybe she was not so tired after all. Maybe she had had enough and more than enough of this world and its tricks and its damned bloody wars.

Major Li would wake with a killing headache, but she would live. Khalida leaned against the wall waiting for the transport, pistol set back to kill, and drafted her letter of resignation in her head—over and over, in a dozen different ways.

Building and street and, for all she could tell, sector were completely deserted. All the people had drained out of it, sucked like infection from a wound.

The deep sense of unease was back, throbbing at the base of her skull. She meant to ignore it, but the thirteenth iteration of her resignation had turned into a rant. She began to delete it, paused, saved instead—absently, as she moved away from Major Li.

The transport was almost there. Khalida set a finder beacon over the psi agent, laid her spare pistol in the slack hand, and went hunting.

Alone, without the taint of Psycorps around her, Khalida walked more easily. The thing she hunted had stopped moving. It was close, though still some little distance through the empty streets.

She must be walking outside the world. The city was too densely populated and the web too pervasive to tolerate this kind of emptiness.

Consider the ramifications, she thought. Psi and non-psi, and then a third thing. Psi-null. A thing the psis had made, that was neither psi nor not, but something...other.

Did they need a worldwrecker out of a pirate vid, or even Pele Syndrome, if they had this?

Plots within plots. Wars and enmities twisting on one another like the turns of a tesseract.

Khalida turned and walked through a wall.

The air was full of stars and singing. Khalida kept walking until the stars went away. She intended to walk until the game ended and she came to whatever point she was meant to come to.

"You must have been an exasperating child."

Mem Aurelia floated in front of her, a cloud of shimmering pixels.

Khalida walked through that, too. "You've hacked the worldweb," she said. "That I can see. Now let me out. Or am I supposed to die here?"

"We want you alive."

That was not Mem Aurelia. She was younger and darker and somewhat less tall. Her hair was a cloud of black curls.

The room was ordinary, in the style of Ostia Magna: walls painted with a dreamlike landscape, floor a holomosaic, furnishings available on web command. The woman occupied a woven mat in front of a low table. On the table was a bouquet of stars.

Khalida sent table and stars flying. "No more," she said. "I've been a pawn in every game that's running on this sinkhole of a world. I'm done. Either settle your war or let the world go to hell. I don't care which."

"I think you do."

"Can you read my mind?"

"You know I can't."

"I think you extrapolate. Cross-reference. Hack. Turn worlds into weapons. Psi was going to be the next stage of human evolution. But it's not the only one, is it? They made you for their use. You'll use them—somehow. I haven't found the answer to that yet."

"You don't think that's fair?"

"I don't know what fair is. I just want to be done with all of you."

"On that," the woman said, "we can certainly agree. Shut down Psycorps, rid this world of them, restore our children, and then it will be over. No more war. No more Corps."

Khalida sighed. "All you want of me is the impossible. Or this world ends."

"Worlds end. Entropy rules. Do you blame us for saying we've had enough?"

No matter how hard she had tried, Khalida was caught in a trap she had been trained strictly to avoid. She must be objective. She must not judge, only adjudicate. Above all, she must not allow herself to fall into sympathy, let alone empathy, with one side of a war.

"I recuse myself," she said. "I withdraw. I refuse."

"You can't do that."

"Watch me," Khalida said.

She turned on her heel, but the woman caught her. The hand on her arm was warm and strong.

"I won't speak of what you owe us," the woman said. "You did the only thing you knew how to do. This time, you know more. I would like you to know everything. To be able to judge fairly."

Khalida turned back to her. "I am the last person you want sitting in judgment over you, or trying to negotiate anything either for or against you. I've already been used to destroy a city. Now I'm to be held accountable for destroying a world."

"That, no," the woman said. "They miscalculated, you know. Invested resources here that can't easily or feasibly be transferred elsewhere. They need this world."

"In a negotiation," Khalida said, "the party that can afford to walk has the upper hand." She shook her head. "They're still playing games with me. Setting impossible conditions. They don't believe they can lose."

"They can't afford to." Finally the woman let her go. "Three days. Then it ends."

One way or the other.

Khalida felt oddly light. Relieved. There was no possible way to meet Rinaldi's conditions before the core tap went rogue. Which absolved her of that responsibility. Of all of them, really.

Except one. Her brother's daughter.

She paused. "You have a name?" she meant to ask.

The room was empty.

More games. More impossibilities. She resisted the urge to spit.

The door, at least, opened, and the city beyond it was the one she knew. The worldweb offered her a map when she asked for it, and a route back to headquarters.

She took it, because there was nowhere else she would rather be. She could think there, in the shielded room. Make arrangements to get Aisha back offworld. Maybe even care enough to find her own way out of this multileveled trap.

33

Rama ran web searches with speed and efficiency that would have impressed even Jamal. Aisha shadowed him. Maybe he was aware and maybe he wasn't, but he didn't block her.

He had the whole planet's maps and surveys drawn up and one spot marked: the Ara Celi. The Altar of Heaven, which the planet was named for.

Aisha flew with him up the virtual valley, while the datastream ran through, repeating over and over what little anyone knew.

Alien. Old. Older than he was by some disputed number of millennia. It stood on what had been a tableland once, but was a column of granite now; the softer rock around it had eroded away.

It looked like a grotto, a cave in a mountain long since gone. Its walls were thick with carvings so worn they were barely visible. Simulations and enhancements offered suggestions, but it was obvious that no one knew what they really were.

Maybe Rama did. He spoke so suddenly Aisha jumped. "Marta. Plot a course to these coordinates, and arrange transport."

"That area is restricted," the not-quite-human voice answered, "and currently closed. The Institute for Psychic Research—"

"I require transport," he said. Calmly. The code he ran through the web as he spoke made Aisha stare.

"That area is restricted," the bot repeated.

"But the rest of the planet is not."

"Approximately thirty-eight percent of the planet's land mass is restricted, proscribed, banned, or uninhabitable," the bot said. "Of the sixty-two percent that remains—"

"Transport," he said. "Hire. Or buy if necessary."

"Planetary law requires that all visitors be escorted by a licensed guide. Restricted, proscribed, banned, or unhabitable areas are—"

"Marta," he said as if to a living person. "If I wanted to be legal or traceable, would I be here?"

"No," the bot said. Then: "Your illegal and untraceable transport will arrive in one hour."

Aisha could have sworn the bot's voice was just a little bit dry. Bots weren't supposed to have personalities, but that didn't mean they didn't.

She was barely making sense, and now she knew when Rama intended to bolt. She slipped out of the web with extreme care.

She was ready when Rama called her out for katas. Ready and packed and as casual as she could possibly be.

He was as easy as Aisha could remember him being, loose and free, but with a snap and power to his movements that told her everything she needed to know. She didn't try to mirror him. She'd have worn herself out. But she kept up, and she was proud of that.

He didn't cut the session short, but he didn't let it go on past time, either. "You rest," he said, still light and free, but underneath he felt like the edge of a sword. "Eat. Sleep if you can."

Aisha bit her tongue before she asked him what he was planning to do. He was going to slip out while she slept. That was as clear as the smile on his face.

He hadn't needed this place to hide in. He could have gone anywhere. He wanted a safe place to stow Aisha. She'd wake up and find her aunt looking down at her, or someone else from MI, and then she'd be picked up and carried back to Mother and Pater. And that would be it for Nevermore.

She'd thought he knew her better than that. She pretended to be as stupid as he thought she was, yawned and stretched and retreated toward her room.

She couldn't feel him watching her. He was preoccupied; he'd already forgotten her.

She gave it a few minutes, to be sure. Then she slipped around the back and down toward the street.

A cubby of a room opened just off the outer door, where a guard might sit, watching who came and went. The screens were mostly dead, but Aisha patched together one in the direction that mattered.

The transport was exactly on time, which surprised her a bit. It was a weird hybrid of a thing, half land vehicle, half aircraft, and she suspected it had armor in places where a legal transport wouldn't have any.

The person who emerged from it was perfectly ordinary and perfectly casual. Nothing furtive about her. She walked past the room Aisha was hiding in, up toward the entry screen and the inner door.

Aisha darted out behind her. The rover had a security lock on it, but Aisha was ready for that. She hit it with Rama's ident code and a spurt of his voice off the web.

The door opened. Aisha started toward it.

The world slid sideways. Everything—the air, the buildings around her, the planet underfoot—melted in a deep and singing roar of absolute pain and despair.

It was agony. And she couldn't die of it. That was the worst part, the part that almost snapped her mind in two. That she had to keep on living, and feeling, and *being*…

The sun exploded around her. The voice in it was familiar beyond memory of names. "Focus. Focus on me."

She didn't have a choice, any more than she'd had to feel—that—

"Focus," he said.

She fixed her eyes on a single dark point in all the blinding light. Little by little it grew, until she recognized Rama's face. There was no mistaking that blade of nose.

She was back in her body again, and it ached. Something or someone had thrown her over the edge of a passenger cradle in a vehicle that was mostly a blur. She crawled down into it.

Someone outside was flapping and squawking. The pilot, she thought. She was proud of herself for being able to think that clearly.

Rama slid into the pilot's cradle, already linked in to the rover's systems. A shimmer of schematics played across the part of his cheek that she could see.

She must be imagining that. Her insides were still shaking from the awfulness of the mindsong.

The rover took to the air with its pilot flailing and screaming below. The web should have been screaming, too, but Rama had a grip on that.

He didn't say a word to Aisha. He didn't throw her out, either. She'd won that round, though she could have done with a little less agony.

The flight plan for the Ara Celi shimmered on the screens, but Rama veered away from it. Aisha could feel the pull in herself, the song that would not stop calling and calling.

He could fight it. He was strong enough. He was flying toward it instead, as straight as time and traffic would let him.

Some of that traffic started howling at them with official rage. He did something—Aisha was too fuzzled to be sure exactly what. Made the rover invisible, maybe. The howling trailed off.

She never had been afraid of Rama, but this made her blink. He honestly didn't care for laws or rules or anything that existed in this time. It was a nightmare to him, that was all. Nothing about it was real.

She had to make it real to him. Somehow. He was awake because of her. He had to wake the rest of the way.

First she had to wake up herself, and get her body under control, while the singing went on and on on the other side of the sun that shielded her. Out there it was getting louder, and strong enough to hum in the rover's hull.

She clawed up out of the cradle and staggered to the nearest viewport. They flew in a long arc over the city, angling toward the actual port, where the shuttles landed, and where spaceships built for planetary atmosphere could come and go.

Nobody came in now, though ships and shuttles went out at scattered intervals. It looked as if they were running away from the planet.

Rama brought the rover in low, in between surface traffic and actual, official airspace. He barely cleared the tops of buildings, or skimmed around them, smooth and so fast Aisha had to remind herself to breathe.

The rover shouldn't have been that fast, even if Rama hadn't flown it that way. Which told her it really was illegal and probably undocumented, and now stolen. Which made them pirates. Or criminals at least, if anybody caught them.

The port opened up just below them, a sudden stretch of open air and clouded light. Rain spattered the viewports. Whole swaths of landing pads were empty, and those that were occupied had many more ships loading than unloading.

"End times," Rama said, so sudden after so long a silence that Aisha jumped.

He seemed to be talking to himself, but she could feel his attention on her, wanting her to hear. "Psycorps' war comes to a head. Culling pirates out of the city; sending the quicker-witted offworld before the cull reaches them. Forcing the enemy's hand. Hoping they'll be the first to blink."

"But they won't," Aisha said. "Will they? Not that I understand much at all, but I heard Aunt talking sometimes, and we hacked her files once. The other side can't give up. It's at the wall. There's nowhere to run."

"Except up and out," Rama said, "leaving devastation behind."

"How long?" Aisha asked.

"Days," he answered.

He sounded calm, but Aisha could feel how tightly he was holding himself in. Whatever he needed to do or see at the Ara Celi, he had to get there before it all went away. And then get away himself, but she couldn't think about that. Because then she'd have to think about what they were getting away from.

Not to mention that they weren't heading toward the Ara at all, but toward something somewhere on this hemisphere of Araceli that was screaming and screaming. Something huge; something completely and utterly alien.

"No," Rama said. His voice was terribly mild.

The song was gone completely. Shut out. Pushed to the other side of a wall so wide and high there was no measuring it.

The rover bucked as if whatever was calling had tried to get hold of it. Rama snapped the controls, first sharply up, then in a steep banking turn.

The screens showed the original flight plan, and a modified one that included the port, and a map of the planet's surface between the port and the Ara. Rama's shoulders didn't relax, but he let out a breath, and so did Aisha.

She wasn't sure how she felt. Not glad, no. Relieved, maybe. Scared. That more than anything.

And guilty. Because whatever had tried to pull them off course had hurt so much, and been so desperate. She didn't know what any of them could do, or how, or even why, but still. Something thought it needed them, and they were running away from it.

34

The Ara might be on the same continent, but there was a great deal of land between it and the port, and most of that had various forms of restricted airspace. Though Rama might not care, whatever he was doing to cloak the rover took energy, and even he had to think about conserving that.

Aisha helped him plot a course that wouldn't trigger any alarms—she hoped—but that would get them where they needed to go in as little time and with as little power usage as possible. They'd have to fly through the night; he wasn't going to stop, still less find a place to sleep.

She was wide awake, though she knew she should rest as much as she could. She foraged in the rover's galley, fed herself and bullied Rama into eating with her. Then she noodled through the web, not really knowing what she was looking for—news, she supposed. Warrants out on a pair of rover thieves.

She didn't find any warrants, but the web was humming. Sweeps had started in the port. Whoever was in charge of the planet was purging pirates, rounding them up or chasing them offworld.

Which explained what Aisha had seen and what she hadn't. Probably no one would have time to run after two nobodies who'd stolen a rover, if they were going for much bigger criminals.

Probably. She kept the stream going, with flags on anything that might have to do with them or the Ara, and curled up in the cradle and let herself doze.

They flew through the night and the rain. Cities came and went below, with larger and larger stretches of open country in between. The maps said they were leaving neutral territory and getting closer to land that, officially or not, belonged to Psycorps. On the map it was labeled *Castellanos Maior.* Greater Castellanos, that meant.

The warning came out of nowhere, sometime before dawn. "Ten minutes. Ten minutes to power shutdown."

Aisha snapped awake. "What— There's no way! We have more than enough power to get where we're going."

"Not if we're shut off from the grid." Rama was as calm as ever.

"But we're not supposed to be *on* the grid."

"Evidently we are," he said under the blare of the rover's system listing available landing places.

There weren't many. The nearest didn't even try to pretend it wasn't a Corps station.

Aisha's mind wanted to spin and spin in hopeless panic. She'd tried to think of everything. The course she'd helped to set, the hacks she'd used, how could they have—

Didn't matter. They were going down, and the Corps would have them. Again. Rama wouldn't make it to the Ara, and the worldwrecker would get triggered, and it would be all over for Araceli, and Nevermore, too.

Rama muttered something to himself. It sounded like swearing, but not in any language she knew. He sat back away from the screens, as if he'd let them go. Aisha felt the grid lock on and start to take control.

The rover bucked once, and the system shut off. Voice, screens, everything. They sat in the dark, with rain rattling on the hull.

Light grew very slowly. Aisha braced for impact, but the rover was still in the air, and still moving.

The light came from Rama. It was low, no more than a shimmer. It made the small hairs of her body prickle, and there was a faint hum in her ears.

That came from him, too. He was singing softly, hardly more than a whisper.

It felt as if the song was holding the rover up and keeping it on course. Which wasn't exactly true, or couldn't be. He was focusing his psi. Letting the music and the words carry them toward the Ara.

Calling the sun into the sky, too, with long shafts of light under the shield of cloud. In the middle of the song he sighed, and the rover speeded up.

They left the clouds behind and flew into a bright and rain-washed morning. The country they'd flown into was stark and rugged, broken into deep rifts and crevices, with sudden sharp uprisings of naked stone.

One of those uprisings stood at the top of a deeper valley than the rest, carved out by a ribbon of river. Aisha recognized it from its virtual image, and the trail of petroglyphs winding up the column, with the deep slot at the top.

It was bigger than she had imagined, and higher. There was room in the grotto for the rover to land, with space left over to get out and walk the circle and peer at the carvings in the old, old stone.

The niche in the deepest part was big enough to pose a statue in. Its edge carried an arch of ancient writing, but the rest was plain, rough and barely worked, like an afterthought.

Rama traced the faded carvings, moving slowly around the grotto. Sometimes he paused.

The carvings weren't in any of the styles of writing that Aisha had seen on Nevermore. That didn't seem to be stopping him. He frowned as he went; his lips moved, as if he had to work out what the letters or characters said.

The ones that framed the arch were different than the rest, to Aisha's eye. They looked more like pictures. Dots and circles, and small spiky things in patterns that made her think of—

"Star systems," she said aloud. "It's a map."

"Yes." Rama had been across the grotto, but now he stood beside her.

Aisha traced the shape of one, and then the one above it. There was a dot between, though when she peered closer, it looked like a tiny spiral. Like a galaxy, but not exactly.

"Subspace route?" she wondered.

"Something like that."

She frowned at him. He was even more than usually hard to read. As best she could tell, he wasn't happy. Disappointed, maybe. He hadn't found what he'd hoped to find. Or not quite what he'd hoped for.

"This is the way," he said, following the star systems up and over and down the arch. "It's as clear as it dares to be. But I can't—there is no way—"

"You need a ship," Aisha said.

"These aren't paths for ships," he said.

"Then what are they?"

"Gates," he said. "Strings of pearls across infinity, each pearl a world, but how the gates were made, or by whom, or for what, no one ever knew." He let out a sharp breath. "It's all here. All the signs. The promise—but there's no gate. It's gone, if it ever was at all."

This was enormous. Aisha couldn't even measure how huge it was. "Is there one on Nevermore?" she asked.

"Not any more," he said. "I fear they're all gone. All broken. No gates left anywhere."

"There has to be one," Aisha said. "Somewhere, one must exist. Or what is all this for? It doesn't make sense."

"It must," he said. "I'm missing data. Misreading the messages. Not understanding some crucial thing, some key—or it's somewhere else. Another system. Another world. A new message, a clue—"

Aisha was still trying to get her mind around it. Gates—like in old stories. Portals from world to world. No need for a ship or a subspace drive. Just step forward and be lightyears away from where you started.

Rama had honestly expected to find one here. Or a guide to one. What that told her about the world he'd come from, the culture that made him—Bronze Age, Pater had estimated, give or take and allowing for differences between worlds and species...

Civilization wasn't just technology. She'd managed to forget that. This living atavism with his golden treasure and his edged weapons was a psi master above anything she'd ever heard of, and now she understood why space travel hadn't baffled him, either. Ships he hadn't known or needed, but interstellar travel was nothing new to him at all.

He thought Psycorps was a pack of amateurs and poorly educated children. Was that what he thought of spaceships, too? Slow and cumbersome and oh, so primitive.

It would have been humiliating if it hadn't been so horribly funny. She couldn't laugh; she was past that. She was even past being scared.

"So," she said. "A ship. Navigation systems can process the maps here, and plot courses from system to system. It won't be instant, but it can be done."

"It could take years," he said. "Lifetimes."

"Or not." She tapped a system halfway up the nearer curve of the arch. "This looks like the one we're in. The one on the bottom, with four others in between—isn't that Nevermore? So we've jumped a handful already. If we figure out how to bypass the rest, and where it's all leading us—what we're supposed to find—it could take no time at all. Relatively speaking."

"That supposes the map is linear," he said, "and the way is straight from world to world. And that this"—he stooped and brushed the bottommost swirl of star-dots on the farther side—"is where we're meant to go."

"That's why we need a ship, and a navigation system. To plot the course and see where it leads."

"It can't be that straightforward," he said, stubborn. "Or they'd have left all this on Nevermore, and not sent me half across the galactic arm to find it."

"So get a ship and run the coordinates," Aisha said. She could be at least as stubborn as he could.

"That easily? On a world at war? That may not even be here tomorrow?"

"Why not?"

He glared. Then he laughed. "By the good god, child, you're starting to talk like me."

"That's a bad thing?"

"Very."

"We'd best get at it," she said. "Can you keep all the maps in your head or do you need web access for that?"

"It's here," he said, but he didn't tap his head; he touched his chest over his heart.

Different culture. Different ways of seeing the world, and the worlds.

"So," she said. "A ship. Back to the port?"

"Maybe," he said. He paused for one last long scan of the Ara, and especially the arch; then he turned toward the rover.

T hey had an instant's warning this time, like a storm wind gathering
itself to roar.

The song that had been silent since they left the port broke over them
with such force that Aisha looked wildly around, expecting to see whatever had
sung it. Then she realized that the rock underfoot was swaying, and a slow crack
spread upward through the carvings in the wall past the arch.

They both dived into the rover. The hull was no protection from the song,
but at least it held together, and the engine fired when Rama hit the controls.

The rover lurched. Stones rattled on the roof. The Ara was coming down.

Aisha couldn't even squeeze her eyes shut, let alone breathe. The passenger
cradle strapped her in, jerkily, while the rover lurched again, then leaped
forward.

There was no flight plan. No plan at all except to get out as fast as mechanically
possible.

The Ara Celi buckled and folded and collapsed on itself. The rover tried to
go down with it, sucked into its vortex, but Rama extracted every last bit of
power out of the straining engine and his own psi, and held it to a rocking,
bucking, groaning hover.

Dust billowed over them, darkened the sun and slowly dissipated. The song still screamed all around them.

Rama aimed the rover straight at it. Aisha might have squawked—she couldn't tell; no other sound in the world could penetrate that vast and appalling cry.

It wasn't growing louder. It took her a long while to realize that. Little by little, it was starting to fade.

When Rama tried to turn the rover aside from it, it erupted again. The rover's hull warped visibly. He wrenched it back in the direction the song wanted him to go.

Everything was completely out of control. Maybe Rama knew what it was all coming to, but Aisha's imagination had lost its ability to keep up.

She ventured a tiny poke at the rover's web access. It was weak and intermittent, fading in and out, but with a little effort she could make it make sense—enough to get the maps working, and activate the forward screen.

They were flying away from the port, deeper into Corps territory. The map called it Montecito: a ring of mountain ranges around a wide flat valley.

The mountains were clear enough, but the valley refused to come into focus. The far west end wouldn't record at all, except as a blur of mist and rogue pixels.

Wrestling with the web helped keep her sane. She teased out a set of older maps that showed the valley more clearly.

Well, she thought. No wonder it was shielded.

It was a spaceport. Part of it looked like the larger port she'd landed in from the *Leda*, but the far end was different. Instead of open landing fields and long, wide, high shuttle bays, it held wells for deep-space ships. Those almost never came down into atmosphere, but when they did, they flew under null-g and settled into gravity-controlled cradles.

It said something for how important this place was, that it had half a dozen of these enormously expensive wells, which meant the tech and the staff and the capabilities that went with them. Psycorps had to have built them, and be using them, too.

She hacked a connection from the old map to the new one, and then patched it in to an observation satellite that had a tiny spark of bandwidth available. The connection was rough and blurry, but she persuaded it to zoom in.

Five of the landing wells were empty. The sixth, the one on the very end, looked like a piece of starless space floating above the deep curve of the well.

Aisha rubbed her eyes. They kept wanting to see the blackness, but when she looked directly at it, all she saw was the shape of a much more ordinary ship in a cradle: long and tubular, with rows of ports like a planetary skyliner.

Spaceships could look like anything they wanted to. This one was downright boring. No frills or nacelles. No shiny metal or clusters of modules like shimmering bubbles, no wings or struts or solar sails—though those wouldn't hold up to a planet's gravity.

The awful song came from the ship, or from something inside it. It was pulling them in.

One of the screens in front of Rama came alive, streaming data off the web. Aisha hadn't done that. Rama had his own hacks going, and she hadn't even picked up that he was doing it.

The stream was a lot of official data: ship's registration, cargo and passenger manifests, flight plans and routes traveled.

Research vessel *Ra-Harakhte*, commissioned out of Beijing Nine, assigned to—

Then like what she'd seen in the well, the stream jumped and lurched and settled, and what it said was completely different.

Experimental ship, commandeered from scientific expedition, passengers and crew detained, interim commander—

Pirated. Though since it was the Corps, which could do whatever it wanted, they used that other word. Commandeered.

The words didn't matter. All that mattered, and all she could hear or see any more, was the song. She felt as if it had lodged in her bones and set her blood on fire.

She fought to see through it. The ship wasn't just sitting there. Things were happening around it. Cars flitting back and forth. Shapes moving on the ground.

Fighting?

"Rama," she tried to say. "Rama, we have to turn around. Or stop. Or something. We can't—"

He ignored her. His back was rigid.

Aisha concentrated on breathing. The rover skimmed the mountaintops and slid down the slopes into the valley, passing over knots and clusters of buildings and the occasional road. Whatever protections the place had—and they must be strong—didn't seem to see or touch them.

The screens kept working. The web feed came clearer now they were in the valley. Energy weapons flashed, and knots of struggling figures pushed up against the landing cradle.

Whatever was in the ship had stopped screaming, but the soft moan of agony made it worse. Rama stopped pretending to operate the controls; he made his way to the rear and dug in a locker back there, coming out with two sidearms and a fistful of charging belts.

Aisha took the ones he handed her. Her fingers felt numb. She knew how to shoot. Mother had insisted on it, as long as she was going to live on a planet full of wildlife and almost empty of humans. The thought of shooting at people made her sick to her stomach.

"You won't be shooting anyone unless they shoot first," Rama said. "Once we're down and out of the rover, stay behind me. Don't break; don't go off on your own. We'll use the fighting as a cover."

"For what?" Aisha demanded.

"We're going in," he answered.

The rover floated down on the far side of the landing well, away from the worst of the fighting. No one tried to stop it.

Rama swayed a little getting out: the first sign Aisha had seen that he was pushing his limits. She'd started to think he didn't have any.

He got his balance and took a breath, then ran lightly along the edge of the well. The ship loomed over him. It was huge: Aisha couldn't even see the top, or either end. From where they were, it blocked out the sky.

The fighting was concentrated on the other side, where the entrance must be. Rama had his eye on something else—cargo port, Aisha guessed, from what she knew of starships.

This one, close up, wasn't like any she'd ever seen, with her eyes or on the web. Its hull was a weird, shifting color, like oil on dark water. The ports looked like eyes: the same kind of liquid curve, and the faintest hint of motion.

That had to be an illusion. The hull curving and flexing toward them—that wasn't. The well curved with it, irising open directly in front of them.

Rama never even hesitated. He ran straight in.

Aisha did stop. It was dark inside except for a faint glow. She couldn't see anything but Rama's shape against it, getting smaller as he ran deeper.

Someone shouted: words she couldn't catch. A knot of people ran toward her down the length of the ship. A fighter buzzed down on them, blasting them with plasma bolts.

She fumbled for the pistol Rama had given her. She didn't have any thought on her head, just a kind of blank *Oh, shit.*

He sprang past her, pushing her back toward the ship with one hand while the other swung up and aimed. Above the running people. At the fighter with its Corps logo.

That wasn't any sidearm bolt. It blasted the fighter out of the sky.

He didn't stay to admire his work. He swept Aisha up, one-handed, and hauled her into the rapidly shrinking port—hatch—whatever it was.

She lay on a faintly yielding, faintly glowing surface and tried to remember how to breathe. Images kept flashing through her mind. How the people on the ground were dressed like ordinary citizens: port staff, workers, the odd person in a suit. And how he'd shot the fighter down, and he hadn't had a weapon in his hand.

She dragged herself to her feet. Rama was already well down the tubular, curving corridor.

The light was getting brighter, or else Aisha's eyes were adapting. There wasn't much to see. No doors. No signs. No apparent way in or out or up or down. Just forward.

The place had a smell. It was faint and rather pleasant, a little like mushrooms and a little like the sea. Earth and salt and something sharply clean.

Starships never smelled like this. *Experimental*, the webstream had said. She was starting to wonder just what the experiment was, and what was being experimented on.

Rama was almost out of sight. She mustered as much speed as she could and plowed after him.

36

There was no rest for the wicked, still less for destroyers of worlds. Khalida had hardly settled into the shielded room with a bottle of local grappa and a plate of something that began, as usual here, with pasta and soared into a savory firmament, when the door pinged.

She ignored it. It opened regardless. She stared sourly at Lieutenant Zhao. "Weren't we supposed to be rid of you?"

He inspected the bottle on the table. His eyes widened slightly. "That's potent stuff."

"So I gather. I haven't tasted it yet." She lifted her laden spoon. "Have you eaten?"

"Thank you," he said, "I have."

He did not sit, which surprised her. He stood like a cadet on review: a little too stiff, and a little too obviously trying not to be.

"Well?" she said when he kept on standing—hovering, to be strictly accurate.

"Captain," he said. He bit his lip. Screwing up his courage, she thought.

He let it go all at once. "Your niece…we seem to have misplaced her."

Khalida had not been expecting that. "I thought you had her stowed safely."

"We thought so, too," he said, "but she's gone. She and the Dreamtimer. They might have gone separately. We suspect they went together."

Khalida drew a slow breath. Bursting apart in a fit of rage and desperate worry would do nothing here, and in this room, no one could pry into her mind to see the fires roaring. She kept her voice low and perfectly steady. "May I ask how that happened?"

"Captain," he said, "we don't know. We had taken them to one of our safe houses, where they were monitored and thoroughly protected. They should not have been able to leave the house, let alone vanish."

"Yet they did."

"Yes," he said in what seemed to be honest misery. "It's a terrible failure. Not to mention the danger they would be in, with a world at war."

"If anything happens to Aisha," Khalida said, "I shall hold you personally responsible."

"As you should," he said. He sat down finally, as if his knees had let go. "Captain, do you have any idea where they might have gone?"

"If I did, do you think I would tell you?"

"Please, Captain," he said. "Sera Nasir is still on this world; that much we can determine. But we haven't been able to discover where she is or how she's traveling."

"I don't know if I believe you," Khalida said.

"Of course you wouldn't," he said. "Nevertheless, Captain, we are deeply concerned, and we will do everything in our power to find her and bring her back to you."

"If you really do want to protect her," Khalida said, "find her and get her back to her parents. All the way to Nevermore, Lieutenant, by the safest and fastest means possible. Promise me that—swear to it by whatever you hold sacred—and I'll answer your question."

Zhao barely hesitated. Which meant that he was either a hardened liar or a complete innocent. "I promise," he said, "on my honor as an officer, that if I succeed in finding her, I will return her, safe and unharmed and as soon as possible, to her family."

"Well then," Khalida said. "Meser Rama has a certain archaeological interest in the Ara Celi. He might have taken it into his head to visit the site."

"It is in a restricted area," Zhao said.

"Do you think that would have stopped him?"

"No," Zhao admitted after a pause. "No, it wouldn't, would it?" He rose with a fraction of his usual grace. "Thank you, Captain. We will do our best. I promise you that."

"You do that," Khalida said.

Then finally she was alone with an unopened bottle of grappa and a plate of congealing pasta. She pushed them both away and lowered her aching head into her hands.

The room might be shielded, but its web connection was MI-grade and she, as commander, had the keys. She applied one, and waited while it worked its way though encrypted channels.

"Captain," Tomiko said. Even on the web her voice was thick with frost.

"Captain," Khalida answered. She could not equal Tomiko's coldness, and she did not want to. "I need a favor."

"Do you?" Tomiko opened the connection enough that Khalida could see her sitting in her quarters with a bottle and a plate of her own, and a vid paused on a scene of ancient warriors standing face to face and sword to sword.

Khalida appreciated the symbolism. "It's all coming to a head here," she said, "and the Corps seems to have misplaced my niece. Will you keep a shuttle on call? The instant we find her, I want her off this planet."

"Only her?" Tomiko inquired.

Khalida chose not to answer that.

"There is one other thing," she said. She had the dataspurt ready: her resignation, locked and coded to file when the call ended. Dumping it off on Tomiko was not exactly kind, but there was no one else in the system whom she trusted to register and execute it.

"Thank you," she said as the data marked itself as sent.

Tomiko's leaned forward, as if she could reach through the connection, get hold of Khalida, and shake her. "Khalida—"

Khalida cut the connection. She had time, she calculated, before her resignation worked its way through all the relevant channels. She had no expectation that it would be accepted, but it would create a diversion.

Meanwhile she was as free as she could remember being—even on Nevermore. No one could read her here; if she wanted the web, she had to open a channel to access it.

She ran a quick scan. The purge in the port continued. Rinaldi was out of the city and off the grid—which might have concerned her if she had not withdrawn herself from his pleasant little game. He could play it through with Colonel Aviram. She was done.

Khalida requisitioned a fresh set of riot arms and armor, and a rover with orbital capability. She waited for alarms to trigger, but her command codes were still valid. People she passed either ignored her or seemed to find nothing unusual about her.

Once she had the rover and a hundred meters of altitude, she said to the console, "Mem Aurelia."

No response. Khalida had not expected one. She set a hook in the search's tail and left it on the web, and programmed the rover with its own search grid.

She could still run MI-level encrypted searches. That was useful for finding one child with a limited web implant, and a man with none.

Her stomach rumbled. *Now* she was hungry. She found a packet of survival rations under the pilot's cradle.

They tasted like sweetened sawdust. She choked down most of a bar and left the rest for later.

The search pinged. Target found, though the time stamp was a planetday old.

It was better than nothing. She locked on. The rover altered its grid to match.

The web tried to scream at her. Rinaldi, Aviram, MI itself—they all erupted on the other side of her barriers. None of them took control of the rover.

Of course not. They could reel her in at any point. Meanwhile, she could search, and they would watch.

She considered shutting that off, but they would only find other ways to do it. This one went both ways, which might turn out to be useful.

Lieutenant Zhao was not in range. Either he had been lying after all, or he was too far ahead of her to catch.

While the rover tracked a flicker on the worldweb, she tracked something else under multiple layers of encryption. It was brain-straining, exacting work, and she had to do it while seeming to doze and while maintaining a façade of harmless coasting on the web.

The targets did some of the hunting for her. She had the connections: Mem Aurelia; the woman with the wonderful hair, whose name was Marta; the network of corporations that manufactured and distributed the devices that, in aggregate, constituted the worldwrecker.

What she needed, and wanted, was the trigger. The entity or person or mechanism that set off the reaction.

MI had run its own exhaustive searches. What they had missed was the human connection: the two women who had left clues for Khalida to interpret.

They wanted her to stop them.

Or not. This could be revenge: torturing her with hints and cryptic bits of patterns too big for a single mind to hold.

Possibly it was both.

Connection met connection. So: Marta, the null. Mem Aurelia, the non— and the genetic parent of the null. Daughter, mother. Torn apart by the Corps, but maintaining contact in defiance of law and tradition. Finding one another when the conspiracy first began, and finding a common level of—genius? Madness? Plain and visceral rage against the Corps?

It could not be this obvious. If Marta was the trigger, or knew what and where it was, she would hardly have thrown herself in front of Khalida. She must be a blind of sorts. A diversion.

Maybe Khalida was the trigger. She had performed the office once already, for the Corps. Why not use her again, this time for the other side?

The web gave her a gift: a stream of Marta not more than an Earthyear ago, singing Old Earth opera onstage on Centrum itself. The set, the costumes, the grand and stately music, struck Khalida with exquisite irony: she was singing that great pseudo-Egyptian tragedy, *Aïda*.

Her voice was glorious. She had both range and control, and passion that made every note tear at the heart.

It washed over Khalida with the clarity of understanding. An opera company, a troupe of singers, a pattern of engagements and performances that took them all over the United Planets—and everywhere they went, they left minute and highly poisonous fragments of code in each world's web.

They could do more than break Araceli. They could bring down the worldsweb—all at once or world by world.

They had not made that threat. Not yet. Not quite; though Khalida was meant to see.

Aïda loved and lost and died. Marta meant to do all three, but she would take the worlds with her.

That was hate, with all of the singer's passion in it. Khalida collected the data in a report capsule and added her conclusions, but did not send it. Not yet. Not until Aisha was safe offworld, on the *Leda* that had its own web and its battery of formidable protections. Not least of which was its captain.

By MI regulations, Khalida was committing treason. Not to mention insubordination, desertion, and sabotage. She found it difficult to care.

The search string for Aisha broke, then re-formed. She had, for a number of hours, disappeared from the web, but that morning she had reappeared, and begun moving rapidly away from the port.

That was what Khalida had been looking for. It was clear where Aisha was going, and all too easy to guess who was taking her there. Voluntarily, Khalida suspected; which was a bit of a disappointment. Abduction she could have come down on with the full force of military and civilian justice.

That might still be possible. She reset the rover's itinerary once again, toward the Ara Celi.

The tubular passage twisted and convulsed and spat them out into a space that Aisha at first took for a cargo bay. But the clusters of screens and the cradles and hoverchairs drifting across it looked more like a ship's bridge.

People stood or sat around the screens, and others clumped together in a transparent-walled pen or roofless compartment near the far bulkhead. The people working the screens wore Psycorps green or black. The ones in the pen looked like civilians.

Both looked frantic in different ways. The screens showed the scene outside: the fighting had gotten worse, and there were still, crumpled shapes on the ground, and stains and pools that Aisha knew, with a sick knot on her middle, were blood.

The Corps officer with seven pips on the collar did something that Aisha felt in the center of that knot. The ship screamed.

She might have screamed with it. She couldn't have heard herself if she had. But she could see, and not just with eyes.

Rama hadn't seemed to move, but he was beside the psi-seven. The others surged toward him.

He disposed of them with a flick of the hand. The psi-seven gaped at him. The man was big, with broad shoulders and a mane of hair the color of summer grass on Nevermore. He looked as if he could fight as well as read people's minds.

Rama for once looked small. He wanted that, Aisha thought. He smiled up at the psi-seven. "Commander Bowen."

"Who in hell's name are you?"

The smile widened to a grin. How he was doing it, while the ship screamed and screamed, Aisha could hardly imagine. "I am Death, destroyer of worlds."

"You are insane."

"That, too," Rama said. He kicked the man's feet out from under him, as easily as if he'd been half the size, and set his knee in the middle of that broad and helpless back. Then he lifted his head and sang.

It didn't matter what the words were or where the song came from. It was a hymn, Aisha knew down deep, and much older than he was. The language it was sung in had been ancient when he was born.

He was using it to link to the ship. To hack into its song of agony with his hymn of healing and peace.

The ship was alive. The screens wired into its neural network, the controls that slaved it to human will, were torture beyond anything Aisha had ever known of.

Rama couldn't rip the grafted-on mechanicals out. That would destroy the ship, mind and body both. He had to reinstall them instead. Smooth out the connections. Shut down the ones that made nothing but pain and neural disruption.

It was the most delicate surgery in the worlds, and he did it with the ship's captain lying limp and barely conscious under his knee.

She crept across that vast expanse of—what? Stomach? Thoracic cavity? Muscle cyst?—and eased over toward the holding pen. The people in it were all lined up along the wall, staring at what must look to them like a scene from a pirate vid.

"You," one of them said when Aisha came close. "Please. Let us out."

Aisha was half in and half out of virtual reality. She had to think hard before she managed spoken words. "Tell me who you are first."

"Dr. Alice Ma," the woman said. "Principal scientist, experimental ship *Ra-Harakhte.*"

"So you're the ones who slaved the ship," Aisha said. "We heard it screaming clear across the continent."

Dr. Ma stared at her. "You can't be Psycorps. Or can they run renegade, too?"

"We are not Psycorps," Aisha said coldly. "I'm not letting you out. You're no better than they are. In fact I think you're worse."

"Now listen here," said one of the other prisoners. "*I'm* not a scientist. I'm just trying to get to Beijing Nine."

The gaggle of people with him quacked and clacked agreement. "We're travelers," he said. "Tourists, if you want to be insulting. We were rounded up and shoved in here two days ago. If you could get a whiff of the facilities—"

"*Ulrich!*" snapped the woman behind him. "That's not what she needs to hear. Here, Sera, let us out, please. This pen is hardwired to the ship's controls. If your friend there shuts those down, that's our life support gone, too."

"But not mine?" Aisha wanted to know.

"You're breathing ship's atmosphere," the woman said. "We aren't."

Aisha wasn't sure she could believe that, but the expressions on the other side of the barrier were fairly convincing. Those people were afraid. The ones in the blue uniforms with the character for wisdom on the collar were downright terrified.

That decided it. Aisha worked her away down the barrier till she found the dimple in the surface that just fit her hand. Though it looked like glass, it was warm and yielding, like skin. She pressed until it folded and shrank away.

The first one out looked down the muzzle of Aisha's pistol. It was Dr. Ma; she stopped and took a sharp breath, but she didn't shriek or flinch.

She didn't knock Aisha down and sit on her, either. Aisha took a breath of her own and stepped aside.

The rest of them came out in more or less orderly fashion, falling into gaggles once they were out. Scientists, passengers, a handful of people who must be crew.

None of them made a break for it. They could all see the screens and the battle still going on outside. They didn't try to stop Rama, either. Aisha wondered if they could understand what he was doing: if they had any way to see or hear what went on underneath the long chant.

It was doing what he meant it to do. He kept his voice steady, but Aisha could feel the strength draining out of him, note by note and syllable by syllable.

Aisha eased Rama off the psi master and kicked one of the hoverchairs over for him, then unwound the cord that tied her robes at the waist and trussed the man up, ankles to wrists. In case he woke enough to find a way out of that, she knelt on the floor, set her pistol to stun and aimed it right between the man's eyes.

She'd been right: he was awake. His eyes rolled, but he held still. A bolt at that range, he knew probably better than she did, would fry his brain.

Rama's chant never paused. The light in the room—compartment—bridge was changing. Growing brighter. A subtle hum rose out of the walls and floor, like a ship powering up.

Aisha thought she might want to be afraid. But she was too busy making sure Captain Bowen didn't attack Rama.

The chant was winding down. The energies had shifted. All the giving had been coming from Rama. Now it flowed the other way. The ship was feeding him, healing him the way he'd been healing it.

That made Aisha happy in a deep and wordless way. It didn't keep her from trying to watch Rama and the captain and the Corps agents and the ex-prisoners and the screens all at once.

The ship rocked underfoot. The screens went dark. Tubes and wires and cables snapped out of the floor and ceiling, dropping like the dead things they were.

Aisha sucked in a breath. Some of the ex-prisoners had fallen down. One or two had started screaming.

Rama was on his feet. He didn't do anything obvious, but the screens came back on. They started off blurry, but they came into focus, sharper than before.

The ship stopped rocking, but the screaming went on. They were well above the fight now, and rising. Fighters buzzed and darted. One bolt came close enough to white out the screen on that side.

When the screen cleared again, the fighter that had fired the bolt was dropping. Spiraling down as if its engines had gone dead.

Rama spoke calmly, without raising his voice. "This engagement is over. Stand down. Or we will do it for you."

The screens' audio erupted in a torrent of voices. No one was firing, but they were closing in. Trying to surround the ship.

"Very well then," Rama said.

They all went down at once. The voices escalated into a frantic babble.

The ship sang. One long, sustained note that reduced everything else to silence.

"It says," said Rama in that silence, "that it will put you down gently. But you will not ride the air again until you learn sense."

"Stand down."

That voice came from inside the ship. It sounded distinctly strained, but the words were clear. "Stand down," Captain Bowen said again. "That is an order. Abort mission. Stand down!"

"Thank you," Rama said dryly. "Aisha, let him up."

Aisha didn't want to, at all, but she untied him. She kept her pistol up and aimed while he got stiffly to his feet. He towered over her.

Aisha refused to be intimidated. She set her pistol to kill, letting him see her do it, and sighted along her forearm: first up, at the throat, and then down at a much easier and more pointed angle.

He frowned at her. Not that she was threatening his hope of future generations; that didn't seem to bother him at all.

He was trying to read her. Almost too late, Aisha remembered to take refuge in the sun.

"Captain," Dr. Ma said.

Aisha had been to busy to notice that the ex-prisoners had come away from the wall. Dr. Ma stood in front of them, perfectly still, radiating cold fury.

She turned her glare from Captain Bowen to Rama. "And you, Meser. If you could possibly explain—"

"I probably can't," Rama said. "Nor am I especially inclined to try. Did it occur to you that what you were doing was torture? Either of you?"

Dr. Ma drew herself up. "We used only the most humane of methods. Most of them were experimental, and therefore somewhat rough or tentative, but we never intended—"

"The ship is alive," Captain Bowen said, "but hardly sentient. Its pain sensors are rudimentary. The controls were wired to areas that were determined to be free of them. We did our utmost to—"

"You," Rama said to Dr. Ma, cutting across the Captain's words, "may excuse your arrogance with ignorance, but *he*—" His teeth clicked together; he looked ready to spit. "*He* should have known. Every psi in the system could hear the ship's agony."

"Every psi in the system could not," Captain Bowen said, "because there was none. There was a little static when we installed the regulators, but—"

She didn't think he was lying. The other psis, who were sitting on the floor holding their heads and trying not to moan, didn't look likely to contradict him.

"Are you really that weak?" Aisha asked. Then bit her tongue.

Luckily nobody was listening. Rama hissed through his teeth. "You are all idiots. Fools and children. Get off this ship."

"What?" Captain Bowen said. "You have no authority—"

"I have the ship," Rama said with terrifying sweetness. "You have shuttles. Take them."

"I will not—"

"I have very little patience," Rama said, "and a very big ship."

The floor rolled under them all. Rama's smile was wide and bright.

Aisha watched Captain Bowen decide to get out now and deal with Rama later. He might have the ship—if he could actually control it, which the Captain doubted—but Captain Bowen had fifty thousand trained psis to call on.

Fools and children, Rama would call those. He kept his smile while the Corps agents picked each other up and made as dignified an exit as they could manage.

That left the ex-prisoners, clumping together and eyeing possible exits. All but Dr. Ma. "I may be an idiot," she said, "but I am not leaving this ship. My life's work is here."

"Your work is done," Rama said. "Your slave is freed. You have nothing left to do here."

"But I do," she said. "If you are telling the truth, this ship is far more than we ever imagined. If you can control it by other than mechanical means—if you have insights into it that we lacked the skills or knowledge to imagine—"

"Or else he's lying." Aisha recognized the tourist who had spoken earlier. He was modified and dressed and accessorized to look like an Old Earth adventurer from a particularly dire era, but his eyes didn't look as if they missed much.

"I don't think he is," one of the others said. He was a scientist, according to his uniform: a middle-sized man, round-faced and innocuous to look at, but the glance he darted at Rama was wickedly intelligent. "Meser Rama. You're all over the worldweb today. Grand theft transport, wanton destruction of historical relics, grand theft again—that's impressive."

"I suppose I should be impressed by your access to the feeds restricted to government and law enforcement," Rama said. "Tell me why I should let any of you stay. The ship is leaving as soon as it may. I doubt it will be amenable to serving as your personal transport."

"This is my work," Dr. Ma repeated. "Wherever it goes."

Most of her colleagues nodded—stiffly, and their eyes looked frankly scared, but they seemed to have made up their minds. The crew mostly did the same, and that surprised Aisha.

The man named Ulrich took off his antique helmet and wiped his forehead with an enormous handkerchief. "Really, we're just passing through. If you'll put us in the way of a transport to Beijing Nine, we'll be most obliged."

"Or anywhere else civilized and not at war," said the woman with him. Her costume was less elaborate than his, but equally ancient. Aisha especially admired the furled lace parasol with the sharp and gleaming point. "You can make it a ransom demand if you like, when PlanSec comes down on you, which I estimate it will any moment now. Get us transport, get rid of us, then go wherever you're minded to go."

"Isabel," Ulrich said, "I really don't think it's wise to—"

"It's extremely wise," said Rama. "There's a shuttle in the bay that, I'm assured, will hold all of you. Take it and go."

"We'll need a pilot," Isabel said, "and clearance. Not to mention—"

"The shuttle will take you to the port," Rama said. "You, Professor— Robrecht, is it? You know the way. Direct them, please."

The round-faced man in blue smiled. He was having a grand time, and he wasn't trying to hide it. "This way, sers and seras."

Some of them actually ran behind him as he strode across the bay. One didn't: Isabel, eyeing Rama narrowly. "You know where we want to go. What about you? Or don't you know?"

"I come from the far side of time," he answered, "and I go to the far ends of the worlds. The ship knows."

She didn't tell him he was insane. Oddly, Aisha didn't think she thought it, either. "Good luck to you, then," she said.

He bowed his head like the king he'd been, a very long time ago. "And to you," he said.

S he'll put you in a book," Aisha said when the tourists and the odd few of
the crew were gone. "The web's in and out—mostly out—but she's famous
enough to come through. She writes books about adventures. Vids, too."

"Pirate vids?" Rama asked.

"Probably." Aisha started to say more, but Rama was starting to sway on his
feet.

If he passed out now, he might not lose his connection with the ship, but the
people still on it might decide to take him hostage.

That was a problem. Pirate kings had mobs of henchmen for a reason. If
they needed to sleep, or pass out, there was always someone to man the tiller.

Someone who knew how to sail the ship. Aisha could feel the connection in
her bones, but the ship wasn't talking to her the way it did to Rama. She didn't
want it to, either. Those same bones knew they'd shake apart if it did.

She had to try to talk to it. Not aloud, where people could hear. She shaped
the thoughts as clearly as she could.

Ship. He needs to rest, but we can't trust the humans here. Or the ones
outside, either. There's no telling when he'll be able to stop. Can you help?

The ship didn't answer that she could tell, but Rama stopped swaying. He
took a deep breath and stood a little straighter.

"You have quarters," he said to Dr. Ma and the others. "I suggest you rest in them."

"Not until we know what we'll find when we wake," Dr. Ma said.

"Sir," one of the crew said before Rama could erupt. He was a big man who looked as if he'd spent a good part of his life outside on rough planets, but his expression was calm and his tone was mild. "It's not just curiosity. You need a crew. If not to fly the ship, then to monitor the screens and, if it comes to that, repel boarders."

"And I should trust you why?" Rama inquired.

"Because if we can't be trusted," the man answered, "we all die."

Rama's brows went up. "Your name, sir?"

"Kirkov," the man said. "Supply officer. Second in Communications. Ship's cook." He paused. "You do eat, sir?"

"Occasionally," Rama said. "May I encourage you to perform that office?"

"Of course," Kirkov said. "So you'll trust me. That's good. Now the rest of them, they're not going to turn on you, either, as long as you're fair and as honest as you can stand to be. Robrecht who's off getting rid of tourists served a term in Military Intelligence before he went sane and became a professor instead. Rinzen over there was our security officer, and pulled duty with Engineering when there was anything to engineer. Abikanile doesn't say where she came from originally, but she can fix anything that's fixable and most things that aren't. As for Soonmi—"

"Soonmi can speak for herself," said that individual, "and she wants you to know that she is insulted by your lack of trust. We may be trapped here by a war and a hijacking, but we are devoted to the cause of staying alive. We will do whatever it takes to get you, and us, and this ship, away from this planet and safe into space where we belong."

Rama scanned all their faces, the ones that now had names attached and the ones that, Aisha was perfectly sure, he would have names for before the day was over. He was doing it for effect, mostly. She could tell. He'd made his mind up while Kirkov was still speaking.

"Very well," he said finally. "I am going where I have to go. The ship agrees to go with me, because I ended its long pain, and because it believes it knows the way. It's very far and may be very long. I ask none of you to follow me; I will ask you more than once to be wise and leave. But until we escape this world and this system, I accept your service."

"None of us said anything about—" Dr. Ma began.

"Doctor," Kirkov said surprisingly gently, "in your way, you did. Besides, you owe the ship, after what you did to it. Don't you think it's the least you can do?"

Her lips were tight and her eyes were angry, but she spread her hands. "Call it what you like. This is my ship. I will not leave it."

"To your quarters, then," Rama said. "You will know if you are needed."

Oh, that was sharp. Dr. Ma thought so, too: Aisha suspected she might have done her best to kill him if she'd had a weapon within reach.

She turned on her heel instead and stalked out, followed by the rest of the scientists. The crew were already getting to work, figuring out the new configurations of the controls and the screens, or heading off to their stations elsewhere on the ship.

The war hadn't stopped because they weren't paying attention to it. Underneath the ship, according to the screens, the civilians who had been fighting on foot had managed to escape, and take their dead and wounded with them. The Corps had taken to the air.

The ship opened a channel to the web when Aisha asked. It had the buzz in the back teeth that said it was encrypted, but she didn't mind that at all.

None of the public traffic had anything to say about a hijacked experimental ship or a battle between Psycorps and a hundred or so civilians. The security channels were full of buzz and crackle about the war—and an ultimatum. The non-psis had set a deadline. Either they got what they wanted, or they broke the planet.

There weren't even two planetdays left. As far as Aisha could see, and she ran so many searches she made herself dizzy, nobody in the Corps was talking about surrender. They were chasing pirates offworld instead, and rounding up nons under cover of safety patrols, and tracking down and neutralizing what they called nulls.

It was more complicated than Aisha could keep straight in her head. She gave it to the ship, for what good that would do, in time to hear Robrecht say over the conn, "Shuttle's loaded and secured. Are we sure we want to let it go?"

Everyone in the bay turned to stare at Rama. He spoke the way he would to any of them, but the person he was talking to was halfway back to the port by now.

"Captain Bowen. We're releasing a shuttleful of noncombatants. May we ask that you vouch for their safety?"

One of the screens that had been dark came alive with a crackle and sputter. Aisha looked through it into the pilot's compartment of a fighter, and Captain Bowen's startled face. "What in the name of—"

"Captain," Rama said. "You heard me. Will you place them under your protection?"

He'd sent a manifest underneath his words, a list of people who were on the shuttle. Captain Bowen scowled at some of the names on it. "I'll vouch for them," he said grudgingly.

"Good, then," Rama said. "What is it your people say, Captain? Godspeed."

Captain Bowen was obviously not amused, but whatever he'd been about to say, the ship—or Rama—cut off. The screen went dark.

"Robrecht," Rama said, still in that calm and casual voice, "let them go."

"Aye, sir," Robrecht said on the comm.

The shuttle showed up on one of the side screens, emerging from a bay that Aisha didn't remember seeing in the ship before she came inside. It dropped fast, then leveled out, turning in a wide arc until it aimed toward the port.

"Now," said Rama, "we go. We'll jump as soon as we clear this planet's gravity well. If you have cradles, I suggest you find them now."

Aisha's heart thudded. He and she didn't even have quarters, let alone jump cradles. Maybe for him it wouldn't matter, but for her it did.

She started to remind him of that, but before she could get the words out, the ship lurched. Screens flashed to life all over the bridge—she hadn't known there were that many.

Black-winged fighters swarmed them on all sides. Something much bigger hovered above.

Command vessel. Military Intelligence, the web told Aisha, with Psycorps agents on board in force. Which told her which side of the war MI was really on.

She looked for some sign of Aunt Khalida, but she didn't recognize any of the names on the ship's manifest. The commanding officer's name was Aviram. What little she had time to catch about who he was didn't reassure her at all.

A voice crackled across the comm. "Command vessel *Shad Iliya* to *Ra-Harakhte*. Stand by for boarding. Stand by."

"I think not," Rama said.

"You are surrounded. We are armed. You are not. Stand by for boarding."

"No," said Rama. "Aisha. Lie down."

The words didn't make sense at first. Or after a minute or two, either. "What—"

"Lie down," he said. "Now."

Aisha obeyed slowly. It wasn't her imagination: the floor was curving up to meet her. Taking the shape of a jump cradle.

All that kept Aisha from running screaming was the fact that there was nowhere to run to. No way she was heading for the Corps.

The floor was warm, not too soft and not too hard. The cradle that grew around her looked like an ordinary one, but didn't smell like it. This smelled green, with an undertone of fresh dirt.

The only way to deal with it was to shut off the part of her that kept trying to make sense of it all, and just let it happen.

"*Ra-Harakhte,*" the *Shad Iliya* said. "On our signal, open aft port. We would prefer not to open it for you."

"I would prefer not to obliterate you," Rama said pleasantly. "Out of my way, if you please."

"Stand by," the MI ship repeated.

"No," Rama said.

That was all he said aloud. Aisha could feel the flow of communication that ran underneath, too deep and complex for words. He asked, and the ship answered.

The answer was a song, deeper than deep. The cradle had almost completely closed around Aisha now, but when she pushed at the lid, it let her keep it open.

The rest of the crew that she could see were in cradles, too, or cysts or whatever they were. All but Rama. The ship had given him a chair to sit in, but he was out in the open, eyes on the screens.

The swarm of fighters was almost on them. One of the screens streamed a warning: *Weapons aimed and locked. Ready to fire.*

"Now," Rama said.

39

The Ara Celi was gone. The maps showed it ahead of Khalida, but on the rover's screen was nothing but empty sky.

It reminded her with surprising vividness of the broken cliff on Nevermore. A finger of granite stood up still. The rest was rubble.

She had been staying off the web, partly to avoid the inevitable screaming and the orders to return to her post, and partly to preserve what sanity she had left. She held her breath as she opened the connection.

Even tightly filtered, it was a deluge. MI was losing its collective mind. Psycorps had received the ultimatum from their slave classes, with uprisings in all the cities. And a rogue army was in the process of hijacking a most peculiar ship.

Ships were still leaving Araceli—loading and running. No one pursued them, or did more than record their essential data. This must be something special, to rate its own priority-level feed.

Science vessel. Experimental ship. Psycorps had it under deep cover—no wonder; they had hijacked it from an expedition out of Beijing Nine. The political implications of that were interesting to say the least.

None of which could possibly matter to Khalida, except that her search string placed Aisha inside the ship. That had to be a scanner error: she must be near or above it.

Khalida was trained to speculate at endless length based on negligible data. She shut that off as best she could. She had one mission: to get Aisha out of there and ship her offworld.

That was not going to be easy. MI had a new set of marching orders from Psycorps: Converge on the ship and secure it. Eliminate any opposition.

The rover qualified as MI, as did Khalida while her resignation continued to be ignored. She set a course toward the shadow spaceport.

While the rover did its own piloting, she hunted down information. If Rama wanted a starship, there were several hundred less heavily protected vessels in this hemisphere alone, and a good few thousand in orbit or close in in the system. Many of which would be delighted to take on a wealthy passenger with a lucrative obsession.

But he had sought out this one, or so she inferred from Aisha's presence near it.

Maybe it was the name that lured him. *Ra-Harakhte*: a fine old Egyptian divinity. There was no manufacturer listed, officially or unofficially.

Nor would there be. The ship had been discovered by a deep-space mission, a coalition of astrophysicists and xenoarchaeologists, searching for remnants of a theoretical but as yet unproved species of interstellar explorers. It had been drifting in a stellar nursery, where it had apparently been feeding on infant stars, until for reasons unknown to the discoverers, it had, essentially, beached itself.

The mission found it by crashing into it, and so damaging their ship that they had no choice but to improvise. They had cannibalized their own ship, slaved the foundling to it, and made their way back to civilized space.

Nowhere in the datastream did anyone remark on the fact that, as far as anyone could determine, the ship was a living thing. The expedition's report declared that it had a rudimentary nervous system, a large but remarkably efficient digestive system that processed and recycled interstellar gas and gorged on the leavings of newborn stars—and functioned, in ways not yet understood, as a powerful and almost inconceivably fast subspace drive—and no discernible brain or functioning intelligence.

Hence, Psycorps. The deeply classified report, signed and cosigned by a gaggle of Sevens and a pair of Nines—including one all too familiar name—maintained at length and in highly technical detail that the living creature commissioned as a ship and named the *Ra-Harakhte* was devoid of sentience.

On which grounds, a new order had come down from the heights of both MI and Psycorps. A joint expedition was to be mounted, to hunt and capture creatures of this new and wonderfully useful species. The hunt would begin in the cradles of stars, but would proceed in subspace as well, under the direction of a psi-ten.

Ten?

Khalida's hunger for data devoured that snippet. Before it could dive for more, the stream broke in a shower of pixels. They stung like shrapnel in the blast of a warning klaxon.

ALL PERSONNEL! ALL PERSONNEL IN THIS AREA! PIRACY IN PROGRESS! ARM AND LAUNCH! ARM AND LAUNCH!

The command code on it made Khalida hiss with a crazy mix of anger and laughter. Colonel Aviram, at least, had wasted no time. He was in command, and these orders superseded any and all that she might have given.

"We'll see about that," she said.

But first, she patched in to the commander's feed. The fighting that she had observed on the ground was more or less bog-standard civil war. This was something else.

The ship had risen out of its well. Fighters completely surrounded it. They looked, in this feed, like a sphere of glistening insects enclosing a large and subtly shimmering shape.

The sphere was not, she realized, intentional on the fighters' part. The ship was generating it.

Colonel Aviram's own ship hovered above it all. It was smaller than the *Leda*, designed for planetary atmosphere and solar-system runs but not, rather to her surprise, deep space.

Someone had not been thinking. Or had been caught flat-footed between a conventional haves-and-have-nots civil war and an act of pirate bravura.

Khalida in her little rover without even near-space capability could relate to that. She did not need to scan the feed to know who the pirate was. Of course Rama could not hire a ship like a sensible citizen. He had to go for the one that would cause the maximum disturbance. In the middle of a war.

She doubted he cared about that, and she would hardly have cared about him except to wish him luck. But Aisha was on that ship.

She started to patch through to the *Ra-Harakhte*, but paused. Panic gave way to cold clear logic.

She and Aisha both were safer if she stayed out of it. Rama would protect the child. He might not promise anything else, but that she was absolutely sure of.

On the screen in front of her, the sphere of fighters collapsed abruptly. The *Ra-Harakhte* was gone.

Khalida was well beyond surprise. She threw up a new link, and that one she let go through. "*Leda.* I need that shuttle now."

She did not wait for an answer. The rover had its return route to the port mapped and locked in. "Execute," she said.

"Don't."

Mem Aurelia sat in the copilot's cradle. Her edges shimmered faintly. "Not the port," she said. "They'll impound this rover before it lands. Send it here."

The map she raised on the screen marked a site so familiar Khalida spat a curse. "I have no time for your games and petty revenge. Get out of my cockpit."

"Maybe it is a game," Mem Aurelia's holo said, "but we play it in earnest. No one will be looking for a shuttle to land in the ruins of Ostia. Do you want to get offworld in one piece or find yourself in a Psycorps detention chamber?"

"I want—" Khalida bit her tongue. "Get out."

Mem Aurelia melted away into the reconstituted air. Her map persisted on the screen. With no joy at all, Khalida reset the rover's course.

She had divided perfectly down the middle, as the rover carried her through day into night. Half of her was grimly calm, prepared for whatever would come. Planning; strategizing. Focusing on the mission.

The other half, all the way down deep, was living that day again and again. Fire coming down. Ash falling like filthy snow. People running. Screaming.

Max and Sonja. Kinuko and John Begay.

When she first knew what she had done, she had had a ritual. She ran the names of all the dead, every one, from beginning to end. She had stopped after she came to Nevermore. She called up the files again now, and ran them in order, as she flew into the fire. It burned her all away, body and mind, grief and guilt and sheer white rage, and cast the ashes on the wind.

The rover's night vision gave her the wasteland she expected: a city blasted to slag, rivers vaporized, a barren crater full of rubble and ash. But its edges were blunted. The planet had already begun to reclaim it. Trees and ferns and grasses grew in a twisted jungle over the ruins.

Radiation scans returned readings that penetrated even her fire-dulled intelligence. They were barely above planetary normal.

That was not possible. The best scrubbers in existence took Earthyears to clear out the detritus of a dirty bomb. Khalida knew exactly what she had hit this city with, and as far as the scanner could tell, though badly scorched and blasted, it was almost completely clean.

"Nobody noticed?" Khalida asked the screen.

It answered with an overlay: no vegetation, naked earth and melted rock, and radiation readings exactly as they should have been.

"Why?"

The rover slowed and angled downward. Half instinctively she hit the cradle's settings, amping them up to crash strength.

Stupid. She could almost hear the nulls laughing at her. They brought the rover in as softly as a fleck of ash falling, and laid it to rest on an undamaged pad in an intact and obviously functioning transport hub.

"You have all this," Khalida said. "Why bother with an ultimatum? Just go undercover and disappear. You can hack the galaxy. Go anywhere you like. Rescue your children—"

Mem Aurelia was physically present on the rover. She had not asked permission to board, and two silent and cold-eyed people kept Khalida from leaving. They were perfectly polite, but the message was clear. Khalida was their involuntary guest.

She had had about enough of that, but training held. She would pretend to cooperate, and acquire what data she could.

Antagonizing her host was not exactly the best strategy. She bit her tongue and swallowed the rest of what she had been going to say.

"We have talents," Mem Aurelia said, "and skills that are remarkable in the scheme of things. What we don't have is power. Political, economic—"

Khalida swept her hand around the rover and by extension the whole of the hub. "This isn't power?"

"This is stolen, smuggled, clandestine, and so far, unique. It ate most of our resources. We've barely been able to use it, and we haven't managed to acquire ships of our own. That one you want to try to chase was our best hope, but we lost it to a bolder pirate than any of us."

"You want me to catch it for you," Khalida said. "In return for what?"

"The trigger," Mem Aurelia answered.

Khalida's teeth clicked together. "The ship is that valuable?"

"It will hold as many of our children as we've been able to find and hope to set free. We believe it's like them: a kind of null, with capabilities that the Corps can't begin to comprehend. If they can be got to safety, and hidden from the Corps, even the end of this world will have been worth the price."

"Suppose that happens. Suppose you get the thing back, and load up your children. Do you plan to stop breeding altogether? There will be more children, and the Corps will keep taking them away. What good will it really do?"

"Whatever the Corps wants with our nulls, we'll take those away. They'll need years to build the program again—and we'll be spending every moment of that time finding ways to stop them."

"That presumes you're alive and capable of higher cognitive functions. What's to prevent them from shredding your minds and locking your bodies in breeding sheds?"

"They'll never catch us all," said Mem Aurelia. "And our children will be free."

"You know I can't help you," Khalida said. "The man who took that ship has no interest whatsoever in this planet's troubles. He certainly will not agree to turn it into an interstellar orphanage."

"Do this and you get the trigger," said Mem Aurelia. "Araceli survives. You won't add another hundred million souls to your account."

That was a blow to the gut. Khalida had to stop and remember how to breathe. "Even if I would or could agree, how do you expect me to get it all done in less than a planetday?"

"I'm sure you'll manage," Mem Aurelia said.

"May the nonexistent gods save us from people with a cause."

Khalida spat the words to empty air. Mem Aurelia and the guards were gone. She was free to leave the rover and meet the shuttle as it came down.

The shuttle was Spaceforce. Letting it know of this place made no sense, or else the Ostians had plans within the plans within their plans. Khalida could hardly tell any longer.

She slung her kit over her shoulder, shoved in a handful of waterbulbs and the rest of the ration bars, and left the rover for, she hoped, the last time.

The *Helen* was a little more than a shuttle. It was a fighting ship in its own right, sleek and fast. The detachment of marines that crewed it included a familiar face or two, but no manacles for Khalida, this time.

Its commander was a message, and one that made Khalida almost want to be happy. The *Leda*'s XO should have been well above running pickup service for stray MI officers, but she grinned as Khalida came onto the bridge. "You ready?"

"Commander Ochoa," Khalida said. "I'm honored."

"*De nada*," Commander Ochoa said. "I was bored, and here's a war to fly in and out of. Now they tell me we're hunting a pirate ship?"

"Better than that," Khalida said. "A living ship. Which managed to jump into subspace in the middle of a full-on fighter attack, from a hundred meters above the surface."

"Better and better," Commander Ochoa said. "Not just an adventure, but an impossible one. Now tell me the fighters belonged to the Corps and I'll be a happy woman."

"Some of them did," Khalida said.

"I'll take it," said Commander Ochoa. "Here, patch in to ship's systems. Do you have a course to lay in?"

Khalida started to say she had no faintest idea, except to get offworld fast. But she did. It was still there: the tracer she had put on Aisha.

There were no miracles. There was technology that worked, and a ship that had to have come out of subspace in time for Khalida to catch the link.

It could jump again of course, but it was still in the system. Very close—orbiting one of Araceli's triad of moons.

Impossible. No ship could jump from a planet to a moon. The interplay of gravities, the complication of solar flares, the risk of damage or collision—

Nothing about this ship was possible. Or its de facto captain, either.

She filed the coordinates. *Helen's* system returned a complex and circuitous course: restricted areas, banned areas, war zones, high-traffic clusters, evacuation zones. Even without the worldwrecker, Araceli was coming apart at the seams.

If she won this gamble, the planet would stay in one piece, at least—whatever happened to the people on it.

The cradle beside the commander's post was empty and waiting for her. So were they all. Even while the straps secured themselves around her, the *Helen* launched herself toward the stratosphere.

"Captain Nasir?"

Khalida had fallen into a doze. Even less than half out of it, she knew the speaker could not be on the *Helen*.

"Captain Nasir," he said again, while the stream beneath the words marked his location and identity. *Zhao, Lieutenant. Psi-Three. Coordinates—* "Request permission to board."

"I'm not the one to ask," Khalida said.

"Actually," he said, "you are." He shot her a spurt: Commander Ochoa spitting at his Corps ID and tossing it off toward the MI officer.

Khalida aimed a glare at Commander Ochoa, who was happily preoccupied with flying her ship through its twister of a course. Zhao was alone, as far as she could determine, and rapidly running out of air.

Any vestige of intelligence would have let him drop away. He was Psycorps: the last thing any of them needed, least of all either Aisha or the walking atavism who had effectively abducted her.

She snarled in frustration and no little self-disgust. "All right. Come aboard. You're not a guest, do you understand? You aren't a prisoner, either, but you damned well will be if I catch you slipping data to your superiors."

"I won't do that," he said. "You have my word."

It might have been her imagination, but he sounded breathless. His shuttle was a maximum altitude and straining to stay there, but he was already outside it, suited and with jets engaged.

Trusting of him. Or suicidal.

Helen's rear hatch opened to take him in. Khalida was halfway there, escalating to a long lope as she hit the half-gravity of the stowage bay.

Lieutenant Zhao out of his suit looked almost wild, and distinctly hollow-eyed.

"Why?" Khalida asked him—calmly, she thought, but he shied like a startled horse.

He answered steadily enough, even so. "I took responsibility for the child."

"I absolve you," Khalida said. "We'll have to keep you until we're done with this; then we'll drop you off at the nearest Corps installation. You will stay out of the way and you will not communicate with the Corps. Do you understand?"

"I understand that you trust me," he said, "and that you have no idea why. Except that you can."

"My head hurts," Khalida said.

He did not laugh at her, which was merciful of him. She turned her back on him and led him up to the bridge.

PART FOUR

RA-HARAKHTE

40

Something about the way the living ship jumped was different. Aside, of course, from the fact that it could jump straight off a planet and end up next to a mini-moon of that same planet.

Which turned out to be more of a space station than a simple moon. System maps didn't say so, either. They just labeled it *Morta* and listed its size, mass, orbital period, and all the rest of the ordinary data.

Everything was different in this universe Aisha had dropped herself into. She wasn't sick the way she usually was during and right after jump, but she wasn't right, either. She kept feeling as if she'd left her skin off.

Rama had been keeping her inside herself since Nevermore. Taking over the ship had pushed him so hard there was nothing left for anything else. Including Aisha.

He was hanging on. He couldn't sleep, but the ship took care of that for him, for now.

She could feel it doing it. She could feel the people on the ship, too, like sparks popping against the inside of her skull, some stronger, some weaker, and some barely there at all.

She had to focus. The near side of this moon had Corps markers all over it, but they were blurred and broken. The far side made her think of the port down below. There were even some of the same people.

Everyone seemed to be screaming at the ship. No one was firing on it, or trying to, which was an improvement.

"Why are we here?" she asked Rama. "I thought we were headed for deep space."

"We were." He sat back in the chair the ship had made for him. Aisha felt it give him another shot of whatever was keeping him awake and able to function. "Ship says we have to stop here. Fueling, it says."

"Why? If it eats star-stuff, what's here?"

"Star-stuff."

Of course it was. Hydrogen and helium were everywhere. Denser in interstellar gas clouds, and densest where stars were being born, but every system had its share. "It's not going to eat the moon, is it?"

"Not if the moon leaves it alone."

"I don't think that's going to happen."

His lips stretched. It wasn't a smile. "I don't, either. Tell me: would you rather I start a war or end one?"

"You have to ask that?"

"*I* would rather do neither. This is none of my world or my people or my concern. But it keeps getting in my way."

While they talked, Aisha had been feeling the people on the bridge: scientists at screens and running data, crew backing them up. They were listening, and they were not happy. Some because they thought him impossibly arrogant. Others because they'd started to understand what he was.

One of them was a complete blank. She was crew. Her name, Aisha gathered from ship's web, was MariAntonia. She'd been part of the original expedition, but past that, her history was as blank as she was. There was an overlay of backstory, which evaporated when Aisha leaned on it. Then nothing.

Except for one thing. She was born on Araceli. There was a smell of the Corps around her, but she wasn't Corps. At all. Even in the blankness that made Aisha's skin itch, that was impossible to mistake.

Aisha moved before MariAntonia did. So did the ship—throwing up a loop that caught MariAntonia securely.

She didn't seem terribly perturbed. "Sir," she said, "you do have a debt to pay."

"By winning your war for you?"

Rama didn't sound angry. He didn't sound sympathetic, either.

"We'll do our own fighting," she said, "but we need something from you."

"I'm not giving you this ship," he said.

"That's not what we're asking."

"I have very little patience," he said, "and none to spare for games of taunt and parry."

"Our apologies," she said. "Two shuttles are coming in. Will you allow them both on board?"

"I have a choice?"

"You can refuse," she said. "The planet will die. You'll go on. Your debt will never be paid. You'll have the whole of U.P. after you no matter what you do. I don't suppose that matters to you, either."

"This is what you call persuasion?"

"Is it working?"

He spread his hands. "The ship isn't going anywhere until it's fed. If it lets the shuttles in, so be it."

"She's talking to somebody by shielded link," Aisha said after the ship had made sure MariAntonia went to her quarters and stayed there. "I can't hack it at all. Can you?"

"I'm not trying." Rama pushed himself up out of the chair. "This is all part of the game they play on this world. They would like to make it bigger—to play it everywhere your people are. They think they can use this ship to make it happen."

He had to know they could hear, if they had a hack in the ship's kludge of a system. He was disgusted, and tired, and pushed to the edge.

Nobody here had the faintest idea how dangerous he was.

At least he was talking. Aisha had to hope that meant he'd listen. Whether it would stop him from blasting them all when he'd finally had enough, she didn't know. All she could do was hope.

Both shuttles came in at once. The one from Spaceforce, with *Leda*'s ID attached, and the one from Araceli with its interestingly complicated set of authorizations. Rama was waiting when they got there, which meant Aisha was there, too, along with most of the crew and a handful of scientists.

Those were studying Rama. He ignored them.

The *Leda's* shuttle had Aunt Khalida in it, and to Aisha's deep dismay, Lieutenant Zhao. The other one, the one that she'd thought belonged to pirates, took its time opening. Then Marta stepped out: the lady from the bar, with her hair braided and caught in a net.

"Well," Rama said to them all with the first hint of humor he'd shown since he set out for the Ara Celi, "and welcome."

"And in good time, too," Marta said with serenity she must practice in front of a mirror. "You know why I've come, I think."

"Suppose I don't," he said.

"We all play games," she said. "Even you. Ask Captain Nasir why she is here."

"I've come for my niece," Aunt Khalida said. She sounded stiff and cold, which meant she was either crying or screaming inside.

"Is that all?" Marta inquired.

Screaming, Aisha thought. Definitely. Though not at Aisha. Yet.

"*You* tell him," Khalida said, biting off each word. "You're the backup, after all. The failsafe."

"The trigger," Marta said.

Khalida rocked back. She couldn't be that shocked, could she?

Maybe she'd had as much to bear as Rama had, in her way. "A line of code? That's what you are? It doesn't make sense."

"We are all made of code," Marta said. "Mine, in combination with certain implants, has an actual, and particular, use."

"You can't be the only one in existence. You can't—"

"Limited resources," Marta said with a graceful lift of the shoulder and turn of the hand.

Khalida met it with deliberate gracelessness. "I don't believe you."

"When you're done sparring," Rama said much too amiably, "do let us know what the match is in aid of. Meanwhile, I believe I'll take the opportunity to rest. I can't remember the last time I did that."

That stopped them both cold.

"I come to claim my debt," Marta said, at the same time Khalida said, "They want you to get their children out of here."

It was like a chorus. Aisha had no trouble telling the voices apart. Neither did Rama.

"Debt I understand," he said. "Pray explain the rest."

Marta was not about to, which left it to Khalida. She wasn't happy about it, either. "They've liberated a shipload of children from the Corps. They want you to get them away from here, and keep them away. The Corps will probably come down on you with the proverbial fire and sword, but Araceli won't blow. Or so they say. I don't know what, or whom, I believe any more."

"They would entrust their children to me?" Rama looked even wilder than usual.

"I don't understand it, either," Khalida said. "But I can't budge them. You open an orphanage, the planet survives. I told them you wouldn't do it."

"Not an orphanage," Marta said. "They're in stasis. We only ask that you take them out of the Corps' reach, and keep them safe until they come there."

"Why? Why trust me?"

"Instinct."

That was not a rational answer. From the expression on Rama's face, it made actual sense to him. "Supposing I would agree to this, where is this safe place you speak of? How far and how long have I to go?"

"As far and long as you choose," Marta answered. "Just get them away from the Corps."

"Which, as the Captain reminds us, will simply lock on and follow."

"I doubt that," Marta said.

"Bargain for bargain," he said. "You come with them. You bring your powers of darkness, all your shields and your defenses. You protect them. I transport them. Otherwise, no. I will not."

"Debt for debt," she said. "I accept."

"One more thing," Khalida said. "The code. You've got what you wanted. Now hand it over."

"I told you," said Marta. "I am the code. I'm going wherever this ship takes me. Araceli lives."

"Unless you come back," Khalida said. "Or another trigger happens to have been made. Or born."

"Both," Marta said. "Does it matter?"

Khalida's eyes narrowed. Her mouth was a thin line. Aisha could feel her thinking, through the static and the blankness and the craziness in this place. Clicking over data. Reckoning up accounts. Calculating options.

Not trusting Marta even slightly. She was playing a bigger game than this one planet, and offering a greater threat to the whole of U.P. Turning her loose might kill far more than a hundred million people. But there was no way to be sure of that.

Kill Araceli for certain. Risk killing who knew how many other planets. Back and forth. Weighing. Measuring. Deciding.

Taking the bargain in front of her. Leaving the rest to whatever gods might exist.

Her mind was a beautiful thing, even with all its broken bits and its jagged edges. Beautiful and terrible. Aisha remembered to get out before she got caught.

She felt eyes on her. Lieutenant Zhao had managed to disappear while the others talked. Watching. Listening.

Thinking. And seeing.

She threw up the old familiar wall. It was too late; she knew that. She still did it.

She hoped she'd given him a mother of a headache.

The ship made a bay for the stasis pods that Marta had brought in her shuttle. There were six hundred of them, and a bit more; they weren't all baby-small, but only a few were big enough to hold a grown person.

They were sad and hopeful at the same time. All those children who might never grow up, but at least they were free.

Ship's web told Aisha what they'd come from. Slaves, in a way. Tools for the Corps to use. Living shields. Enough of them in one place would make it invisible to anyone with psi.

Even in stasis, they were enough to do the same for the ship. That was a gift. Aisha was sure it was intentional.

The ship was taking a long time to feed, and it wouldn't be hurried. People, even crew, straggled off to bunks and berths. Rama was one of the few who stayed awake and on the bridge.

Aisha stayed close by him. She mostly stayed awake. She kept thinking she was dreaming, that the living ship and the planetary war and the ancient king were all in her imagination. Then she snapped awake, and it was as real as the kink in her neck.

A whole lot of people were trying to hail the ship. They couldn't find it, but the ship's communications systems picked up the signals. The Corps and MI and half the Spaceforce ships in the system were melting down.

The only thing that wasn't was Araceli. The worldwrecker was still there—she could trace the millions of devices that made up its parts—but the trigger was off.

"Aren't you afraid the Corps will kill all your people?" Aisha asked Marta. "Or worse?"

Marta had made herself a station near one end of the bridge, set up a cradle and a screen and gone to work on Aisha couldn't quite see what. It wasn't harmful was all she could tell. It looked as if she was studying an opera score.

She glanced up from it when Aisha spoke. Aisha was still in the black robes, but she hadn't had the veil on in a while. She put up with Marta searching her face, though what there was to see, she couldn't think. Marking points for ID, maybe.

"The Corps will do nothing," Marta said. "We've scrambled their web systems from here to Outer Pradesh. They'll be planetyears sorting it out."

"Wonderful," Aisha said. "You've made them mad. They'll hunt you to the ends of the universe, just on general principle."

"I'm sure they will. They'll have to find us first. And that needs the systems we've worked hardest to scramble."

"All they need is hostages, and you've left them a planet full."

Marta turned to face her. "This planet is full of farmers, artisans, builders, engineers. Infrastructure, Sera Nasir. Their lovely country houses, their endless supply of foodstuffs, the roads they travel and the machines they depend on and the web they use for communications because mind to mind takes an excess of energy and requires a plethora of shields—take away the people who make all these things happen, and what's left? A nest of parasites without a host."

"I don't think it's going to be that easy," Aisha said.

"Nothing ever is." Marta turned back to her screen. It was opera: she had the music set to a tight feed, but Aisha caught the edge of it. Grand, roaring stuff. She would have listened if she'd had time, but the twisting in her stomach told her the not-easy was about to get a lot harder.

Rama went down so slowly Aisha didn't realize what was happening until the ship lurched.

He was sitting upright as he had been for hours. His hands were on his knees. His eyes were open.

Empty.

He was in there somewhere. Deep down, curled up tight, sleeping deep.

The ship rocked again, less sharply. It was almost done feeding, and starting to feel another hunger, to be moving—sailing—swimming through infinite space.

Without Rama to keep it focused, it didn't care about the swarm of microbes running up and down its insides. It was starting a long roll, powering up for another subspace leap. A bigger one this time. All the way out of the system.

That was what they wanted. Wasn't it?

"*Stop!*" Aisha shouted—screeched, really. "Ship, stop now. Wait."

There was no reason for it to listen. It had a bond with Rama, which he had earned. She had nothing but desperation.

She pushed at it till her head ached. It had stopped rolling, which was good, she hoped. It still wanted to dive deep.

Somebody's hand closed over hers. She felt a rush of something like wind and something like the one sip of brandy she'd ever managed to sneak when her father wasn't looking.

"Hold on," he said. "Breathe."

It wasn't Rama. This voice was too soft and light. It was Lieutenant Zhao.

Part of her wanted to rip free and run to the other end of the universe. The rest drank his strength and used it to lean on the ship.

It didn't stop wanting to dive, but it decided to feed a little more around the edges of this moon. Aisha's knees tried to let go.

Lieutenant Zhao held her up. She shrank away from him.

"I won't hurt you," he said. "Or sell you to the Corps, either."

"No. You'll just sign me over, and the law will make me go."

"From here?"

She worked her arm free of his hand. It was hard, because she wanted to like him. He wasn't a bad person at all. He was just...

"Corps." He was reading her. She'd been too badly thrown off to remember how to stop him.

"He helped you with the test, didn't he?" he said. He tilted his head toward Rama, who hadn't moved at all. "Of course he would."

"He'll never let you have me," she said.

"I didn't come to take you to the Corps," he said, "but to your mother and father."

Her body went rigid. It didn't stop her brain from working. "You're not getting your hands on me again. Ever. You understand?"

"Even to take you back to Nevermore?"

"I'll go back when I'm ready to go back." She stepped away from him. "You leave me alone."

He took a breath as if he might have said something else, but in the end decided not to. Not that she would have listened anyway.

They were still in deep trouble. Rama was not responding, the ship was just barely under control, and Aisha had no idea what to do. There wasn't anybody she could trust, to ask.

Even Aunt.

It hurt to realize that. Aunt was part of the reason why Araceli was such a nightmare. Aisha couldn't be sure Aunt would hold together if anybody pushed, especially MI. Or the Corps.

She'd belonged to them once. They'd messed her up and thrown her out. She was broken.

There was one person Aisha might talk to. She was not on this ship, but her XO was.

The Spaceforce shuttle sat at the end of the bay, with its whole crew still on board. Aunt, too.

Aisha never got that far. People waited at the entrance to the bay. They were all crew, and they weren't about to move.

In a vid she'd whip out her swords and swashbuckle her way through. In real life she was half the size of half of them, and half the age of the rest, and her swords were plasteel.

They didn't necessarily know about the second two, but the first was obvious. Even standing up straight, she had to tip her head back to glare at the big one named Kirkov.

He wasn't the one who got in her face. MariAntonia was almost as small as Aisha, but she didn't seem to care.

Aisha could learn from that. "Let me by," she said.

"So you can sell us out to Spaceforce? I don't think so."

"Oh," said Aisha. "Is that what you'd do? My aunt's on that shuttle. I want to see her."

"No," said MariAntonia.

Aisha walked through her. She gave way, which surprised Aisha, but Kirkov didn't. It was like running into a wall.

She leaned back till she could see his face. "You think you're taking over the ship now?"

"I think you need help, and you don't know where to find it."

"It's that obvious?"

"I'm not psi," he said, "but I connect data for a living. Your friend or employer or whatever he is may be able to control this ship, but if he wants to get anywhere with it, he has to have help. That means crew. You think Spaceforce will or can give you that?"

"I'm not asking Spaceforce," Aisha said.

"Someone in the Force, then," MariAntonia said. "When will it sink in that you can't trust any of them? Even relatives. Especially relatives. They want you back home with Mummy and Daddy, and they'll do whatever it takes to make that happen."

They were getting some of it wrong, but enough was right that Aisha had a serious thought about pitching the same kind of fit she'd pitched when she was three years old.

She couldn't do that. She had to make herself calm, and then force herself to think. She wasn't getting to the *Helen* from this direction. What she was getting was an offer she maybe couldn't afford to refuse.

"All right," she said. "Tell me why I should believe you."

Because you don't have a choice.

She could read that one in MariAntonia's face, but Kirkov wasn't quite so blunt. "I'll let you read me," he said.

"But I don't—" Aisha bit her tongue. She was in so deep she couldn't imagine how to get out. Now they all thought she was psi.

She was. She could face that. But she didn't have the first idea how to *be* it.

It felt as if the crewpeople around Kirkov were closing in. Their eyes were hungry.

All she could think of to say was, "I'll do it. But not here."

"Yes, here," MariAntonia said. "You don't get to stall us."

There was no Rama to help her. Aisha was all alone.

"Kneel down," she said to Kirkov.

She thought MariAntonia might squawk, but she didn't. Kirkov dropped down to where Aisha didn't have to strain to see his face.

His eyes were calm. They looked kind. She thought about them the way she did about a web portal, a set of access codes that opened a new stream of data.

At first she wasn't sure it was working. She might be on the web, more or less by accident, but if she was, it was a weird, staticky, now blurry and now painfully sharp connection.

The static eased up a bit. The sharpness smoothed out. The stream had an undertone of words—a lot of words—but what she focused on was the way it felt.

He was nervous, but clamping it down. Trying to make sure he was focused and coherent. Hoping she wouldn't find—what?

A mob of children in a dirty street on a world with a greenish sun. The air had a smell to it, a bit like burning and a bit like sulfur. His pants were down and his backside was cold and he was so embarrassed he wanted to die.

She backed up fast. Up, and sideways, just like navigating webstreams. She followed the feelings. Not just the ones on top, that he was trying to make her see. The others, running underneath. The fears and worries. Anger—he had plenty of that.

It wasn't at her, or anything that would hurt her. Psycorps, Spaceforce, that was different. The things they'd done to him…

She pulled back again. She had what she needed. She could get out, she was sure. Just keep pretending his mind was a webstream, find the portal and shut it.

Except it kept sliding away. The stream wanted her to go down into the parts he was trying to keep from her, the deep swirls and eddies where the mind stopped making sense and started making its own rules.

"Up here."

Brisk. Sharp. It might seem angry, but that was fear honed to a keen edge.

It wasn't Lieutenant Zhao. Aisha didn't know who it was at first, because it was so unexpected.

It was Aunt Khalida. Her voice guided Aisha up through levels like sucking mud, toward something she decided to see as light. Once she made the decision, it was light: the soft, faintly underwater glow that lit the inside of the ship.

Aisha was still on her feet, but once she realized that, her knees gave way.

Kirkov held her up. She could still feel him, partly inside and partly through his big warm hand. "You're trustworthy," she said. "That doesn't mean anyone else is. Say you'll take responsibility for them."

His answer was steady, though inside he wasn't quite so sure. "I'll speak for all of them. We're in this together. We'll help you get out of this system, and crew the ship at least as far as the nearest free station."

"Which is how far?"

"That depends," MariAntonia said.

Kirkov shot her a look. "Simplest route would take us to Tien Shan."

"Which is glaringly obvious and promises us a welcoming committee," MariAntonia said. "I'd head for Novy Novotny, myself."

"I see," Aisha said. She hoped she sounded neutral. She wasn't about to tell them the ship might have its own ideas, and Rama definitely did. Would. When he woke up.

She'd stopped the beginnings of an argument, at least. "I'm going to see my aunt," she said. She tilted her chin at Kirkov and then, after a pause, MariAntonia. "You can come. Just be quiet."

Kirkov wasn't offended. MariAntonia obviously was. Aisha didn't care. She walked between them, and let out a breath when neither tried to block her.

Commander Ochoa's ping woke Khalida out of a dream in which she had been walking in a man's mind beside Aisha, guiding her up and out and into the light. It was an odd dream, not because it was strange, but because it felt so ordinary. As if she did such things every day, with as much ease as if she were running the web or piloting a shuttle.

The dream scattered. "Captain," Ochoa said. "You need to see this."

Khalida swung out of the bunk and onto the bridge. The main screen was running a data feed that notably lacked the usual MI hallmarks.

"Hacked?" she asked Ochoa.

The Commander nodded. "It's running everywhere in this system."

It must have been set to release as soon as the children were safe. Khalida had seen most of it, or heard it from Mem Aurelia.

It was slanted, of course, for maximum shock and outrage. MI itself could hardly have done better.

"I would say," Ochoa said, "that things just got ugly."

"Ugly," Khalida said, "and extremely, and intentionally, distracting. You'd better get off this ship, Commander. Unless you want to go wherever it's going."

"'You'?"

Khalida had not made a decision, exactly. One of the secondary screens showed three figures striding across the shuttle bay: two strangers, and a small but upright figure in alien black.

"I'm done," she said. "I did what MI said it wanted. I defused the trigger; I kept Araceli from being killed, though what happens to it now, I don't know or care."

"This just got a whole lot bigger than Araceli," Ochoa said.

"So it did." Khalida shouldered her kit. "Good luck to you, Commander. Give my best to Captain Hashimoto."

Anyone else might have tried to talk Khalida out of it. Commander Ochoa did not even try. And that, Khalida thought, was one more reason why Tomiko had sent her.

Messages within messages. She snapped a salute—for the last time, maybe. Commander Ochoa returned it; and so, to her surprise, did the rest of the crew on the bridge.

Her throat was unexpectedly tight. She walked out without interference, through the shuttle and down the ramp and into the bay just in time to meet Aisha and her escort.

"Aunt," Aisha said.

Her face was stiff and looked cold, which meant she was close to tears. Khalida was not a person for hugging or comforting, but then neither was Aisha.

"You have quarters?" Khalida asked.

"I don't—"

"She does," said the big man with her. "Follow me."

Aisha stiffened as if she might rebel, but Khalida swept her around and aimed her toward the man's retreating back.

The cabin in which he left them would have been quite ordinary if one had not known that it was formed of living substance. Khalida suspected that it had been intended for scientific staff: its many connectors, now disabled, would have allowed for the running of multiple experiments, and its half-dozen bunks, all convertible into jump cradles, showed signs of having been used as specimen storage.

Two meals were laid out on the table by the far wall, each contained in a micro-stasis field. Khalida had no appetite, but Aisha fell on her share, even while she burst out in a flare of pent-up temper. "I wanted to talk to Commander Ochoa!"

"Commander Ochoa will be on her way back to the *Leda* as soon as the ship lets her go," Khalida said. "What were you going to say to her that you can't say to me?"

"Everything!"

Khalida paused to let the ringing in her ears subside. "I quit, you know. Resigned. Left. I'm out of MI."

Aisha stopped with chopsticks halfway to her mouth. "You what?"

"If you're looking for help from Spaceforce, I don't think you'll get it. A planetload of ordure just hit the fan out there, and every ship in the system will be called to fend it off."

Aishal set her chopsticks down. Her eyes flickered: accessing ship's web, and maybe something more. "Oh," she said. "Oh my. They really want us to get away without anyone chasing us, don't they?"

"They really do," Khalida said.

"That's the problem," Aisha said. She breathed deep, then let it go. "The only one who can control this ship is Rama. And he's out—just gone. Though he'll come back. I think. I got the ship to keep feeding for a little while, but I won't be able to hold it for long. Then I don't know what's going to happen."

Khalida took her time digesting that. "Do you know where he wants to go?"

"I know he has star maps," Aisha answered. "I saved them. But which ones matter, or where they eventually go, I can't tell you. I'm not even sure he can."

"I believe this is what's called a fine mess." Khalida was almost happy, saying it. It was not MI's mess, or hers, unless she made it so. She raised her voice slightly and pitched it to carry outward. "I know you're listening. Come in and join us. If we're all in it together, we may as well be honest about it."

It was a while before anyone responded to Khalida's invitation. She took the opportunity to eat, having found her appetite after all. She needed fuel, if this adventure was going to continue.

Ship's web, she discovered, was open for her access. She idled through it, searching out its nooks and corners. Aisha's star maps waited for her at the end of a search string, linked to downloads from Araceli's worldweb of the carvings on the Ara Celi.

They suggested no pattern to her. A sequence of separate systems and clusters of systems, curving up and over a stone arch, but leading nowhere she could discern. The distances from Araceli seemed random, the routes as suggested by the web equally disconnected. There was no telling in which direction they were meant to run, or even where the progression began.

Either they really were random, or they were a code for which she had no key. The key was sitting on the bridge, apparently in a trance, and no one dared to wake him.

People were coming: the ship sent a shiver along her arm, like feet walking down one of its corridors. Khalida saved the maps to a file of her own.

As she slid out of the web, the ship shuddered.

Khalida was on her feet and running. Aisha ran ahead of her, trailing black robes and tightly controlled panic.

They passed a handful of people: the big man from the shuttle bay and the woman who had been with him, and one or two in science-team uniform. One of the latter fell as the ship lurched again. Khalida kept her balance, hurdled the fallen body, and sprinted onto the bridge.

Rama sat upright and motionless in the captain's cradle. People swirled around him: crew, scientists, Marta from Araceli in a trail of virtual stars. Lieutenant Zhao from the Corps, as blankly shocked as the rest of them.

The screens showed no changes outside the ship: the moon below, Araceli floating in the distance, and a faint, disconcerting shimmer that might be a cloaking field. Then what—

The forward screen flicked off. While Khalida stared at the darkness where it had been, a new image formed: the bridge of a Psycorps cutter, a blur on the edges that must be crew, and Rinaldi in the center, for once in Corps black with nine pips on his collar, smiling. "There you are," he said.

Khalida spun and clipped Zhao alongside the ear. He dropped. Rinaldi's image, unfortunately, did not.

"You don't think I'd be that obvious, do you?" he said. "We'll be boarding now. Don't trouble with an escort. We'll find our own way in."

"They've got a tractor beam on us," Kirkov said from one of the side stations.

"Yes," said Aisha, "and ship doesn't like it." Her face was tight, as if her head hurt.

Khalida sent a quick query on ship's web. *Helen* was still in the shuttle bay; the ship had not yet released her. It allowed Khalida to open a link.

It was a poor connection, full of extraneous noise. Pain, she thought. The ship was in pain.

Commander Ochoa met her stare through the link. Khalida shot her a burst of data. Not orders, exactly. Unless she chose to interpret them as such.

She caught the burst, scanned it. "Got it," she said.

Khalida jerked a nod that was half a salute. "Godspeed," she said.

Khalida's instant on the web had seen little change on the bridge. Aisha had moved, that was all. Edging toward one of the crew, the woman whom Khalida had seen with Aisha in the shuttle bay. She seemed unaware that she was being stalked, intent on the screen in front of her.

Khalida's mind was moving almost too quickly to keep up with itself. That was it. The weak link. The connection to Rinaldi. MariAntonia—that was her name.

The ship's pain had mounted. While Aisha descended on MariAntonia, Khalida aimed for the screen.

Aisha sprang, bringing the spy down bodily while Khalida confronted what the spy had done: opening the link to Rinaldi; restoring the Corps' modifications to the ship.

Not all of them; there had barely been time. The shields first. The jump drive and the basic controls were still incomplete.

There was no safe way to rip them out. The ship kept a memory of what Rama had done—the bright one, it called him; the living sun. It was well beyond any capabilities Khalida might have had.

She tried speaking directly to the ship. "Wake him up. You need him."

The pain was too strong. It could maintain essential functions, life support, even opening the port that released *Helen* into space, but nothing more complex.

She scanned the bridge. No one was doing anything useful, except Aisha, and the big crewman, who had moved past Aisha to lock MariAntonia in a set of shackles. Khalida would have been interested to know where those came from on a research vessel, but a Corps slave ship—now that made perfect sense.

What came to mind made no sense at all. It was simply there, out of nowhere, except possibly the ship.

"Marta," she said to the woman sat quiet in the midst of the commotion, listening and taking it in without offering to add to it.

Marta lifted her chin. It was answer enough. "Come here," Khalida said, moving as she spoke, toward the other center of stillness.

He was as immobile as that statue of him on Nevermore. The carved stone had been more alive than his living face.

"Sing," Khalida said to Marta.

Marta's eyes widened slightly, but she offered no argument. She drew breath, paused, then released it in a torrent of sound.

That voice was trained to fill the cavernous spaces of an ancient opera house. *Ra-Harakhte*'s bridge was larger than the command centers of most Spaceforce destroyers, but not nearly as large as that. Every cell in Khalida's body sprang to attention. Her ears rang, and kept on ringing, as Marta transformed that first note into a cascade of melismas and intricate flourishes.

Khalida felt him wake. Consciousness soared from unimaginable depths to a blaze of living light. Eyes opened, with nothing human in them; nothing mortal at all, seething and swirling like the surface of a sun.

They blinked; darkened. Became a man's eyes, white and iris and pupil, but the sun still lived in them.

Khalida had all but forgotten the fore screen and the image that still flickered on it, Rinaldi shaking his head and trying to laugh through evident pain. His lips moved; she did not trouble to read them. Something witty, no doubt. Marta's aria drowned them out.

Marta's aria, and the ship's pain. Cutting off MariAntonia had been too little and too late. Boarding parties stung like blisters along the hull. Two, six—ten. Rinaldi was taking no chances.

"That will be enough," Rama said, soft, as if to himself. He should not have been audible. He was perfectly clear.

His eyes met Khalida's. "Shield yourself," he said.

She should not have known what that meant, but it too was perfectly clear. Aisha, and even Zhao, had fixed on him. Like a firewall on the web, Khalida thought. Layers on layers of encryption. Closing in her mind; sealing this thing she had become.

He nodded. Warmth brushed past her like the flicker of a smile. Then the world was hard and sharp and globed in glass.

Rinaldi screamed.

It was incomprehensible at first. Blood streamed from eyes, nose, ears. His body convulsed.

He was not dying. Dying was a gift. He would live. On and on. In agony.

Psis of the Corps had felt none of the ship's pain. Until Rama gave it to them. All of it. In all its vastness and its unfathomable depths.

Justice.

Khalida laughed. Roared; howled. Rolled on the floor like a mad thing, till there was nothing to do but lie hiccoughing, with tears streaming down her face, and Rinaldi's screams fading beneath the whoop of the boarding klaxon—his, not *Ra-Harakhte's*.

Ochoa had gone to arrest him for high crimes and misdemeanors. It was a crazy thing, and should have been a dangerous thing, but not any more. No psi in this system was a danger to anyone but herself, now and for who knew how long.

Forever, Khalida hoped, though she knew better than to expect it.

Rinaldi's screams cut off. One of Ochoa's medics had dropped him with a tranq.

Ochoa was in battle armor with the helmet pushed back. Even through the dicey connection, she looked faintly green around the edges. "What in the name of the twenty hells did you do?"

Rama spoke before Khalida could find the words. "Their eyes opened, and they learned to see."

"Stop talking like that," Aisha said, startling them all. "He means they were giving the ship such pain it was almost out of its mind. They didn't know. Now they do."

"All of them," Khalida said as the datastream caught up with her. "Every psi-five and higher, all through this system. Every three with any claims to be an empath, and even the ones, if they had enough of that capability to do anything with. It's a massacre."

"Not one of them is dead," Rama said.

"No," said Khalida. "They only wish they were."

He barely hinted at a shrug. He felt no more guilt than she did, and no more grief, either.

What guilt she felt was for feeling none. Every psi in the system could not have known or colluded in torturing the ship. Some of them might even have been innocents.

They were Corps. The children in stasis—those were on their account, too. The planet that had nearly died. The corruption that ran through MI. And more, much more, that she did not know and could not prove but had heard or suspected.

Justice.

She met Ochoa's stare. The feed had steadied, though it was still grainy and visibly pixelated. "Tell Captain Hashimoto I wish her luck."

"She'll rip me a new one for letting you go," Ochoa said. She did not sound terribly perturbed. "Try to stay alive, will you?"

"I'll do my best," Khalida said. Slightly to her surprise, she meant it.

Ochoa nodded. "Better get out of here while you can. Nobody's chasing anybody for a while, but once the thrashing and blaming stops…"

"…they'll blame me." Rama sounded almost pleased with the prospect. "We understand, Commander."

Ochoa's salute included him as well as Khalida, with a fair portion of respect. The screen blanked, then opened again to a field of stars.

Khalida drew a long breath. She felt strangely light. Empty; free.

43

The ship had settled down now the Corps was done torturing it. Rama gave it a course that it was happy enough to set: toward a system called Kom Ombo, out toward the edge of United Planets' space.

Under the euphemisms that clouded the web stream, Aisha recognized an old and almost completely worn out-warning. The system belonged to pirates.

Free traders. That was what they called themselves. Most of the stream was perfectly dull: missing taxes and shipments that didn't add up. But a little was at least distantly like a pirate vid. Smugglers, chases, the occasional arrest. U.P. usually gave up after a while and issued letters of marque, and then the system ran itself.

Kom Ombo had been running itself for a long time. There weren't any Earthlike planets in the system, but a cluster of planetoids orbited its sun at a usable distance. Those had grown, with the addition of a web of stations and orbital colonies, into a trading hub for that whole part of the Outer Reaches.

It would be a while before they reached it. The ship was still in orbit around Araceli's moon, but its systems had shifted into jump mode.

Rama called them all together in a space the scientists had been using as a lab. It was smaller than the bridge but ample for everyone who was awake and out of stasis.

He was still stretched thin, but Aisha didn't think anyone else could see it. He'd stopped talking in gnomic utterances, which was a good thing. Mostly he looked like the Rama she'd known on Nevermore: solid, sturdy, and blessedly clear-eyed.

He scanned them all. Crew, scientists, recent additions—even Lieutenant Zhao, who was managing to hold himself together.

They scanned him back. Crew and scientists especially. Dr. Ma looked as if she would have liked to dissect him on one of the tables pushed against the wall.

When they'd all had a chance to decide what they thought of each other, Rama said, "Before we reach Kom Ombo, it's time we turned ourselves into a functioning ship. We can't afford another adventure like the one we just, somewhat miraculously and with thanks to my friend here, managed to survive."

It dawned on Aisha that he was talking about her. Heat flooded her face; she had to work to keep her head up and not duck and try to hide.

"Agreed," said the crewman named Kirkov, "but as far as I know, you're the only one with psi high enough to control the ship. Unless you're planning to install the slave circuits again?"

The ship shuddered. Aisha braced herself, but the movement stopped. Rama had calmed it down.

Not everybody had felt the tremor. Zhao had, and Aunt Khalida: they both looked slightly wild. Kirkov might have. It was hard to tell.

"No more slavery," Rama said. "It lets us ride it; but it needs a certain slant of mind."

"Psi," Kirkov said.

"Not necessarily," said Rama. "You've ridden land animals, yes? Horses?"

"A long time ago," Kirkov said.

He was wary, but Aisha could tell he was interested. One or two of the science staff were, too, though maybe not in the right way.

"When we're in jump," Rama said, "I'll teach as many of you as can learn."

"And the rest of us?" Dr. Ma inquired. "Are we to keep to our quarters and stay out of your way?"

"That depends," he said. "I'll be learning myself what goes into the running of a ship. Is that something you can teach?"

"I might," she said.

She hadn't thawed even slightly, but Rama smiled as if she had. "Go now, prepare for jump. We'll gather again once we're all safe in subspace."

Some of them would ride out jump here: the remains of the maintenance crew, the lab techs, a handful of people who looked after the kitchens and the storage bays. Rama would want to know them all by name, Aisha thought, because he was like that.

But first they had to begin the deep dive. The ship was ready. It wouldn't wait much longer.

Subspace was its native habitat. She could feel how it yearned to go back. It had come out like a whale breaching, to feed in the harsh dry wastes of what she knew as space; but its home, its sea, was the endless deep below.

It went down soft and slow, sliding seamlessly through the layers of the multiverse. No mechanical ship could ever do what this living creature did. It knew the exact angle and the precise speed. It was beautiful.

Aisha had let the ship feed her a light dose of drugs, but she barely needed it. She could feel Rama riding the way he did his antelope on Nevermore: quiet, balanced, letting the ship move the way it was born to move. All he did was ask it to go where he needed to go.

Because he asked and didn't compel, it was happy to oblige. It was young—a baby. Still growing; still learning how to be itself.

Subspace was different from inside a living ship. Aisha could hear the singing clearly. She could almost understand what it meant.

She wanted to lie in her bunk and just listen, but there was too much to do. There were crews and duties and rosters, and everyone had to help.

Even Rama, though Aisha didn't think anyone asked him. He did it, that was all. Taking a turn on kitchen duty. Inventorying cargo. Presenting himself as lab assistant.

"No," said Dr. Ma.

Aisha had been enlisted to record data streaming off a set of sensors. She wasn't told what it referred to, but a quick search told her they were measuring the ship's responses to shifts in the external environment. Which was subspace, but to the ship it was real space.

She didn't tell that to Professor Robrecht, who took the data after she'd organized it, and went away to mutter and scowl and tear out what hair he had left. The datastream was mostly running itself by the time Rama came in and took a station over by the sample-analysis bay.

He'd already started in with a set of samples when Dr. Ma stopped him. "It's not appropriate," she said.

"For whom?" he inquired.

For some reason Aisha could not understand, Rama didn't hate Dr. Ma. He found her interesting; he wasn't insulted when she snapped at him.

She did not return his sentiments. At best she was frostily polite. At worst, she looked ready to take his head off and run it through a scanner to see what it was made of.

She had that expression now. "You belong on the bridge," she said, "Captain."

"I belong wherever I'm needed," he said. "The ship knows where to go. The bridge crew has nothing to do but watch the monitors and wait for emergence."

"I don't need you here," she said.

"Why not?"

"Have you any scientific training at all?"

"That depends on your definition of science."

In a vid, they'd keep fighting till one of them grabbed the other and the kissing began. That wasn't going to happen here. Not in a thousand years. Or six thousand.

Dr. Ma closed her eyes. She seemed to be counting at least that far, to calm herself down. "When you hijacked this ship, we had no choice but to accept it. That places me under no obligation to accept you as anything but the pirate captain you chose to make yourself."

"When I rescued this living creature from pain unimaginable, I only did what I must in order to set it free."

Even on the other side of the room, Aisha felt the force of that. Dr. Ma, in front of him, braced as if she stood in a strong gale.

It barely swayed her. "So you say," she said. "I don't see you turning it loose. In fact, it seems you've found a way to use it for yourself."

"I asked," he said. "It chose to help."

"Prove it," she said.

His white smile lit up the lab. "Ah! Science!"

"Always," she said.

"I'll teach you to ride it," he said. "Then you'll have your proof."

Aisha bit her lips before she burst out laughing. He had trapped Dr. Ma perfectly. Now she had to do what he wanted, to get the proof she said she needed.

Dr. Ma saluted him. "Well played, sir."

He bowed to the compliment. "I will need your help, and the help of some of your colleagues. The links you'll need can be made, I'm told, but they won't be simple, and they're not the usual configurations."

"That's not my specialty," she said.

"No, but you can advise as to whose it is." Rama was as polite as ever, but he wasn't going to let up.

It was obvious that he didn't need her to tell him anything. But he wanted her to.

She was too curious—too much a scientist—to keep resisting him. She made an exasperated face, but she gave him what he asked for.

She came to the first lesson, too. Aisha had more than half expected to see everybody there, but it was just Rama and Dr. Ma, Kirkov, the scientist named Robrecht who used to be MI, and Aunt Khalida and, not surprising but not welcome either, Lieutenant Zhao.

Not Lieutenant any more. The Corps was broken and he was a deserter. Or kidnapped—it didn't matter which.

Just Zhao, then. Pale and much too still, with hands that shook when he wasn't paying attention.

"Are you sure you can do this?" Aisha asked him when they were all together in a smaller space just off the bridge.

He stared at her as if he barely recognized her. "No," he said. "No, I'm not sure. I'm not sure I can't, either."

"You can," Rama said. "You will."

He stood in front of a set of screens. They weren't showing anything that made sense. Ship's web had the same feel to it: vague, sort of empty, but not really.

Waiting.

The ship was aware of them. Aisha didn't know if she should call it that, but she couldn't think of anything else. It liked being *Ship*, as long as it got to choose when the tiny creatures inside it tried to make it do things.

It was like a horse that way. Intelligent, very. Focused on eating and moving and someday making new ones. When humans asked it to carry them places, it was just as happy to do that, if they let it eat as much as it needed, and swim the deep seas under space, which it also needed.

Rama had taken its pain away. That was like rescuing a horse from a bad owner. It looked to him for the things that made it feel good. It took starstuff out of him, a little, the way a horse would take sugar from a human's hand: because it was sweet, and if it did more of what he wanted, it could have more of the sweet.

Humans who were not Rama couldn't give it that, but Rama, with the techs who were still telling one other that what he'd asked them to do was *not possible*, had rigged Ship's web to feed it small sparks of hydrogen and helium when the person at the helm needed or wanted to offer a reward.

The screens in the training room were the old backup screens from the bridge. In place of slave circuits, they connected with the ship's neural network through thin filaments that looked like human nerve cells. Ship had grown them, and insulated them. Rama didn't say so, but Aisha knew that if anyone tried to slave the ship to their commands ever again, the loop would feed straight back into the pilot's own head.

That was what had happened to the Corps in Araceli. He hadn't done a thing to them—just given them what the ship felt. The raw feed. No filters.

Ship was comfortable now, happy to be swimming through the deep sea, and curious about the humans who one by one, shakily, tried touching it through the web. Each time, the screens lit up, not showing anything yet, just light. Clear and bright for Aisha and Robrecht and Kirkov. Darker for Aunt Khalida, with a shimmer in the back of it, like moon on water. Deep gold for Dr. Ma: striking and beautiful.

Zhao was last. His face was pale; his lips were tight. His hands shook. He knew, Aisha thought. One wrong move and he'd go the way of the rest of the Corps.

She watched him almost decide to do it. To finish it. Then he wouldn't have to hurt any more.

"Focus," Rama said. His voice was soft and surprisingly gentle. "Think of light. No more. No less. Just that."

Zhao's face twisted. He lashed out with his mind, and near flattened Aisha—like the worst headache she'd ever imagined. Like a spike through the skull.

She only got the edge of it. Rama took it head-on. He hissed, but held still. The screen behind him blazed so bright it blinded.

Ship kicked: a snap of protest; a wave across the screen, dark shot with stars. Zhao went down without a sound.

Rama hauled him up and slapped him back to what senses he had. When he could stand on his own feet, Rama let him go. "Grieve as you please. Hate me at your leisure. Slit your own throat if you must. But spare this creature that consents to carry us."

Zhao jerked as if he'd been shot. Which in a way he had: straight to the center of his guilt.

"Again," Rama said. "Properly this time."

He was sullen, but he did it. His light was softer than Aisha's, which surprised her. He was trying not to hurt the ship again.

"Good," Rama said.

He asked as much as Zhao could stand to give, and a little bit over. As they set to learning how to access the screens and then how to ask Ship to do simple things, he did the same to all of them. Aisha, too.

They each had a screen, and they each keyed it in whatever way felt right. For some it was like a straight web connection. Aunt Khalida made it like a pilot's console.

Aisha set her screen for ship's web, because that seemed simplest, but when she closed her eyes, what she saw and felt was a horse like one of the herd on Nevermore.

That hurt in ways she completely hadn't expected. She missed Jinni suddenly, with a pain like grief. It barely helped to tell herself she was doing what she had to do, and she had every intention of going back home when she was done. When she'd made sure there was a home to go back to.

The twisting in her gut didn't care about that. Behind her eyelids she saw the long rolling grassland and the bitter-blue sky. She rode a horse she didn't know, big and glistening black. The mane on its neck swirled and streamed like a solar storm.

It was a strong horse, with a mind of its own. It wanted to run through the endless grass. It was happy to carry her, but it wasn't particularly interested in doing what she asked it to do.

Other horses crowded around her. The field was full of them, grazing and dancing and mating and dreaming. They ran in herds or wandered off alone.

The one she rode felt like a young thing, old enough to ride but not much more, a little awkward and not as confident as the others. It was bright and curious and eager to explore, which was how it had surfaced from its native space where it had, and been beached and then caught.

Instead of pulling it around when she wanted it to turn, she started asking it with shifts of weight or turns of her own body. It turned then because it had to, and she was there to keep it from falling over.

It was more patient than a horse would be, especially with six other people taking turns poking at it. When Aisha's screen went down, she watched the others, trying to see and feel what they were doing.

The sea of grass stayed in the back of her mind, and all the creatures in it. Subspace was empty, people thought. Void without substance. Too alien for the human mind to understand. Even computers could barely begin to give shape to it.

But it wasn't like that at all. Any more than Ship was a mindless tube full of holes and compartments, capable of generating breathable atmosphere and maintaining human-tolerable temperature, but incapable of feeling anything so sophisticated as pain.

"How did you manage to be so blind?" Aisha asked Zhao while he waited his turn, too.

"We weren't looking," he answered.

She hadn't expected him to have an actual answer. That changed how she felt, a little bit. "Not looking in the right places, you mean," she said.

His eyes flickered: a yes. "We fell into the trap of thinking we knew far more than we did. Because we had a set of gifts, a hierarchy, and a system, we thought that was all there was. We didn't allow for the size of the universe. Or," he said, "the multiverse."

"I'm sorry," Aisha said. Not for that, exactly. For everything.

He understood. His eyelids lowered; his head bowed slightly. "We did it to ourselves."

She couldn't argue with that. Then it was her turn again, and Ship seemed glad, and she let his sadness slip away beyond the sea of grass.

44

"Why?" Khalida asked.

The null was still in shackles. That was petty, maybe, but Khalida was not moved to take them off.

The cell had been made for this prisoner. It was slightly smaller than crew quarters, with a bunk grown out of the wall, and a protrusion like a chair, on which Khalida sat.

The null's name was MariAntonia. Khalida wanted to render her nameless in the ancient way, but if there was to be a record, there had to be ID. Ship's web gave her what data was to be had: name, rank and position, performance reviews. No history. Where one should have been was a blank: *Redacted.*

Even her past was null.

Maybe Marta knew what was behind the wall. Khalida had no particular need to know.

"Why did you sell us out to the Corps?"

MariAntonia pulled her knees up to her chest and hid her face against them. Her shoulders were stiff.

"What did they have on you? Or did they buy you?"

The voice that came out of the rigid knot was both muffled and defiant. "You're not MI any more. What are you now, then? Torturer in chief to a pirate king?"

"Do you wish I were?"

MariAntonia raised her head. "How did he buy you? Or do you just have a finely honed death wish?"

"I thought I did," Khalida said. "So they bought you. I hope they paid a living wage."

"Or a dying one?"

"I know what I'm atoning for. You?"

The null twitched: half shrug, half raw nerves. "So what's the sentence? Death? Worse?"

"As far as I know," Khalida said, "nobody's given much thought to you since you were shut up here. The ship feeds you and sees to your needs. When it gets tired of that, it will do whatever it pleases."

Khalida knew what unvarnished truth could do, but MariAntonia surprised her even so with the vehemence of her reaction. She looked ready to spit acid. "That's a lie."

"You know it's not."

"I sold this ship and all its contents to the Corps. Almost succeeded, too. If it hadn't been for—whatever that is, out there on the bridge."

"I know what he is," Khalida said. "Now I know what you are. You bet on the wrong hand. So did the rest of the Corps."

"I am—not—Corps."

"Of course you are." Khalida stood. "If it were up to me I'd space you. But that's the ship's to decide. You might try bargaining with it. I don't know if it can understand you, without psi or a working web connection. If it can, and if you do talk it into letting you go, then you can worry about the rest of us."

MariAntonia curled back into her knot again. Defensive posture, Khalida thought. She was no stranger to it herself.

She should have left well enough alone. That was the residue of MI: wanting to sound out the prisoner, to extract what truth there was.

There was nothing there. No point in trying to find anything, except to wonder if some or all of the nulls in stasis had had this same programming: to turn against their own. If so, she hoped she was far away when they woke.

The scientists had come out of their shock at the hijacking of the ship to find themselves in a kind of heaven. With their instruments properly calibrated to the ship's systems, and the ship actively cooperating with them, they were making discoveries that would, at the very least, secure their careers for life. Or kill those same careers, if what they discovered contradicted enough of the accepted wisdom.

Either way, they were gloriously content.

"Were you always a patron of the arts?" Khalida asked Rama toward the middle of the third shipday in jumpspace.

"Yes," he said. "And the sciences."

He had been pulling galley duty, running the cleaners in the crew's mess. It was one of the things he did that made some of them exquisitely uncomfortable.

Now he was done, but Khalida had stopped him before he went on to something else. She pulled a pair of cups out of stores, and filled them with coffee that was hot, fresh, and wonderfully real. She pushed one toward him as they sat at one of the long tables.

"You're corrupting me," he said, grimacing slightly as he sipped. "Who knew bitter could be bliss?"

"That's a lesson for all occasions," she said.

He watched her as she tackled her own cup. After a while he said, "You're healing."

"Scabbing over."

"Yes."

She met his dark stare. "You, too."

She thought he might look away, but he held steady. She should be afraid, maybe. Knowing what he was capable of.

He was only dangerous if she got in his way. "Did you do that before, too? Work in the kitchens and give the staff fits?"

It was a risk to ask him that, but she was bored. She would welcome an argument, even a fight.

He gave her neither. "Sometimes I did. People didn't expect it, even more than here. But there were so many more of them, and the world was so much bigger than this ship. I could go for a whole day, sometimes, without being recognized."

"So you looked like everyone else."

That was transparent. His lips twitched: a flicker of a smile. "I look like my mother. She looked like her whole tribe. Smaller—that was her mother's blood; that lady had been like the people who remain on my world. It was a state marriage: an attempt at alliance that ultimately failed." He drained his cup and set it down. "Old wars. Politics so ancient even I barely remember them. What they were; why they mattered."

"Maybe someone remembers," Khalida said. "Wherever we're going, if we find your people—"

"Somehow I doubt they'll care for the petty details of a tiny kingdom at the back of beyond, that was a thousand years gone by the time they abandoned the world," Rama said.

"They remembered you," said Khalida.

"Oh, but I was a great monster," he said. "I'm sure there were legends. Horrors real and imagined. Nightmares for children and their more delicate elders."

"They left a message for you," she pointed out. "Whatever they might have thought of you, they believed they needed you."

"No doubt to kill something," he said.

"Or save it."

"I don't think," he said, "that that was my reputation."

There was not much she could say to that. She changed the subject instead. "Have you figured out where you need to go?"

"Not yet," he said. "The map from the Ara was left for me, I'm sure of it, but I don't know how I'm supposed to read it."

"It must be keyed to you somehow," Khalida said, "if it's aimed at you."

He sighed and rubbed his eyes. Tired, she thought. "I may be thinking too hard. If I could slow down, stop—not lost in the ship; just be..."

"This is as good a place and time as you'll get," she said. "Rest, then let your mind find its way."

"I don't think—" He bit back what looked like a snap of temper. "This place, this space, is not restful. It teems with life, or what might be life if it were in that other face of the universe. It sings—so many songs. So many voices. Even when I ward myself, when I go down as far as I dare, I still hear them."

That Khalida had not expected. "Here? In jumpspace? But—"

"The space we come from is infinitely quieter," he said.

"So you can hear the songs."

Khalida had neither heard nor felt Marta come into the mess. Rama had: he regarded her without surprise. "You, too?"

"Yes." Marta fetched her own coffee and sat a handful of seats down from Khalida, where she could see both of them but not intrude on their space. "Somewhere in this is a very serious scientific paper on the hitherto unexplored range and variety of psi. In the space we call normal, I'm null. Here, there's so much music I can hardly hear myself think."

"I can't hear anything," Khalida said with what she realized was a flicker of regret. "Just a little human babble. And the ship. It's singing, off and on. Humming to itself."

"That would be restful," Rama said. He slanted a glance at Marta. "You're not really null—not empty of psi. You have strong natural shields. What's beneath is, in its way, equally strong."

"You can see," she said. She did not sound completely comfortable with the thought.

"I can hear," he said. "When you sing. Music concentrates what we are."

"You sang your way to command of this ship."

"Do you find that objectionable?"

"You know I don't." Marta smiled, sweet and deceptively vague. "Someday you'll have to tell me your story."

"So that you can put it to music?"

"Of course."

"Someday," he said. "In the meantime, how well can you read a star map?"

"I'm not a pilot," Marta said, "but I've traveled enough, and been curious enough, to learn a little. What would you like me to see?"

"Something that I'm missing," Rama said.

He called up the maps on one of the screens by the far wall. There was no mistaking where they had come from: the first set of images showed the Ara with its carvings; then the star maps extrapolated from them.

Marta approached the screen with her face intent. "So. That's what you were doing there. Did you deliberately bring it down, once you'd finished scanning it?"

"No."

There was no telling if she believed him. She studied the maps from all angles.

Khalida expected nothing. She went for a fresh cup of coffee, and thought about wandering off. She had a turn on watch, but not for another few hours.

Rama stared at the maps as he must have stared at them over and over since he first recorded them. He must know every dot and symbol, down to the cracks in the stone in which they were carved.

After a while Marta said, "I can't see anything useful, but in Kom Ombo, there are people who may."

"I had hoped for that," he said.

"Some of them know me," she said. "I'll speak to them for you, if you like."

"I would like," he said.

It had not struck Khalida yet how long his search might be. Longer than he had left to live, maybe.

He caught the thought: his glance flicked past her. "I don't think so," he said. "If these maps were left for me to find, they were meant to guide me as straight as may be. Unfortunately, that route is no longer direct. I'm condemned to take the long way. Still…"

"More direct than jumpspace?" Khalida asked.

He seemed to ignore her. The screen shifted the star maps to a corner and began to flicker through sets of images. Ancient sites on various worlds. Remnants of cultures, some of which had survived, while others were long gone.

There were no apparent connections between them. Some were alien, some had been some form of human. They were scattered through the United Planets and in the space beyond.

None of them fit with the star maps from the Ara Celi. As far as Khalida could tell, they were completely random.

Then each image narrowed and focused. They were different spaces—rooms, caverns, gatehouses, the gates themselves, and here and the bones of a ruin. Marks were cut or carved or somehow turned into the substance of the ruins.

It was the same set of star maps, over and over. Some were so worn and faded they were barely visible; others were as clear as if they had been carved within living memory.

The system collated them, matched them, and filled the screen with the results. There were small differences, minor slips or—

Khalida left the table and moved closer to the screen. "These are calibrated," she said. "Oriented to, or from, each system. Which means…" She shifted her voice to command mode. "Ship. Extrapolate the age of each map. Then arrange from oldest to newest."

She held her breath. The image remained unchanged for so long that she had to breathe after all, and then a dozen breaths more.

The shift at first was almost too subtle to see. Then it fell into place.

"Now," she said, "extrapolate. New sequence based on existing pattern."

That took longer than the first, but this time she was prepared. Rama and Marta were perfectly silent, watching.

One by one, the maps fell into place on the screen. Each was labeled with the name of a system.

Khalida held on to hope for as long as she could. But as the images piled one on top of the other, she sagged. "It's completely random. There's no pattern."

"No," Rama said, slipping past her and stopping almost inside the screen. It oriented itself to him, wrapping around him, so that he stood in a globe of nearly identical star maps.

He turned slowly, arm outstretched. The maps turned with him.

Spiraled.

"This isn't a map," he said, "exactly. It's an itinerary."

"An itinerary designed by a random generator," she said with a touch of bitterness. "It doesn't go anywhere. It jumps from one end of the galaxy to another, in no perceptible order."

"Ship," he said, "track destinations by jump routes. Add wormholes and spatial distortions."

Khalida was holding her breath again. She had fallen into the error of thinking like a conventional pilot. This was not a conventional mission. But— "Wormholes? Those were never viable. Once we discovered how to access jumpspace—"

"—we stopped exploring other options." Marta had joined them by the screen. "This is fascinating. May I ask what you're trying to find?"

"I don't know," Rama answered.

"Look," Khalida said. "Here's the beginning."

Nevermore. Of course. Then a succession of worlds in no apparent order— until the pattern of wormholes and jump routes overlaid it.

Something else appeared over the pattern. A succession of points, each glowing brightly and then dying away like an ember. One after another, world by world, ruin by ruin.

The jump alarm went off.

45

Kirkov had been practicing flying Ship, using the virtual modules that it had developed to teach the student pilots. Aisha, having nothing better to do, was half napping in the pilots' bay, half picking through a plate of pastries that one of the cooks had been experimenting with.

The jump alarm throbbed straight through her bones. "*Kirkov!* What did you—"

"Nothing!"

It was true, he hadn't done anything. The lesson had nothing to do with the alarm. Ship was jumping back into realspace.

Kirkov was already gone, diving for his jump cradle. Aisha bolted for her own.

Her mind babbled around and around inside itself. Three days, only three days, was supposed to be a tenday, where are we coming out, what are we—

Ship gave her calm. It was more than the drugs in the jump cradle: it was a sense that they were going where they were supposed to go, there was nothing wrong, everything was the way it should be.

All she could do was accept. And hope Ship was telling the truth.

They had come out on the edge of Kom Ombo's system, outside the usual lanes of traffic, but still close enough to receive a hail from system center.

In three days of jump from Araceli.

"We calculated based on our own ships," Kirkov said. "We didn't stop to think that this living creature might be different."

Which was stupid, Aisha thought but didn't say. Thinking human machines were the universal standard.

She hadn't thought otherwise, either. Till Ship proved how wrong they all were.

It was amused—that was the best way she could describe the feeling it sent her. Humans had so much to learn.

It was showing off. Aisha felt Rama step in, soft but firm, and ease it on course toward the center of the system. Marta answered the hail: "*Ra-Harakhte* to Kom Ombo. Request berth at Central."

The voice on the other end paused, then said, "Marta? Is that you?"

"Yes, Jonathan," she said. Aisha could hear the smile.

"You have the shipment, then? Already?"

"Already," she answered.

He got control of himself—the hint of excited babble disappeared, and he said crisply, "Sending course heading via datastream."

While that was busy coming through, Rama pinged Dr. Ma on the pilots' stream. "Doctor. Would you like to take us in?"

Aisha held her breath. She more than half expected Dr. Ma to say she would not. But she came through promptly. "Yes. Yes, I would."

They were all on the bridge as the ship made its careful way toward Central. Dr. Ma had the conn; Rama stood in front of one of the screens to the side, scanning the system.

It was a cluster of stations and ships and planetoids and odd bits of space debris that had been turned into habitats. The original asteroid belt was still mostly there, and mostly occupied, where it hadn't been mined out for everything from iron to water.

This was the wildest place Aisha had ever been. Nevermore was wild, but it was well within U.P. space. Kom Ombo stood on the edge of the unexplored.

People who ventured past it had no federation of worlds to help them. They were out on their own, or traveling in relays, running supply lines back to what civilization there was.

For the edge of nowhere, it was a remarkably crowded place. Free traders ran in and out. Explorers used it as a base. Bits and pieces of U.P. showed up here and there: an embassy, a handful of consulates, a military installation that wasn't allowed to dominate anyone.

Aisha was sure it tried. It knew they were coming: Ship caught the ping and routed it to the pilots' screens. A whole stream of data unreeled from the ping, a hack that made Aisha widen her eyes in respect.

She heard Aunt Khalida choke, but couldn't tell if it was laughter or outrage. Probably laughter.

Meanwhile they sailed on along the route that Central had set, aiming toward the heart of it all, the planetoid that had been the first settlement in this system. It was a full-on space station now, surrounded by a webwork of docking bays and biospheres: habitat modules for alien as well as human species.

The bay they'd been assigned was on the outer level above the planetoid's south pole. It had been built to hold a starship; it was just big enough for Ship.

Ship was happy enough. There was star-stuff to feed on, thin enough here, but the bay was positioned to catch the wind from Kom Ombo's sun. It was like a terrestrial whale floating in an ocean current, waiting for plankton to stream past.

While they docked, Rama left the screen he'd been monitoring and moved toward the conn. Dr. Ma let him have it.

"Central," he said. "May we come aboard?"

"We were just about to say," said the voice on the feed. "By all means. A shuttle will be ready for you when docking is complete."

The shuttle was actually a sort of elevator: a string of cars on cables that connected the bay to the outer level of the station. Most of the crew would stay on Ship until Rama was sure of what was below, but he couldn't stop Aisha from going, and Aunt Khalida didn't intend to stay behind, either. He took Marta, who knew people in Kom Ombo, and to Aisha's not entirely pleasant surprise, the former Lieutenant Zhao.

He left Kirkov and Robrecht and Dr. Ma in charge of the ship—balancing each other out, Aisha thought. Nobody would hijack it in any case. It wouldn't go unless Rama asked it to.

They were a nicely piratical collection of people. Aisha even wore her swords; nobody said anything about them, and there didn't seem to be any restrictions against them. Unlike energy weapons, which were supposed to be peace-bonded, or projectile weapons, which were outright banned.

Central's web ran a stream of what regulations there were, along with information, instructions, and so much advertising for goods and services that it made Aisha dizzy. Most of Central, as far as she could tell, was one huge open bazaar, where a person could buy just about anything, and just about anything was legal, as long as admin got a cut of the take.

Aunt Khalida shut that off before Aisha could test it. "Not till we're down," she said. "Everything on this feed is jacked for the tourists."

"They get tourists out here?"

"Tourists are everywhere." Khalida sounded almost cheerful. She'd been terribly quiet since they left Araceli, but something about this place had opened her up—or made her stop caring.

Aisha eyed her warily, but there wasn't anything to be done here. All she could do was watch and wait.

The shuttle passed through the outer levels, then through a tunnel into Central itself. Everything was pitch black except for the faint glow of emergency lights and a glimmer around Rama that Aisha almost might have thought she was imagining. Then suddenly they burst out into light: clear and bright, shaded more toward the blue spectrum than the suns of Earth or Nevermore, but still not so far along that it made her eyes hurt.

The whole world was hollow. Bubbles floated in it, full of people and buildings and machines, and some that were empty except for water and greenery. Cars hummed and darted and swarmed in patterns controlled by the worldweb, flowing all around and about and into the bubbles.

A car was waiting for them when they came out the shuttle, with a pilot who greeted Marta as if they were long-lost cousins. Aisha didn't think they were technically related, and the web wasn't helpful when she asked, but they obviously went back a while.

He was a smallish man, no taller than Rama, and built square, with black hair cut short, and bright black eyes. He took them all in with transparent pleasure. "Welcome!" he said, spreading his arms wide. "Welcome to Kom Ombo!"

"Meser Abaad," Aunt Khalida said. "We're honored."

"The honor is mine," he said. "Come, there's someone who's eager to meet you."

Aisha followed the rest into the car with the pilot who was actually, the worldsweb said, one of the principals of Kom Ombo. That being what they called someone who ran the system.

He didn't act like any important person Aisha had ever met. He was easy, casual, and full of information as they flew in a long arc toward the center of Central. The bubble there was almost big enough to be a planetoid in its own right. There was a whole city inside, and a lake on the bottom, surrounded by deep green woods.

The car flew through the surface of the bubble—slowing a little and stretching the bubble until the world outside blurred and then came clear again—and wove into a swarm of traffic, aiming down toward the lake.

Marta called Meser Abaad Jonathan. He didn't feel like a null, but he didn't feel ordinary, either. Sometimes when Aisha turned away to look out at the city floating past, and then looked back again, there seemed to be two of him: one laid over the other, as if he rode in a bubble of his own.

She'd never met a grown person who was so happy without being impaired somehow. The city he flew through made the port of Araceli look clean and simple, and he was in charge of it. It didn't seem to taint him at all.

The car slowed as it descended toward the lake. The water was dark and looked deep, but Aisha could see something moving in it. Something huge, though not as big as Ship.

"My dear," Jonathan said, and this time he wasn't speaking to anyone in the car, "our guests are here. When you're ready…"

A voice even brighter than his came lilting over the comm. "My dear! Of course I'm ready. Bring them in, if you please."

"Immediately, my dear," Jonathan said, sweeping a smile around the car. "Going down," he said.

By which he meant into the water: nose down, diving straight, with the searchlight arrowing ahead of him.

Aisha had never been in a submarine. She didn't think Aunt Khalida had, either, and Rama was no seafarer. Neither of them allowed any expression to show, but Aunt gripped the arms of her seat so hard the padding bulged.

There was something about the pressure of water on a hull. No pressure at all, in space, or whatever weirdness jumpspace was made of, didn't feel as perfectly dangerous as this.

Strands and coils of weed curled up past the searchlight. Small shiny creatures darted out of the way. They weren't fish, exactly, but close enough.

Something rose up from below. At first Aisha thought it was more of the weed, but it moved differently. Its undulations weren't random. It was swimming.

She'd seen something like it in an aquarium on Earth. A lionfish: an explosion of shimmering striped fins and spines, daring the world to try, just try, to get in its way.

This was enormous. Bigger than the car, and its eyes were bright gold, flaring like a cat's when the light struck them.

"My dear!" Jonathan cried.

"My dear," the voice on the comm trilled. It came from the thing in the water, which had stopped swimming upward to hover in front of them.

Aisha could see it perfectly well. The car's hull had gone transparent. They floated in a bubble, with nothing between them and the dark water but a few millimeters of glasteel.

"Sers and seras," Jonathan said, "this is my beloved, my dear one, my sweet Alexandra."

They all murmured polite things. Aisha felt faintly stunned. She'd seen aliens before, of course she had. She'd been through enough spaceports and traveled on enough ships. But never one like this.

"My dears," Alexandra said. Her voice must be synthetic, but it sounded wonderfully real. "You're most welcome. I do apologize for dragging you here without even a pause for a rest or a bite. I've been waiting so long, you see. I'm just a little overeager."

"That's easily remedied," Jonathan said. He waved his hands like a stage magician. It all came out of the blanked storage bins, of course: water and wine and something light and fizzy and alarmingly good, and boxes that opened into smaller boxes full of food.

Aisha didn't want to imagine that the creature called Alexandra ate for dinner. She was hungry enough to not particularly care.

Even Zhao ate a little, under the force of Jonathan's good humor and Alexandra's luminous eyes. They were being studied, and no one pretended otherwise. It was all very open and uncomplicated.

It was weird. Aisha should have been ready to crawl out of her skin, but she was as comfortable as if she'd been at home on Nevermore.

Even that didn't hurt as much as usual. She breathed past the too-familiar pain in her heart, and focused on the food in front of her and the alien now wrapped partway around the car.

"Dear Marta," Alexandra said after they'd been eating for a while and were starting to slow down, "would it be terribly rude of me to ask if you would sing for us while you're in Central?"

"Not rude at all," Marta said smiling, "and of course I will. Only tell me when and where."

"We'll do that," Jonathan said. Then Aisha caught a glimpse of his other side, crisp and professional, before he shifted back to his happy self. "My dear, shall I take them to Home Above now, and let them rest?"

"By all means," Alexandra said. "You've all been most kind."

46

Ihat was one of the stranger meals Khalida had eaten. They were on display to the alien who was also, obviously, the human principal's lover and lifemate. What the creature really thought, or why it was so important that they be brought to her in her own habitat, Khalida lacked the data to know.

It was a test, she supposed. She noticed that no one had much to say while they ate, and Rama had not spoken a word since he left the *Ra-Harakhte*.

He was not in the fugue state that had taken him down on Araceli. His eyes were alert and his movements as light and powerful as ever. He was in observation mode, even while he was being observed.

Khalida for one was glad to leave the lake behind and be delivered to a house halfway up the curve of the city's bubble. It was a near-perfect replica of an early Industrial Age villa in Luxor in Old Egypt, complete with palm trees and mock Pharaonic columns.

Aisha laughed when she saw it. Fortunately their host took no offense. "Isn't it delightful?" he said to her.

"It looks like my grandfather's house," she said. "You really live here?"

"I really do," he answered. "Now you will be my guests while you're in Central. The house is keyed to all of you; you have only to ask and it will provide."

"A bed," Aisha said promptly. "Sleep."

"As madam wishes," the wall said. It sounded exactly like Khalida's father's major-domo.

She suppressed the start of recognition. That was a test, too. Everything here was a test. She did not know what it led to, but she meant to pass, or at least to come out intact.

The guests, however willing or unwilling they might be, were housed along a corridor on the second story. Aisha made sure to claim one of the rooms next to Rama's, and Khalida tossed her kit into the one on the other side.

The others seemed happy to put themselves to bed once their rooms were sorted, but Khalida had no sleep in her. She prowled the house, investigating its nooks and corners, and made note of which doors failed to open when she approached.

When she set an alert on Aisha, the house was cooperative. It had no objection to her going out, either.

Their host was long gone. Being a principal, she supposed. Or being lifemate to his alien beloved. It was none of her business either way, unless it threatened her or her niece.

Central's web was extremely well designed and impeccably maintained. For a pirate network on the edge of nowhere, it compared favorably with Centrum itself—and probably intentionally, considering the name.

It provided her with a detailed map of the city, though not of the people in it, except in terms of traffic patterns and, here and there, species. Not every sector had human-breathable atmosphere.

She was almost tempted to test one of those, but her mood was not quite that contrary. She found her way to the center, to the Mercado as it was called here: the bazaar, they would have said at home in Egypt.

Odd that she was thinking of Egypt as home. She had stopped that along about the time she enlisted in MI. Now that she was out, old habits seemed to be coming back.

She had her sidearm tucked in a pocket—no one had shown any interest in relieving her of it, in spite of the regulations that had been streamed at them on the shuttle. Her jacket and pants with the insignia removed were still a little too obviously MI, but if any eyes took note of it, they slid on by.

She was not being stalked, either, that she could detect. Predators tended to go for the weak, and she had never projected that, even as a raw young recruit with more temper than sense. She was anonymous, and somewhat surprisingly safe.

She turned in to one of the dozen bars along that particular stretch of street. It was an honest dive, not trying to be anything else: walls held up by a combination of grime and smoke and the smell of ancient beer, screens showing random streams from the worldweb, and a holobar tended by a person of approximately the same vintage and provenance as Vikram on Nevermore. The radiation scars if anything were thicker, the skin was darker, and the gender indeterminate, but the voice was smoky sweet and so was the brown-golden liquid the bartender set in front of Khalida.

She tipped back the shot and paused while the liquor burned its way to her stomach. A low whistle escaped her. "That was pure peat. Not the real Lagavulin?"

"All the way out here?" The bartender grinned, baring teeth inlaid with chips of space iron. "A shot of that would cost you half a planetoid."

Heshe meant that literally. Khalida held out the glass for another shot. A connoisseur could probably have determined to the last molecule where the imitation departed from the original, but to her untutored palate, it was close enough.

While she dealt with the second glass more slowly, she took note of the patrons in the bar: the ones who seemed to be regulars, staked out at tables around the room; the tourists, who were not numerous and who were transparently convinced—and half hoping—that any moment they would be slugged and rolled and sold off to pirates; and those just passing through as she was, alone or in pairs along the bar or settled against the walls where they could watch all possible entrances.

None of them triggered her inner alarms. Maybe she was a tourist after all: she was a little sorry. She might have welcomed a spark of danger, if not a full-blown bar fight.

She was not quite bored enough to wander back to Meser Abaad's house. She switched to beer after the third shot and kept half an eye on the nearest screen, which had run through a game of null-g soccer and shifted to a documentary on extra-U.P. exploration.

The hereditary archaeologist in her could not help but lock on. The buzz of synth-Lagavulin and the bitterness of local beer added an air of surreality to the rambling narration and the panoramas of dead worlds and deserted systems.

There seemed to be a great number of those. Through the faint golden fog, she let her mind pull in data from the web, from her own cache, and from wherever else it happened to think of. Nothing came back at first but random hits and *Data Not Found.*

Then patterns started to emerge. The vid ranged far—clear to the edge of the galactic arm. She had not even known that was possible.

Maybe it was not. But the pattern persisted, even when she tried to exclude that last bit of data.

It was not quite the same, but similar to Rama's star maps. Similar distribution of points across space. Similar jumps and backtrackings. As if someone, or some thing, had followed the same set of parameters, and left a ruin or an abandoned settlement exactly there.

Sometimes there was nothing but space where the ruin should have been. Suns grew old and died—swelled into giants or went nova. Wandering wormholes swallowed planets and systems. Planets collapsed upon themselves, or broke apart under stresses that sometimes could be known, and often not.

She was dizzy with the immensity of the universe. She stood on the edge, on the last world, looking up at a sky empty of stars but dotted with the swirls of galaxies.

In her dream or hallucination, she stepped through a doorway that stood in the emptiness. It was made of stone, with carvings worn almost to nothing.

The world behind was barren, endless tracts of dusty waste and crumbling stone. Water had long since vanished, and dust had blown into the tracks that it had left, sweeping the planet clean.

On the other side of the door was light. Yellow sunlight, no brighter than Earth. Green, and falling water. The song of something like a bird.

Someone knelt by the waterfall, bending to drink. Fall of blue-black hair, long curve of blue-black back and haunches.

It was not Rama. Oh, no. Rama was never so tall or so lean, or so very female.

The woman looked up from the water. Her eyes met Khalida's: dark and bright at the same time, with a glint of humor and a flicker of curiosity. Khalida opened her mouth to speak, and willed her foot to step forward out of the door.

Darkness fell. Khalida snapped awake, glowering at the bar and the screen and her half-empty glass of beer.

The dream wanted to cling. She pushed it away. She was unreasonably and unexpectedly angry. Because it was a dream. Because she wanted it to be real.

The pattern stayed in her head, saved to her personal cache. The most immediately useful datum was the provenance of the vid: a company owned by her hosts in Central.

The villa was quiet when Khalida came back to it. House net marked everyone as asleep. She was still ferociously awake, as the buzz of the liquor wore off and the dull ache in her head set in.

She found the kitchen and the supply of drinking water, and drank until she felt ready to serve as the habitat for another of Alexandra's species.

As if the thought had conjured her up, a screen woke in front of Khalida. Alexandra's golden eyes stared blandly at her. They were on stalks, Khalida happened to notice, and capable of focusing wherever they pleased.

The eyes shrank until the whole creature fit into the screen, frills undulating and spines rising and falling in an almost hypnotic rhythm. "Sera Nasir," Alexandra said.

Khalida saluted her with the empty water bottle. "Sera. You have interesting hobbies. Do you physically track down ancient ruins, or do you delegate?"

"You might be surprised," Alexandra said. Her tone was amiable, however unreadable her physical expression happened to be. "Fascinating, isn't it, how many worlds show signs of habitation, but no indication of who or what, or how those worlds or those structures were destroyed."

"Fascinating," Khalida agreed, "and puzzling. Because none of those worlds seems to have been generally inhabited. Outposts, the ruins seem to be. Way stations. Markers on the way to—who knows?"

"Ah," said Alexandra. "You do have your family's tropism toward the archaeological."

"Bred in the bone," Khalida said, without quite the edge of sarcasm that she was used to giving it. "You targeted that vid at me. Didn't you?"

"Not necessarily at you," Alexandra said, "but it seemed that you should see it."

It was not really Khalida's place to do this, but she had the data. Her gut might be well pickled with synth-Lagavulin but her mind was clear enough. She sent what she had in a dataspurt, all of it, patterns and speculations and extrapolations, though not either the dream in the bar or the truth about the being they all called Rama.

There was enough there to make Alexandra's frills flush bright gold. "Oh! Oh, my dear! This is astonishing."

"We were hoping," Khalida said, "that you might help us decipher the patterns. They're a map, we think, or an itinerary. But we don't know where it leads."

"My dear," said Alexandra, "this is the kind of thing we live for. For you, after what you've done, it's the very least we can do."

Khalida had no expectations. When she left Araceli, she had gone outside of time and space.

It was a kind of freedom. It made her smile at the alien in the screen, retrieve a new bottle of water, and reflect that now, maybe, she could sleep.

47

When everyone had had a chance to catch up on sleep, the house that had seemed so quiet started to fill with people.

Some of them came for Meser Abaad or his lifemate, who lived in the web as well as in the lake. Some came for Marta, because everyone here seemed to know and love her.

The rest were simply curious. It might seem odd that the largest outpost of explorers and free traders would even notice yet another handful of strangers, but strangers who came in a living ship were something different.

Aisha had grown up never knowing who she might run into wandering down a passageway or waiting in a sitting room. It went with living in big houses in the middle of archaeological sites.

Still, it was a little startling to go in search of breakfast and find her way blocked by an assortment of large and dangerous-looking persons. They looked like pirates from every vid she'd ever seen, dressed on the far end of last decade's high fashion on Centrum and bristling with things that looked like weapons, but they were a delegation from the musicians' union in Central, armed with their instruments. Looking for Marta, of course. Wanting her to sing.

Marta took care of that, herding them all into the garden that filled the whole middle of the house. Aisha slipped on past.

When she came back with her belly comfortably full and a cup of chai warming her hands, there were even more people in the garden with Marta. And Rama—Aisha could feel him.

He wasn't angry, but he wasn't calm, either. Aisha slipped through the crowd of larger bodies, toward the middle where Marta sat under a trellis of blood-red roses. "I want you to sing with me," she said.

Rama leaned against one of the supports of the trellis, seeming lazy and casual. He smiled as he said, "I'm not what you'd call a master of your art."

"Oh, but you are," she said. "I'd like to try a new piece, and it needs a particular range of voice. Please try, ser. I promise you won't be pelted with rotten fruit if you're not perfect."

"Oh, no," one of the large persons said. "We lean toward throwing knives and the odd blowgun."

Rama's grin had too many teeth in it. "Now that's a game I'd play."

"Sers," Marta said with quelling sternness. "Hiroshi, there will be no weapons in my concert hall. Meser Rama, will you look at my music? It needs your voice."

Rama might know exactly what she was doing, but he was not immune. He bowed. "If there are blades and darts, I'll do my best to defend you."

Hiroshi laughed. So did most of the others.

Aisha took note of the rest. They might not be worth noting, but she liked to be sure. There were undertones, and things that weren't being said. Marta wasn't just doing this on a whim. It meant something.

Aisha would have dreaded singing in front of who knew how many total strangers. Maybe Rama didn't care so much. It couldn't have been any worse than leading armies into battle.

He was making them pay attention to him now. Asking questions. Listening to the answers. Managing to make it seem as if he was interested in every person there.

She didn't listen to the words. She watched the expressions, and the feelings that ran beneath. The ones who'd been skeptical were starting to think he maybe was, at least, interesting. The ones who'd thought so to start with were moving from interest toward fascination.

Marta was watching, too. Listening. Being amused. Turning what she saw and heard to music.

Aisha caught a skein of it, a bit of melody floating through the worldweb. Words drifted underneath. "He sang a psi master into submission. What could he do here?"

"What do you want him to do?" Aisha asked.

She didn't get an answer. Not then. She would eventually, she was sure.

Rama escaped without making anyone think he was running away. He wheedled Marta into singing an aria from one of her most famous roles, and while she sang, he slipped out.

The aria was the one she'd sung when they first saw her, back on Araceli. Aisha wanted to hang back and listen, but Rama was almost out of sight.

He was headed for the street. She didn't think he had any plan in mind, just to get out and see where they were. Aunt Khalida had done that when everyone else was asleep. Now Rama wanted a turn.

He wasn't headed for a bar, and he didn't want to drink himself out of whatever funk he happened to be in. He had thinking to do.

Aisha settled herself in his shadow. Rama didn't object. Probably because he knew it wouldn't do any good, but he seemed content with it.

Aisha kept track of where they were on the city's grid. Parts of it weren't so well monitored as others. Rama aimed for one of those, down toward the lake.

It was midday, Central time, and the streets were not maybe as crowded as they would be after the virtual sun went down. People wandered in and around the shops and restaurants, though the bars were quiet at this hour.

Rama didn't stop anywhere. He was doing a walking meditation as Pater called it. Moving to keep his mind moving. Processing.

Up one street, down another. Around a proscribed area: nonhuman habitat, atmosphere toxic to humans. Getting the shape of this place.

"Madhusudana Rama?"

He stopped. Nobody ever used the whole of his presumed name.

Unless they were MI, and blocking the way. The one in charge was a sturdy, grizzled man with a look of perpetual tired. "We'd like to speak with you, Meser Rama, if you don't mind."

The sergeant wasn't any taller than he was, but Rama managed to look as if he sneered down his nose at the man. "I believe I do mind."

"It will only take a few minutes," the sergeant said. "This way, ser."

"I think not."

The sergeant's troops closed in. There were more than Aisha had thought at first. They weren't taking any chances.

"You have no authority here," she said sharply.

"Actually, we do," the sergeant said. "We'll be wanting to speak to you, too, Sera Nasir. If you'll come with us."

"By treaty with Kom Ombo," Rama said, sounding just as casual as he'd been in the garden with Marta, "kidnapping, if proved, and if the victim is of appropriate age and family, is a crime without borders. That's his authority."

"Nobody kidnapped me," Aisha snapped. "I stowed away. Stowing away isn't a crime without borders, is it, Sergeant? You can't touch either of us."

"That remains to be proved," the sergeant said.

"Exactly," said Rama. "When you have proof, lodge a complaint with Central. In the meantime, if you don't mind..."

Obviously the sergeant did. Unlike Rama, he cared if he lived or died. And he had rules to live by.

He snapped a nod. His soldiers stepped back.

Rama saluted them. Aisha thought about it, but that might be too much. She settled for making sure they could see that she was armed, and staring down the sergeant on the way by.

"That was a pretext," Aisha said when they were out of sight and into a market square. All the booths had free trader marks on them, family crests and company logos and the black slash of the ancient syndicate called Anonymous. U.P. wouldn't dare make a move here.

"Of course it was a pretext," Rama said, pausing to inspect a table full of sharp and deadly things. "Your father wants you home. The Corps wants me stripped down to the last molecule, in as much pain as mortally possible."

He wasn't any more afraid of that than he was of anything else in this universe he hadn't asked to wake into. "I want to go home," Aisha said, "but not now. Not till I'm done. I'll send Pater a message. I've been ducking it. I should stop."

"That would be a good thing," he said.

Of course they'd keep coming after him anyway, because of what he'd done to the Corps. But Aisha would feel bettesr.

He wandered down through the market. He was making sure to be seen, Aisha realized: the same as he'd been in the garden. Buying a trinket here and a cup of exotic liquor there. Feeding pastries to his shadow, who had to eat under her veil.

It was all theater. She didn't know why, unless for its own sake. He had as much crew as he needed. More, in her opinion. Wherever he went next, it wouldn't have anything to do with this nest of free traders.

"A commander never wastes resources," his voice said in her head. "These might be useful someday."

Aisha couldn't very well argue with that. It was more entertaining than sitting in the principal's house, and she got to see actual aliens—walking right out in the street, sometimes in atmo-suits and sometimes with breathing mechanisms and sometimes simply walking or crawling or slithering or fluttering like any other oxygen-breather.

Like Rama. Which made her wonder how many other apparent humans in this place were not actually from Earth stock.

Her head had started to hurt again. The sun's image that Rama had taught her helped a little, but it was getting harder to keep her thoughts in and everybody else's out.

She was tired, and she wanted to go home. That was all it was. This adventure went on and on, but they were closer to an end, and an answer, than they'd been before.

She tripped and almost fell, but caught herself before anybody noticed. The map on the web had them nearly back to the principal's house.

MI was waiting outside. Besides the sergeant and his unit who had tried to stop them before, there was a lieutenant and a major and two more units. They blocked the streets on all sides and spilled over into doorways and down alleys.

They didn't try to stop Rama from going in. The way to the door was clear. Equally clearly, once he went in, he wouldn't get out again.

He laughed. It was the purest mirth Aisha had ever heard, and it was perfectly terrifying. He sauntered down the narrow path, mocking them with every line of him.

They weren't used to being laughed at. Some looked ready to leap when he went by. They closed in behind him, rank by rank, until the door was in front of him and opening to admit him.

He turned in it. A shiver ran across Aisha's skin, but she felt as if she'd been brushed with fire. "Go home," he said. "All of you, go."

Their faces went perfectly blank. They turned in formation and marched. Away. Every one of them. Not one even hesitated.

Once he was inside, Rama staggered. Fire brushed over Aisha again, but different this time: stronger. It felt like Ship, and like the sun on which Ship was feeding.

Rama steadied. It was beginning to sink in on Aisha what he'd done to the MI units, and what kinds of trouble they could all be in because of it.

She tried to say something, but he was already most of the way to his room, and there were people coming and going, looking for the principal. The moment slipped away.

She waited another moment. Then she went down the hall and through the door before he could shut it.

"That was stupid," she said. So was saying it, knowing what he'd just done, but she didn't let that stop her.

"I used to have patience for idiots," he said. "I slept too long. Time is short. I won't stay here any longer than my promise keeps me."

"That won't stop U.P. from going after you," she said. "The Corps wants your blood. You've made sure they want your brain, too. In a vat. Slaved to them forever."

He dropped onto the bed that must be meant for honored guests: it was huge, and the wood it was carved from must have cost a fortune to bring all the way out here. "They think I'm better than a living ship now?"

"After what you just did? If they can control that, they've got more power than they dared to dream of. When they find out what else you can do—"

"What else can I do?"

"That's what they'll want to know."

"I don't care."

"I know you don't." Aisha pulled off her veils and dropped them on the floor. "I hope you learn to care about something again. Someday. In the meantime, could you at least try not to get anyone else killed or mind-slaved? Not that you care, but we do."

He lifted himself on his elbow. "So now you're done with me."

"Don't you wish." She dropped her swords on top of the veils. She'd have dropped her robe, too, but all she had on under it was a shift. "If time is really that short, you don't need to waste any more of it fighting the Corps."

"What should I do, then? Apologize?"

He really seemed to want to know the answer. "It's awfully late for that," she said. Then paused. "Did you send them *all* the way home?"

His eyelids lowered: a yes.

"Can you make sure they don't let the Corps know what happened until they get there? If they haven't already?"

"It was stupid of me to do what I did, and now you want me to do more of it?"

"That was stupid," she said. "This is damage control. I can hack their system, I think. Or Aunt can. If you'll do the rest of what's needed."

"That would make you a criminal," he said.

"Not if we do it right." She wasn't as sure as she tried to sound. But she had a very bad feeling about what would happen if she didn't do it.

He dropped back flat. At first she thought he was asleep. Then she felt the shiver under her skin again.

Making magic. Or using psi. There wasn't any difference.

48

W hat does he mean, time is short?"

Khalida had heard Aisha out with a certain sense of inevitability. From the moment she realized what the being called Rama was, she had expected something like this. Destroying the Corps to end a war—that was justice. Mind-bending an entire MI garrison was no more or less than royal whim.

MI's access codes were not especially hard to find, if one still had one's own codes that with the slowness of subspace communications had not yet been voided. She simply wanted to prevent the troops here from notifying Centrum that they were abandoning Kom Ombo. Centrum would get that news when the ships emerged from jump.

Fifteen Earthdays. Then another fifteen at least before Kom Ombo could expect a reprisal. Longer, probably, with the amount of chaos Rama had already caused.

That was a given. What caught her attention now was that he was feeling the pressure of time. After six millennia and a handful of tendays, suddenly he was in a hurry to find whatever he had set out to find.

"Why?" she asked Aisha; not expecting the child to know.

But Aisha surprised her. "When he woke up, it was like tripping a trigger. Something started. He has to get to the end before—whatever else does."

"You don't know what that is. Does he?"

"Not as far as I can tell."

"Lovely." Khalida rubbed her eyes not because they were aching but because they were not. She felt strange.

Alive.

She could leave Rama to it. Let him live or die on his own. The Corps would gut him if it could.

She would gut the Corps if she could. If helping Rama solve his mystery would make that happen, she was glad to do it.

For the first time since her first tour to Araceli, she had a mission she was actually glad of.

That was what was strange. She was happy. It was dark and full of shadows, but there was no mistaking what it was.

"Right, then," she said. "I'll take care of communications. You watch him. If he tries to take off without us, don't let him. He's going to need backup wherever he goes. No matter what he thinks."

Aisha nodded. "He has enormous powers, but they're not unlimited. He does these impossible things, and then he crashes. He'll never find what he's looking for if he tries to do it alone."

"*You* should go home while you can," Khalida should have said. The words would not come. If Rashid ever got hold of her, he would throttle her for keeping quiet.

Maybe Marina would, or maybe she would not. Aisha was young, but she knew her own mind. Marina would understand that.

Khalida understood familial duty. She also understood the need to do what was necessary. Rashid was a man, and traditional at that—a long and ancient tradition of protecting the women and children. Regardless of whether the women and children either wanted or needed protection.

None of which Aisha needed to hear. Khalida said instead, "I don't think he'll go before the concert. His honor won't let him, even if his ego would."

"I'll watch him anyway," Aisha said.

"You do that."

Aisha went off to be a guard. Khalida had a different kind of guarding to do, once she had worked her way into MI's web and set the codes that needed to be set.

Whatever Rama had done, he had done it thoroughly. MI was pulling out of the system altogether—calling in scouts and surveillance vessels, shutting down bases. Packing up all their kit and loading it for transport.

"Impossible," Khalida said through the heavily shielded uplink to the *Ra-Harakhte*'s web. "Six thousand trained personnel with all their support staff and infrastructure, and another ten thousand shadow ops agents scattered across the system and out into the Great Beyond. All following orders without a word of objection. All—"

The former Lieutenant Zhao had not been visibly pleased to receive her ping, but he was conditioned to be amenable. He heard her out, until she stopped in frustration.

"All chipped," he said. "Linked to MI's systems. Connected on the web."

"What does that have to do with anything?" she demanded—angrier than she wanted to be, but unable to help herself. "You're a psi-three. Beside him you're a spark in a plains fire, but you understand these things. The kind of manipulation that can move an army—how is he still on his feet? Why hasn't he burned himself out?"

Zhao sighed over the link. He sounded terribly tired. "This is nothing I have ever heard of, let alone seen, but I can tell you the expenditure of psi was minimal. I barely felt it. It was like a tug on the hem of my mind: enough to notice, but certainly not strong enough to bend my will as he bent theirs."

"You never knew the ship was in pain, either," Khalida said. "I don't know why I expected you to be any different with this."

He flicked the link from audio-only to visual. She saw the matte darkness of one of the ship's bulkheads, and a screen full of stars, and almost incidentally, his worn and hollow-eyed face.

"You are not seeing the obvious," he said. He was trying to be severe, but it was not in him. It came across as prim. "They are all chipped. Connected on the web. He hacked their implants, Captain. It's no more complicated than that."

"Those implants are not hackable. There is no way—" Khalida broke off. "All right. Suppose he could do that, and even manage to keep my implants out of it, which implies a level of control that—well." She hauled herself back on course. "Between what he's learned from my excessively talented young relations, and what he's seen of the rebels on Araceli, he might have had examples to follow. But the sophistication of it—it's downright elegant. It reads as orders from Centrum. Properly formatted, solidly supported, and absolutely incontrovertible. Centrum says withdraw. Therefore they withdraw."

"'Theirs not to reason why,'" Zhao said.

She snarled at him, but absently. She had been thinking mind control in the raw sense of psi acting on the human consciousness. This was much more. The Bronze Age warlord had not only taken to cyber technology, he had treated it like a subset of psionics.

That, she could not say to this agent of the Corps. "I'm surprised your people haven't tried it."

"It's banned," Zhao said, and he seemed honestly horrified.

"That would stop them?"

He blinked. She was pushing, she knew it, but no Corps agent deserved better. "You must have had the same lessons in manipulation that I did. The most effective intelligence agent thinks faster, thinks deeper, and thinks around corners. She steps beyond the tidy box of *everyone knows*. She stands outside and looks in, and sees what those inside lack the perspective to see."

More than that, she thought as Zhao frowned, pondering what she had said. The being called Rama was an alien in a universe and a time that meant nothing, that was all new, without ingrained understanding or underlying assumptions. He took the nulls, the Corps, and the web, and turned all their variations on power into a weapon that could empty a system of its military presence.

"Genius," Zhao said slowly.

For a moment Khalida was sure he had read her mind, but then she remembered to breathe again. If he had, he would never have been so close to calm.

"Really," said Zhao. "It's brilliant. He's run a master con on an entire system's worth of armed forces, cleared the system for long enough to do what he has in mind, and then he'll go. By the time United Planets can begin to act, he'll be long gone."

"And us with him," Khalida said.

He peered at her through the link. She could feel him trying to reach into her mind after all: a sensation like a limb going numb, a faint, vaguely uncomfortable tingle. She met it with blankness and the polished surface of a mirror.

He flinched. She hoped, not kindly, that he had a headache. "Aren't you even a little bit afraid?" he asked with the first hint of temper she had seen in him.

"Of Rama?" She snorted. "Compared to what we had to cope with on Araceli? Not particularly. He doesn't mean us any harm, unless we get in his way."

"I wish," said Zhao, "I could be trusted with the truth. There's no sign of anyone or anything like him, anywhere within United Planets. *Anywhere.* He's not a child; I believe—I know—he's older than he looks. Where did he come from? How did we never have to contend with him? Because, Captain, the kind of man he is, he would never be content with obscurity. Tides of events swirl around him. He shapes those tides. He makes them turn to his will."

"Why," Khalida said, "you're a poet. And a precog. Aren't you?"

He bent his head. "It's not my strongest talent. I don't see clearly. Shapes, patterns, movement and change: I feel them. This man, this being, whatever he is, is like a shockwave. Where he goes, worlds change. I think—sometimes—they die."

Across the connection between them, her own familiar files began to stream. Star maps, patterns half-formed, traces of ruins across known and unknown space.

"He didn't make those," she said.

"Are you sure?"

"Moderately," she answered.

"It's a riddle," he said. "Isn't it? There has to be a key. A code that opens the—whatever it is. Files. Door. Jump point."

"You've been spying," she said.

"And thinking," he said without shame, which surprised her slightly. "That's my talent. Synthesis. I could help you, if you would let me. If you would trust me."

"I don't know," she said. "I'd have to think about it."

"That's fair," he said steadily. The sadness beneath was not intended to incite pity, she thought. Or no more so than he could help.

"Did you dream?" Khalida asked. "While you were asleep?"

Rama had not been awake for long. Khalida had camped in his room, with coffee on order for the moment he cracked an eyelid. Which, when she had almost dropped off herself, he finally did.

"I dreamed a panther stalked me. Just as it was about to spring, I woke up."

Khalida showed him her teeth. "Not just now. Then. When you were asleep in the rock. Did you dream?"

His eyes were the darkest she had ever seen, but they always had a light inside: a brightness in the heart. That brightness went abruptly dark.

"I have a reason for asking," she said. She gave it to him on the web, or in her mind if he preferred that.

A fragment, a few bytes in the stream of data that Zhao had run past her. A collection of children's stories from a multitude of worlds. A tale from an all but abandoned world, told by members of a forgotten tribe. How a terrible enchanter, half a demon, had been trapped by his mortal father and his lover and their children, and shut up in stone, and condemned to sleep forever, or until he dreamed his way out.

The light sparked again, as Rama's brows twitched upward. "A children's story?"

"Children get the truth when everyone else has forgotten. It's wrapped in story, but it's there. Did you dream?"

"Incessantly."

"Of what?"

"When I wasn't living my last day over and over?" He sat up, clasping his knees. He looked so young she was almost sucked in, but she was too old in paranoia for that. "I dreamed of suns and stars. Suns in multitudes. Stars wheeling in ranks like armies—galaxies, I know now. Then—nothing."

"Emptiness?"

"Nothing. No thing. No suns. No stars. Absolute blackness. And then..."

He paused so long that Khalida caught herself leaning forward until she almost fell over. "And then?"

"Light," he said, "at the utmost end of time. Where the stars have all died or were never born. Except one. With...something...in its heart. Something that I could never see."

"Never?"

"Not ever," he said. "Except..."

This time she waited. He had a long, long run of dreams to remember.

When he spoke, it was in his own language, a swift flow of words that gradually resolved into something she could understand. "I was cast into sleep because I saw only light and darkness, and nothing between. Light was perfect; darkness was evil. I was absolutely convinced of it—as only the true believer can be. I nearly brought down half a world.

"I deserved my sentence. But something was out there. Something beyond any of our gods or even our night terrors. Something that would cause our people to empty the world and sweep away a moon, to destroy it. Or," he said slowly, "to lure it. To draw it away. To trap it, and bind it. Because that was all they could do. Or all they dared do."

"Because none of them was as strong as you?"

"I doubt it was the strength," he said, dry as his bones should have been after six thousand years. "I was—I am—a weapon. A mindless, deadly thing. A power that can, and without compunction will, destroy—and not care if it is destroyed."

"You're not mindless," Khalida said.

"Am I not?"

She had nothing to say to that. Instead she focused on another part of this inherently preposterous story. "What is so terrible that it needs the sacrifice of a whole world?"

"Not just one world," he said. "All those worlds, all those ruins—world after world, star after star. It took them all. Until my people stopped it. Wiping out all trace of who they were, that was part of it. The mystery. The void that beckoned. And beckoning, became a trap."

She could almost make sense of that. "So—what? They left a trail for you? It's not just random worlds?"

"Not random at all," he said. "Each world was a destination, and a point of departure. A gate. We hadn't mapped them, but we knew of them. After I was gone...I think our world became a nexus. A gathering place, a port—like this place. But not for ships; for worldgates. Then something came through. Something that could only be stopped by destroying them all."

"Or that destroyed them all, once it had gone through." Khalida had stopped trying to suspend disbelief; she had proof enough that something was out there, or had been. "If that all happened a thousand years after you went into stasis, why is it so urgent that you find the answer now? You're no part of whatever it was. You were awakened by accident."

"Was I?"

"Aisha miscalculated the quantity of explosives. She was only trying to open a door."

"Yes."

Khalida throttled back a strong urge to hit him. "My niece has nothing to do with you or your world or your people."

"Your niece is a strong psi, as you would put it. If it was time, and she was there..."

"I don't believe in destiny," Khalida said. "Or in divine will."

"Or fate, either, I would presume." Rama reached for the coffee that had been steaming in its mini-stasis field, and grimaced as he drank it. "You are all godless heathen, and my old self would have given you a choice: to be converted to the one true faith, or killed."

"Really?"

"No." After coffee there was breakfast: enough for three. He ate it all, methodically. Fueling. Just as the *Ra-Harakhte* fueled itself for a voyage to the edge of nowhere. "Our kind of holy war was not about conversion. It was about who was demonstrably right."

"Which you were?"

"Until I was manifestly wrong."

"Do you think you might be wrong now?"

"I think I have to go where I'm directed to go. I'm no use to this universe otherwise."

"Everyone is of some use," Khalida said. "If only to fertilize a field."

He stared; then laughed. "You would have done well in the world I come from."

"I am a bit of an atavism, aren't I?" She stood. "You have an opera to rehearse. I have a set of patterns to stare at, and try to make a little more sense of."

"Why?"

"Why rehearse? Because you need to know where to stand, and when not to start singing."

He shook that off. "Why do you help me? What's in it for you?"

"Knowledge."

He pondered that. After a while he nodded. "It's in your blood."

"Tomb robbing. Since before even you were born."

"Searching not for gold but for understanding. Yes. Your niece is the same."

Sudden anger gusted, catching Khalida by surprise. "My niece is nothing like me. She's clean."

"Of what?"

Khalida could not bring herself to answer that. She left him sitting there with the empty cup in his hand.

Aisha had been capturing and filing all her messages from Nevermore since she came out of jump on the *Leda*. She hadn't opened any of them. She knew what they said. She wasn't sure she could handle the way she'd feel when she finally read them.

Now she'd promised Rama, and she kept her promises. Even when she hated to even think about it.

There were many more messages than she remembered, most from Pater. Nothing from Mother. Only two from Jamal, and one of them was the most recent of all the messages in the file.

They'd probably put him up to it, hoping she'd answer him if she wouldn't go near them. They were right. He'd filter them anyway, and he might have something to say other than How Dare You and What Were You Thinking and Get Back Home Right Now.

The message was plain data, no enhancements. Just words.

They've been freaking since they found out where you went. I know you can't come back, but you'd better say something to them before they finish ripping my head off and feeding it to me sideways.

I'm on lockdown. I can't even go outside the house unless somebody goes with me. Not that I mind, really, but they keep trying to restrict my web access, and that

I do mind. Did you know we got our hackitude from Mother? Not just from Aunt Khalida? She put an actual tracer on my searchbots. Took me two whole Earthdays to get rid of it.

Aisha had known about Mother and the web, and she suspected that what Jamal had got rid of was just a decoy. But she wouldn't tell him that. Some things a person had to learn for himself.

Everything's crazy here. The horses are all impossible without you and Aunt Khalida to keep them in line, and Mother's too busy with everything else to take the time. The antelope are actually less trouble than the horses. Malia comes and goes and keeps them mostly from climbing walls and breaking down fences. Pater wants to turn them loose, but Mother won't let him. She still wants to write that paper.

The new interns are an exceptionally incompetent collection of miseducated acephalic organisms, Pater says. U.P. tried to cancel the grant for the season, which just happened to happen after you turned up on the Leda. We've been descended on by a shipful of tourists who aren't, if you know what I mean. I think some of them are Psycorps agents pretending to be Centrum richidiots, and the rest are MI and maybe even black ops. It's like a vid, with more screaming.

Aisha was almost jealous. Life on Nevermore had never been that interesting when she was there.

Look, Jamal said. *Send something, all right? Just so they'll calm down a little bit. Which we will.*

That wasn't Jamal. Aisha let go the breath she'd been holding. Mother came through in text, but with her image attached, eyes steady on Aisha as if she could actually see her. *Daughter of mine, I won't tell you anything you don't already expect, except this. If you need help, or backup, or more advice, good or bad, than you can ever use, send a message with the code I've embedded. Direct it to any tradeship in or out of U.P. space. They'll give you what you ask.*

Now that Aisha hadn't been expecting. She knew a little about Mother before she met Pater—how she was crew on a tradeship because she didn't have the funding to be a research scholar. She'd met Pater on one of the ship's runs, while he was still setting up the expedition to Nevermore.

That was very romantic, though like Nevermore at the moment, with more screaming than one mostly saw in stories. What Aisha hadn't known was that Mother still kept her contacts with the tradeships.

Odd to think of Mother as someone with secrets. Odder to get an offer of help, instead of a demand that she come home.

Stay sensible, Mother said. *Take notes. Your first doctorate is in there somewhere.*

Aisha broke down and bawled. Not too long. Just to howl a little bit. Let it all out. Wish she could be home again—for an hour or a night.

Then she could be sensible again, the way Mother said. She kept the message-within-a-message with its encrypted code that she didn't expect she'd ever use.

It was the thought that counted. She put together her own message, just a short one.

Dear Mother and Pater and Jamal and Vikram and everybody, I'm well, really I am. Aunt Khalida is here and keeping me in line. We're looking for ways to save Nevermore. We'll come back when we find them. That's a promise.

P.S. Mother, I'm taking notes.

That was the best she could do. She marked it to send the next time the subspace packet went out, which would probably be when MI left the system.

She still felt odd and weepy. She went to watch rehearsals, to have something to do that wasn't on the web or inside her own head.

Marta's piece played as part of an opera, with chorus and instrumentals and virtual sets and costuming. They were putting it all together when Aisha slipped into the hall.

It was dark, and quiet except for the shimmer of music far away. Aisha could feel the people in the big high room, the bodies moving and breathing and thinking. They didn't matter, any more than the air around her or the floor under her feet. Everything was about the music.

It grew slowly, bringing light with it. Faint at first, like dawn on Earth, or on Nevermore. But the setting was neither. It was a landscape of rock and ruins, stripped of anything living. The dark overhead was a sky without stars, but that changed, too, little by little.

What rose was not the sun but a wheel of stars, a spiral galaxy climbing over the barren horizon. The music swelled from instruments into voices.

Under the wheel of stars was a wheel of stone. It was broken: parts of it had fallen into rubble. But the arch held, and on the other side was white light.

The voice that soared above the chorus was Marta's, pure and strong and high. It was singing in a language Aisha almost recognized: a little like ancient Egyptian, a little like the old language of Nevermore.

The words weren't important. The music said everything it needed to say. Grief and loss. Anger and sorrow. So many years. So many worlds. So many lives poured away into the unforgiving rock.

When the voice changed, it was so natural and inevitable that Aisha almost felt safe. But this wasn't about safety. It was about something so terrible that it had no name, and so powerful that it had broken whole worlds.

He stood in the light, distilled out of it: as dark as the darkness, but full of the fire of suns. His voice was dark and bright and harsh and sweet. It was trained—he'd been too humble about that—but the way it wrapped around the notes was completely different. Not of Earth or the worlds that looked toward Earth. Alien.

He sang in web-common, which was like all languages piled together and made into a matrix for data. He'd thrown his own words into that, and along with the rest they made more sense than they had any right to make.

They translated in her mind as images. The endless rolling grasslands of Nevermore. The vanished cities, the people gone, every face, every voice, every name. The moons that had been; the one that was left, broken and barren. As barren as the world around him on the stage.

He stood on the edge of infinity, staring down and down. She knew he would jump—he had to jump. There was nowhere else to go.

He soared instead. Up and up. Into the sun. Through the sun. Into darkness and quiet and a far glimmer of green.

Marta's voice found him again, there on the other side of spacetime. They sang the light back into the universe, populating the sky with stars, and the stars with planets, and the planets with life in infinite variety.

When silence fell, it was perfect. Aisha remembered to start breathing again.

Everyone had the same blank, stunned expression. Even Marta—though she shook herself out of it. "That will do," she said. "With a few small adjustments. The blocking of the sets—"

"I've seen a face like that before."

Aisha was still recovering. She'd known what Rama could do with his voice, but Marta had turned it into something even stronger. It was almost terrifying.

She blinked at the person in front of her. It was one of the techs, a very tall person, very pale, like something carved in ice. Heshe was staring at Rama, whom Marta was talking to low and fast, while other techs and the musicians swirled around them.

"Those proportions," the tech said, "are almost human, but they're not. Are they? Not quite. I've seen them in one other place."

Aisha sucked in a breath. This was huge, if heshe was telling the truth. Though why would heshe not? "Where?" she asked.

"Very far away," the tech said, sweeping hiser long thin hand outward and upward, the way Rama had flown out of the abyss. "Out toward the farthest station, on the edge of human space. It was just for a moment, in passing in the zocalo, but I'll never forget."

"Did you record it?" Aisha asked. "Can you show me?"

"No," the tech said with real regret. "It was too fast, and I was too startled. It's only in my head."

Aisha knew someone who could view that. Several someones. She couldn't make herself say so. It felt too strange.

"Will you come?" she said. "And tell him?"

The tech stiffened. "I couldn't—I don't have much to—"

"He'll want to know," she said.

Heshe dithered, but Aisha waited himer out. After a while heshe twitched toward Rama. Aisha led himer the rest of the way.

Marta had let Rama go while she went into conference with the musicians. He had the odd, closed look he got sometimes, turning inside himself and facing things Aisha didn't want to imagine.

"Rama," she said.

Her voice brought him back out of his head. He smiled at her, and slanted an inquiring glance at the person with her.

"Rama," she said, "Mesera Pereira wants to tell you something."

Mesera Pereira looked ready to bolt, but Rama's smile held himer immobile. It was like bathing in sunlight. Aisha was used to it, and she could still just bask; for someone new, it must be overwhelming.

"Mesera," he said.

"Meser," heshe answered. "I said to your friend—your sib—your crewperson? I saw someone. A face like yours. It's not—it's hard to forget."

He went perfectly still. The warmth was still in him, consciously so; he was trying not to spook the tech. But all his focus had gathered and fixed. "You have seen one like me? Where?"

"A station," Mesera Pereira said, "very far out. Starsend, it's called."

"Will you show me?" Rama asked.

He did it so gently, and so warmly, that the tech could only nod. Aisha felt him go in, gliding like a fish through deep water, and finding the one thing he wanted, that floated up near the surface.

She saw it, too, pulled along in his wake. A crowded marketplace under a few sparse stars, a swirl of faces, and then that one. The one that—yes, it looked like Rama.

It was just a glimpse as the tech had said. A person walking fast between market stalls, not acknowledging anyone nearby, going from here to there with as much speed as traffic and long legs would allow.

It was a very tall person. Much taller than Rama, but the profile was strikingly like his, and the skin like black glass, and even the way it—heshe? No, she—held her head and turned her shoulders, as if she ruled the world.

Rama paused the memory like a vid, to bring out details that the tech might not have consciously recalled, but they were there. Hair in braids strung with copper beads. Rings swinging in the ears. Clothes almost disappointingly ordinary, but brightened with embroidery.

Real embroidery: thread stitched on cloth, rimming collar and fastenings and sleeves and hem of the closely fitted coat. Glint of metal under and over it: at least two necklaces and a collar made of hammered plates—copper, maybe; in that light was hard to tell. The rest Aisha couldn't see; the woman was too far away and there were too many people in the way.

Rama let out a long, slow breath. Aisha blinked: she was out in the physical world again, and Mesera Pereira was staring at them both, puzzled and a little dazed.

"Thank you," Rama said, and he meant it. "From my heart, I thank you."

The tech didn't seem to know what to say to that. Rama dazzled himer with a smile several solar magnitudes brighter than the one he'd had before, and one way and another, got himer moving toward the rest of the techs and the rehearsal that was still going on.

For Aisha it was over. For Rama, too, though he wasn't inclined, just yet, to leave.

"Is it?" she asked him. "Is it really? But if it is, how—"

"Yes," he said. "It is. Really. There can be no mistake. As to how—that's a question to which we will have to find the answer."

We. She liked that. Unless he was being royal, in which case she had no intention of being left behind.

"You can't go now," she said. "Not till after the performance."

"No," he said. "Not until then. But as soon as it's over—"

"We'll be ready," she said.

While the *Ra-Harakhte*'s captain made music in Central, his crew had been taking shore leave in shifts. Khalida found herself functioning more or less as his XO, not through any effort of her own; it just seemed to happen.

She still had MI clearances, with Kom Ombo clearances on top of those, and more experience on the bridge of a starship than anyone else on the ship. With one thing and another, various bits of administrivia devolved to her; as she dealt with them, more appeared. She had every intention of tossing them all into Rama's lap when he finally deigned to come back aboard, but in the meantime, it did pass the time.

Robrecht had also fallen into executive-officer duties; when he came down, she went up, onto a ship gone oddly silent with so few personnel on board. Even the scientists had gone below. A skeleton crew manned the bridge and watched over the cargo in its shielded bays.

She appreciated the quiet. The ship was in feeding mode, which was somewhat like sleep. The two members of the crew at the screens were not far from sleep themselves; they were only there to respond if something unexpected happened.

She could as easily monitor them and the ship from quarters as from the bridge, but there was something oddly comforting about sitting in the captain's cradle and staring at the dynamic sameness of traffic in and out of Central. The webfeed streamed through, with the occasional blip or near-miss, but nothing to do with this ship.

What alerted her, at first she hardly knew. A slight anomaly running underneath the feed. A blip that had nothing to do with external traffic.

Something was trying to hack into the ship's web. That was not particularly unusual—except that it came from on board.

All of the crew were either off the ship or doing their duty, or else, in one or two cases, asleep. Khalida tracked the anomaly with one of her own, and hissed.

Of course. Everyone had forgotten the prisoner in the ship's brig. The ship fed and monitored her, but seemed not to have bothered to stop her when she found her way into its web.

Khalida entertained the thought of simply shutting off life support to the brig. But she had done enough killing.

She waited instead, and observed. The anomaly was a very small and subtle bot, exploring specific sites.

Not necessarily the ones she would have expected. Free ships in search of crew, yes. Deep-cover sites for MI and the Corps—of course. But also archaeological journals, news of the weird and the outré, and statistics related to the trade, both legal and illegal, in alien artifacts.

Khalida set her own bot to shadow MariAntonia's. When that was taken care of, she happened to pass by another stream of the web, a feed from crew quarters.

The former Lieutenant Zhao had been keeping to himself. Aside from that one ping from the station four days ago, Khalida had barely paused to think of him. For a person whose whole world had imploded, he was not doing too badly.

Or so she had thought. Without the Corps behind him, he was a more or less harmlessly pretty thing with just enough psi to be noticeable. It had not burned out with the rest on Araceli—the ship had shielded him, and Rama, too, as far as Khalida knew.

And now there was survivor's guilt, which she knew much too well, and grief, and shock, and all the rest of the aftermath of an intensely personal disaster. With no one to care enough to get him mended, even if Khalida had believed in such a thing after the little good such therapies had done her.

He was asleep, and he did not intend to wake. She would have left him to it—his life to waste or lose—but some vestige of childhood training brought her to her feet.

Crew quarters had grown down toward the ship's ventral sections, clusters of three- and four-meter globes strung along tubular passages like grapes on a vine. She found Zhao in the farthest of these, drawn into a fetal knot.

The ship was as willing to shock him awake as it had been to send him into a gradually deepening coma. She would have to do something about that, she thought as he thrashed and flailed. The ship did not, yet, know how to distinguish between actual pilot's duties and suicidal stupidity.

Zhao's convulsions quieted slowly enough to knot Khalida's stomach. She had not set out to damage him, though she had not tried terribly hard not to, either.

Ship's web scanned him, but apart from a headache and some cognitive confusion, found nothing out of order. He lay shaking, sucking in breaths.

"Idiot," Khalida said.

He blinked at her. His face twitched; he shuddered. "What did you— Why—"

"I didn't get to die after what I did," she said. "Neither do you."

"What I—I didn't do anything!"

"Tell that to the children you dragged in for indoctrination. The ones who went on to become good soldiers. The ones who wouldn't surrender; who were neutered and thrown back out."

"The ones your alien beast stripped of mind and sense and left to go mad inside their own skulls?"

That might have been the first truly honest thing he had ever said. "All he did," Khalida said, "was give them back what they had given."

Zhao shuddered again. "I wish I could hate him."

Khalida's brows lifted. "Don't you?"

"I hate myself."

He was drawing into a knot again. She slapped him hard enough that his ears must be ringing, but not so hard that he lost consciousness.

"Get up!" she snapped at him. "Get out. Walk!"

He had been conditioned to do what he was told. He got up; he lurched toward the door.

Khalida hauled him back. "Not toward an airlock, damn you. You're coming to the bridge with me, and you're making yourself useful. No more hiding. No more wallowing."

"Talking to yourself now, Captain?"

"Is it working, Lieutenant?"

"No." But he stood straighter. When she pushed him forward, he walked, and did not try to escape.

She had had nothing in mind for him to do, but by the time she herded him onto the bridge, she thrust him in front of a screen and said, "Monitor traffic. Out as well as in. If anything makes a move that doesn't feel right, alert me."

He blinked at her. "Something wrong? What do you—"

"Ordinary and sensible precautions," she said, "and a feeling in my gut."

He nodded. "I'll keep watch."

Maybe he would. Maybe he would fall back down into despair, or maybe he would wander off when he grew tired. But he was disposed of for the moment.

Part of the feeling in her gut was hunger. She dealt with that, and considered sleep, but the thought of leaving the bridge made her shoulders twitch.

She still had patterns to ponder, and a mystery that needed solving. Too much, her old self would have said, before it ran to hide. This new self, after Araceli, let it all run together.

"Captain."

Khalida snapped out of a half-dream. In it, she had been swimming through a sea full of stars, following a shadow that sometimes had no shape at all, and sometimes looked back at her with a woman's face.

Zhao was still at his screen, but his voice spoke directly in her ear, through a focused weblink. "What do you make of this?"

The feed he sent seemed unexceptional. Flow and ebb of traffic. MI ships reaching jump points and vanishing from the system. Other ships coming in— free traders, a cruise ship, a freighter or two.

"Not out there," Zhao said. "In here."

He meant around the docking bay, not inside the ship. Inside was quiet, even in the brig.

Every bay had its quota of human traffic, even at this upper level. Inspectors inspecting, travelers traveling, the occasional random explorer. Khalida's scans had allowed for this. What they had not considered was an explorer of apparent alien origin who happened to be a mask for—on quick count—fifteen all but perfectly shielded human bodies.

They moved slowly, but their trajectory was not difficult to see. They were aiming toward the shuttle hatch, which was well down along the docking bay.

If the ship had been a simple mechanical object, they would have had a reasonable chance of breaking in and doing whatever they had in mind. The *Ra-Harakhte* was neither simple nor mechanical.

Khalida paused in alerting the ship. There would be no hatch anywhere on its hull, if she warned it to keep the intruders out. If they tried to burn their way in, the ship would react appropriately. There might be something left of them: a drift of ash, a coil of smoke.

She sent an alert, but not the one that first came to mind. The second message she sent was directed toward Zhao and, after a slight pause, the prisoner in the brig.

Khalida went armed. So, under duress, did Zhao. MariAntonia went in shackles, without a word or a glance. No protests, either, which Khalida took note of.

Two and a hostage against fifteen was poor odds, but the two of them had the *Ra-Harakhte* at their backs. Once they were in the bay, the entrance smoothed behind them, growing back into the body of the ship.

Ship's web showed her the vaguely amorphous alien shape oozing toward the hatch. It was an interesting construct: evidently alive, and almost perfectly concealing the humans inside. Someone had been experimenting, or gengineering.

The latter, she hoped, but considering what MI and the Corps had tried to do to the *Ra-Harakhte*, she would not have bet on it.

The hatch opened as the intruder approached. It paused: suspicious, she supposed. The interior was lit like the rest of the ship: bright enough for human eyes, and therefore welcoming.

She was not visible; a jut of wall just happened to cast a shadow across her and her companions. They were still, Zhao by choice, MariAntonia because the ship had wrapped a pseudopod around her mouth and neck. It could, it made clear, cover her nose if she moved.

Her eyes were flat, and unafraid. Khalida knew that look. She had nothing to lose.

That made her even more dangerous. Khalida smiled with honest warmth, and dipped her head: acknowledgment; amusement.

The ship played its part well, seeming to resist, and forcing the intruders to work to get in. It had shifted pain receptors elsewhere, and hardened the hull, but not to impermeability. This was a trap, after all. Not a fortification.

The glow of a beam grew slowly near the edge of the usual hatch. Khalida found she had shifted to fighting stance. She drew a breath and settled back to relaxed, casual, but ready to leap.

It took the beam a good while to cut through, and then the invaders had to pry an opening large enough to admit a human body. Even knowing that the ship allowed this, and felt little more than pressure, as if anesthetized, Khalida grimaced.

The first intruder thrust her way in with beam rifle at the ready. Her armor seemed to be of generic make without insignia, but there was no effective way to hide the profile. MI. As were the rest who followed her and fanned across the bay, scanning the apparently empty space with helmet cams and rifle barrels.

The last one in had his rifle slung behind him and a control console in his hand. Khalida recognized the make and shape. Larger versions had been wired into the *Ra-Harakhte*'s nervous system.

Size, at this level of technology, was never particularly relevant. She felt the ship shudder underfoot. It recognized the thing, too.

Khalida recognized the man who held it. It was like a beam in the vitals.

She held still. Not yet. Not yet.

She watched the invaders realize they were in a blind pouch, with nothing in it but patches of light and shadow. They circled back to their commander.

His fingers flicked across the console. A filament shot out of it, aiming toward the ceiling.

The ceiling pulsed upward. The filament fell short, but snapped up again, stretching higher.

Khalida shot it down.

Fifteen beam rifles swung toward her. She stepped into the light. A handful of barrels flickered, charging to fire.

"I wouldn't do that," she said.

"Captain Nasir," the commander said, as coldly calm as she was trying to seem.

"Colonel Aviram," she answered. "You travel fast."

"As do you."

"I know how I got here. You? More experiments, like the thing you hid behind to get in here?"

"That would be classified information," he said.

While they spoke, she was sharply aware of the two still in shadow. Zhao breathed shallowly, tensely. She could not hear MariAntonia at all, or sense her. But the ship knew she was there.

The ship inhabited a different zone of consciousness than the humans inside it. Khalida had known that. She had not, until just now, understood it.

It was important. She had no time to think about it. Aviram and his unit were positioning themselves, with exquisite slowness, to dispose of her and finish slaving the ship all over again—more effectively this time. More completely. Though not with any less pain.

That was important, too, in a way that churned her stomach. The Corps had always been ugly at the core. MI, not much less. But the pattern here went beyond institutional awfulness. Experimentation on living creatures—humans; sentient aliens. There had been laws against that since before the first spacecraft left Earth's surface.

The ship could dispose of these, and the mole who had brought them in. All Khalida had to do was drag Zhao with her through the wall and leave them to it.

That would have been the rational thing to do. She faced down those fifteen gently flickering barrels and inquired, "Don't you have orders to vacate this system with all personnel and equipment?"

Aviram's stare was perfectly flat. "Who manufactured those? You?"

"I'm flattered," she said, "but I don't have anything like that level of skill. Not to mention the ability to convince several thousand trained troops and staff that those orders are valid."

"I didn't think so," Aviram said. "You realize that—whatever he, or it, is—is a threat to everything United Planets stands for."

There was no point in pretending to misunderstand. "There is no threat. He doesn't care what we are or what we represent. All he wants is to get free of us and go on about his business."

"Pity he's wanted for high crimes and misdemeanors, hijacking, hacking, grand theft, abuse and misuse of psi, unregulated psi…"

"He doesn't care," Khalida said again. "Neither do I. I'd wonder how you managed to escape the compulsion to get out. More experiments, I suppose. It doesn't matter. You can leave now, or I'll leave you here and let the ship dispose of you."

"That would be murder," Aviram said. His eyes flickered, maybe. The light was not terribly bright, and Khalida was not terribly interested.

"I have a quarter of million lives on my conscience," she said. "What's a few more?"

There, she thought. That was the key. Not to care. He might order her shot; that was the tightness between her shoulders, though the ship was watching.

One rifle did pulse, but the beam dissipated in midair. The ship swallowed it—not delighted with the taste, but glad enough of the nourishment.

"Stand down!" Aviram snapped. "Barrels up. Disengage."

MariAntonia darted past Khalida. Zhao plunged in pursuit. Khalida caught him. Crossed beams caught MariAntonia.

Khalida gagged on the savory scent of roasted flesh. Zhao doubled up with dry heaves.

"Take that with you when you go," Khalida said.

She sounded cold even to herself. Colder by far than she felt.

Aviram caught the shooters' glances. They moved in just slowly enough to register reluctance, lifted the charred carcass and carried it through the hatch that had, obligingly, opened in front of them.

None of them spoke. Not even Aviram.

He was last to go. When he looked ready to pause, the hatch curved around him and thrust him firmly out.

Screens showed him in the bay, staring at a smooth and unmarred hull. He wore no expression at all.

"She chose that," Zhao said, still gagging. Tears streamed down his face. "She killed herself."

"She had nowhere else to go." Khalida directed the ship to clear the air; when she took another breath, there was only a hint of roasted flesh left. With the next inhalation, that was gone.

"We're not done with Aviram," Zhao said, "or with U.P. They want us too badly to ever let us go."

"Are you planning to stay here?" she asked.

He frowned. "No. No, I'm not staying. Why would I—"

"Where we're going, U.P. has no jurisdiction. It might try to claim us, because we used to belong to it. It won't be able to hold us. Not without more backup than it could afford, that far out—and with its bases here gutted and its personnel gone, its lines of supply have thinned to vanishing. We're not safe, Lieutenant, but we're not in danger, either. We're as free as we can hope to be."

He did not believe her. He was a child of the inner worlds: he had only known the full power of the systems he used to serve.

He would learn. Or he would die. They all might die, out there, before Rama found what he was hunting.

Khalida was looking forward to it.

Aisha could not stop twitching. The performance was today, and then they would all go back to the ship. Everyone was ready—Aisha as much as anyone. There was no reason to fidget and fuss.

She was still wearing her black robe because it was all she had. The veils and swords were still on Rama's floor, for all she knew. Which left her without a weapon, except the one inside her head.

She thought about requisitioning something. She got as far as opening a web connection, but then she stopped. She didn't know why.

She asked for something else instead. Clothes—sensible things, and nothing in black. She didn't know that she'd ever want to wear black again.

When the Pay Now screen came up, it flashed once and disappeared. She dived after it, and ran into Alexandra's shimmering, floating icon.

"My dear," the rich voice said, "it's our pleasure."

"I can't," Aisha said.

"But you will," said Alexandra. "It's not a bribe, if that worries you. You need these. It's our gift."

"Why?"

Alexandra wasn't human. She didn't blink at Aisha's straight thrust. "You need them. We can give them."

"And?"

"Maybe we wish you well," Alexandra said. "Maybe we want you to be properly outfitted, wherever you are going."

"We don't know where we're going."

"Yet." Alexandra's smile wrapped around her like a warm woolen hug. "Someday we'll all know. And that will be wonderful."

"Or terrible."

"Terrible has wonder in it, too," said Alexandra.

She slipped out of the link. Aisha felt unexpectedly cold and a little lonely. She shouldn't trust anybody, especially out here; she knew that. But she really wanted to trust this alien.

Go with your gut. That was one of Mother's sayings. It didn't always work, but Aisha thought it might, this time. She hoped.

After all that preparation, the performance came up startlingly fast. One minute they were all running around finishing up the last-minute crises. Then everybody crowded into the concert hall in the center of Central, perched on a promontory above Alexandra's lake.

The hall was full. So was the feed to the rest of the system. Marta was that famous out here, and people were that curious about her new production.

Aisha stood backstage, pressed up against a strut while chaos whirled around her. She'd much rather have been high up in the balconies, like being in a starship on the edge of a system, where she could see everything and everybody, and look down on the stage. But unless she learned to fly and not just float above her bed at night, that was much too far away from Rama.

She could feel the pressure of watchers on the web feed, with more coming in the closer they got to showtime. Ship was there, too, more awake than it had been in a while. Watching. Curious. Interested. A little wary.

There was no telling what would happen once the performance began. Aisha was ready for anything, or nothing. They would all be leaving as soon as it was over—they were packed and ready, and their shuttle was booked.

Rama had done that, abruptly, this morning. He wasn't twitching the way Aisha was, but he was done here. If it hadn't been for his promise, he'd already be gone.

Aisha stayed as close to him as she could, dressed in the most practical clothes Alexandra had sent her—close enough to riding clothes that she found herself missing her horse.

She wished she'd kept her swords, too. But she had the web and her brains, and her eyes keeping track of the hall as it filled.

The musicians trooped down into their bay. The hum and buzz of people moving and settling started to slow down.

The lights dimmed. Silence fell. Aisha realized she was holding her breath. She let it go.

She'd seen all the pieces of the performance before, but not together. Not with the sets in place and the lighting all working and the music doing what it was supposed to.

She had to work to keep from getting caught up in it. To stay alert, and keep watching.

The beginning was all Marta and the musicians' guild. Her songs, their music. Those were wonderful, but no one was here just for them. They were waiting for the new piece and the new singer.

Word was out. People had heard about the traveler with the living ship.

MI was mostly out of the system, but not quite. There was no telling which agents were still there undercover, or which agency they reported to.

It might not just be U.P., either. Ship was something different—something valuable. So was Rama, if anyone knew or guessed.

Everything was quiet on the web. The music wound on. Marta wasn't making the magic she could make. She was just a beautiful voice, singing beautiful songs.

She'd deliberately ramped the performance down. Or maybe she was saving it for the second half.

In the intermission, the shuffle and shift of people had an unusual quality to it. They were holding their breath. Nobody went too far or stayed away too long, even on the web.

When the lights went out, the hall was absolutely silent. No one so much as breathed.

Aisha had thought they might dress Rama in something spectacular, but he came out in the same plain black robe he'd worn in rehearsals.

It was all he needed. His voice seemed so soft, but it filled every corner of the hall, and soared out onto the web, and echoed in the system.

He could have been his own statue, or a broken shard of a pedestal, or a featureless cylinder like Ship, and it wouldn't have mattered, once that sound began to pour out of him.

He was singing to the stars. Marta's music was only the beginning. When he shifted to Old Language, that was another music altogether. His music. Music from a world only he remembered.

It was a call. A challenge. I am here. Where have you gone? Show your faces. Lead me onward.

He put all his power into it. He drew from the sun, and from every starship's drive and engine in Kom Ombo, and from Ship, which gave even while it fed.

No one moved, anywhere. The hall and the web were absolutely silent. Absolutely rapt.

It was a wild, crazy, lethal gamble. If his people had had to destroy every shred of evidence about themselves and their history, filling truespace and subspace with their music, in their language, with his of all voices, was completely insane.

That was why he did it. He always did the wild thing, the crazy thing.

When it was the right thing, as far as he could know. It might be completely and hopelessly wrong, but he had to trust that it wasn't.

He sang till his heart must be like to burst, till his bones turned to stellar dust and his veins were laced with fire.

Finally Aisha saw him clear, without his masks and his grief and his eons-old exhaustion. He was terrifying, but she wasn't afraid.

The attack came straight down through the roof and in through every entrance.

They'd put everything they had into it. The web crashed, taking the lights and most of the life support. System traffic ground to a halt.

The people in the hall didn't panic. Aisha noticed that particularly. In the pale blue of the emergency lights, they stayed put. A rumble rolled through the crowd, like a mass growl, but no one attacked the attackers.

There must have been fifty of them in riot gear with night-vision helmets, running down the aisles and rappelling off the roof. They aimed for the stage.

Rama stood as still as the audience. Pale gold light shimmered over him. His head was lifted, his eyes following the attackers as they converged on him. He smiled.

He was the only light in that place. He seemed to glow brighter, the longer the dark lasted.

Boots thudded on the stage. A bolt flashed off into the rafters. Rama's voice said in Aisha's ear, "Stay close. Be quiet."

She nearly jumped out of her skin. He held her down with his hand on her shoulder. As far as she could see or feel, they were alone backstage. The musicians and Marta and all the techs and stagehands had disappeared.

He *was* there. But she could see—

—through the one on stage. When she really, deeply looked. The one next to her was solid, warm and breathing.

More and more invaders crowded the stage. Rama's fetch stood in a circle of empty space. It flashed a grin, and laughed, and said, "Catch me if you can!"

It flew straight up, just as the roof directly above came down and the floor of the stage curved to meet it. The snap of beam fire flickered like lightning, most of it inside, a few out: blasting the smooth curved surface that had been a stage and a dome.

The rumble in the floor swelled to a deep, angry roar. Shadowy figures surged up and over the handful of invaders who'd eluded the trap.

Rama tugged at Aisha's shoulder. In the open space that had been the roof, a shuttle hovered. A line snaked out of it, glimmering in the dark. Rama caught it in one hand and Aisha on the other arm and swung up into the air.

Aisha laughed. It was the worst possible place and time to do that, but she was flying through the air on the arm of a pirate. Jamal would be horrendously jealous.

They arced out over the place where the stage had been. It sank away below the floor of the hall. While she stared, astonished, the floor closed over it with a bone-shaking boom.

The audience erupted in applause and cheers. Faint underneath it, Aisha heard Jonathan calling from the shuttle: "Here, up!"

Rama surged as if he'd spread wings. Aisha's skin prickled all over, almost sharp enough for pain. They flew up the last few meters, and landed lightly inside the shuttle.

Jonathan turned in the pilot's cradle and smiled his sweet, serene smile. In a fist-sized cradle above his head, an image of Alexandra floated in a silver bubble. "My dears!" she sang. "Oh, my dears! Wasn't that glorious?"

Aisha had no words. She tripped and fell into the cradle nearest the hatch, while Rama claimed the one beside Jonathan.

The hatch irised shut. The shuttle flew straight up and out through the hollow center of Central.

Aisha took time to just breathe. Finally she had enough breath to ask, "Marta?"

"Safe." Rama sounded like himself—or the self he'd been since Araceli. Calm. Somewhat remote. "She's making her own way to the ship."

Aisha sucked in another handful of breaths. "What just happened down there? What—"

"We closed a trap," Rama said. "Before you ask, all the civilians got out. MI is truly done in this system—with all its allies, including some who hadn't been open about it before. It won't be following us when we go."

"I don't believe you."

The stare he aimed at her was a little more sincerely there than she'd seen in a while.

She aimed her own straight back, and the thrust of words with it. "Everything you do makes sure they'll keep coming after you. You can't stop them. They won't ever let go. Now you've got this system on their kill list, too. And they will kill it. They won't have a choice."

"We have our own kill list," Alexandra said. Her voice was as musical as ever, but it had stopped with the soaring sweetness. "We're fighting our own war. If this hadn't happened, something else would have. We've been waiting. Planning. Hoping. This is a gift, and we are glad to take it. And oh, what a beautiful show we gave our people!"

"Legendary," Jonathan agreed.

The universe was bigger than Aisha could ever understand. She knew that. People were more complicated, too. Which she had to keep reminding herself.

"Still," she said. "This is bad."

"So is United Planets," Alexandra said.

She hated them. Really, deeply hated them. That was another revelation. Aisha slumped back into her cradle and tried to wrap her mind around all of it.

It wasn't easy. Her head hurt, again. Bad enough that she had to swallow hard to keep from throwing up.

While she fought to keep her stomach where it belonged, Jonathan said to Rama, "You're cleared for immediate departure. Any personnel left behind, we'll keep safe for you."

"As safe as we can," Alexandra said.

The shuttle lurched. Aisha started out of her own head.

They were flying through the middle of the sphere, aiming straight toward Ship's bay. Another flier had buzzed them—accidentally, maybe.

It veered off. The shuttle kept going. Jonathan's face had gone still, but his hands were steady on the controls.

He was flying on manual—crazy in this tight and crowded space, but what did Aisha know? She wasn't a pilot.

All she knew was that they were on their way out of Kom Ombo. System's web wasn't saying anything about the concert hall that had turned into a trap, and maybe a tomb. Everything was quiet.

She had to stop seeing awfulness ahead for this system. She wasn't precog. She was just scared, and completely out of her depth.

"My dear," Alexandra said. She spoke through the top layer of the web, on a tight connection: as private as those things got. "We won't let harm come to you here. Or to ourselves, either. U.P. has enough troubles of its own to keep it busy for years. It's not going to come after us at any time soon."

"I hope you're right," Aisha said.

"I am always right," said Alexandra. She was laughing, but not at Aisha. "You will go out there and see things no one of your world has ever seen. I'm jealous."

"We'll report back," Aisha said, "if we can."

"I know." Alexandra's web presence was warm, like a smile. "Swim well. Swim far. May the great-toothed ones glide past and the sweet-tasting ones dart into your jaws."

That was strange and rather bloodthirsty. Alien. But weirdly comforting. "Stay with God," Aisha managed to answer. "Stay safe."

"Always," said Alexandra.

Ship was ready. Its stomach tanks were full; sparks of spare energy ran up and down its sides.

Those also happened to function very well as shields. They parted just enough to clear a hatch and let the shuttle in, then quickly out again.

Rama didn't wait for goodbyes. He was gone almost before there was a space for him to get out of the shuttle, aiming for the bridge.

Aisha needed to go, but wanted to say something. She couldn't think what.

"Go," Jonathan said. "Quickly."

She was barely out of the shuttle before it backed through the already closing hatch and out into Central.

53

Khalida had been prepared for a rapid departure, and she knew the ship was capable of entering jump from anywhere it pleased, but she was still taken aback by the speed of the exit from Kom Ombo.

There was no pursuit that she could detect. The system was quiet. She could almost swear that there was a sense of satisfaction about the ship, as if it had completed a successful hunt and fed well on the quarry.

The *Ra-Harakhte* had set a course toward Starsend. The distance was as far as most ships could manage in a single jump, but this was not an ordinary ship. It was fully fueled, strong and, in its alien way, eager.

Just as they entered jump, she happened to be in her cradle, downloading what amounted to a passenger manifest. The data blurred and stretched and disintegrated into random bits and bytes.

In the midst of jump they fell into the configurations of a star map. She had almost recognized it when the distortions of jump settled into the dead-air calm of jumpspace.

The map faded like the memory of a dream. She counted names on the manifest, and hissed half in temper and half in appreciation. Nearly all of the science team had happened to be in Central when the ship left. Only Dr. Ma was still on board, along with Robrecht and Kirkov and one or two of the lab techs.

Most of the crew had managed to come back in time. The ship had its full complement of immediately useful personnel.

The nulls in stasis were safe in their bays. So was Marta, who had come in by shuttle somewhat before Rama and retreated to her quarters, apparently to sleep through as much of this jump as she could.

"Well done," Khalida said.

It had taken her some little time to catch Rama away from at least one or two of the crew. She found him in one of the now deserted labs, throwing up star maps on an array of screens.

The sight of those woke a memory of Khalida's dream during jump. Not enough to make any sense of; it was a buzzing in the back of her skull, no more.

At sound of her voice, Rama glanced over his shoulder. "Thank you," he said. "I think."

"You should have left the nulls, too," she said.

He zoomed in on one of the maps, bringing a triple-star system into planetary orbit. The tangle of planets there sorted into a complex dance of orbit and counterorbit in a nearly empty field of stars.

"I would have left them if there had been anywhere to put them," he said as the map's viewpoint focused on a glorious monster of a gas giant, almost a star in its own right.

"Don't dump them *there*," Khalida said.

His lips twitched. He was freer, she thought. Wound up tight still, with all he had ahead of him, but he had an actual destination. A place that was not a distraction or an obstacle.

"This is a universe of wonders," he said. The gas giant stayed in focus, but the rest of the star maps merged. The walls had vanished. They stood as if in interstellar space.

"Is it true," he asked, "that the universe is not singular? That there are an infinity of them?"

He was not speaking to Khalida. Dr. Ma came to sit in the middle of the galactic arm, with more distant galaxies scattered like jewels all around her.

"That is the most widely accepted theory," she said.

"It's never been proved?"

"Never to anyone's satisfaction." Her brow rose slightly. "Is this idle curiosity? Or is there a reason?"

"I don't know."

Not an answer she might have been expecting. Both brows went up. "The mathematics support it. There have been glimpses, hints. But no one has ever managed to penetrate the wall; to enter, reliably and provably, another universe. Or, if that has been done, to return."

"Not even your psi masters?"

"Don't mock," she said.

"What if one didn't want to enter one of the many? What if one wanted to perceive them all? As we see the stars—in multitudes."

"I don't think the human brain is capable of that," she said.

"Ah," he said. "It needs a god."

"If you believe in such things."

Khalida held her breath. The priest of an ancient and forgotten god smiled ever so softly. "What would you call a being that stands above the multiverse?"

"Most likely nonexistent."

"What would your mathematics say?"

"That the scale may be too vast to calculate."

"Even with your infinite numbers?"

"Yours are different?"

He had stung her into temper. It was deliberate, Khalida thought. "Doctor, when I was born, we counted in thousands. Stars were the eyes of the gods, and the sun was the greatest of them. We knew more of what you call psi than your Corps has begun to imagine, but our understanding of more practical processes tended to be, in root and branch, practical. The theoretical sciences had barely been thought of."

Khalida went still. Of course he had to do this. They all had to know before they went much farther, what they were doing and with whom.

She might not have chosen to begin with Dr. Ma. Which was why he had done it. Being what and who he was.

"When you were born?" Dr. Ma asked. "Some ten Earthyears after me? Even if you are longer-lived than the human norm, that hardly begins to—"

"Six thousand Earthyears," he said, "and many lightyears from that world. Endros Avaryan, we called it. You would call it MEP 1403."

"Nevermore," Khalida said.

Dr. Ma took a long time to ponder that. She did not try to deny it or argue with it. When she finally spoke, she was perfectly calm. "All the crew should know."

"Yes," Rama said. "Those that are still with us after Starsend."

"Now," Dr. Ma said. "While there's still time for a choice."

"Yes: to end their voyage. I'll go on alone."

"You plan to leave them behind. As you did with my teams at Kom Ombo."

"I don't need them," he said, "or any of the rest."

"No?"

"No."

"Were you alone before, then? Completely solitary?"

"Of course not," Khalida said. Her voice sounded harsh in her own ears, like the scream of a bird of prey over the plains of Nevermore. "He had armies."

"That was another world," he said, "and a time so long dead, there's none left to remember."

"Now there," said Dr. Ma, "is why you need us. To remember."

"Stasis," Kirkov said. "You had stasis."

None of the crew were archaeologists. They were not trying to eat Rama alive for his knowledge of ancient mysteries. They were not denying what he was, either, which Khalida found fascinating.

Rama sat on a table in the middle of them all, still in the dining hall where he began. Strangely enough, he seemed to be in his element. He had always been different, Khalida thought. Always stared at and set apart.

"We had stasis," he agreed. "We had swords and spears, and weapons of the mind that could shatter a world."

"And worldgates," Khalida said. "Passage from world to world, without ships or jumpspace. Whatever emptied the planet had something to do with that."

"We think," Rama said. "And I think…possibly also something to do with the theory of the multiverse."

"How do you calculate that?" Kirkov wanted to know.

Rama shrugged. "Jumpspace is full of life, though maybe not as your science understands it. What if there is life outside the universes? Something so vast it's beyond our comprehension. Something that feeds on universes."

"Universes as plankton?" Dr. Ma was smiling—almost laughing. But not mocking him. "If we're being fed on, how can we even know? We're less than molecules. We certainly can't hope to stop whatever it is. If it is."

"Maybe that's too large a scale," Rama conceded. He tucked up his feet, eyes brighter than Khalida had ever seen them, leaning toward Dr. Ma. "Maybe it's only as large as a darter in a pond, and we're the algae it feeds on. And maybe some of the algae learn to produce toxins that repel or even kill the darter. Maybe that's what we're looking at. Or for."

"Speculation," Dr. Ma said. "There could be nothing there."

"Something emptied a planet," Kirkov pointed out. "Something seems to have tripped a timer and pulled you out of stasis. Now something's dropping clues to lead you on. Do you necessarily need Starsend? Why not just go on past?"

"It could be a trap," Dr. Ma said, "or a delusion."

"It could." Rama seemed delighted at the prospect. "Starsend holds a message. I'll claim that, and I hope decipher it. And then go on. And on."

"We," Dr. Ma said.

"You could die. In fact it's quite likely. Or disappear forever, beyond the ends of time."

"Recording every step of it," she said, "and doing my best to understand it."

"We'd have called you mad, when I was as young as I look."

"What, you had no scientists?"

"We had philosophers," he said, "and madmen."

"Explorers," Aisha said. She had been so quiet that Khalida had not even realized she was there. "Adventurers. Conquerors. People who couldn't stop until they knew what was over the next hill."

"Then wept when there were no more?" Rama asked.

"Did you?"

"My world was wider than that. I ran out of sanity before I came to the end of it."

Khalida watched the crew watch him. None of them looked afraid. Wary, yes, and fascinated. Trying to understand.

They traveled through space in the bowels of a sentient starship. An ancient king roused out of stasis to chase a myth from one universe into another—that was as likely as any other impossibility.

"You seem to have run out of madness when you ran out of time," Zhao said. "Though what is sane, and what is not…who in any world knows?"

PART FIVE

STARS' END

54

Starsend was what Aisha had expected Kom Ombo to be: an outpost on the edge of the abyss. It was a domed city on an ice moon that orbited a gas giant so huge it was almost a star. The star itself glimmered faint and far away.

It was near enough for Ship to feed on. Ship came in hungry and barely wanted to listen to the microbes inside it, but Rama persuaded it to settle into orbit around the moon.

There were no other ships. The city was deserted. Its web was shut down, and any beacons that might have marked the system were gone.

It was all too much like Nevermore. No one here had tried to hide any images, but without the web or any communications system up or running, the only way to access them was by going directly into the city.

Nobody was stupid enough to say the obvious thing. This was a trap, of course it was. Every vid they'd ever seen said so.

"I'll go down," Khalida said. "Kirkov, Zhao—"

"And I," Rama said. He was ever so gentle. "This trap was laid for me. I'll walk into it, and see how it springs."

"I don't think it is a trap." Aisha bit her tongue. She hadn't meant to say that aloud.

Now everybody was staring at her, and she had to say the rest. "It's a message," she said. "With clues in it."

"That's a trap." Rama was already halfway off the bridge. Aisha shut her mouth and went after him.

Aunt Khalida insisted on taking point from the shuttle bay into the dome. There were no barriers. The airlocks opened silently, without challenge.

Life support was on, they'd made sure of that before they went in—and brought breathers in case it shut off unexpectedly. The dome was lit with bioluminescence: colonies of microorganisms deployed overhead and underfoot, brighter in some sectors, dimmer in others.

The silence was eerie. Even the smells were strange: vacant, empty. No one walked in the streets. No voice spoke, and nothing moved except the reconnaissance party making its wary way across the city.

Somebody had power, Aisha thought, to be able to do this. The shops were empty. The windows they peered into showed vacant rooms. Everything was gone. Starsend's people had left nothing behind.

In the middle of the city was the hub from which the streets ran like spokes. Screens walled it in, and one arched overhead.

They were blank, until Rama came into the center. Then they came alive.

Aisha jumped like a startled antelope. So did the others. Even Rama reared back a fraction.

There were screens on screens all around them, and screens within screens, all showing desolation, and the wreckage of worldgates. World after world. System after system.

They had an order to them. One after another. In the very middle, a place Aisha recognized: the tower above Blackroot village.

That image had to have been made long before the village, or long after it—because who knew? Whoever had done this might be traveling in time.

It was night there, on the screen, and the stars were different, too: subtly shifted and changed. Five thousand years' worth, maybe. Give or take.

Farther along, closer to Rama, was the Ara Celi still intact. And farther still, the wheel of stars over the wheel of stone that Aisha had seen, in virtual form, in Kom Ombo.

Here were Aunt Khalida's star maps all in order, one by one. Past the wheel of stone was one more: the gas giant that loomed above the dome at Starsend.

And then nothing. Absolute blackness. Emptiness deeper than truespace and jumpspace together.

That was the clue. Aisha bit her tongue. What she was thinking was so wild, so far off what could possibly be likely, that she wasn't even sure she should say it.

A face took shape in the blackness. It was so dark at first that she thought her eyes were bored and inventing shapes of their own. But then she realized: it was a face like Rama's.

The same face she'd seen in Mesera Pereira's memory—here, at Starsend.

Aunt Khalida hissed and lurched forward. She recognized it, too. Though where she might have seen it, Aisha didn't know.

Dreams. The voice in her head had no name or person on it. Just the raw understanding.

Aisha glanced at Rama. His eyelids had lowered and his chin come up.

"There is no way in but through," the woman said.

She was speaking Old Language—softened in places and changed in places, but understandable. There was no life in her voice; it was purely mechanical.

"Do you know," Rama said to no one in particular, "how very much I hate riddles and coy mysteries? Give it to me straight, damn you. Or don't give it at all."

The AI had gone flat and slightly pixelated while he spoke, as if its programming couldn't both sustain the image and process the auditory data. He spun away from it in disgust.

The AI started to sing. The language was older than Old Language, too old for Aisha to understand; all she could tell was its age, and that it had the rhythms and timbres of Nevermore. It was a chant, a long slow roll of syllables like a wave on a shore.

That voice was alive. Rama had stopped, and his shoulders gone stiff.

The chant ended on the hint of an up note. He answered it almost angrily, but slowing down as he went on, falling into the same stately rhythm.

Recitative. Response. The voice in the darkness answered his answer, and he answered it again. Back and forth.

He turned to face the singer. She *was* alive, but surrounded by a sense of unimaginable distance. "So," she said in Old Language. "It is you."

"You doubted it?"

"Not any longer." She looked him in the eye, dark to dark, and each with a terrible brightness deep inside. "You know the way. Now come."

Aisha knew the way, too. In her bones, along with the meaning of the chant. It was old, yes, so very old. It was a hymn: to the sun and to the dark. They were brother and sister in that world, twinborn, back to back and spirit to spirit.

They were universes, too. Back to back. The gate between shone overhead, a giant planet with an almost-sun at its core.

"No wonder they all left," she said as it all came clear.

Rama was halfway gone already, looking so far ahead she could barely follow. But he heard her. He answered her.

"I leave destruction wherever I go."

He wasn't sad about it. He'd left that behind. He was a little bitter, maybe. A little wry.

"Oh, no, you don't," she said. "Don't you go forgetting what you are."

"I never forget," he said. "This is what I am. Destroyer of worlds."

"That's Lord Shiva," she said with a snap in it. "You're going to save what's left of your world. Remember that."

"By destroying this planet," he said, "and taking part of the system with me."

"Are you sure?"

"Aren't you?"

"Maybe there's a way," Aisha said. "Why don't you ask your science people?"

"My—" He almost laughed. "They're not my people. My people are out there."

"Your people are wherever they happen to be. And whoever they happen to be. Whether you want them or not."

He opened his mouth. She glared him down. "Do you want to change something? Be something else? Ask for help. Maybe you'll get it."

"Or maybe not." Dr. Ma frowned out of the screen in front of him, and Aunt Khalida had an expression that dared Rama to do anything about it.

"Damn you," he said to them all impartially. Then: "Well? I suppose you know what I'm about to do. Can it be done without taking out the system?"

Another person came up behind Dr. Ma: Robrecht, the professor who'd been MI once. He'd been keeping quiet and keeping his head down, but now he said, "Give us the data. Route it to engineering."

"And while you do that," Aisha said, "figure out how that woman showed up in the zocalo at Starsend without breaking the planet. If she did it, why can't we?"

"Magic," Rama said, but he was only half laughing.

"Or projection," Robrecht said. "A holographic image projected through the wormhole or gate or whatever you like to call it. If you can project yourself in the opposite direction—"

"That would be relatively simple," said Rama. "I have to go there in the body. What they need me to do will require all of me. If not more."

"You know what that is?" Aisha asked.

"Don't you?"

She didn't, really. Or she didn't want to.

Until now, this had been an adventure. Inconvenient. Sometimes dangerous—people shooting, and waging wars. And the Corps doing terrible things to people and other sentients.

What it hadn't been, in her mind, was immediately and personally deadly. Rama was going to try to cross between universes.

He, and whoever went with him, could die. Or worse than die. Be trapped. Or erased. There was no way to know until it was done.

They were all beyond crazy now. This was real.

55

The *Ra-Harakhte* orbited the moon called Starsend, which orbited the gas giant called Acheron. Khalida appreciated the symbolism.

"Was this a worldgate?" she asked Rama after he returned to the bridge.

"Maybe," he said.

He paced while the scientists and some of the crew huddled around a cluster of screens. Their conversation was forbiddingly technical and, as far as Khalida could tell, getting exactly nowhere.

"Do you know how those were made?"

"No." He bit off the word.

"Can you guess?"

"No!" But then, while she nursed the mental blisters from that blaze of temper: "There were no gates in the middle of stars. Or almost-stars. They were all on planets. And no, none of them showed signs of having been constructed from the corpses of stars. They were just there."

"They were gates within this universe," Dr. Ma said. She had left the latest round of getting-nowhere, retrieved a pot of coffee and was on her way back. "I gather you didn't know of any that connected adjacent universes."

Khalida held her breath, but Rama seemed to have recovered his temper. "I was never a master of gates. My arts and talents were elsewhere. Still…"

"Your masters of gates," Dr. Ma said when the silence stretched. "They were psi masters. Yes?"

"Yes."

"Not engineers, then. Not physicists. Though they manipulated matter and energy. Are we coming at it from the wrong direction? Should we be addressing this with psionics?"

"Such as we have," Zhao said. His soft voice was flat. Which was an improvement over bitter, Khalida supposed.

"We may not have much," she said, "but you do." Her eyes caught Rama. "If you were passing through a gate, how would you go about it?"

He frowned. He was not angry, or not much. "I would walk through. Because it was already there."

"Just walk through? Just like that?"

"Not exactly. There were guardians and guides. The places between could be dangerous—more than jumpspace, though that maybe was because we didn't have ships to shield us."

"You have a ship," Khalida said. "You have shields."

"The nulls? Yes, they may protect us. But the planet, the moon—"

"A gate had two sides," Zhao said. "Someone guarded either end, yes? While you went through. Someone must have been keeping the gate from swallowing the planet around it. Or something."

"Something," Rama said. "A structure. Stone. Bones of the earth—whichever earth it was." He shook his head. "There's no stone here. It's all gas."

"Not at Starsend," Khalida said. "The core is nickel and iron. Or does cold iron kill magic for you as it used to for us?"

"Only if it's forged into a blade," Rama said with the faintest flicker of humor.

"If you can show us what you know of how gates were constructed," Robrecht said in his precise and careful way, "we may be able to use Starsend as the anchor point. Then when you aim the *Ra-Harakhte* to the core of Acheron, the whole thing will be a gate, and it should hold stable. Provided, of course, there's another anchor point on the other side."

"I think we have to take that on faith," Rama said.

"Flying on a guess and a prayer," said Khalida. "It's almost suicidal enough to be worth doing."

Rama's eyes glinted. "Almost?"

"We might actually survive," she said.

"We would hope to," he conceded. "For the sake of whoever, and whatever, is on the other side."

The engineers and the scientists were in their version of heaven, creating a structure that might not be possible, for a purpose that no one precisely understood. Even, Khalida suspected, Rama.

He was going to try to leave them all behind and take the ship ahead alone. She could tell, looking at him, and seeing how he drew back little by little from their discussions.

It made a reasonable amount of sense. He had been placed in stasis alone and would be presumed to have waked alone. Whatever was needed of him, it must be unique to him.

Still, she persisted in feeling that there was more to all this. Something else that had not figured into their calculations. The woman in the zocalo: she was an anomaly. Or, possibly, a key.

Khalida retreated to her cabin. No one took any notice: they were all focused elsewhere.

She needed quiet, and sleep if she could get it. Once she had the first, the second was no easier or quicker than she had expected.

She lay on her back, staring at the faintly glistening, subtly organic arch of the ceiling. It would have shown her starfields if she had asked, or the sky of any planet in the database, or an arch of branches, for that matter.

Branches, she thought. Green leaves, long and delicate. A tracery of flowers as pale as her own Earth's moon, but these had never grown under it.

She turned her head. She knew that fall of water, that slant of yellow sunlight.

That figure kneeling by the water, watching her. Waiting to be seen.

"How?" she asked.

Of all the things she might have said, it was probably the most obvious. Or the least.

The answer of course was obvious.

"Magic," said the woman from the other side of the gate.

She must be a figment of Khalida's imagination. She was too much like Rama, even to the wry twist with which she said the word.

"I am quite real," she said. "Are you?"

"As far as I can tell," Khalida answered.

"Listen to me," the woman said. "When you begin, remember this. Keep it firm in your memory. No matter what you see or think you see, no matter what seems to happen around you, don't lose focus. Stay fixed on me."

"Why? I'm not the one you've been waiting for."

"No?"

She was fading—letting go. Khalida tried to hold the image, the presence, whatever indescribable thing it was, but it slipped away. All but the memory. That was perfectly and indelibly clear.

Khalida only rested for an hour after the dream or vision passed, but she surprised herself with how refreshed she felt. She made her way back to the bridge, and found the ship's whole waking, walking complement there. Even Marta had emerged from her quarters.

They were all fixed on Rama. Eyes intent; faces grim or stern or studiously blank. And one almost exalted: Zhao, whose grief had mutated into a pure and glorious deathwish.

"We will do this," Rama said. "All the science staff who are left, and all the crew, will disembark into Starsend, and the nulls with them. Marta, Zhao, you build the gate between you. When the gate is made, the ship and I will make the jump—into Acheron, and if the gods will, out beyond."

"Oh, no," said Zhao. "No. I'll be on the ship."

"You will not," Rama said. "You are the only psi with any semblance of training. Without you, there will be no gate. The nulls alone can't do it. Marta can't. It has to be you."

"It might kill you," Marta said. She was cool, dispassionate. "It probably will."

"And you? And your children?" Zhao looked ready to shatter.

"If you do your part as I'll show you," Rama said, "the power will route into and past them, but not through. They'll be safe."

"I don't want anyone else to die," Zhao said, "or any more minds to break."

"Hold to that," said Rama. "Make it your shield and your armor. Try not to die, if you please."

"Yes, do that," Khalida said. "We'll be needing you when we come back."

Rama's glance was quite as wild as she had expected. Of course he had no expectation of returning. This was his suicide mission even more than it was Zhao's.

"There is no *we*," he said. "I'm leaving all of you here—you, too; you have no training, but you have power, and you will feed it to this man."

"I don't think so," Khalida said. "You don't know for sure where you're going. I do."

She had to give him credit: he suppressed the reflex to deny what she had said. "Do you? How is that?"

"I had another dream," she said. She gave it to him as best she knew how—sloppily, she knew; she had no training. Zhao caught it, too, and Aisha.

Aisha was not surprised. That interested Khalida. Rama was—and that was also interesting.

She could not tell if he was jealous. Bemused, certainly. Maybe a little put out. "I see," he said, "that there is more to this than I thought. Very well, then. You're our pilot. As soon as everyone is settled in Starsend, we go."

So soon?

That was foolish. It could hardly be soon enough.

Khalida reminded herself to breathe. The woman whose name she had never thought to ask was waiting.

She might be an AI after all. Or an illusion. A lure or a trap or an entity long dead and set at the gate to guide the traveler through.

She felt real. She must be. Khalida would accept no other possibility.

56

Aisha her mouth shut while everyone sorted out what they would do and where they would be. She wasn't going to let herself be left behind. No more than Aunt Khalida was.

The other one who refused to leave the ship was Dr. Ma. She and Kirkov were polite but immovable. "Robrecht will take charge of Starsend," she said. "We will go. This is our mission as much as yours."

Rama shrugged. "I've never in my waking life done anything alone. Why would now be any different?"

"Believe me," Dr. Ma said, "solitude is vastly overrated."

"I wouldn't know."

He was more wry than annoyed. He went to help load the nulls on the shuttle that Robrecht had commandeered from Starsend, and Dr. Ma kept on collating data in her array of screens.

Aisha stayed on the bridge. Invisibility was her plan, until they'd left Starsend and headed into Acheron.

She should have known she wouldn't be that lucky. Aunt Khalida was supposed to be supervising the loading along with Rama, but she turned up here instead, dropping into the captain's cradle and fixing Aisha with a hard eye.

"I'm not leaving the ship," Aisha said.

"I didn't think you would." Khalida looked tired all of a sudden. Or dizzy. "Did you know about—her? On the other side?"

Aisha shivered a little. "Not really. Just what I heard in Central."

"I don't believe you."

"It's true!" Aisha ramped herself down before she squealed any higher. "I keep thinking she's family. Which can't be possible."

"No," Khalida said. "No, it can't, can it?"

"You think it can."

"There is no way."

"Worldgates," Aisha said. "Somehow. A very long time ago, if it did happen. People could be related anywhere and everywhere. It would explain—"

"Nothing. It explains nothing." Khalida launched herself out of the captain's cradle and dived for the door.

Aisha wasn't sure she wanted to understand. She went to her quarters instead, and lay on her bunk and turned her face to the wall.

It wasn't that she was afraid. She was lightyears past that. She'd had enough, that was all. She was full. Overloaded.

By this time tomorrow, ship's time, she could be dead or evaporated or rendered into antimatter. Or she'd be on the other side, in another universe. Doing Rama's god knew what. Saving Nevermore, she could hope.

She pulled the covers up over her head. She missed Jamal just then. His annoying voice. His even more annoying finicky fussing about anything and everything. His familiar presence and his particular way of seeing things.

He would tell her to get out of there right now and not look back. He'd be right, too. He had all the caution between the two of them. Aisha had all the craziness.

This was the craziest thing either of them could have imagined doing. Crazier than blowing up a cliff or chasing lightning or riding through jump without drugs. Even crazier than stowing away on a Starforce ship.

She could sleep. Ship would wake her before it started its jump. She might dream, but then she might not. She still had the sun inside her, that protected her from the Corps. It could protect her from nightmares, too.

It was time.

Everybody had settled in Starsend except the handful who wouldn't go. The nulls in their stasis pods were stowed at the city's core, in one of its vaults. Marta and the crew guarded them.

And Zhao, because without him to anchor this side, the transition couldn't happen.

That was a fragile branch to hang a world on.

Aisha went looking for him before he left the ship. No one else seemed to care about him, and that didn't seem fair. He'd traveled a long way from anything he knew or was, and he might die here.

"Or be broken the way my wife and my family were," he said when she found him in the passage beyond the bridge, staring out the port at the curve of Acheron.

He wasn't bitter. It was the simple truth.

"I'm sorry," Aisha said.

He glanced at her. He was still pretty, but his bones were visible now under the ivory skin. "We aren't evil, you know. Most of us are just trying to do what we feel is right."

"Right for you, or right for the Corps?"

He winced. "You've never been hated, have you? Never had people cross the street to avoid you, or spit on the road behind you. Mothers hide their children from us. Sometimes we're shot on sight."

Aisha could have answered all of that, but she set her lips together and let it go. The truth was, if he hadn't been Corps, she would have liked him. He was a gentle thing, and he tried to be kind.

"I don't hate you," she said. She let him see it, if he was looking. "I think what you're doing is a brave and powerful thing."

"Thank you," he said. He meant it. "I won't break before I've done what you need me to do. I promise you that."

"Don't break at all," she said. "Promise."

"I don't know—"

"Promise," Aisha said again. She leaned on him inside.

He leaned back. He was strong: she had to push hard.

"I will try not to break," he said finally.

She nodded. "That will do."

It had taken longer to get ready than Rama liked. Long enough for Aisha to have a solid sleep and a belly-load of breakfast, and even to start to wake up.

Rama had stopped twitching and gone dangerously still. He was building power: Aisha could feel it crackling along her skin. The back of her skull felt strange, as if something was trying to get in—or out.

Most of the screens showed the system, such starfield as there was, Acheron and Starsend. The ones in front of Rama shifted, focusing on the people at the core of Starsend.

Nobody spoke. For all of them, this was the last breath before the long dive. Maybe one of the last they ever took.

Rama bowed to them, a deep and formal gesture. They nodded in return. Marta smiled with sudden, startling brilliance.

That brightness seemed to hang in the air as she moved with the ship's crew toward their own bank of screens. Robrecht raised the meteor-deflector shields, for what good they could do if the planet blew.

Zhao took his place last, strapping himself into a modified jump cradle. He wasn't smiling, but he touched Aisha with a hint of warmth. Wishing her well. Remembering the promise he'd made. Then he was gone from inside her mind, as his focus narrowed and shifted.

Aisha more or less understood what he would be doing. It was basically the same thing as a deflector shield, but with psi. Marta would connect him to the nulls, and they would build a wall of energy around him. He would be an anchor, which Rama and Ship and everyone in it would hook on to. Then they would jump.

She had a moment of fear for him; of knowing this was all going to fail. They were going to die.

It was only fear. Not foreseeing. She pulled herself together.

A faint shimmer rose around Zhao in his cradle, hardly enough to see. His face was pale and still. He looked deep asleep, or dead.

He was neither. She could feel him inside his wall, like a twisting core of flame in a globe of glass.

She could feel Rama, too, the rioting fire he'd always been, like a captive sun. And Aunt Khalida. Aunt Khalida was the map, a living set of coordinates.

She had her own anchor on the other side. The line to it stretched vanishing thin through the planet's core.

"We are going to have to train you," Rama said inside Aisha's head—calmly, and calming her by not being either nervous or afraid. He'd left all that behind. There was only the battle ahead, that he intended to win.

"Her, too," Aisha said, flicking her consciousness toward Khalida.

"Both of you." He was already withdrawing, focusing on the jump.

They were all in cradles but Rama. He'd finally stopped pretending to need one. His feet were braced on the deck. He had his *gi* on, his fighting clothes.

Aisha was dressed to dig in the dirt on Nevermore. Shirt and pants and sturdy boots. Hat tucked into her tool belt.

It had felt a little bit stupid when she put it on, because she wasn't likely to need any of it on a starship, but wherever she was going, if she got there, had some form of outdoors. She meant to be prepared.

There was nothing she could do to prepare for this jump, except lie in her cradle and keep her mind open to ship's web and the other web, the one made of psi. Ship was powered up to the brim, and so was Rama.

The connection with Starsend locked on and held. Zhao was stronger than Aisha had thought, and steadier. The nulls fed him in ways even he might not have expected, and protected him, too.

They were like a bow. Ship was the arrow, and Rama was its point. The target loomed over them: the vast red-gold-silver bulk of Acheron.

The archer was Khalida. She had the map inside her.

"Now," she said.

Acheron swelled until it there was nothing in the universe but swirls of glowing gas with a heart of fire. The forces outside Ship, the buffet of winds strong enough to break a lesser world, the relentless pull of gravity, didn't touch the people inside at all. They were safe. Surrounded. Protected.

Diving deep. Into the fire. Swallowing it. Being swallowed by it. Catching the point at the very middle, the space, the place, the instant in which universes touched. Flowed; fought.

The anchor's connection frayed. The map blurred. Matter dissolved into energy. Energy into—

There were no words.

It was like jump—the weirdness; the senses all turned inside out and backwards. The feeling of being broken down into atoms and then put back together again.

But it was different. Part of her rode through it as she always had. Another part—grew. Opened up. Saw/felt/smelled/heard/tasted worlds on worlds on worlds on…

They were like bubbles, a little. Enough to give her mind something to hold on to. Drifting and floating and swirling and touching. So many—so vast.

Too vast. She was too small. It was too much for her tiny mind to contain.

A strong hand caught hers. Then another, almost as strong.

Rama. Khalida. They gave her boundaries. They guided her back toward shape and solidity. They anchored her behind and drew her through ahead, from bubble to bubble among the countless masses of them.

Khalida knew which one they were going to. Rama knew where they'd come from, and he'd locked on to Khalida's view ahead. Aisha was exactly in the middle.

She balanced them. She didn't know what she was doing or how. Ship surrounded her and kept her from disappearing into the mass of bubbles.

Universes. Worlds and worlds and worlds. Every one different. Some by a little, some by so much that there was no wrapping her understanding around them.

She fixed on Khalida, on where she was going and what she was going to. Here in this not-space, she could barely resist the temptation to fall forever and ever and ever. In between the worlds. Never moving, growing, changing.

Until—

Ship was dizzy with freedom. It wanted to dive, too, filling itself with the energies of worlds, sweeping through them all until its bays were full and its skin ready to burst.

Then it would *become*. That was the word that came to her. It would shed its skin and unfold and grow and change. It was a larva, a nymph. What it would be when it became—

Not yet.

Rama reined it in with gentle firmness. It bucked and twisted, but he rode it until it settled. It was not happy; still, it knew he was right. It was much too young. It had other and lesser becoming to do first, and much traveling and learning and feeding.

Beginning here, ahead of them, where Khalida's anchor was. Her goal; her guide. A bubble that touched their own, then slipped away, but still kept that thread of connection.

Other threads wove through the multiverse. Aisha pulled herself back before she followed any of them. They were oh so beautiful. Oh so tempting.

Her mind was going to break. She had to wall it in. Focus it. Make it tight and small and clear.

Then she could see. Finally, she knew what Khalida knew. Where to go; how to get there.

She reached out with Ship and Khalida and Rama and all, and dived down into that one of all the bubbles that were.

57

They rode through a field of stars—huge, gleaming swirls and sweeps of them. Those were galaxies, crowding together, full of newborn suns.

Ship brought them to perfect emptiness, except for a thin scatter of suns. One gleamed directly ahead, deceptively familiar: M-class, yellow, like Earth's sun, like the sun of Nevermore. It shared its stretch of void with a scattering of sister stars and a handful of planets: a gas giant or two, a ringed beauty, a bare and meteor-pocked globe of greyish rock.

That last had a moon nearly as large as it was, and the moon wore a familiar face: swirls of clouds, blue of oceans, green and brown of land masses.

Aisha's whole body and mind let go at sight of that, like a long release of breath, or the unlocking of muscles clenched to pain.

Rama, too. His knees buckled. She could swear she saw tears in his eyes before he shook them fiercely away.

"There's your moon," Khalida said. "It's reading gravity on the scale of Nevermore, though it's not near the size or density. Or the orbital speed to make up for either."

"Magic," Rama said with the flash of a smile.

"Gravity generators," said Dr. Ma, quellingly simple.

Ship swam toward the moon while they went back and forth like fencers. This space was not empty for its senses; there were energy sources all around, some so strong it shivered. It was hungry—starving. Swimming between universes was the hardest work it had ever done.

It fed carefully, too wise to gorge. While it fed, it swam, and the blue-and-silver-and-green moon grew larger in the screens.

Dr. Ma and Kirkov ran scans of the moon and its planet. Aisha would be interested in their composition later. Now she only wanted to know what evidence there was of living things—people, animals, anything that grew or moved.

"No sign of a worldweb," Khalida said, "or electronic signatures, or any other indication of what we call civilization."

"You're looking at the wrong things," Aisha said. She wasn't tactful, which she realized too late. "With the wrong instruments. Use your mind."

She did it herself now she thought of it, imagining a web like a worldweb, but made of psi. At first she thought she was as wrong as her aunt was—that there was nothing; the moon was empty.

Then it lit up like a galaxy full of suns. Hundreds, thousands—minds with strong psi, minds with just barely enough to wake a spark, even the dead zone of a null here and there, and every possible range in between.

The moon was not just inhabited; it was dense with people. Whatever tech they had didn't register on Ship's sensors, but that didn't mean there was none. It wasn't electronic was all.

Khalida had lost her beacon in the mass of them, but Aisha felt her find it again and lock on. It was clear, and focused, and aware of them.

It wasn't friendly. It was calm and open but distinctly wary. It might have called them, but it wasn't at all sure that they were to be trusted.

All they could do was keep on toward the moon, settle into orbit around it, and ready the shuttle for descent. There were no spacecraft in orbit with them, no stations, nothing but the emptiness of an uncharted system.

Rama piloted them all down in the shuttle—even Dr. Ma. Khalida or Kirkov could have done it, but one look at his face and they both found cradles in back of the pilot's station.

Aisha ended up in the cradle beside him, because no one else would go there. She wasn't altogether comfortable about it, either, but she'd never been afraid of him.

He went completely still as the shuttle descended. His face in profile looked as if it was carved in obsidian, all sharp planes and fierce angles.

She'd thought he might put on whatever a king wore in his world, to show himself to the descendants of the people he'd ruled, but he'd gone the other way. He was in the first clothes he'd found on Nevermore, the faded red shirt and the hand-me-down Spaceforce trousers and the well-worn riding boots. And gold, plenty of it: ring and bracelets, torque and earrings.

It said what it needed to say. What his people would think, Aisha couldn't know.

She'd dressed for practicality herself, in her digging clothes. No weapon. If they needed any, they had Rama, whose whole self was a weapon.

When they touched atmosphere, Aisha caught her breath. It felt like fire running across her skin.

At the same time her hands were cold. She kept reminding herself to breathe. "Steady."

She almost thought she'd imagined it, but Rama's eye was on her, with the hint of a smile.

He was as scared as she was. Being Rama, he built walls around it and locked the gates against anyone who tried to get in.

Behind Aisha, Dr. Ma was talking to Kirkov, softly. "This is a universe being born. All those clusters of galaxies and infant stars—we're at the beginning. It's possible we've traveled in time as well as in—and beyond—space."

"That's not possible, is it?" Kirkov said, but not as if he was really arguing.

"Theoretically it may be," she said. "If every universe is different, however subtly, why not one at the beginning of its cycle?"

"But time travel—"

"What would you call the space—place—continuum—that exists between universes? Does spacetime follow the same rules there? Might time be as simple to traverse as space? Could we—"

"You're giddy," Kirkov said.

"I am never giddy." Her voice was pure frost. "This is scientific euphoria. I need the worldsweb, with all its data and its computational powers, but I think—I hypothesize—I theorize—"

"You know we're not likely ever to get back there," Kirkov said. "All you have is the ship's web and what's inside your own head."

"I'll make do," she said.

Aisha had to admire her. She was not easy to like, but she had passion. As for what Kirkov had said...

Aisha refused to believe it. They would get back. Somehow. They'd find a way. After they finished whatever they'd been called to do on this lost moon of Nevermore.

58

When the shuttle touched atmosphere, what felt to Khalida like a tractor beam locked on. No voice came on the conn; no planetary security system issued a challenge. They were simply and effectively trapped and held.

Rama tried an evasive maneuver or two, met an invisible wall. He shrugged and folded his hands and let be.

Once when Khalida was visiting Nevermore, before Araceli broke her inside, the expedition had been invaded by one of the giant plains cats, a young one looking for its own territory. It had badly injured one of the interns and killed a mare and her foal.

Marina and Vikram had got the rest together to build a trap and half lure, half herd the cat into it, with a young antelope for bait and all the available transports to make sure it went where it was supposed to. Then once it was trapped, they had flown it, in the cage, to a far and unclaimed corner of the plains.

This felt like that. Bait for the predator; a route constructed to bring him to it.

They flew over the widest of the moon's several continents, a rolling expanse of brown and green, mountain and plain, that reminded Khalida almost painfully of Nevermore. She looked down on a tracery of rivers and a deep green of forest, and in among them, the regular shapes of roofs and walls, streets and plazas.

Roads connected the towns and cities. The shuttle flew too high for its passengers to see people moving there, but flocks of winged things passed below. Khalida's mind was almost antic enough to wonder if any of those was large enough to carry a human rider.

She would have thought the shuttle would be drawn toward one of the larger cities, but whatever was in control piloted them toward a complex structure perched on the sides and summit of a mountain above the blue bowl of a lake. The walled interior of the mountaintop looked like a park: an intricate pattern of stone and greenery bounded on the farthest edge by a waterfall that plunged half a hundred meters into the lake below.

Khalida knew that fall. There was no sign, visual or otherwise, of the guide who had brought them from one universe to another.

The shuttle came down on the long field beside the upper reach of the fall. People waited there: a dozen standing together.

If Rashid could see…

Only one of them was like the tribes who still remained on Nevermore: smaller than the rest, all ivory and gold, with a smooth oval face and wide golden eyes. Three towered over them all, dark and eagle-faced like Rama but as tall as the woman in her dream. The rest were short or tall, brown or bronze.

None was their guide. These were strangers, standing very still, with expressions ranging from somber to grim.

They were afraid. Not of the shuttle; that barely troubled them at all. Of the man who walked out of it, with the rest trailing behind.

He was amused, with a distinct, dark edge.

He halted between the shuttle and the welcoming party, giving them time to get the measure of him. Khalida doubted that any of them could see him clearly through the lens of legend and dire history.

After what felt like a long while, the man in the middle spoke. He was tall though not nearly as tall as the dark ones, with red-bronze skin and narrow dark eyes and proud and somber features, crowned with striking, shoulder-long, fire-red hair. But for that last, he could have been a man of Earth.

"Kalendros," he said.

That was Old Language, or close enough. A title. Not quite *King. Majesty,* maybe. With a faint but unmistakable suggestion of *Tyrant.* Or *Royal Monster.*

"I see my reputation precedes me," Rama said. He sounded light, easy. "What do you have for me, then? A war to fight? A dragon to slay?"

"We thought you'd bring an army," one of the tall ones said. He was young, Khalida thought, and less afraid than the others—maybe because he was still young enough not to know better.

"I did," Rama answered him, flicking a hand toward the others behind him. "There's much more to them than meets the eye."

Khalida realized that she had stiffened and come to attention. She fixed the young giant with a hard, cold stare, as if he had been a particularly callow recruit.

He had the grace to blink and look away. One of the others, square and sturdy and remarkably like a woman Khalida knew from Old Tibet, stepped forward and met Rama eye to eye. She was slightly taller.

They were all psi masters. Khalida could feel the force of it under her skin. That one, the woman who had the least fear of Rama, was the strongest.

She might even be stronger than Rama. Khalida lacked the knowledge to be sure.

"So," the woman said. "The Sun's son found his way to the other side of the sky. You're saner than I expected."

"And shorter?"

Her lips twitched. "That part of the story came near enough to the truth."

"It's a dragon, then, isn't it? Not a war. You seem remarkably peaceful here."

"We work at it," she said. "Come. Majesty. If it pleases you."

She might be mocking him with the title and the courtesy. She might not. Rama took it calmly either way. "I'm no king in this world. They call me Rama in this age. And you?"

"Elti," she said.

He bowed slightly. "Elti," he repeated.

"Come," Elti said.

Yes, this was a cage for a predator. It had the amenities of a palace, with of course no machines, but a company of mute and efficient servants. Its walls were made of energy as well as stone—a forcefield maintained by the powers of the mind. Their hosts—she could not quite bring herself to call them captors— were taking no chances.

Rama seemed neither wounded or angry at the mistrust of his own people. He had gone into a kind of trance, light and yet hyperalert, as if his every move was a form of katas.

The archaeologist in Khalida was enthralled by the palace: from architecture to furnishings to frescoes and mosaics and works of art on walls and floors and displayed in niches and courtyards, to whole rooms constructed like galleries in a museum. That maybe was what it had been before it became a monster's prison: a place not meant for living in, though the beds in the high airy rooms were wonderfully comfortable.

A pair of silent servants led them to one of the galleries, where a table was spread with the makings of a feast. They set out the plates and cups and bowls, bowed the guests to seats at the table, and mutely withdrew.

The food was close enough to the tastes of the tribes on Nevermore that Khalida could guess at some of what was in it. The room was like nothing she had seen on that planet. Sculptures lined the frescoed walls. Human figures of all the kinds and peoples of Nevermore sat and lounged and whirled and leaped, dancing, feasting, making love: as if in stripping their own world of any such thing, they had brought it all here.

It was too frenetic for Khalida's stomach. She ate what she could of bread and sharp cheese and roasted vegetables and drank a little of the too-sweet wine, then sat back in the elaborately carved chair while the others satisfied less finicky appetites.

Rama could be a delicate eater, too: he took most of his energy from the sun, or from the ship when he was in space. On this night of the moon's short day, he ate as if he were fueling for a race. Or, she thought, a battle.

No one had much to say. Aisha was the most talkative: she was teaching Kirkov and Dr. Ma bits of Old Language, naming the various items of furniture and describing the most exuberant of the frescoes, color by color and figure by figure.

They were being watched. It began as a prickle in Khalida's nape and grew to a crawling sensation across her shoulder blades.

Rama ate one last bite and thrust his plate away. Then, quite calmly, he said, "Come out and face us. We're not animals in your menagerie."

"No?"

Elti emerged from the shadows, with a much taller shadow behind her.

Khalida's breath stopped. There was the woman of her dream. Here in the room, in living presence, she was even taller than Khalida had expected. As tall as any of the men who had met the shuttle.

She carried that height well, with easy grace. She wore a long embroidered coat over closely fitted trousers. The coat was open; her breasts were bare, firm and high though she must be at least as old as Rama seemed to be. Her hair was straight and shining and braided down her back; she wore a torque, deceptively plain, made of what must be pure silver.

Khalida had to remember how to breathe, and then to see. There were others with the two women: a man, walnut-brown, very old and withered with sparse white hair, and a pair of young persons helping him hobble into the light and settling him in a cushioned chair.

If the others they had met were psi masters, this was something more. Khalida could barely describe to herself what it felt like to be so close to him. Like waiting for a storm to break. Like standing inside the warp drive of a starship.

Rama sat motionless at the table, relaxed, visibly at ease. Khalida had always known that he was damped down, suppressed; still in large part asleep, lost in a long dark dream.

Now he was waking. He might, she thought, be angry.

Or not. She would hardly know. He was no king or kin of hers.

"No?" The tall woman read Khalida's thought as easily as if she had spoken it aloud. "Worldgates opened on your world once. One of his descendants, it's said, met a woman there, a queen."

"Of course a queen," Khalida said, not meaning to be cutting, but she could not help herself.

"Why not?" the woman said. "He was a king. Or had been. By then he'd abdicated. Retired to tend his flocks. Until there was a crisis of gates, and he was trapped on the far side of one. You have his blood—his genes, is that your word? Far and far away, but perceptible still."

Khalida opened her mouth to argue, but memory silenced her. The results of a test. Contamination, she had thought. Maybe, after all, not.

"So that's how," Aisha said farther down the table. "It wasn't just Rama making the connection to come here. It was us."

"Yes," the woman said.

She was speaking PanTerran. Khalida had been too focused on her and on what she said to absorb the meaning of that. Now it struck words out of her. "That *was* you at Starsend."

"A projection," she said. "You know firsthand how difficult physical passage is. Mental, however…"

"Daiyan," Elti said.

It was interesting to see that proud person reined in by an evident superior. Commanding officer? Mother abbess?

"You'll speak again," the old man said in Old Language. "Later. Now there must be apologies: to you, majesty, for treating you like a wild beast, and to you, strangers from far worlds, for our lack of courtesy and proper welcome."

Now Elti was visibly brought up short. Daiyan, not so much; she had an air of vindication.

"I do understand," Rama said with an inflection of careful respect, "why you might be cautious. I was not a tame creature when my own kin captured and bound me."

"Nor are you now," the old man said, "but your dreams taught you a little. You understand why our people protect themselves. It still reflects poorly on us. We called you for our great need, and locked you in a cage."

"A surpassingly comfortable one," Rama said.

He rose. Elti and the two children flinched. Daiyan, Khalida noticed, did not. Nor did the old man, but she had expected that.

Rama circled the table to stand in front of the old man. Narrow dark eyes met wide and preternaturally clear, even darker ones. Rama held out his hand: the right, with its—whatever it was. Manifestation of psi, magic, divine power. Image or projection or his own gods knew what, of the sun of Nevermore.

The old man blinked. So: he did not know everything. "It has changed," he said.

"You've seen another?" Rama asked. Breathlessly, maybe. Hopeful; or apprehensive.

"No." The old man sounded honestly regretful. "Your last descendant died to bring us here and to guard against what we fled. We have no kings or emperors now. We left that on her grave. It's memory only, and images in the temples."

Rama sighed faintly. "Of course; no dynasty endures forever. A thousand years, was it? That's a fair run."

"Very fair," the old man said.

"And still you remember."

"We could hardly forget. We keep the time here in the old way, as we can. Nine hundred years of the world we left, and nine cycles of this moon as it was once, and nine days of the old world. As was foretold."

Khalida opened her mouth to speak, but shut it again, carefully.

"Nine hundred years?" Rama began to laugh. Threw back his head and roared, until the old man's acolytes crouched with their arms over their heads, and the two women braced as if against a gale. Only the old man sat still and apparently unmoved.

When Rama's laughter finally died, he stood with tears running down his face—and they were not all tears of mirth. "Oh, master of mages," he said. "Oh, there's a grand jest of the undying gods. Six thousand years I slept. Six thousand years of the long dream."

"Ah," the old man said. There was a world of meaning in the sound.

"Strange are the ways of time and the gods," Rama said.

"It's physics," said Aisha. She was all eyes and appetite, taking in this world as if she would swallow it whole. "Spacetime warps in between universes. It goes the other way, or it wouldn't be possible to project an image into Starsend. So it's consistent."

"It serves the gods," the old man said, "and may save us. You are not what we feared."

"He may be worse," said Elti. "You know what the council—"

The old man ignored her. "Majesty," he said. "May I ride in your shuttle?"

He spoke the word in PanTerran, carefully, enunciating each syllable.

Elti stiffened as if in protest, but no one paid attention to that, either. "You may," Rama said.

"Now, then," the old man said.

59

The old man's name was long and complicated. "Most of it is titles," he told Aisha as they carried him in a chair through the palace and out into the unexpectedly chilly night. "The rest is family. One part actually belongs to me. That part you may have. I am Umizad."

"And I am Aisha," she said, trying not to be too stiff. His version of Old Language was older than the one she knew, but the changes made sense if she put her mind to it.

"Aisha," he said.

"There's more to it," she said, relaxing a little into the language, "but that's the part you can have."

He bowed in his chair. His smile made him look a great deal younger and quite mischievous.

"You aren't supposed to be doing this, are you?" she said.

"No." He was almost laughing. "We are to keep his majesty closely caged and strictly limited in what he may know or do. That being the decision of the council, which is both wise and just."

"It's wise enough," Rama said. He had an end of one of the chair's poles on his shoulder—and the shock when he had done that had made him laugh again so he could hardly hold himself up. "I'm a dangerous animal. I might eat someone."

"You do eat souls," Elti said. Snarled. She was not stooping to carry anything; she left that to Rama and Daiyan and Khalida and to Umizad's acolytes, who shared the end of a pole. Aisha had tried to take that one but been glared away.

"Not your soul," he said. "I'm partial to sweeter vintages."

She almost spat at him. "You should not be alive. You should have died however many thousands of years ago. You are a monster and an abomination, and I deplore the necessity that compels us to use you."

"Yes," he said. "I am all of that. But you need me."

"We need you," she said in utter disgust.

Umizad in the shuttle was like a little boy, all big eyes and cries of wonder. It wasn't an act, Aisha thought. He might be old and his body was failing, but he had joy. It always filled him; here in this machine from another universe, it overflowed.

Flying didn't either surprise or frighten him. He was more interested in the way Rama operated the controls, and in the screens that showed the moon and the planet and the space around them, and Ship in its orbit, dark and ever so faintly gleaming.

With him on board, the shuttle could fly where its pilot wanted to send it. Which, under Umizad's instruction, was up into low orbit, well below Ship but above the atmosphere.

When they were stable in orbit, Umizad still bubbled with delight, but his face went somber. Though Elti in the cradle behind him looked ready to strangle him, she didn't have the courage—or the strength. All she could do was sit and glower and promise, on all the levels Aisha could sense, that every word and move would be carried back to the council she was part of.

Neither Rama nor Umizad cared about that. Rama turned in his cradle to face Umizad. Umizad sat for a long while, studying him inside and out, while he sat perfectly still.

Finally Umizad said, "Look there."

His glance pointed to the screen off to his right, the one that looked toward and past the system's sun. There were no stars in that field, and no galaxies. Only perfect blackness.

Space was never an absolute void. It might be empty to human sight, but it was full of dust and debris and background radiation and particles both random and not. It even had a smell, like burning metal.

Out there was nothing. Not one thing.

It had a boundary. The shuttle's sensors weren't powerful enough to trace it exactly, but Ship knew. Ship could feel it, and it made Ship's skin twitch. Ship needed space to be full of matter and energy; that was how it lived and fed.

"We made that," Umizad said. "We brought it here and trapped it. And there it stays."

"What is it?" Aisha asked, since nobody else seemed inclined to.

"We don't really know," Umizad answered. "We know what it does. It eats—everything. All that is."

"Tell me," Rama said.

Umizad could do better. He showed them.

It played like a vid inside their heads. Aisha closed her eyes to see it better, and remembered to breathe while she spun down into a world both alien and weirdly familiar.

She'd seen that city in dreams, with its walls intact and people in its streets. She'd dug up potsherds from its ruins.

Over the vault they'd opened before she left, where Rama's statue had waited for them to find it, was—not a temple, exactly. A place where people like Umizad lived and worked together. Corps headquarters, in a manner of speaking.

"Mages of gates," Umizad's voice said in the air. "They monitored travel in and out and through, and kept track of the worlds. And, more occasionally than you might think, dealt with threats to the gates or the worlds they served."

Aisha saw the shape of it. She saw the people who did it, too. She'd seen faces like theirs waiting for the shuttle, and riding in it now.

They came from different parts of this world, studied and taught here. This was a major city, though not the capital—it had been once, but not for centuries. It had been here since the tower on the cliff was built, the fortress with no way in, where the Sleeper was.

In the time of the memory—a memory almost a thousand years old in this world—there had been no threats to gates for well over a century. The guardians knew better than to let themselves get slack, but none of them had any experience of real danger, either.

When it first came, they took it for the return of an old enemy, a tide of darkness that swallowed gates and conquered worlds. Rama's descendants, with the psi masters of his world, had fought it and won—and one of them had gone all the way to Earth and left a memory there.

So that was true. Aisha wasn't sure how she felt about it. That she was part of that family, in a distant and diluted way.

This was her world, too, then—this world her mother had named Nevermore. What came toward it was something so huge and so destructive that there was no comprehending it.

In the beginning it came through a gate—drawn to it, maybe, or sucked into it, from somewhere else. Like Ship, in its way.

It ate the gate, and the world on which the gate had been. Then it swallowed the rest of the planets in the system, and the star.

One by one and then in threes and fours and tens, gates disappeared. Where the worlds had been was empty space. Even their stars were gone.

Late one night in a high cold tower on Nevermore, a psi master—a mage of gates—woke from a dream so terrible his mind was never the same after. In his dream, the eater of gates had a mind and a will. It ate what tasted sweet, and what made it happy. Stars were both. The more it ate, the more it wanted. It was drunk on star-stuff.

That dream was true.

The dreamer led an attack through gates. His army of mages cornered the eater on a world that was already mostly barren, where the sun had burned out. They bound it in the star's cold, dead core.

The dreamer burned out his own mind in binding the eater. The mages who survived brought back his body and laid it under his tower, and celebrated the victory across every gate and world that was left.

A generation passed, then two. Nevermore's mages grew comfortable again. They waged wars; they made peace. They watched over their gates and worked their magic and never gave thought to the fallen enemy.

The eater woke. Its bindings had frayed with time and the absence of magic to keep them strong. They broke when it reared up in its prison and roared at the stars.

It was starving, and it was enraged. It knew what had trapped it: powerful psi, which as a creature of energy it recognized as being like itself. It knew its enemy had come through gates. The same gates that had trapped it in this universe, and that it had been feeding on.

"Or so we suppose," Umizad said in Aisha's mind. "This we are sure of: It didn't know who the mages were, or exactly where their world was in the chain of gates. It went hunting them."

They had warning. Its hunt was slow; it paused to search each world, hunting for any sign of psi. It left animals and plants, and anything sentient that lacked a particular kind of psi—the kind that Nevermore's masters had. Anything endowed with that flavor of psi, even the slightest hint of it, it ripped apart, molecule by molecule, and dined on the fragments.

"Each world it found, it stripped of magic," Umizad said. "When it was done, it hunted through the world's gates one by one, searching for its next feeding ground. It learned as it went: it began to look for certain shapes and species. The closer a species was to the people or powers of our world, the more avidly it hunted, and the more messily it fed."

Aisha could see. She could feel. She had slipped inside its thoughts the way she could with Ship.

It was not the same kind of creature as Ship. It couldn't be. Ship was bright and open and clean. This was dark, dark, dark.

And huge. Most of it didn't even exist in that particular universe. Only its consciousness, the part of it that lived and felt and fed.

It liked pain. Pain was sharp and hot and sweet. It learned to crave pulling the soul out of a body after it had sucked the body's psi to a husk. It left whole worlds full of empty, shriveled bodies. Nothing remotely human-like survived.

One world tried to communicate with it. They hoped that if it knew they were fellow sentients, it might go back to eating stars, and let them be.

Maybe once it might have, but it had the taste of magic now, and a long memory for the time of its captivity. It had to eat, it wanted to eat, and this was rich, and easy, hunting.

Fear was the spice that sharpened the sweetness. Any weapon that might turn on it only fed it.

On Nevermore, everyone knew it was coming. They still had monarchies, mostly, and tribal rulers, though the mages elected their leaders from the strongest and the most skilled.

Even with all their wars and squabbles, between the network of gates all over the planet and the psi masters in even the tiniest hamlet, their communications were almost as fast and almost as complete as if they'd had a worldweb. That web conceived a plan.

"We can't sacrifice an entire world."

The most powerful of them all had met in the guildhouse in the old city, in the circular hall that in this age was carved and painted with images of great mages and great workings and the many wonders of gates. Aisha could have stopped there, just to marvel at the beauty of the place, but the half-dozen people seated in a circle spoke of harrowing things.

The one who had just spoken was younger than the others. He reminded her of Zhao: earnest and pretty, and near tears with the awfulness of what the rest wanted to do.

"We don't have a choice," one of his elders said. Half her face was beautiful, as if carved in bronze. The other half was burned away. She fixed him with one dark eye and one milky white. "This is the penance we pay for all the worlds that died because our ancestors were not the great saviors they wanted to be. There is no other way, and no other hope."

"What hope is that?" the young one cried. "All our people—not only mages; whole tribes and nations of innocents. They'll all die, and worse than die, if we do this. There won't even be a ghost left to wander the ruins."

"We will save as many as we can," the tallest and darkest of them said. He was huge, with a beard that spread across his massive chest, and eyes that held all the sadness in the worlds. The deep rumble of his voice vibrated in Aisha's bones. "We will move them beyond gates for as long as gates are open, which pray the good god will be long enough. No one will stay who has not chosen to stay."

The young mage tossed his gold-curled head. "What if it doesn't work? What if it's not enough? What if—"

"We die," the burned one said. The hand she raised was a claw, the fingers fused together. "We'll die if we do nothing. I know which I'd rather choose."

The council of mages whirled away. Time speeded up; images passed by too fast to catch. But Aisha could see the pattern in them all.

The mages of Nevermore dangled themselves as bait for the eater of souls. They taunted and teased it with their psi that it so well remembered: darting and out of gates, setting off fireworks of magic on abandoned worlds, and leaving bits of energy like crumbs along a path. Then, just as the eater was about to find them, they snatched the bait out of its jaws. Disappeared. Vanished completely.

But they always left a hint, a clue, a new trail for it to follow. A trail of gates that led through barren worlds.

Some were left from the old enemy. Some had simply died. The masters and rulers and educated minds in the web mapped and charted the way.

The burnt mage died on an airless rock that orbited a near-dead sun. The young one almost escaped—almost made it back alive. But the eater swallowed him just before he passed the gate. Then it ate the gate.

On Nevermore, most of the ordinary people were gone, taken away to what their leaders hoped was safety: shifting through gates to worlds that could support them—empty worlds or worlds with few inhabitants, where they could make lives for themselves. They had, voluntarily or otherwise, agreed to a terrible and necessary thing: to forget the world they came from, and even more terrible, to give up psi if they had it. To make themselves invisible and inedible to the eater of souls.

Those who had stayed, who were mostly mages, devoted their lives to removing all evidence of themselves from their world. It took ten years of Nevermore. Ten years of destroying every image and every hint of the human creatures who lived there.

Out of that whole world, a few thousand psi masters stayed to the end. They moved everything they could to the larger of their moons, the one that was a planet in its own right, with air to breathe and water to drink—both of which they made better and stronger and more plentiful with psi.

The eater came before they were completely ready. Nevermore was empty except for the Sleeper in his heavily shielded tower, and a tribe of warriors born and bred to be nulls, who would wait for him and guard the planet.

So far the memory or history or whatever it was had been like a vid. It was vivid and close, but Aisha sat outside of it, watching and listening.

Now she found herself inside. Living it. She floated in the mind of one of the masters: born to the arts and the powers, and raised to fight this most terrible of all enemies.

They called her the ruler of the country in which the Sleeper slept. She thought of herself as its servant.

Her deepest name, her true name, was Estari. It came with the memory of a man's voice, soft and deep, speaking over her head from a father's height.

Her mind was as sharp and clear as a castle made of crystal. Aisha saw and felt the kind of person she was, not only the strength but the weaknesses that made her moral and fallible. She was strong and skilled, but she had a temper. She had no patience for people who were slower of mind than she was, a flaw in her character that caused her no end of trouble.

She took care to show her people only her most calm and confident face. Inside, she was terrified. At night, alone in her high and royal bed, she cried herself to sleep because there was nothing she could do to save her world or her people.

Rama didn't cry, that was burned out of him, but like him, she was full of the sun. She was keyed to it, and it fed her and made her strong.

She didn't think she was strong enough. She thought the Sleeper might be, but she had some gift of prescience, and it warned her not to disturb him. His time would come.

She wrote down what she knew of that time, in the book that would go with them on the long chase. Aisha saw her hand with the pen in it, a sharpened reed, simple and perfect: narrow, long fingers, as dark as Rama's. There was a lightning-tree of a scar across the back, from an old accident with psi and fire-making.

The alarm went off just then. The eater was coming. It had passed the last gate seeded with sparks of psi—skipping a dozen in between. Which was not good news for such plan as they had.

They had, by their calculation, a handful of days while the eater fed, before it came through the gate to Nevermore. The queen—no, empress; that was the title she held in this world—no longer trusted that. She stood up in the small crowded workroom, lifted her head and called with all that was in her, mind and body both.

Everything was as ready as it would be. The last of the people were safe beyond gates. Everyone who was left had trained specifically for this—and each of them had some art or craft that they would need if they survived. Farmers, fisherfolk, artisans. Leaders, too, but even those had functional skills. Hunters. Smiths. Masters and teachers.

Some of them set wards on the planet. The rest wound the moon in a web of psi, protecting its atmosphere and preserving its gravity. On the empress' command, they launched it through the gate that they had made.

Estari didn't take part of that great working. She was the sentinel, the guardian on the mountaintop. She watched, and held on, and waited.

What she hadn't told any of the others—though some surely knew—was that she couldn't do what she had to do if she rode the moon through the gate. She stepped out of her workroom onto the plains of Nevermore's northern continent, beside the river that flowed past the Sleeper's tower.

It was tall then, and sharp, black stone polished as smooth as glass, with a golden sun on the pinnacle. It had no door or window. The only way in or out was through psi—and it had to be a particular kind, of a particular genetic heritage.

She had it, but she wasn't looking to go in. The Sleeper slept, and dreamed, she hoped, of sanity and peace.

She was all alone in this world except for a handful of bred-warriors wandering far away, and a herd of antelope grazing farther down along the river. Some of those had been tame once, but they had already forgotten.

There was no grief in her. They'd all done what they knew was necessary. If she succeeded in what she meant to do, the people could come back. The world would be safe.

If not...

The eater was too vast to see or even really understand. The best Estari's senses could give her, even with psi, was the image of an unimaginably enormous sea creature in a cloud of dark ink, with tentacles innumerable, and huge eyes full of cold intelligence, and a beak sharpened on the edges of mortal souls.

She meant to let it eat her, and then, from inside, alter it. Shift its polarities was as close as Aisha could come to understanding it. Turn it into its own prey, and trick it into feeding on itself.

She stood alone under the sun that was her father and her lover and her self. She made herself a beacon. "Come and get me! See, I'm sweet, I'm strong, I'm everything you hunger for. Come and swallow me!"

It came down out of the sun. It was beautiful and terrible and absolutely alien. There was nothing human in it at all—until it ate her whole.

Her body flared to ash, but her spirit held together by pure indomitable will. The eater staggered, drunk on the splendor of her. She reached through every part of it, and twisted.

Space warped. Time turned on itself. The eater lunged toward its own extremities, and swallowed them.

She dared to be glad; to taste a sweetness that was victory. To think that now, at last, she could let go.

The eater convulsed. She hadn't gone far enough, or held on long enough. Nor could she. She'd given all she had. There was nothing left.

Except for one thing. Her plan had failed. The other one, the one all the mages had shared, was still there. With the last disintegrating fragments of herself, she turned the eater toward the gate that was almost shut, and gave it the scent of the mages' bait.

She had weakened it just enough," Umizad said, "that we were able to stay ahead of it down the track we'd set. We meant to stop at the stars' end, but it drove us on—and out and through, into this place beyond all places that we ever knew. We bound it here, made a cage for it out of the dark behind the stars. We meant to destroy it, but none of us had the strength, singly or together. With her we might have. But she was gone."

They still mourned her, nine hundred of their years later. That mourning tightened in Aisha's middle and made her throat ache.

"We were bound here, too," he said, "out of time and space, on guard over the captive, with no way to kill it, and no hope of finding our way home. None of us is strong enough to do either."

"Do you believe I am?" Rama asked.

"I don't know," Umizad said. "I only know what she wrote in the book she left us. That you would wake, and hunt us beyond the edges of the world. That you would have dreamed so long that your soul would have been burned clean, and your heart would be a pure cold thing. Only the pure, she said, can destroy what we brought here."

"Pure? Of what? Humanity?"

"I don't know that, either," said Umizad. "She had the malady of seers, which is to speak in riddles."

"Because sight is never clear," Rama said. "I am all too human. I may have dreamed myself to some semblance of sanity, but my flaws have never changed."

"Pride and ambition and the conviction that you and only you are right."

Rama bent his head. He was almost smiling. "I see what she tried to do. It wasn't about strength. It was about focus."

"Are you saying she lacked it?"

"She had not had six thousand years and one very long night to concentrate her mind."

"Can you do what she failed to do?"

"Probably not," Rama said.

Not only Umizad sagged at that. They all did, even Elti.

That was his revenge for the way they'd treated him. He let them steep in it for a while. Then he said, "But I will try. I'll need your library and your best rememberers. And I will need to be free in this world."

"Are you bargaining with us?" Elti demanded.

"I don't bargain," he said. "That is what I need."

"And if we won't give it to you?"

He smiled, sweet and wild and gleefully mad. "I'll take it."

She was mad, too, in her way. In all the various ways of the word. "You are not our emperor. Do you understand that? You do not rule us. We are not your subjects."

"I understand," he said. "The son of the Sun is dead. I am a pirate captain from a long-forgotten world, and maybe I can finish what the one you loved began."

"I suppose you'll want to be paid," said Daiyan. Her tone was dry and her expression sardonic. For her, Aisha thought, this was as good as a play on a stage.

"I owe my world a debt," he said, "for what I almost did to it. Consider this the payment."

Daiyan bowed in her cradle. He'd startled her. She could see him now: not as the monster from the children's tales, but as a person. The empress' ancestor, with the same powers and the same bred-in obligations.

"Don't let him suck you in," Elti said, sharp and harsh. "He was the greatest courtesan of his age. He could seduce anyone into anything."

"Not anyone," Rama said with a touch of old, old sadness. "Not quite."

Rama brought the shuttle down on the far side of the moon from the cage that had been built for him. That continent was full of cities, built along rivers and chains of lakes, with high mountains like a spine down the middle.

One city was not the largest, but it was the brightest when Aisha shut her eyes and looked in that other way that was getting easier the more she did it. It was full of psi masters.

He came down through their layers of defenses, precisely in the middle of the central square. It was dawn here, the sun still hidden behind the mountain wall. Swirls of galaxies shone dim in the brightening sky. Directly above the mountains, the absolute darkness of empty space seemed to swallow the tops of the peaks.

No welcoming committee waited for them, except for a sleepy person with a cart full of what looked and smelled like fresh-baked bread. She stared at the machine and the people who came out of it, transparently thought about bolting, then got hold of herself.

It was the sight of Umizad that did it. Elti, too, maybe, but the old man had much more power here than she did. That was obvious even to a complete stranger.

"Ah," Umizad said. "Shendi. Are your wares all spoken for? Would you have a loaf or two to spare for hungry travelers?"

Shendi rolled her cart forward, eyeing the shuttle sideways but not as if she was afraid of it. She hadn't seen anything like it before.

Her bread was fresh, and tasted wonderful. Elti had to pay for it, too, which made Aisha unreasonably happy. While Shendi went off to her usual customers, Umizad and Rama and the rest settled down a circle of stone benches around a fountain, to eat their breakfast and wait on what would happen next.

It wasn't a market day, Umizad told them, but as the city woke up, people started to fill the streets and the square. They circled the shuttle with curiosity but as little fear as Umizad or Shendi had shown.

Rama had locked it, which meant no one could get inside. More than one person tried. Some had a fair blast of psi in them, but the shuttle just absorbed it.

The sun finally rose over the mountain. Rama lifted his face to it and breathed deep.

Aisha felt it under her feet and all around her, like a fire on her skin. He was drawing the light to him, feeding the way Ship did.

He did it here because he wanted these psi masters to see. Which, in ones and twos and dozens and hundreds, they did.

Nobody tried to blast him the way they'd blasted the shuttle. They were completely silent, watching with more than eyes. She couldn't tell what they were thinking. Some were afraid, that she could feel, but the rest was too complicated to make sense of.

When the square was full except for a wide open circle around Rama, he lowered his eyes from the sun and scanned them all. "I'll speak to your council now," he said.

"They're not here," Elti said. "They're on the other side of—"

"They will come," Umizad said. He was enjoying himself as immensely as ever. "Lord Rama, while you wait, there's a place where we can go, and be in comfort."

"I'll stay here," he said, politely but without any yielding in him. "You go; rest. I'll be sure not to do anything interesting until you come back."

Umizad laughed. "That's a promise to be glad of! But I'll stay, too. They'll be here soon enough."

Aisha thought he might shame Rama into leaving, but Rama had another answer. In very short order, people had raised a canopy over them and padded the stone benches with cushions and brought water and wine and something dizzyingly sweet.

"Mead," Khalida said, plucking the cup out of her hand. "And that's the last you'll taste of it till you're a good few Earthyears older."

Food came a little bit after that, a proper breakfast, and then someone with a box, and in it a book that made Elti hiss in outrage. "How dare you—"

"Who has more right to read the Book of the Empress than the empress' firstfather?"

That wasn't Umizad; it was Daiyan. By which Aisha knew that she'd had something to do with it; and that she was choosing sides. She stared Elti down. Elti's glare promised consequences—and not pleasant ones.

Daiyan steadfastly refused to be intimidated. She focused on Rama instead, as he took the book out of the box and opened it, turning the pages slowly, reading bits here and there.

It was an interesting book. Tall and thin, with pages stitched on the right side. He read it from bottom to top and from back to front. The archaeologist in Aisha took note of what he did, and of the language and alphabet in which it was written.

With pictures. Drawings in colored inks that seemed to shimmer on the page, as if they wanted to pull free and hover in the air. Her fingers itched to get hold of it, but she sat on them and made herself be patient.

Everyone watched him. Not with fear, here. Not as if he was a dangerous animal. But not in comfort, either.

They all knew too much about him, and too little. He was history to them. Seeing him in front of them, alive and breathing and all too real, must be almost unbearable.

Rama fed on that the way he fed on the sun. Aisha could feel what he was feeling. All the tangled emotions. Some she didn't have a word for. Sadness so deep it was like happiness. Grief, rage, resignation. Fear—even he could be afraid of what he'd agreed to do.

Irony, too. His whole life before he slept had been a battle against the dark. There above him, washed out the sun's light, was the darkest of all darkness. A great enemy beyond anything his earlier self could have imagined.

He'd let that self go while he dreamed. Learned to see shades between dark and light. Now he needed what he'd been before: the blind belief. The perfect dogma.

He couldn't do it. He wasn't that holy warrior any more. He'd dreamed too long.

"Are you sure?" Aisha asked him under the surface of her mind.

He surprised her by not being angry. "I am sure," he answered her in the same way.

"I mean," she said, "are you sure you can't do it? Maybe it needs you to be complicated."

"*Pure*, she said. I'm not purely anything. Except possibly," he said with a twist she felt in her middle, "foolish."

"She was guessing," Aisha said, "and prophesying, which is more or less the same thing."

He laughed, a ripple of warmth down her spine. "I'm no stronger than she was. But I do have something she didn't have."

"Science." Aisha felt it unfolding, a kind of dizzy delight, a vision of the universe that bent at right angles to the one he'd be born to—not in a way that broke or denied it, but that made it bigger. Grander. More complete.

Psi, or magic, had one way of mapping the universe. Science had another. When he put them together, he had something much bigger than either. Something that might make it possible for him to keep his promise.

"We need Ship," Aisha said. "And Dr. Ma and the others."

"Yes." He was thinking ahead of her now—but not so far she couldn't keep up.

It was dizzying, like a mad gallop across the plains, with war behind and battle ahead and every breath the sweeter because it might be their last.

Now the plains were fields of stars, and the battle was as wide as universes. *Finally*, his ancient self said: *a battle worthy of me.*

His present self laughed at that, but didn't argue with it, either. This was what he'd come for. He spread his arms and swept it in.

61

Khalida felt the change in Rama like a seismic shift. All the systems that had been damped down suddenly were open wide.

As far as the eye could tell, nothing had changed. He sat under the canopy while the sun rose higher, reading the book that the psi masters had brought him.

That Daiyan had brought. Khalida kept her eyes on Rama and peripherally on Aisha who, as the hours wore on, curled up at his feet and seemed to go to sleep, but she was keenly aware of every breath and every shift in Daiyan's long elegant body.

She knew exactly what was happening. She also knew how to shut it off.

She did not want to. That was a choice, clear and conscious. She wanted to feel what she was feeling.

Training kept her still, and something else, half instinct, half intuition, kept her thoughts deep inside where only she could know. On a world of psi masters, that was a difficult and possibly dangerous exercise, but she had a tropism toward difficult and dangerous.

She was a pirate at heart. That made her laugh.

She was catching Rama's joy that bubbled up and over them all. In her mind she saw him on the plains of Nevermore on the back of his coal-black antelope, no bridle, no saddle, galloping headlong toward an army bristling with spears. He was laughing like a mad thing.

This was dangerous, the cold deep part of her observed. He had the power to sweep a world along with him. And he would do it, because that was what he was.

There is no other way.

That soft inner voice was not Khalida's, nor was it Rama's. Khalida caught Daiyan's eye. In the flush of heat from head to foot, she acknowledged the truth. About Rama, and about Daiyan.

The council arrived in a most interesting way: riding in bubbles that looked as if they were constructed of air and water, but that had the apparent stability of the *Ra-Harakhte*'s shuttle. The dozen who had met the shuttle came together. The rest traveled singly or in twos and threes.

As each bubble touched the paving of the plaza, it melted into the sunlight. Khalida counted fifty personages in all, and not all were psi masters. Some smelled almost purely of politics; others had the carriage of aristocrats whether born or made.

Rama surveyed them with a perilously bright eye. They advanced warily, in order that spoke of precedence. The handful in front were not the leaders. Those held back a few paces, letting the lesser luminaries serve as a shield.

They were more afraid now than they had been when they dared to hope that their cage could hold him. Foolish; but Khalida had never had much respect for the political classes.

When they had come as close as they dared, which was a good ten meters from the edge of the canopy, people emerged from the crowd, carrying chairs and benches. Quietly, without too much evident amusement, they made a sort of gallery, a semicircle focused on Rama.

It took a while for them to agree on positions. He waited patiently, as he must have done a thousand times in front of such gatherings, with an air that made her skin shiver.

You do not rule us, Elti had said.

Maybe. And maybe he had no desire to. But he still ruled. He could not help himself.

After the dignitaries were seated, and everyone from end to end of the plaza and in the streets beyond had gone silent, Rama left his seat and stepped out into the sun.

Khalida saw him the way they must see him. A rather ordinary man of one of their nations, much smaller than most, neither beautiful nor ugly, but simply himself. His plain worn clothes in their odd fashion, his antique gold, reminded them that he was not one of them.

For those with the eyes and the power, he was something else altogether. Something strong; something terrible. Something that they had been fools to try to control.

He spoke quietly, making no effort to raise his voice. Everyone heard; he made sure of that.

"I have read your book. I will read more, and think upon it. While I do that, I have a thing to ask of you."

They all waited. Some in the council thought of speaking—Khalida saw eyes flicker and jaws clench. But none of them dared.

"I ask," he said, "that you give me one gift, and only once. That when I ask, when the moment comes, all of you, all together, give me what strength you have. Not to death—that I will not allow. But as much as you may, without hesitation, without question."

"All of us?"

Elti asked that. Of course. Elti, Khalida had concluded a while since, was this world's speaker of the truth. The one who said what no else had the spine to say.

Rama knew that, too. He regarded with her with something very like affection. "All of you," he said.

"And if we won't? Or can't?"

He raised his hands. The one that was like anyone else's. The one that, visibly and perceptibly, was not. "Then you won't. I will do what I can to keep my promise. If I fail, maybe you'll find your own way. Maybe that's what you're meant to do—having outgrown your need for heroes and conquerors."

"Now you're mocking us," she said.

"Isn't it the truth?"

"If you fail," she said, "you'll go the way of your descendant whom we loved. You'll be dead in every possible manner."

"Yes."

"You're not afraid?"

"Would it matter if I were?"

"It would to me."

"I am afraid."

She searched his face, narrow-eyed as if against the sun. Whatever she saw there, she set her lips and turned away.

"We will give you what you ask."

The speaker was one of the council, a woman of indeterminate age and indeterminate nation, round and small and dressed plainly as such things went here. Khalida would have taken her for an aide or a functionary, but Khalida had been trained to see through the façade. This was a power in this world.

The woman was small enough that when she stood in front of Rama, she had to look up. She had taken the measure of him the moment she arrived, of course, but she allowed herself a proper while to confirm it.

He allowed her her proper while. He had no discomfort with being stared at. It was the way of every world he knew.

At length she said, "We have waited for you, and prepared for you. All of us have studied and trained and done everything we may—to help you or destroy you. Whichever is necessary."

"Whatever you know of this thing you brought here," he said, "I would know."

"Ask," she answered, "and it shall be given."

He bowed to her. She accepted his respect. She had her own fair share of what made leaders and kings.

They brought all their knowledge to him, in books or in the minds of people who knew. Or he went to them—in his shuttle for the most part, though he took an almost childlike delight in riding in one of their bubbles that was made of air and water and psi working on them both.

"Magic!" he said. Which Khalida was willing to concede.

By the morning of the third day on the moon that had become a world in its own right, Kirkov and Dr. Ma came down from the *Ra-Harakhte*. The ship remained in orbit, empty but firmly connected to its captain, feeding with rising urgency as he moved closer to fulfilling his promise.

The scientists needed an interpreter, and pressed Aisha into service. Khalida could have joined them, but she found herself charged with ferrying books and scholars to the mages' city.

That threw her together with Daiyan as often as not. Daiyan was a mage of rank, and also an aristocrat; when she was not gleaning information from archives or sending her virtual self across universes, she served on the council of a federation of cities near the northern pole.

She wore it all easily, an ease that Khalida suspected she had worked for. She knew where most of the texts Rama needed were kept, and where the sages and scholars lived, as well as how to persuade some of the more fearful or the more hostile to venture within the Sleeper's reach.

"He may be right, you know," Khalida said as she piloted the shuttle toward an island in the larger sea. There were storms brewing, and the winds were treacherous, but nothing that need absorb all of her concentration. "You probably don't need him. He's an atavism—a relic of a state of mind that you've left behind."

"Have we?" Daiyan asked. Her long body was coiled in the copilot's cradle; she looked as boneless as a cat, and as paradoxically comfortable. "Do you know exactly what he is?"

"No," said Khalida, "but I have an inkling. He was an infamous conqueror; he is a psi master of unusual strength. He managed to found an empire that lasted the better part of a millennium—which is vanishingly rare. He appears to have a mutation that makes him uniquely qualified to deal with this thing that brought you all here. I don't know what that mutation is, or how it works, but it did breed on, didn't it? Until the last of his descendants died trying to do what he's come here, or been brought here, to do."

"More than an inkling," Daiyan said. She bowed in her cradle, half in amusement, half in respect. "Our ancestors said, and some of us still say, that he was the son of our sun-god. Maybe it was the sun that caused him to be what he is. His powers, or his psi as you say, certainly seem to come from that direction."

"I've heard of stranger things," Khalida said. "Still. All of you together, with your combined skills and powers, ought to be able to do anything that one man can. If that thing out there feeds on stars, and his psi is keyed to them, can't you do something similar? If you study him as he studies you, can you learn to do what he does?"

"With time enough, maybe. I don't think we have that much left."

Khalida had been catching hints of this. She had not been paying attention. There was too much else to focus on.

Out here, with clouds boiling above and the sea tossing below, it seemed suddenly both urgent and immediate. "Why? What's happening?"

Daiyan was as calm as ever. Her voice smoothed the rough edges of Khalida's mood, though the words offered no comfort. "When you came through the wall, it knew. It had been asleep; it woke. It's working its way free, now. We've tripled the guard on its prison, but the guards are barely holding on. We've lost seven already. Four of them since yesterday morning."

Khalida searched her face. The lines of it were subtly alien and yet subtly familiar, as if she had always known them. "It was waking before we came. Wasn't it?"

"Yes. But your coming roused it fully."

"He's your bait this time. Your sacrifice, that you hope will buy you the time and strength to put an end to it forever."

Daiyan bent her head. She was not ashamed, but she was not proud, either.

"He knows," Khalida said. "I'm sure of it."

"As am I," said Daiyan. "We're fools, aren't we?"

"You're desperate. You gave up everything, even your world, for a gamble that might still fail."

"It didn't fail," Daiyan said. "Even if we all die here, we did what we set out to do. Our only fear is that it might go back where we came from, and undo it all."

"Ah," said Khalida. She had not reasoned all the way through to that. She should have; it was a failure of training that she had not.

Daiyan brushed a finger down Khalida's cheek. It felt like a kiss of cool fire. "I thought he would come alone, or with an army of blackrobes. I never expected you."

"Even in dreams?"

"I didn't believe them."

"I thought mages were great believers in dreams."

"That one made me too happy. I was sure it had to be false."

Khalida's breath was coming short. "Are you sorry it wasn't?"

"If we fail, and we all die," said Daiyan, "I will be."

The shuttle bucked and yawed. Khalida dived for the controls. Daiyan reclaimed her hand, but the memory of her touch lingered.

Khalida was too happy. She knew it, just as she knew that there was no way it could last. But she could not make herself care.

62

D r. Ma could have died and gone to Paradise and been in less bliss than she was on this rogue moon of Nevermore, trying to make sense out of data that ranged between improbable and impossible. Even more wonderful, she had to gather what she could through a child translator who did not speak the language perfectly—and that language was like Old Earth Latin or classical Mandarin, an artifact as ancient as the Sleeper in his tower.

Aisha could appreciate how she felt. Pater and Mother would have killed to be here. Aisha was more tired than anything, and her head hurt with the effort of bringing psi and science together.

Her psi, too. Being surrounded with it made it want to spread and push and grow. It felt as if it was trying to crack her skull open.

Sometimes she got to sleep. On the third night or maybe the fourth, she stumbled into the room she'd been given, near the long-disused barn that the scientists had set up as a laboratory, ready to drop into the oversized and excessively comfortable bed.

That was not going to happen. Aunt Khalida sat in the chair by the window with her head resting on her hand. She looked asleep, but her eyes opened when Aisha stopped in front of her. "What's wrong?" she asked. "Did you have a fight with Daiyan?"

Khalida blushed, which made Aisha want to laugh. But she didn't dare. "Daiyan is wrangling mages who have no intention of being wrangled. I wanted a little quiet."

"In my room?"

"The wrangle is happening in mine." Khalida yawned. "I suppose I could curl up in a corner of the lab. I've slept in worse places."

Aisha was tired. That made her irritable. "Don't be stupid. This bed is big enough for six. Just don't hog all the covers."

"I promise," Khalida said.

"Do you think we'll ever go home?" Aisha asked Khalida.

Once she was in bed, of course she couldn't sleep. Her aunt was awake, too, turned away from her, lying very still.

Khalida rolled over when Aisha spoke. "I don't know," she answered.

One thing about Aunt Khalida. She didn't soften the truth to spare the children.

"We aren't, are we?" Aisha said. That had kept her awake: that fear, even more than fear of the soul-eater. "This is where we'll always be."

"Not necessarily," Khalida said. "We are in a different universe, but Dr. Ma thinks we made a gate when we came through, and that we might have the coordinates to open it again. Though we can't do it until that thing out there is dealt with, because it feeds on gates. We're purely lucky it didn't wake before we closed the gate."

"We weren't lucky," Aisha said. "Rama and Ship were doing something— shielding, hiding—to make sure nothing caught us. I think Rama knew what we were coming to. Or guessed. Remember when he talked about a fish in a pond?"

"And algae," Khalida said. "I do remember. I wonder…maybe the thing wasn't just feeding on gates and stars. It was like our ship: it was in the wrong place at the wrong time, and a gate caught it. It ate the gate the way an animal chews off its foot to get out of a trap. But the trap surrounded it, and eating the gate pushed it through another gate, and on and on. The harder it tried to get back to wherever it came from, the deeper into the trap it went. Breaking out into this universe didn't help. It's still caught. It can't get free."

"Don't tell me you feel sorry for it," Aisha said.

"Think about it," Khalida said. "If I'm right, it's squeezed into this tiny single cell of a universe, and it can't get out. Of course it wants to tear up anything that stops it. It went after the people who were in charge of the gates, and not only did it not manage to destroy them, they made its situation worse."

Aisha still wasn't convinced. "Umizad told us people of another world tried to communicate. It ate them all."

"Would you notice if an amoeba tried to talk to you?"

Aisha folded her arms behind her head and frowned up at the beams of the ceiling. She was annoyed that she hadn't thought of it herself. From what everyone had been saying and reading and theorizing, it made sense.

"We should tell Rama," she said.

"I'm sure he already knows."

Now Aisha was sleepy, suddenly and almost completely. It let down her guard so far that she said to the air, "You do know, don't you?"

It felt as if he was there with them, but he lay in his own bed on the other side of the house. Aisha heard his voice clearly.

"I haven't conceived it exactly as you put it together," he said. "That it fell through a gate, and the gate trapped it—that it encompassed universes, and was forced down into a single one—that succession of thoughts I hadn't come to."

"That was our error," Khalida said: "to think inside the boundaries of a universe. Even when we allowed for two, we didn't reckon on something that belongs outside, that was never meant to shrink itself so small."

"But if we make a gate big enough for it," Aisha said, "won't we risk blowing this universe wide open? And maybe the other one, too, through the gate we made?"

"Maybe there's another way," Rama said.

"Such as?"

"I don't know yet."

He left them with that, closing himself off, leaving silence where his voice had been.

Aisha should try to get up. She'd put an idea in his head. God knew how far or fast he might run with it.

She couldn't force herself to move. She had to sleep. If he flew off into another universe before she woke up, there was nothing she could do about it.

For the second time in as many days, Aisha opened her eyes to find Rama standing over her. She was sprawled across the bed, still in her rumpled clothes. There was no sign of Aunt Khalida.

"We're leaving tonight," he said.

She sat up blearily. "*We?*"

"You weren't going to insist?"

"Would you care if I did?"

He didn't answer. He was gone as if he hadn't ever been there. Which in the body, she realized as she woke up a little, he hadn't been.

Nobody else knew. She stumbled out of bed and got herself as ready for the day as she could get. She was wanted in the lab; she had to pretend there was nothing different about this morning than about any of the others.

It didn't make sense for him to leave in secret if he wanted them all to help him with the eater. Unless he wanted to avoid a fuss at the start. Or had a plan that didn't include a planetful of psi masters arguing over what to do.

They were doing that outside the lab this morning. Aunt Khalida had brought back another shuttleload of sages, wild-eyed and wild-haired men and women from an island without beach or harbor; it could only be reached from the air.

Aisha doubted they had anything new to bring Rama, except entertainment. And maybe understanding.

He was learning what made them what they were. Not just their psi; their thoughts, and what they wanted, and what they dreamed of.

Their nightmares he already knew. He was one of them. The eater was another.

Her day in the lab ended early. Dr. Ma was running data that didn't need translation, and Kirkov and a handful of mages had a new experiment set up that involved telescopes and linked screens, focused on the star nurseries deeper into this universe's core.

What that had to do with the eater, Aisha didn't know. It didn't matter. She would be gone when the eater's prison rose over the mountain.

Ship was ready. It waited in orbit, full and shimmering with the stuff of stars.

It knew what they were going to do. It was afraid, but it hadn't dived into subspace or bolted for the other end of the universe. It was like the rest of them. Rama led, and it followed.

They were all crazy. She ate as much as she could make herself eat, put on clean clothes and packed what she could carry without seeming obvious. Then she went to find Rama.

It was a longer hunt than she had planned. The light was getting long and people were leaving the streets and the markets when she tracked him down to the master mage's house.

Umizad's acolytes had the lamps lit though it was still daylight outside, and were feeding Umizad and Rama and Khalida and Daiyan in the small dining room that opened on the back garden. People here loved gardens, and Umizad's though small was considered to be very fine.

They weren't enjoying it tonight. Umizad was getting himself in trouble, and having much too splendid a time doing it.

"I am going with you," he said to Rama, "and you two"—to Khalida and Daiyan—"will stay here. I'm the connection you need to this world, and they will be my—conduits, is that your word? I love that word. Conduits."

"Not *my* word," Rama said. "I'm older than you, and my death wish is more finely honed. You are not coming with me."

"Of course I am," Umizad said. His smile was as terribly sweet as Rama's could be. "We had better leave before too long. Some of my colleagues aren't as dense as we would wish them to be. They'll be catching wind of what you're up to."

"Then what will they do? Herd me into another cage?"

"Don't underestimate them," Umizad said. "They're not all idiots, and some of them are very nearly as strong as you. When you call them, they won't hesitate to answer."

"If they don't prevent me from going at all."

"There is that," said Umizad. He raised himself laboriously from his chair. "Shall we go?"

63

Aunt Khalida only argued halfway to the death about staying behind while Rama went to get himself killed. Aisha looked at Daiyan and knew why.

She felt sorry for Captain Hashimoto, a little. But that hadn't ever been going anywhere. This had even less chance, especially if the eater ate them all.

Khalida might not trouble herself about that, but she did care about Aisha going on Ship with Rama.

"This one you don't get," she said.

"It's not for you to say," he said before Aisha could open her mouth.

He could be cold, but this was iron and old stone. He was turning inward, getting ready for the battle that would probably be the last one he ever fought.

"You bastard," Khalida said. "You think she has something you can use. What? Her genetics? Some long-hidden power that you can turn into a weapon?"

"I don't know," he said. "Prophecy was never my gift."

"Oh, no," Khalida said. "You don't get to sidestep and dance merrily off. She's not going with you."

Aisha had had enough. "Aunt," she said. "Just stop."

Khalida spun on her. She backed up a step, but she kept her glare steady.

"Stop," she said again. "I'm going. You can't talk me out of it."

"Why?"

"Because I have to," Aisha answered. "If we do this, and we survive, and make it home with proof of what we've found, we'll have what we need. Nevermore will be safe. The expedition won't have to leave."

"Child," Khalida said, and the word was cutting, "politics don't work that way, either in United Planets or here. It won't be that simple—any more than he is. He doesn't care about what you want or what you hope for. He's using you."

Aisha refused to let that break or even bend her. Even if it might be true. "So am I using him. I'm doing it for Nevermore, Aunt. There's no way you can stop me."

Khalida's breath hissed, but she couldn't win and she obviously knew it. She turned her anger back on Rama. "I'll kill you," she said. "I'll rip you apart with my bare hands, if you don't bring her back alive and in one sane, conscious, functioning piece."

"I will do my best," he said.

That was as good as Khalida was going to get. Aisha hugged her aunt, though Khalida was as responsive as one of the beams in the barn.

Aisha's eyes were blurry. She turned away quickly, before they brimmed over.

It was a relief to help lift Umizad into the shuttle, while his acolytes stood by with tears running down their cheeks, and watch the hatch close on the darkened field outside of the mages' city. Except for the acolytes, no one watched them go. No one in this world knew, except the two children in the field and the two women in the city.

The shuttle was already in the air when Aisha dropped into her cradle. Rama had cut himself loose from the people below. She didn't quite know how to do that, but she tried focusing on the dark bulk of Ship in orbit above them.

Eventually it worked, more or less. Umizad was even happier up here than he'd been in the shuttle before. She let herself be happy with him, and push everything else out of her mind.

Ship was happy, too, to have Rama back inside it. The others it barely noticed, though it might have sparked faintly when Aisha connected with it.

It was very quiet with only three people on board. They camped on the bridge, rather than scatter to the empty corridors and the deserted quarters and labs and common spaces.

Aisha linked to Ship, as backup for Rama. Umizad, after watching them for a while, made his own link, which was much smoother and subtler than either of theirs.

He didn't mean to show them up. He was a psi master; this was a thing he'd been trained to do since he was younger than Aisha.

Someday, Aisha thought, she would have training like that. She'd find a way to get it.

She caught herself. There wasn't going to be a someday. What was out there would eat them all. If they were lucky, they would damage it enough first that it never ate another gate or world or soul.

Her eyes came to rest on Rama. He was completely focused on Ship and on the thing out there. Everything else had slipped away.

She'd seen that expression when he did katas. Perfect intensity. Everything in body and mind fixed on what he meant to do.

The eater was nearly free of its prison. She could almost see it, almost get a glimpse of what it really looked like.

She caught herself. There was no way a human mind could contain what that thing was. It was like a neutron star, it was so compressed and constrained by this space that was too infinitely small for its real self.

And yet a human device had trapped it. It was an accident, which Aisha understood all too well. But it gave her a little hope that they could, maybe, do something besides die trying.

"Courage," Umizad said.

His voice sounded different. In the space Aisha was in, halfway between the physical body and Ship's web, he wasn't ancient at all. He was a sturdy person, not tall but square and solid, with a plain and unremarkable face, and a hint of wickedness in his smile. His hair startled her: it was curly and thick and goldy-red.

For an instant she saw an even younger version of him in what looked like a stableyard, scowling at a mountain of manure that he'd been ordered to move, and eyeing the grossly inadequate cart and shovel that he'd been given for the job. He wasn't a power in the world then. He didn't even know he was a mage.

He did know he had a mountain to move, and he was angry and frustrated and life was horribly unfair. He threw all of that at the mountain, for pure spite, because he *knew* nothing would come of it. And the mountain blew apart. The results were stinking and filthy and glorious.

Aisha laughed. Her terror hadn't grown any less, but its grip on her had loosened.

She met Umizad's eyes. They were the same no matter what face he wore. They had always made her feel warm.

"Humans tell stories," he said, "because the universe is so vast and they so small. This is a story of a thing that we can imagine without actually understanding. It tangled itself in a web we wove."

"Some webs can't ever be untangled," Aisha said.

"But we have to try."

She shivered. Much of that was her own fear, but Ship was feeling it, too. Though it went willingly where Rama asked, it knew what was ahead of it. It recognized the eater.

Stories. Ship had a story, too: a thing that ate its kind. Which, when it thought of them, it saw as much larger and older and stronger than itself. Sometimes they came out between universes, and this thing, or its relatives, hunted and ate them.

Rama spoke quietly across the jangle of fears. "We can't kill it. Anything we do will only feed it, or make it more furious, or both. I want to try something else. I'll need your fears, all of you, and your anger. And, when the moment comes, your connections with the world we left behind."

"What—"

Aisha stopped. Ship twitched. Space pulsed.

The eater was free.

"Now," Rama said. Quiet. Calm as ever.

Aisha sucked in the deepest breath she'd ever taken in her life, then let it go completely. All her anger. All her fear. All her grief and guilt and homesickness. Everything. Outward, at that thing that covered itself in absolute darkness.

Everything. Hundreds, thousands poured their terror through her, and through Umizad.

There was a story. Older than Rama, as old as Earth and Nevermore. A beast, a monster, a dragon, made of darkness and elemental fire. A warrior came to fight it: young or old, king or commoner, woman or man, it was different with every telling.

The warrior always had a weapon. They were that weapon. Sword or spear or rifle or laser cannon. Whatever they most needed to be.

The beast opened its jaws wide to swallow them, flame them, destroy them with deadly venom. Rama looked into its one eye, or two, or a multitude. What he saw there made him laugh with pure exhilarating terror.

It saw him. The force of its seeing nearly shook him apart.

They held him together, all of them. All through Aisha—even Umizad, who was meant to be the focus.

She didn't know how. She couldn't—

"Steady." Umizad set the example for her. It felt like a firm hand in hers, and feet braced squarely against an unyielding floor.

Someone else gripped her other hand—someone far away, under a shield of atmosphere. Aunt Khalida's face glimmered behind her eyes, and Daiyan's a shadow behind it. They were strong, and perfectly, immovably still.

They kept her from breaking. She held on to Rama with her mind and will, and to Ship that shuddered all around them.

In the story outside of them all, the warrior leveled his spear. His armor was made of a million mortal souls. Their psi was his spear, flashing and twisting like a bolt of lightning.

The beast reared over him. It fought the story it was in; it tried to be its real self.

He had to keep control. *Focus*, Aisha willed him and herself. Or prayed. *Focus*.

The beast lunged. He struck at it with his spear.

Its laughter shook the sky. *Yes! Yes, smite me!*

Rama staggered. His edges frayed. Scales of armor melted away.

The beast swallowed them. And grew.

Nothing he did could stop it. Or kill it. Or in any way defeat it. He couldn't even trap it. Not any more. It was wise to anything a human could think of.

"Are you?" Rama leaned on his spear. His armor was threadbare in some places and ragged in others, but it held. The spear crackled and threw off sparks.

"Catch me if you can," said Rama.

He turned and ran.

He ran to the ends of the universe through waves of shattered spacetime, spurning the nurseries of stars underfoot and sending galaxies spinning. He was vaster than worlds and stronger than suns. The universe was barely big enough to hold him.

That was one story.

In another, a warrior on a black antelope with blood-red eyes—neither stallion nor mare; Ship didn't do binary—led the beast on a long chase across endless rolling plains. The beast had wings, but the antelope was lighter and faster, and when it had to, it could fly.

It was starting to tire. The warrior's spear was dimming.

The beast never tired. It would catch them when they couldn't run any longer. Then it would eat them all.

Rama stopped without warning and whirled to face the beast. It roared toward him.

He flung the spear.

It missed.

And almost shook apart with the force of Aisha's shock.

In the third story, the story in which she rode in a living ship with two mages from Nevermore, Umizad held her up. The wave of psi turned and lashed through him.

He held on. He was trained. He knew how.

He was old and his body was failing. It couldn't withstand that much power. There was no way—

Aisha reached inside herself. She went down so far and so deep that she knew she might never come up again.

At the very bottom was a tiny spark of light. An image, or a memory. A familiar room. Familiar faces. Mother, Pater, Jamal. Vikram. Malia.

They sat around the table in the family dining room, eating and talking. It didn't matter what they ate or what they said. What mattered was that they were there.

Khalida came in from the door to the roof, hand in hand with Daiyan. No one seemed surprised to see either of them. They sat with the others and joined hands, closing the circle.

That was Aisha's strength. Those were her anchors. She rooted herself in them, and gave that strength to Umizad.

Darkness swallowed them. Darkness absolute. Complete absence of anything at all.

Total sensory deprivation. There was no beast. No universe. No story. Nothing. Absolutely nothing.

The darkness split apart. Light flooded over her. Annihilated her.

Far, far, far down the endless road, a tiny figure struggled toward her. It was Rama in the ragged remnants of his armor, on a battered and limping antelope. He had his spear back.

It was broken. Light dripped from it. He raised it.

His arm shook. He was almost done. They all were.

The beast hovered over him. Its wings spanned the world.

He aimed again and loosed the fire. As straight as he could, as strongly as he could.

Past the beast, again.

The beast laughed and swooped down on him.

The sky split in two.

In Aisha's story, Ship was completely out of control, diving into a nursery of stars. This universe they were in was new, so small it had barely begun to expand. They'd found its center.

Omphalos, Mother would say. Navel of the world. Gate of gods and the powers above and below.

Gate.

Ship lurched aside, wrenching every molecule. Parts of it tore free; it bled solar plasma, long swirls of it dripping down into the gate.

The beast crashed into the singularity. Spacetime twisted.

Rama thrust with the last fading fragment of his spear, direct to the heart of beast and gate. All the souls in the spear screamed at once, ripping through Aisha, catching on a single desperate thread of self and psi: Khalida, who was too damned stubborn and too damned mad to give way.

Umizad reached past Aisha and the straining, struggling remnant that was her aunt. He was as poor a rag as the spear, but he was beautifully calm and perfectly focused. He knew exactly what he was doing.

He pushed.

The beast swallowed the gate. The gate swallowed the beast.

Rama flung the fire of himself at the gate. But Umizad was there first.

He blazed up like a dying star. Stars fed him; galaxies gave him their strength.

The gate collapsed on itself. Ship rode the shockwave outward, helpless as a twig in a flood.

Rama clawed his way up out of his cradle, scraping the last of his psi. He turned Ship, somehow. Aimed it. Dropped, unconscious, dead—Aisha couldn't tell. She couldn't move. She could barely think.

She was a pair of eyes and a shred of consciousness. All she knew was that the gate was gone. The beast was gone. The universe—she didn't know. She might never know.

64

Umizad was dead. Aisha and Rama almost were. The others, down on the moon—she couldn't tell. She couldn't reach that far.

She woke with the great-grandmother of a headache and the feeling that her skin was blistering off her bones. When she could make her eyes work, she couldn't see any sign of burns, but every part of her hurt.

She was breathing air, which meant Ship was alive. She crawled out of her cradle past the cold still shape of Umizad. The captain's cradle was empty. Rama was gone. Was—

Stupid. He hadn't flamed into nothingness like his descendant. He was lying beyond the cradle, sprawled on his back, covered in grey ash.

Those had been his clothes. He still had his antique gold—and raw, blistered skin under it.

Aisha dropped down beside him. She was suddenly, ferociously angry. He was not dead. There was no way he could be dead.

She shook him so hard his head rocked on his neck. "Wake up. Wake up, damn you."

He didn't move or breathe. She hauled back to deliver a full-bore face-slap.

His hand snapped up and caught her wrist.

His eyes were open. There were galaxies in them. Swirls of suns.

He blinked. The suns sank back into the depths.

Aisha wrenched free. "You couldn't even die like a decent person."

"Who ever said I was decent?"

That was Rama. Awake, aware, and as sane as he ever was. He sat up, and reeled.

Aisha caught him. For an instant she was someone else, and he was Rama. Always.

Then she was Aisha again, and memory faded. So did anger. Suddenly she was impossibly tired, and terribly calm.

"We won," she said, "I think. I have no idea where we are. Or even if we're in the same universe we started in."

"We are," he said. "That thing isn't."

"Is it dead?"

"It can't die. It won't come back, either. It's learned its lesson."

"You hope." Aisha pushed herself to her feet. "We need to eat. So does Ship. Then find our way back."

If there was anywhere to go back to. But she didn't say that.

Aisha wasn't going to think about what would happen to the two of them in this universe without a human world or human people. With ship's stores that were finite. And—

Rama retreated to his quarters to wash off the ash and put on new clothes. Aisha stayed on the bridge next to Umizad's body.

It was empty, a shriveled husk, like a leaf in a winter wood. She made herself remember what he used to be before she knew him in this life: not the master mage or the gifted student but the boy in the barnyard, just discovering that he had magic. That was his deepest self, his true self.

"Ship," she said, not even stopping to think whether it would listen, let alone do what she asked. "Make a cradle for him, please. Keep him whole and safe, until we can bring him home."

Ship didn't answer, but the cradle he was in grew and blossomed like a flower, rising on a stem as thick as Aisha's whole body, till it stopped level with her eyes. Then it grew shimmering petals, pale blue and palest green and the faintest tinge of red-gold. They folded over what was left of Umizad, and went still.

Aisha found her voice, eventually. "Thank you, Ship. Thank you."

The bridge was full of Umizad's memory. Aisha couldn't stay there, not without losing what control she had left and crying herself dry.

She retreated to the crew's galley. She hadn't thought she was hungry, but once she was off the bridge, she realized she was starving.

She rooted in cupboards and bins and coolers, and threw together what she found, more or less at random, the way she used to do with Jamal when it was their turn to cook.

By the time Rama came out of his room, dressed in his *gi*, she'd eaten about as much as she could stand. He sat down across the table from her and ate everything that she hadn't devoured.

He didn't complain about her more creative combinations. Just raised his eyebrows and kept on going.

It was the kind of food she'd made on Nevermore, the kind she hadn't eaten in ages. At least since Araceli. She'd been missing the food of her own people, and the people, too.

She wanted to go home.

Ship fed for a whole shipday. Aisha slept through much of it. So, as far as she knew, did Rama. There wasn't anything else they could do. Until Ship was fueled, nothing much more than life support would work.

When Aisha was awake, she went into ship's web in search of Aunt Khalida's navigation protocols. The web was in a knot, with some systems down and others corrupted, but she managed to sort it out bit by bit.

Finally she found the files she wanted. Getting them to open was another adventure. Rama helped with that, emerging from his quarters after she'd started to think he'd collapsed the way he had after he first rescued Ship.

He'd done that alone. For this he'd had all that was left of his people. Whether there still were any, neither of them knew.

He had closed in on himself again. "We should be celebrating," Aisha said. "The eater is gone."

"Not till we know the price," Rama said, even while he sorted out a string of navigation files and got one of the star maps to stop turning itself inside out.

Aisha leaped on it. "There! That's the orientation we came in at."

She triangulated maps and observations. That gave them a course to set.

Ship couldn't jump yet, but it could make fair enough speed swimming through this part of space, which was rich with stellar gases. They had time to rest and get their own strength back.

Two shipdays. Three. Four. Aisha had the web running the way it should, and she had repaired some of the damaged systems. Ship was healing the wounds in its hull, though sometimes, when it itched or the healing tissues stretched, everything inside went strange: the smell of the air, the quality of the light.

She'd thought Rama was finding things of his own to do, till it dawned on her that she hadn't seen him since the second shipday. She tracked him down to his quarters, in the kind of panic that left her barely able to see where she was going.

He wasn't lying dead in his bed or hanging from a nonexistent rafter. He sat with his feet tucked up, back straight, hands on knees.

Aisha sagged against the door. His eyes were open, wide and blank. Still, he was breathing. When she stepped into his line of sight, he blinked.

"I can't find them," he said.

She knew who he meant. "Because they're too far?"

"No."

"Then why—"

"I think I burned myself out."

He was perfectly calm. Too calm. The kind of calm that meant he was screaming underneath.

Aisha shook her head firmly. "That's not true. You went right into ship's web, didn't to use an interface. Your psi is still there."

"Barely. I can't see past the hull at all, except through the screens. I can't find anything out there. I can't see, or feel, or hear—"

She'd never heard him talk like this. He was shaking: holding on by a thread.

"It will come back," she said, though she didn't know if that was true. "You drained the cup, that's all. It will fill up. A day or two in the sun, a few days' rest…"

"This is worse. This is scraped down to the bare bone. What if it never comes back?"

"I don't believe that," Aisha said. "I refuse to believe it. And even if it's true, does it matter? You're alive. You have Ship. We'll find your people."

"If they live. If they haven't all—if I didn't—"

"Stop." Aisha caught hold of his hand. It was the one that held the sun. She turned it palm up.

The sun was still there. Dim, clouded, the swirls of plasma sluggish and slow. But it wasn't gone.

"Look," she said. "Can you feel it? Is it burning?"

"It always burns."

"The rest will come back." She folded the fingers over it and held it in both of her hands. He didn't pull away, which surprised her. "Ship will help. So will I. And the mages when we find them. Between all of us and the sun, you'll get yourself back."

"Is that my self? Is that all I am? That burning thing?"

She would never say so, but he was acting like Jamal. Complete with whiny fit. Which was disconcerting, because she wanted to laugh, and that would not be a good thing at all.

"What did you used to be?" she asked him. "When you were only you?"

"I was—" He claimed his hand back finally, but used it to catch one of hers and pull her closer. He peered into her face. "I was never *only* anything."

"Maybe that's the problem."

She'd gone too far. His breath hissed between his teeth.

She pushed just a little bit further. "Maybe it's time you learned to be a person like anyone else. Nobody out there wants or needs a king."

He could kill her. He was close enough and strong enough. He could snap her neck before she had a chance to move.

She held herself still. Trusting him. Daring him to get over himself.

He rocked back on his heels. She watched rage chase tiredness past the first unwilling flicker of laughter across his face. "Damn you," he said, but mildly.

"Come out and eat," she said. "Ship says we're almost where we want to go."

"Ship says?" His brow quirked upward. "It talks to you now?"

"It always did."

"I don't think I'm surprised."

"But you are jealous." She danced back out of reach. "It's your turn to cook. Better make something fast. I'm hungry."

He lunged after her. She darted ahead of him. He might catch her, and she might get a bruise or two, but it would be worth it. She'd kicked him out of his pity party. With luck he wouldn't fall back into it before they came to the rogue moon.

65

They circled around from the sun side of the barren planet, into a night that was both emptier and fuller than it had been before. The eater's prison was gone. The blackness of space was already filling with dust and gases and bits of stars streaming into the void.

Sparks of light glimmered from the moon, tracing the shapes of cities and the lines of rivers. Someone was alive down there.

Aisha couldn't hear anyone thinking. Ship walled her off from anything that might have come in from outside.

Maybe she was burned out, too. It didn't matter as much to her as it did to Rama. She'd be better off without it, if she ever made it home. If she didn't, not much of anything would matter.

Rama insisted he could pilot the shuttle. Since Aisha had never done it, there wasn't much choice.

He seemed to have calmed down. His eyes were clear and his hands steady on the controls. The course he laid in took them back the way they came, to the field outside the mages' city.

They touched down just before sunrise. The field was empty and damp with rain that had fallen in the night. The air smelled rich and green.

Aisha still couldn't hear anything outside her own head. It was a muffled feeling, like walking around with her ears blocked. What it must be like for Rama, she could hardly imagine.

As they came closer to the city, Aisha started to smell baking bread. At first she was sure she'd imagined it. But it grew stronger. Then she heard someone singing, painfully and blessedly off key.

Rama heard it, too. He lurched forward, then stopped cold.

Aisha didn't want to leave him, as badly as she needed to see for herself that people were still alive. At least Shendi was, making the day's bread, which meant there must be people to sell it to.

"Rama," she said.

He wasn't listening. "I can smell them," he said. "Hear them. Feel them, like sun on my skin. But I can't—"

"You can feel them? It's coming back, then."

He tossed his head the way his people did, not quite a headshake. "It's not the same."

"It will be." She thought about pulling him forward, but the tightness in his shoulders warned her not to touch him.

Someone came toward them down the road, a shadow against the rising sun. Aisha recognized the height and the way it moved, like a big cat.

Her name burst out of Aisha. "Daiyan! Where is my aunt?"

Daiyan didn't break into a run, but she could walk very fast with those long legs. "Umizad?"

"You first," Aisha said.

Daiyan dipped her head: half bow, half concession. "We had casualties. Most survived."

"We had one," Aisha said, and watched Daiyan's face stiffen—as if she hadn't known it the moment she saw Aisha and Rama alone on the road. "He's on the ship. We'll bring him down now we know there's something to bring him to." She advanced a step. Her voice lowered, almost a growl. "Where is my aunt?"

"Alive," Daiyan said. Aisha sagged, but didn't quite fall. "She's still recovering."

"So are we," Aisha said, once she had her legs back under her. "Are we welcome here?"

"Here and in every city and town and village in our world," Daiyan said, bowing and spreading her hands in a gesture that took in Aisha and Rama together. "We didn't feel you coming, or we would have given you a proper welcome."

"So you were just going for a walk in the morning?"

"Khalida tossed me out," Daiyan said. "She said I was hovering. And that I should look for something in the field."

Aisha found she could remember how to breathe. That was her aunt exactly. Whatever had happened to her, she was still herself.

Rama didn't move or speak, but something Aisha couldn't see or sense made Daiyan look past her to the darkness of him in the swelling light.

Her expression went blank. She dropped to her knees and then to her face. "*Kalendros.*"

"Don't call me that." Rama sounded exhausted beyond telling. "I wasn't your king before. I won't be your king now."

"Not everyone will agree with that," Daiyan said. She was back on her feet again, and back to herself, too—though she looked as tired as Rama sounded. "Come and have breakfast. Anything else you want or need, we'll be happy to provide that, too. We owe you this world and everything in it."

"You owe me nothing. Without all of you, I'd have failed."

"Without you, that thing would still be up there, getting ready to swallow this universe whole." Daiyan bowed again, much less deeply, and waved him on. "Come and eat."

They went by back ways to Daiyan's house, but people knew. People always knew. By the time they reached the door, there were eyes in every window, and random persons just happening to wander by.

Nobody tried to storm the doors. Aisha was glad to be inside in the cool dimness shot with rays of early light.

She was gladder to see her aunt sitting in the central room, waiting for them. Khalida had looked worse when she came to Nevermore from Araceli, but not by much.

She was alive, at least, and worn out but not visibly damaged. She was even hungry, which was amazing.

"I dreamed we fought a dragon," Khalida said when breakfast was mostly done. "And I was the haft of the spear."

"Magic works in metaphors," Daiyan said.

"Or psi," said Rama. "You were all there. I felt every one of you. I needed every one. To the very smallest and least." His eyes flicked toward Daiyan. "I'll want the count of the dead, to honor them."

"It will be done," she said.

She used the formal phrase. Aisha had enough of the language now to recognize it. It meant she hadn't let go what she'd said in the field. Rama had won back what he'd lost, whether he wanted it or not.

He didn't want it. She could feel him, a little—like someone singing far away. The song was in a minor key, but it wasn't terribly sad. Just tired.

After six thousand years asleep, he finally, really wanted to sleep again. Though not nearly so long. A tenday would be enough.

He caught that. He was startled, and then amused. And then, very tentatively, hopeful.

"I told you it would come back," she said inside.

A messenger from the council brought Rama the roll of the dead from all over the world. There were seven hundred and sixty and three. Not so many compared to how many survived, but he spent a good tenday learning about each one. Name and age and where each lived, family, friends, anything that mattered.

At the end of the tenday he began a long flight from city to city, to honor each one of the dead, and the living, too. He spoke to as many of the survivors as he could, and to the friends and kin and loved ones of those who had died.

Aisha went with him, to make sure he slept and ate, and to keep him from draining himself dry.

For the people it was a victory procession. They celebrated, as they should. A terrible thing was gone, and they all had helped to send it away.

For him it was penance.

"Should I find you a whip and a hair shirt?" Aisha asked him one evening, after he'd been gracious enough to sit at the feast that the people of ten towns and villages had got together to make for him. He barely ate and only pretended to sip the wine that was the pride of the region.

They'd given him the largest house in the largest town, and shown him to the largest room in the house. The bed was enormous and so new it still smelled of paint.

He wanted to sleep on the floor. Aisha wanted to kick him. "What's with the holy martyrdom? Haven't you just saved your world?"

"Yes," he said, "after nearly destroying it once. Now people have died once more through my fault. In my old life I lost count of my dead. I won't do that again. I'll remember every one."

"You've spent too much time with my aunt," Aisha said.

"She has a conscience."

"Yes," said Aisha, "and how has that ever helped her? I liked you better before. You were too crazy to care about most things, but you weren't always moping and glooming."

That struck home. "I am not—"

"Oh, aren't you?"

He glared at her. "What do you want me to do? Dance on a pile of skulls?"

"Wrong Govindan divinity," Aisha said.

He sank down on the floor, drawing into a knot of pure, unrelenting *No*.

She was just about ready to throw up her hands and leave him to it. "Maybe I'm the idiot. The more you wallow, the more people think you're the great tragic hero. People love tragic. They adore it. Just a little bit more and they'll give you anything you want. Make you king. Worship you like a god."

He spoke through clenched teeth, enunciating each word with vicious precision. "If I still had my power, you would never have dared to say such things to me."

"Of course I would," Aisha said. "I'm an idiot, remember?"

She did leave him with that, before she really lost her temper and started to scream at him. She didn't even try to see inside, to know what he was feeling. She didn't care.

In the morning he looked for once as if he'd slept. He was maybe a little less morose. Aisha didn't let herself hope she'd woke him up to himself, but there did seem to be a difference.

He kept on with his pilgrimage, town by town and name by name of the honored dead. When he came to the council's own capital, on the other side of the world from the mages' city, they were waiting for him with the offer he could hardly have failed to expect.

"No," he said.

They tried to trap him into it. Lay in wait for him in a huge green bowl like an amphitheater, full and spilling over with wildly cheering people. Even for the rites of the dead they could barely keep their jubilation in check.

He wouldn't put on the gold and silks and jewels that people kept trying to give him. He'd let Daiyan have a coat made for him, terribly plain as things went here: a sturdy construction, made for use, black embroidered with red and gold. The belt was only slightly ornate, and the trousers that went with it were plain soft leather, tucked into high boots that matched the coat.

He looked much better than he wanted to, with his ancient gold. Nearly everyone out-glittered him, which only made him more noticeable.

The councilor who had been rudest of all had her own penance to pay: she knelt in front of Rama and said, "My lord, we have all decided. We will accept your rule. You are king and emperor. We bow before you."

And he said, "No."

They hadn't expected that. They hadn't been paying attention.

People like that, Aisha had noticed, knew what they knew. These were completely shocked, or pretending to be. "Majesty!" said Elti.

"No," Rama said again.

"You refuse the wish and prayer of all the people?"

"With gratitude and deep respect, I do refuse it."

She narrowed her eyes. Her old self was back, striking sparks off him, and daring him to punish her for it. "What will you do, then?"

He smiled. Aisha hadn't seen him do that since before he fought the beast. He turned his face to the sun and said, "Go home."

A long sigh ran through the crowd. Not of homesickness. They were too far from Nevermore, too many years, too many generations. Still, it was a powerful word.

"There is no way back," Elti said.

"There is if I can find one," said Rama.

"You'll abandon us, then? Leave us alone on the far side of the sky?"

"Did I say that?"

Elti rocked back on her heels. "You won't rule us, but you'll lead us out of this place?"

"I'm a pirate captain," he said. "I have a ship. It won't hold all of you, but those who really want to go, who really want to see…"

"Who really want to die," Elti said. "You can't do it."

Rama laughed. Aisha hadn't heard that, either, in much too long. "Oh, you know how to make me spark and snap! Maybe I can't. But if I can—if it is at all possible—I will do it."

"I don't think it is possible," Daiyan said.

They'd come back to the mages' city that morning. Tomorrow they would take the shuttle to Ship and bring Umizad's body down, and honor him last of all the dead.

Tonight they sat in Daiyan's house. Here of all the places they'd been, nobody crowded in on them. Mages—psi masters—had that courtesy.

"It is theoretically possible to go back the way we came," Dr. Ma said through Aisha. "The mathematics and physics are complicated to say the least, and our psionics are so rudimentary as to be effectively useless, but—"

Kirkov rode smoothly past her toward a conceivable point. "She means that if we can find a way to restore the link, then lock in a course, we may be able to do what we did in reverse."

"It won't be the same route," said Dr. Ma. "Orientations will have changed. Distances. Relative locations. We could aim in what we think is the right direction, and find ourselves in a universe even less hospitable than this one."

"The link is key," Kirkov said. "Our command of psionics is miserably bad, but this world has been developing and studying it for centuries. You said yourself, if we combine forces—"

"There is still a gate," said Rama. "We closed it, but the connections remain. Here, and there."

"Are you sure?" Khalida asked. "There was a very real possibility that the anchors would be killed when we broke through."

"Zhao, you mean," said Kirkov. "Our one and only trained psi. With the nulls as deflectors."

"He was alive when we came through," Rama said.

"But is he alive now?" Khalida stared them all down. "We can't go back physically unless we have a connection on the other side."

"Yes," said Daiyan. Her voice was quiet, but Khalida, for a wonder, shut her mouth and lowered her eyes. "It's a gamble, though maybe less of one now the eater is gone. Isn't it worth taking?"

"Maybe not for me," Khalida said.

They'd had that argument before, Aisha could tell.

Daiyan's lips tightened, but she kept going. "We can't take this world with us. That, when it was first done, needed more mages than we have, and the eater's power to draw on—and the willingness to strip the energy of suns as we went. We're not desperate any longer. We're not trying to save a universe."

"Only to go back to a world you abandoned millennia ago," said Khalida. "There's nothing left. Don't you get that? It's barely even ruins. They've all fallen into the grass, or the sea, or under the rubble of mountains."

"But it's ours," Daiyan said.

"Was yours. Six thousand of your years ago."

"Less than a thousand of mine." Daiyan touched her shoulder lightly, a simple brush of a finger.

Khalida erupted out of her chair and bolted.

They all sat mute for a while after that. Aisha felt as if a bomb had gone off.

Finally Rama said, "I am going to try it. I don't care if it kills me. I promised to take Aisha home. I will do that."

"And then what?" Aisha demanded—surprising herself. She wasn't angry like Khalida or, for that matter, Elti. But she did want to know.

He raised his hands. "I don't know. Does it matter?"

"It does to me."

If he touched her the way Daiyan had touched Khalida, she would knock him flat. Or try to.

He didn't touch her. Which was disappointing. "I don't know what I will do. Do I have to decide now?"

"Decide to say alive," she said. "Start there."

"I can try."

That was a promise. She intended to hold him to it.

It was not as easy to have something to live for as Khalida might have expected. The aftermath of cosmic battle left her feeling both more solid and more fragile than she had ever felt. She had done impossible things. She had helped to save a world.

Physically she would heal. Psionically, too, these masters assured her. She was stripped to the metal, that was all. Time and training would mend her.

It was her heart, her emotions, that left her in a state of furious confusion. Daiyan took it all in stride, as if she had always expected to fall in love with an alien from the other side of the sky. Most likely she had; she was a moderately strong precog, as the Corps would say.

Daiyan was a world in herself. She had children. Grandchildren. A whole tribe, and two men who were not her husbands and for whom she felt nothing of what she felt for Khalida, but they were able lovers, she said. And dear friends.

She would leave them all behind. Not without a second thought—she was hardly that cold—but they had their own worlds to conquer. She wanted to walk living on the far side of the sky, and set foot on the world of her ancestors.

Khalida wanted that. She wanted her own world back, if it could be done. Considering what she had aided and abetted Rama in the doing of, her piece of it might be three square meters of high-security prison.

The terror that kept her up at night, that made her heart beat so hard she thought it might burst, was that, having found Daiyan, she would lose her again in the not-space between universes. Her own death was nothing to be afraid of. Daiyan's death—that, she could not endure.

"Life is a grand gamble," Daiyan said.

She had taken her time leaving the breakfast gathering. She found Khalida in the room they shared, sitting stiffly on the ledge by the window. Mountains soared above her and a grand storm piled up over the peaks, but she barely saw it.

Daiyan's arm circled her shoulders. Daiyan's lips brushed her hair. "If we die, we'll die together. I plan to live. I expect you to do the same."

"I'm out of the habit of that," Khalida said.

"Then it's time you got back in."

Khalida wanted to snarl, but Daiyan would laugh. She pushed herself away instead, and said, "All right then. Where does this expedition start?"

"With the rite of the dead," Daiyan answered, "and a gathering of mages."

"Psi masters."

Daiyan's smile was her only response.

They laid Umizad to rest high on the mountain, where the masters of mages were set in a cave without door or barrier to the wind and the rain and any animals that fed on the bodies of the dead. The bones of his predecessors were arranged tidily in niches, skull beside skull and femur beside femur.

Khalida the archaeologist had much to observe and compare. Khalida the renegade and lover helped lay the mage's body on the stone table in the center of the cave. It was cold and stiff and unexpectedly light.

She was more than a little sorry that they had removed it from the ship's strange and beautiful storage chamber. That would have been a marvel in this place. But tradition was stronger than alien wonders.

Carrion birds were already circling as the mages began their ritual. That particular chant must serve as a summons, and the interplay of light and psionically manipulated air only served to keep them from closing in before the rite ended.

They played his life in the cave, images of Umizad as child and man, novice mage and journeyman and master. He was older than Khalida might have believed, though not quite as old as the crossing into this universe. He had done wonderful things, and terrible things, and one last, splendid, deadly thing. Now he rested, and they left him to it, descending on foot as they had ascended, back to the city and the preparations for departure.

A thousand would go. The *Ra-Harakhte* could hold that many, with the stores they needed. Many more would have gone, but if this insanity succeeded, and the gate held, it would only be the first expedition.

Khalida refrained from contemplating the ramifications of that. She had enough to do with ferrying supplies and then people up to the ship, and keeping her mouth shut when she was near either Rama or Daiyan.

They were set on this course. So apparently was everyone else here. She might have suggested that they take a smaller number, and look less like an army and more like a scouting force, but Rama answered that for her in her hearing.

Dr. Ma had doubts, too, having to do with cargo mass and availability of fuel. Rama replied, "The more psi masters we have with us, the more likely we are to be able to do this. The ship is our life support. Our propulsion, and our jump drive, is the combined power of all these mages."

Dr. Ma grimaced. "That word," she said. "Even realizing it's a translation, it makes my head ache. We're not conditioned to make these conceptual connections."

"You're doing very well," he said.

He had not comforted her, from the sourness of her expression. Khalida followed him out of the lab, intending to run through a stream of questions that various persons had prevailed on her to ask, but a delegation from one of the cities waylaid him before she could begin.

King or not, he was spending an exceptional amount of time hearing people out and answering questions and settling disputes. They seemed unable to help themselves, and he lacked the will or the capacity to refuse.

She had a few hours before the next shuttle run, and no task urgently demanding she do it. She retreated to her room, with nothing more elaborate than sleep in mind.

Daiyan was not there. She had her own considerable part in this adventure, and it ate even more of her time and energy than it did Khalida's.

Khalida stretched out on the bed. It smelled of the herbs the cleaning staff sprinkled on it every morning, and faintly of Daiyan: a little musk, a little sweetness. Slightly but distinctly alien and blessedly familiar.

She was half asleep already, drifting down to the edge of dream. Lately she had been dreaming of stars: not the crowded galaxies and infant stars and vast expanses of undifferentiated dust and gases that made up this universe, but the stars of home. An older universe, well expanded, mapped by the peoples who inhabited it, and named in their various languages.

Because she was human and inclined by nature and culture to perceive herself as the center of it all, she focused on that infinitesimal part of it which constituted human-inhabited space. Earth-human, she corrected herself; the stars she mapped carried human names and human designations.

The map from the Ara Celi was part of it. So was the route through Kom Ombo to Starsend. In her dream there were layers of space, with truespace in the middle and jumpspace below and…something…above. Skin of the bubble. Boundary of the universe.

Because she was dreaming, she took it all in without either doubt or disbelief. She was nearly as vast as the eater of souls, but infinitely less predatory. She could have been the ship's elder sister, swimming through the layers of space, taking it all in and focusing, simply because she could, on Starsend.

To the senses of her dream, the near-abandoned habitat was a dim glow of clustered lights. Human minds and human bodies, most so faint as to be almost dark.

Those would be the nulls in stasis. Their protectors shone brighter, but they were very few. The one who was brightest lay on the edge of the inhabited zone, and the quality of the light told her he too was dreaming.

She spoke his name in the dream. "Zhao."

He roused sluggishly. He had been deep asleep, and his dream was nightmare: fire and screaming, and unbearable pain, and mind after mind burning to ash.

He dreamed the fall of the Corps in Araceli. Khalida almost left him to it, but her dream-self paused. "Zhao," she said again.

The fire retreated. "Captain Nasir?"

"Lieutenant Zhao," she said, since they were exchanging defunct titles.

He focused sharply, suddenly. He was almost awake. "You're alive? This really is you?"

"Don't wake up!" she warned him. "I'm alive. On the other side of the sky."

He held on with some difficulty to the state between waking and sleep, where psi was strongest—or so the mages said. "You survived? All of you? The thing you followed—is it—"

"Gone."

He almost lost control and woke. But not quite. "Where are you? How are you finding me?"

Khalida did not have exact answers for that. "Here," she said. She had a hand, she realized, and there was a line in it, a length of braided rope, like a horse's lead. "Take this. Don't let it go."

He took it. Wound it around his hand, to hold it fast.

If there had been a horse on the other end, that would have been a very bad idea.

Magic is metaphor.

She heard it in Daiyan's voice. Daiyan, whom she had found in dreams.

Her dream was fading. "Don't let go," she said, though he was already far away. "Don't—let—"

I've got it," Khalida said.

She stumbled out of bed toward the solar flare that was Rama, not caring who else was around him. Only after she had spoken did she see the inner council of this world, and Elti glaring at her for interrupting what must have been a grand rant.

What Khalida had to say mattered more than any demands or arguments or objections that these people might be indulging in. "I found the way," she said. "I'm hooked on, but I don't know how long I can hold it."

Rama was not the rioting fire that he had been. The fight with the eater of souls had drained him dry. He might recover most of it with time, but what had come back so far was a quieter strength, with less of the crazy edge that had got him into so much trouble both before and after he was locked down in stasis.

He was still a psi master. Training trumped talent, MI's instructors never failed to remind recruits. He saw what Khalida gave him to see.

Once he had it, they all did. Elti's mouth shut with a click that seemed to echo in the sudden silence.

"Yes," he said with deep satisfaction and a distinct sense of relief. "You have it. Now we can go."

No one else could hold the link, though others could feed Khalida strength. Even with that, she had not been lying. She could not hold it indefinitely.

Everyone who was already on the ship would go. Anyone who had not embarked on the shuttles would stay. There was no more time. They went now, or they never went at all.

Khalida's life was one departure after another. This might the strangest. It might also be the last.

She could not both pilot the final shuttle and keep the link straight in her head. She flew as passenger with Rama in the pilot's cradle, and Aisha and Daiyan on either side of her. The shuttle's hold was full of supplies and the last few dozen travelers, some still in nightclothes with their baggage in hasty bundles.

One of those travelers was Elti. That had startled Khalida, and dismayed her profoundly. Of all things they did not need, that contentious personage ranked high.

Yet there she was, silent for once and camped by one of the ports, watching her world drop away below. She had more than enough psi to fill the berth, and more than enough ambition to hope to rule the homeworld once they had returned to it.

Khalida could not keep alien politics in her head along with the link across universes. She shut her eyes and let herself drift back to the outer edge of dream.

The *Ra-Harakhte* was ready and eager to fly. It had fed deeply and well, and the addition of so many psi masters made it frankly giddy. If it had been a horse it would have been running in mad circles with occasional leaps and twists.

Rama had all he could do to keep it under control. He laid in the scientists' course with Khalida's refinements, paused to be sure it was locked in, and let the ship go.

It knew the way with a surety that nothing human could match. It had the taste and the feel of that other universe in it, pulling it through the edge/surface/interface of this one.

Aisha had been the interface on the way out. She was there now, quiet, holding steady. She was the key. Khalida was the hand that turned it, and the lock in which it turned—both at once, interchangeably.

Words were not enough. Searching a worldweb came closer, and piloting a conventional starship in some ways closest of all. It was a shiver in the skin and a prickle in the back of the skull, and a dream that lingered long after the dreamer woke.

The temptation to fly apart in the moment of transition was even stronger than it had been on the way out. All the universes begged her to flow into them. She could be everything, and in everything. She could be vaster than the eater of souls.

"Khalida."

Daiyan's voice, soft on the edge of the infinite. Calling her back to the thread that connected her to one universe of them all, and to the body in which her vastness was, however briefly and uncomfortably, contained.

She rode the waves of her name from universe to universe, into the heart of an almost-sun. The ship dived straight through, sleek as a dolphin in a sea, and leaped joyfully into open space.

The link still held, the thread of connection that had brought them through. Khalida adjusted the ship's course, aiming more directly toward it.

One of the forward screens in the bridge came alive. Zhao stared out of it, thin to gauntness but both alive and conscious. Marta stood behind him; the warm of her smile washed over them all. She opened her mouth to speak.

The screen went blank. The ship rolled. The course Khalida had set disintegrated and re-formed, veering away from Starsend. Jump alarms whooped and shrilled.

In the instant of shock before jump, Khalida felt something break away from the ship's web. A dataspurt, directed—

Jump blinded and deafened her. The thread that had bound her to Zhao snapped, flinging her headlong into the dark.

Khalida woke in the soundless cacophony of jumpspace. It seemed unusually full, or else she was unusually sensitive to the things that swam those incalculable seas.

Memory flooded. She stemmed the tide and sorted the flotsam.

They should be orbiting Starsend. Not in the middle of jump.

What—

She extricated herself from the cradle. The bridge was in jump mode: deserted, the screens dormant.

All but one. Aisha perched in front of it, absorbed in what looked like an academic dissertation.

It was, Khalida realized, a collection of writings from the rogue moon. She was building a guide to the language, and to its writing that was sometimes a set of ideographs and sometimes an alphabet. Khalida had not studied it enough to understand the logic behind it.

She was not going to begin now. She knotted her hands together to keep from hauling the child up and pinning her against the bulkhead. She armed her voice instead, and blasted Aisha with it.

Gently. "What did you do? What was that databurst you sent?"

Aisha looked up from the screen. Her eyes were wide and innocent. "I didn't put us in jump. That was Rama and the mages."

"The databurst," Khalida said. "What was it?"

"A message," Aisha answered without perceptible hesitation. "Using Mother's code. To the nearest tradeship, to come and help the people at Starsend."

"Help them do what?"

"Whatever they need."

Khalida sank down in the cradle next to her. "Now I'm embarrassed by what I was thinking."

"We're all on edge," Aisha said. "We're going to Nevermore."

"I figured that," said Khalida. "This ship is wanted from one end of U.P. to the other. Its captain is wanted, if possible, even worse. Best we get in as fast as we can, get the cargo delivered, and then get out. Unless we're planning to be arrested and charged with every crime the Corps can think of."

"I cling to optimism."

Khalida spun. Rama had appeared as he had a habit of doing. He summoned a hoverchair and sat in it.

He tilted his head toward Aisha's screen. "*Amosh,* there. Not *Elosh.*"

Aisha made a face. "I always get those two confused." She keyed in the correction while Khalida simmered.

Rama smiled at them both. "I have no intention of spending all or even a fraction of my remaining days in the Corps' custody."

"You should have thought of that while you were burning your way through United Planets' space," Khalida said sourly.

"I regret very little," he said, "and what I did to the Corps is not in that category."

"Nor in mine," Khalida admitted. "We'd better hope they haven't laid an ambush for us around Nevermore."

"Why would they? I'm known to be heading outward. If they go hunting origins, they'll aim for Dreamtime."

"Or Govinda," Aisha said. "There's nothing official to connect him with Nevermore."

"Unless they're tracing him everywhere he might be found."

"You're MI," Aisha said. "You're thinking things through. I don't think they are."

"They followed us as far as Kom Ombo," Khalida said. "Nobody thought they'd do that, either."

"We disappeared from this universe," said Rama. "We won't be reappearing anywhere, or anywhen, that is possible according to what your science thinks it knows."

"Except Dr. Ma," Aisha said.

Khalida gave it up. "What will be will be. I hope at least some of your mages can fight."

"Oh, they can," Rama said. He sounded as if he relished the thought.

In the process of thinking things through, Khalida ran head-on into the prospect of several hundred psi masters appearing on Nevermore. When U.P. got wind of that, or MI, or ye gods, the Corps...

Rama could hardly have failed to think of that. He had not let it stop or even slow him. His world had been there millennia before U.P. existed. It belonged to him and to his people. What U.P. thought, or what they might do, he honestly did not care.

"You should," she said when she could catch him alone. That was hard: the ship was full of his people.

She managed it by tracking him to his quarters on a rare occasion when he would agree to rest. It was cruel and she was merciless and he deserved it.

"A few hundred of you," she said, "even with what powers your people have, can't hold against trillions of us."

"We don't need to," he said. "Remember the status of this world designated MEP 1403. A status which, as I understand, Dr. Kanakarides insisted on, and fought for, even to Centrum and the Senate."

"How did you know that?"

"I know everything that concerns me," he said.

"Now that I almost believe."

He bowed slightly and set about undressing.

She got the message. She elected to ignore it. "Nevermore is a restricted planet—a permanent preserve. No one can colonize it or build on it."

"Except its native peoples. Which," he said, "we are."

"Marina didn't know that. She's not psi. Or precog, either. What she is is protective. To the death. And you can bet that torque you cling to, that Centrum will come down on us all."

"She won't die for us," Rama said. "I promise you that."

"You had better keep that promise," Khalida said.

68

Finally it was happening. The long jump was almost over.

The mages were more than ready. Even for people with their talents, who could spend jump practicing and honing them, jump was a tedious and often maddening place to be. Not because it was a place of madness, but because they couldn't be outside the ship, exploring and learning and feeling the way Ship did.

Someday, Aisha thought, one of them would figure out how to jump without a ship. They were already talking about it, and asking the scientists questions that half drove them crazy and half made them dive into their databases in search of progressively more complicated solutions.

Now, with their voyage almost ended, the mages had gone silent. Waiting. Hardly breathing.

She wasn't breathing all that well herself. What she'd found was so much bigger than she'd imagined, and so much stranger.

That was wonderful and amazing and satisfying. But more than that, she was coming home. Where Mother and Pater were. And Jamal and Vikram and Malia and Jinni and—

"Steady," Rama said. He'd taken his place to the bridge just before jump, along with the scientists and Aunt Khalida. Daiyan and Elti and a handful of the others had come in with him, who were too curious or too excited to stay in their quarters.

There weren't enough cradles for them all. She wanted to say so, but the words wouldn't come out.

The jump alarms went off. The Earthfolk dived for their cradles. Some of the mages did, but most caught hold of struts and screen supports and went on staring at the screens.

Rama wasn't pretending to need a cradle, either. Aisha had a moment's temptation to climb out and stand beside him, but she wasn't that brave yet. She stayed where she was, with the hatch open as always.

The universe warped and then twisted itself straight again. Through the haze of drugs and jump, the mages were completely solid. Rama most of all. As if, while the universe shifted around them, they stayed in one place and one state.

There was a truth in that. About psi. About people from Nevermore.

She made a new note on the long list, to find answers when she could. Now they'd settled into orbit around Nevermore, and the familiar land masses and seas rolled below. They'd come out directly above the planet, not pretending to need open space for jump, any more than they had on Araceli.

Ship sent out its own hail. It had learned to do that while the humans were busy elsewhere. "Research vessel *Ra-Harakhte*, Tsinghua University, Beijing Nine."

"Research Vessel *Ra-Harakhte*," Nevermore replied. "State your business here."

That was Vikram's voice. Ship didn't answer; it hadn't learned that part yet.

Nobody else said anything, either. They were all either recovering from jump, getting ready to land, or not able to speak PanTerran.

Aisha took a deep breath. "*Ra-Harakhte* greets MEP 1403. We're bringing the ship all the way down with a load of cargo."

She tried to deepen her voice and sound more like a grown woman, but Vikram's ears were much too sharp for that. "Aisha? Aisha Nasir Kanakarides? Is that you?"

"And Aunt Khalida," Aisha said. "Captain Nasir, I mean. Will you let us come down?"

"What in the name of all that's unholy are you doing—" Vikram broke off as if he'd remembered his Spaceforce training. When he spoke again, he clipped out the words in proper professional style. "Stand by for landing coordinates."

They came down on the plain outside the ruined city, where tourist ships usually went, and the ground had been leveled to hold them. Ship was much bigger than any ship or shuttle that had landed there yet, but there was room for it, just.

It could dive through the heart of a star. This planet's atmosphere and gravity were nothing to it, as long as it had the sun to fuel it. It was happy enough to let the planet hold it up.

Aisha had been going to put on the good clothes Alexandra had bought for her in Kom Ombo, the pretty blue dress and the headscarf with the gold sequins, but at the last minute she decided to go with her plain ordinary digging clothes. Rama had the same idea, but Aunt Khalida had gone the other way, with an embroidered coat she'd found on the rogue moon, and the rest of the outfit to match. The boots had copper heels.

She looked like one of them, with her narrow brown face and her wide dark eyes, except for her clipped hair. She was making a statement with that, probably. Aunt Khalida always had to dare people to argue with her.

Aisha's hands were cold and her mouth was dry. One way and another she found herself in the lead while they waited for the hatch to open in the shuttle bay, that being the only part of Ship that could hold all eight hundred of them at once.

She was alone in front of them all, with no time or room to escape. Dr. Ma stood close behind, and Kirkov. Everybody else hung back, even Elti. Especially Aunt Khalida and Rama.

Aisha felt like a scout probe. If she blew up, the rest would know not to go out there.

She was not going to blow up. Everybody had come to meet them: the whole expedition, running to the landing field on foot or in rovers the way they always did on the rare occasion when a ship came by this part of the universe. That would be the new interns, most of the usual staff, and Vikram and Shenliu. And Jamal and Mother and Pater.

Maybe she would blow up after all. She reminded herself to breathe.

Sunlight flooded through the opening hatch. A cold wind blew in, bringing smells of earth and grass and melting snow. It was early spring here, which meant that time had passed a bit faster than it had on the other side.

That was better than what Aisha had secretly been dreading, which was that their handful of tendays on the moon had added up to centuries here. They were more or less in sync after all.

Aisha stepped forward. She wasn't noticing anything now but the people outside.

Not just the expedition. Most of Blackroot tribe was there, and a scattering of people from other tribes. They stood back the way the people on the ship stood behind Aisha. Waiting. Taking it all in.

Winter-dry grass crackled under Aisha's feet. She drank a deep gulp of the clean cold air. She wanted to run toward Mother and Pater and even Jamal, but there was something she had to do and say first.

She turned back to face the people in the ship. In Old Language she said, "From light into dark you went, and from dark into light you return. Be welcome, people of the lost world. Be welcome, and be home."

She hadn't bobbled it too badly. Rama could have sung it, but he was being obstinately silent.

She turned again and faced the daylight. This time there was movement behind her: people walking slowly out of the ship and into their ancestors' world.

Aisha thought about hiding until it all blew over, but Nevermore's part of it would take years, and her part would not end in this life.

She faced the inquisition that night. It was late and everyone was ready to fall over, but Pater had a thing about sitting down for a meal no matter what the distractions. If no one but the family managed it, that was enough to satisfy him.

Tonight it was just what Aisha wanted. She cooked, which was as much hiding from everyone as she meant to do. When the parents and Jamal came in, sparking with all they'd heard and seen and had to look forward to, she had the lamps lit in the family dining room and the food on the table.

Her heart beat so hard she could barely hear herself think. Her hands were shaky and cold. She'd gnawed through half a loaf of new-baked bread to try to calm herself down, and now her stomach felt bloated and sore.

They all stopped just inside the room. Nobody looked at anybody else, but they sat down in their usual places and started passing bowls and platters.

She'd made too much. Mostly it was nerves, and some was habit. She was used to cooking for a mob.

She couldn't eat. Watching them fix eyes on plates and shovel in bread and pilaf made her want to climb up in the rafters and scream.

She slammed her hands down on the table. Everything jumped, even Pater. "That's it. That's enough. Just sentence me to house arrest for the rest of my natural life and get it over with."

Jamal went back to shoveling in vegetables, but his eyes were on her for a change. They were angry. "Next time you plot to save the world, don't ditch me. I could have helped."

Aisha flinched. She'd had that coming. It didn't stop her from shooting back, "You could have died. I made sure you were safe. Even if the expedition got kicked off Nevermore, you'd still be alive."

"But you wouldn't!"

They glared at each other, breathing hard. Jamal's eyes spilled over with tears. Aisha refused to cry. "I *didn't* die. Here I am. Right here. I did what I went to do. I helped solve the mystery. Now the expedition can't be shut down. The mages won't let it. They need us to help them find their way in this new universe. No one else can do it as well as we can. And they know it."

"Until U.P. shows up with a fleet of destroyers," Jamal said.

"That's enough, I think," Mother said. Her tone was terrifyingly mild. "Aisha, you did an amazing thing and I'm proud of you for that, but I am your mother, and there are certain standards I'm expected to meet. You'll be receiving your worldsweb implant as soon as it's practicable to get one shipped here. That will make you much easier to track. In the meantime, you're confined to the boundaries of this city. You may, with my express permission, visit Blackroot village. That's as far as you're traveling, except for such time as the—mages—" She had a hard time saying it; most of the adults did. She shook her head and tried again. "If the mages need your services, they will have them. And that will be all, unless and until you prove you can be trusted."

That was much better than Aisha had been expecting. She couldn't let anybody see how relieved she was, but she managed to say, "Thank you, Mother. I won't disappoint you."

"I would hope not," Mother said.

Aisha could feel what Mother was feeling: a complicated mix of love, grief, anger, and pride. Her own feelings weren't too different, except that there was less anger.

All this time, Pater hadn't said a word. He was usually the one who started shouting first. Aisha raised her eyes and made herself look into his face.

He always scowled. He used to do it, Mother had told her once, because he was so young to be the head of a major expedition, and he had to do whatever he could to back people down. Now he really was older and eminent and had such authoritative eyebrows, he couldn't help himself.

He had been so scared. She didn't mean to see and feel that, but there it was. Every morning he'd prayed that she would come home alive. At first he'd wanted her mind and body whole, too. Then he would just settle for having her back.

She launched herself over the table—she flew; and she couldn't help that, either. His arms opened to catch her.

She clung to him and wailed. "I'm sorry, I'm sorry!"

He held her close and let her howl herself out. That took a while. It had been building up since before she left.

Now she was back and she had saved the world, or enough to keep the expedition on it for another season or two at least. That was a good thing, but she'd hurt people in doing it. She'd hurt Pater. He'd never forgive her, ever.

That came out in her wail. Pater answered it in his soft rumble of a voice, in Arabic that had been first language she ever heard. "God always forgives. Should I refuse to follow his example?"

She pushed back till his grip loosened, so she could see his face. There were tears on it.

Pater, crying. She gaped at him, all the drama shocked out of her.

He actually smiled. It was like sun breaking out after one of the ferocious storms that tore across the plains. "We're good, then?" he said.

She swallowed. Her throat ached too much for speech. She nodded.

"Good," Pater said, and now he looked and sounded like himself again. "Good. Now get to bed. Morning comes early, and you have work to do."

69

When the rest of the universe caught up with the *Ra-Harakhte's* whereabouts, a whole chorus of hammers would fall. But the beginning brought so much archaeological and anthropological euphoria that Khalida could glide along all but unnoticed.

The mages put up a tent city beside the river and moved all their baggage into it, along with their stores. They would not ask anyone to help or feed them, but the tribes came on their own, bringing whatever they could spare after the winter.

It was a gift, and the mages accepted it. It helped them find their feet in this new-old world, and proved that they were welcome.

When they planted the first of the year's crops, the tribes worked beside them. The land was hard to farm, the sod was so thick and the grassroots so densely knotted, but the mages had ways to take care of that. No shyness about it, either, and no reason to think they needed any.

They were an ongoing revelation for the expedition. Rashid looked absolutely furious, which was his way of expressing joy incomparable. He closed down excavations and concentrated on the living artifacts instead, setting his teams to helping the arrivals as they could, and recording every action and word.

"Your brother has the scholar's passion," Daiyan said in the evening a tenday after the arrival. There had been no formal banquet yet, and no rituals of welcome beyond what little had marked the arrival, but mages and expedition had begun to cross-fertilize.

On this first nearly warm night of spring, Daiyan and a handful of her fellow mages had come to dinner in the compound. Khalida had invited Daiyan; the others had followed, somewhat to Khalida's dismay.

That was short-lived. What intentions she had had for the ritual of meeting the family were better served by this more casual gathering. It was hardly the first time any of the mages had been inside the compound, but it was the first meal they had eaten there.

It was warm enough with heaters for everyone to eat on the roof. For once there was no storm within sight or sense; the stars were out, and the moon was nearly full.

Rashid was deep in conversation with Elti and a pair of twin mages who happened to be Daiyan's cousins: identically tall, identically dark, and very differently minded when it came to the finer points of the sacred language. Rashid already had his own views, now he had access to the texts and the history behind them, and he was in no way shy about expressing them.

"Are you laughing at him?" Khalida asked.

"No," Daiyan answered. "We admire passion. As you should know."

She made no physical move, but Khalida felt the warmth of her down deep. It was a promise, for later.

For now there were worlds meeting, and a world changing. Even the precogs could not predict where it would go.

Aisha's voice rose above the babble of conversation. She was talking to Shenliu and her mother and a cluster of interns. "I've started a dictionary and a grammar of the common language, which is based on a combination of languages starting with Old Language. Now I've got back to a system set up for something besides the hard sciences, I'll be able to get somewhere with it."

"Oh, come now," Kirkov said from farther down the table. "You were doing perfectly well with ship's web before you patched it all into the system here."

"Patches and kludges," she said. "Though it was useful for translating science into psi and back again."

"You really did that?" one of the interns asked. "Put the two together?"

"That's how we found our way back. Psi alone couldn't do it, and science didn't know where to start."

Someone slid onto the bench beside Khalida. She glanced at him and started.

Rama had been as close to invisible as it was possible for him to be. He had been avoiding gatherings and keeping his head down in the fields or among the tents. Khalida doubted that Rashid even knew he was there, though she suspected Marina did. To everyone else he was simply one more alien among the hundreds. Most assumed that if the pirate who had hijacked the *Ra-Harakhte* was on the planet at all, he was safely and discreetly confined to the ship.

His presence here tonight reminded her poignantly of dinners on the roof before they went on the long hunt. She felt profoundly different now.

He looked the same, even to the slightly ragged clothes and the air of not quite being in the world. But he too had changed. The shock of waking had eased. He had made his peace with this universe, if not yet with himself.

She passed him what was left of the platter of roast not-quite-lamb, and Daiyan handed him a cup filled with vineberry juice. It could, if one tilted one's perception just so, almost seem to resemble wine.

"Not too appallingly bad," he said of that. He said it in PanTerran, which Daiyan was undertaking to learn.

Vikram passed by on his way to the sweets table. His stride checked; he stopped. "So," he said. "I did see you working in the farthest field the other day."

Rama smiled up at him. "Good evening, Vikram."

"Good evening to you, too," Vikram said. "I can't say I'm sorry to see you survived. Though I should be. You're wanted in all the hundred human and affiliated systems, did you know that?"

"I did," Rama answered. "Will you be arresting me?"

"Not tonight." Vikram sketched a salute and went back to his quest for Marina's baklava.

Khalida left Daiyan asleep in her bed and wandered down to the kitchen for coffee. On impulse she took the long way back, up along the wall that overlooked the stable.

The sun was barely up. She shivered in her light robe. There was a bite of frost in the air, though it promised warmth again later.

She saw Rama in the riding arena below, riding leisurely figures on the antelope stallion.

"He's been here every morning," Marina said behind Khalida. Khalida jumped, then forced herself to relax as Marina came up beside her. "It's as if he never went away."

Khalida wrapped her hands around her mug for warmth, and took a long sip of blissful bitterness. "Does Rashid know?"

"Not that he'll admit to."

"Probably wise of him," Khalida said. "Otherwise he'll have to confront the issue of harboring a fugitive."

"Technically," Marina said, "he's not. As long as the fugitive is on a restricted world, and as long as he can prove that he's a native, he's not subject to U.P. law."

"You think that will stop the bastards who are after him?"

"Once they know he's shown up with almost a thousand of his own species and laid claim to the planet the bastards have been trying to sink their claws into since they first realized it existed? Not for a nanosecond."

"My money's on the thousand," Khalida said.

"So they really are psi masters," said Marina.

"Oh yes. Every last one. Even the children."

"Even the one in your bed?"

"Especially the one in my bed," Khalida said through the hot and sudden flush.

Marina was kind enough not to remark on it. "She looks interesting," she said. "I'll look forward to knowing her better."

"She said the same of you," said Khalida.

Marina laughed. "Why don't we start with breakfast, then. I'll get it going. Go down and tell his majesty that he's to join us. If, of course, it pleases his royal self."

"He's not a king any more," Khalida said.

Marina's smile expressed her opinion of that, before she retreated to the warmth of the house.

Rama had no objection to accepting Marina's invitation. Khalida lent him a hand with the antelope's saddle and watched while he cooled the animal out and curried the sweat from his coat. It was peaceful work in the rising morning, while the interns assigned to the stables stumbled yawning in to clean stalls and discover that Rama had already fed the horses.

When Rama was done and the stallion returned to his harem, Khalida blocked his path to the house. "So," she said. "You'll be staying here. What happens when the Corps comes hunting?"

"I'll be gone," he said, "with a nice ripe trail for them to follow."

Khalida's brows went up. "You'll be gone? Where?"

"Wherever my fancy takes me."

That was the old antic temper. He moved to step past her. She moved with him. "They'll capture you the minute you clear this planet's atmosphere."

"Not if I'm on board the *Ra-Harakhte* under the flag of Beijing Nine. I've contracted with the good doctor to retrieve the rest of her people from their various sanctuaries, then to assist them in continuing their research wherever and however we may judge best."

"The Corps will laugh at your flag and your mission."

"I don't think so."

"Are we laying bets on it?"

"I'll win," he said. "Consider that I know both the identity and the location of the trigger for Araceli's worldwrecker. I also know that the free traders have no love whatsoever for the Corps. Nor do a remarkable number of scientists and academics. I don't think Spaceforce is terribly fond of it, either."

"You're talking about sedition," she said. "Insurrection. Attacking U.P. from within and without."

"Isn't it a lovely prospect?"

"It's a horrendous and chaotic prospect. I thought you'd gone sane after you dealt with the eater of souls. You're crazier than ever."

"And you aren't?"

"I'm not going with you. I'm staying here. There's a whole new world to build and protect. Which considering what you're plotting, may be the only one left by the time Aisha is old enough for university."

"All the more reason to protect the universities," Rama said. "Would she want Beijing Nine, then? I'd have thought she'd be more interested in the university in Cairo."

"You've been talking to Marina."

"I've been talking to Dr. Ma. She's taken an interest in a child so determined to solve an archaeological mystery that she'll follow it into the next universe. That's a born scholar, she says."

"Or a born insurrectionist." Khalida stepped aside at last, to let him go.

He stayed where he was.

Understanding dawned. "You're leaving today."

"Tonight."

Khalida surprised herself with the twist of pain in her center. She had no love for this living relic, but she was used to him. She would miss that particular focus for her temper. "Why? Is something coming?"

"Not yet. When it does, it will follow me. This world will escape its notice for a while."

"Not a very long one. We're already in U.P.'s sights. If they don't get here first and shut us all down, the first tradeship that comes through, or the first shipload of tourists, will blast the news to the universe."

"News that, as far as the Corps knows, has nothing to do with the pirate who destroyed them on Araceli. They'll be much too busy and much too far away, hunting a ghost."

"An angry one, I hope."

He showed her his teeth. He had too many, and they were too sharp to be strictly human. "None angrier."

If she had had any pity in her, she might have spared a drop or two for the Corps. This was a bad enemy. Now he had a world to defend, with his own people on it.

She was almost tempted to throw in her lot with him again. Embark on the living ship. Commit herself to a life of adventure.

She had that here, a thousand times over. She would travel in space again, but not for a while. There was too much to do.

He bent his head to her: acknowledgment, respect.

No love, no. But they understood one another.

A isha didn't need to eavesdrop to know what Rama was up to. She felt it inside, where he always was.

She waited all day to catch him alone. That was hard: he was saying goodbye without telling anyone, wandering all over the tent city and the expedition's compound. He spent a long time with the antelope, but the stable was full of mages asking endless questions about the horses, and interns trying to take care of the horses while that went on, and Malia half answering the questions and half translating the interns' and Vikram's answers. Malia had shown a talent for translating, and was well on her way to being indispensable.

At about the time Aisha decided to grab him and drag him off into the nearest empty room, he slipped away. She almost missed it. One minute he was standing with his forehead against the antelope stallion's. The next, he was gone.

Then she saw him slipping around a corner, and darted after him.

He was fast, but she knew the territory. She also knew where he was going—and how to go straight there while he took the long, wandering, goodbye tour.

She was sitting on the top of the hill when he got there, watching a flock of plains doves swarm and swirl over the rubble of his tower. Something had flushed them: a raptor, probably.

"Plains cat," he said, dropping down beside her.

"Oh, no," she said. "That's bad. We'd better tell Vikram before it gets wind of the horses. Or the interns."

"It won't," said Rama. "Though your father might not mind about the interns."

Aisha couldn't help the snort of laughter at that. "You can talk to it?"

"Plains cats are highly intelligent. One adopted my son when it and he were very young. It was never tame, exactly, but it was more loyal than any human guard. This one knows our people have come back. She'll have her cubs up there, and send them to find companions among the mages."

"Not if Vikram shoots her first."

"Vikram will not be shooting anything without the mages' leave. It's their world now."

"Not yours?"

"It will always be my world," he said.

"But you're leaving it."

There. She'd said it. She glared across the plain and refused to look at him.

"Aisha," he said with tight-stretched patience. "I have to go. I've left too much undone. I have to finish it."

"What, getting yourself killed?"

"I would hope not."

"So you do want to live? Then stay here. You'll be safe."

"Nowhere is safe as long as the Corps keeps your people ignorant and stunted. I'm going to finish bringing them down."

"Nobody can do that. They're everywhere. They're like a virus in the system."

"So they are. What do you do, or Jamal, when you run into a virus? You kill it. You scour the system and wipe it out."

Finally she turned and strafed him with her glare. "I'm sorry we ever taught you what a computer was."

He grinned at her. She couldn't remember the last time she'd seen him that lighthearted.

Damn him. She wanted to cry. He was laughing. He couldn't wait to get away from here—and from her.

"Oh, no," he said, reading her as easily as he ever had. "I'll never be glad to leave you."

"You won't. If you go, I go."

"No," he said.

She set her chin and her mind. She didn't want to go. She wanted to stay here and learn all there was to learn; study everything she could study, and get ready for university. She had doctorates to get. Archaeology and xenoanthropology. Cosmology. Interuniversal physics. But—

But.

"You will get your doctorates," Rama said. "That's your path. Mine is out there, honoring my promises and atoning for my sins."

"My path is with you," Aisha said out of the bottom of her self. "It's always been with you. From life to life."

"Not yet," he said. It was hard for him to say it. She could feel it in the pit of her own stomach. "Maybe not at all in this life. You have so much to do and be. You'll find whole worlds to conquer. You'll forget me."

"I will not." She thought about hitting him, but that was too weak for what she was feeling. She wanted to blast him to ash.

"Aisha," he said, sealing her with her name in this world. Because names had power. "Meritamon. Beloved of the Sun. I'll come back. I promise."

"Alive?"

He blinked. He should have expected that. He knew her well enough. "Alive and as well as possible," he said.

"I'll hold you to that."

"From life into life," he said.

"Oh, no. You don't get to slither out from under. You'll find me in this life, or I'll find you. I won't sit around waiting for you. Don't you even think about me doing that."

"I wouldn't dream of it," he said.

Ship hovered just above the grass, glimmering in the starlight. A storm was brewing, a last hard blow of winter, but the sky was clear overhead, and the air was still. The only sign of what was coming was a thin line of cloud along the northern horizon.

The mages had protected their tender new crops with what looked like sheets of plastine. Dr. Ma was almost persuaded to stay after all, to find out what it was and how they made it, but she had a universe to study, and a grant that she didn't want to lose.

The scientists were on board and cradled in. So were six blackrobes from the tribes, who had appeared that afternoon with their kit and a message for Rama from the grandmother. "These you have earned. They're to follow wherever you lead. Don't waste them."

That was a gift Rama couldn't refuse, even if he wanted to. He handed them over to one of the mages who would go with him, and made sure they were settled in the ship.

Ship would jump as soon as it lifted above atmosphere. Rama hadn't stayed for goodbyes. Aisha hadn't wanted him to. She still wanted to be here, watching Ship power up for launch.

Mother and Pater were there, too. Jamal, of course. And Vikram. And Khalida and Daiyan and a few other mages. Elti. Some of the tribes.

None of them said anything. There wasn't anything to say.

Something blew warm breath on the back of Aisha's neck. Something big.

She turned very, very carefully. The antelope stallion butted her gently and lowered his head for her to scratch between his horns.

She'd wondered, somewhat distantly, why he hadn't galloped and screamed this time and raised holy hell because Rama was leaving. He'd been suspiciously quiet, now she thought about it.

He leaned on her, not hard enough to knock her down, but he was definite about it. They would both sleep in in the morning, what with the late night and the snow. Tomorrow she had better be in the arena, and she had better be ready to work. He wasn't spending another half a year waiting for someone to wake up and pay attention.

"Did he put you up to his?" she asked him.

He snorted wetly all over her clean shirt. *He* had to go and ride that outsized space fish. She was here. She knew how to ride, more or less. She would do perfectly well.

"Until he comes back."

Maybe, the antelope said. Or felt. Or wanted her to feel.

This psi thing was hard to put words to. Impossible, most of the time.

She meant to make it easier. Some of the mages had promised to teach her. Daiyan especially. Aisha was half dreading it, and half beside herself with excitement.

The stallion shifted until he was beside her, and leaned again, so that she had to drape her arm over his back or fall down. He was warm and his winter coat, though shedding, was still thick, and he smelled of dust and grass and clean animal.

Ship lifted without warning, straight up. The sight of it blocking the stars brought a brief, fierce memory of the eater's prison rising over the mountain on the rogue moon.

This was no eater of souls. It was a swimmer of seas beyond human understanding.

Unless that human was Rama. The humans on Ship were already drugged and dreaming, but he was wide awake.

Aisha could see him in her mind, standing on the bridge with the screens around him, all showing stars and planets and moon. In her mind he met her stare and smiled.

He would always be there, deep inside, wherever he went and however far away he was. Psi and spacetime—that was another study for Dr. Ma and her scientists.

Maybe it would be Aisha who studied it. The best way to get a job done, Vikram always said, was to do it yourself.

She stayed till Ship was long out of sight. The others had left by then, all but the antelope.

When it was finally gone, diving into jumpspace with an eruption of joy like a whale's tail slapping the sea, Aisha turned to go, and ran into the antelope.

He knelt, inviting her. She was probably crazy, but the wind was picking up and it was a fair way home. She climbed onto his back and let him carry her toward the first faint light of dawn, and the warmth of the stable, and so much to do and learn and be that she could hardly get her mind around it.

The stallion bucked under her, not enough to send her flying, but enough to make her pay attention. Be, yes. Be now. Later would come when it came.

That was a good rule to live by.

She crouched down over his neck and wound her fingers in his mane. He belled into the wind, loud clear antelope laughter, and stretched into a gallop, and carried her home.

ABOUT THE AUTHOR

Judith Tarr holds a PhD in Medieval Studies from Yale. She is the author of over three dozen novels and many works of short fiction. She has been nominated for the World Fantasy Award, and has won the Crawford Award for The Isle of Glass and its sequels. She lives near Tucson, Arizona, where she raises and trains Lipizzan horses.

ABOUT BOOK VIEW CAFÉ

Book View Café is a professional authors' cooperative offering DRM-free ebooks in multiple formats to readers around the world. With authors in a variety of genres including mystery, romance, fantasy, and science fiction, Book View Café has something for everyone.

Book View Café is good for readers because you can enjoy high-quality DRM-free ebooks from your favorite authors at a reasonable price.

Book View Café is good for writers because 95% of the profit goes directly to the book's author.

Book View Café authors include Nebula and Hugo Award winners, Philip K. Dick and Rita award winners, and New York Times bestsellers and notable book authors.

www.bookviewcafe.com

CPSIA information can be obtained
at www.ICGtesting.com
Printed in the USA
LVOW04s2218051216

515889LV00010B/1458/P